# Praise for the Metta Valley Gospel Series

"ZACHARY HELTON'S ENGAGING ADAPTATION of Jesus's story, '*Metta Valley Gospel*,' opens the imagination to the depths of our shared histories, emphasizing the interconnected and universal nature of wisdom and compassion."
—**Sharon Salzberg, author of *Lovingkindness and Real Life***

"*Metta Valley Gospel* is a rare contribution in the landscape of contemporary spirituality, especially after religious deconstruction. Its approach to God is especially refreshing... For anyone navigating deconstruction or searching for an authentic spiritual path that does not abandon science or self honesty, *Metta Valley Gospel* is a welcome companion and absolutely has the stamp of approval from *No Nonsense Spirituality*."
—**Brittney L. Hartley, author of *No Nonsense Spirituality: All the Tools No Belief Required***

"Zachary has given us a story that dares to imagine Jesus—not as a distant, dogmatic figure—but as a wounded and curious human. Metta Valley Gospel goes beyond narratives of control and fear, instead offering a compassionate vision wide enough to hold all our doubts and longings. For anyone healing from fundamentalism, this book feels like freedom."
—**Cindy Wang Brandt, author of *Parenting Forward: How to Raise Children with Justice, Mercy, and Kindness***

"Not since Christopher Moore's *Lamb* has there been a fictionalized retelling of the Jesus story that had this much imagination, style, and punch. *Metta Valley Gospel* asks profound questions ('What if Jesus' genius was the result of spiritual abuse?') while at the same time telling a rip-roaring story about a young Jesus trying to find himself...and his calling. Metta Valley Gospel is the most fun you can have with Jesus outside the monastery. Don't miss it."
—**Rev. Dr. John R. Mabry, author of the award-winning novel** *The Worship of Mystery,* **and** *Growing Into God: A Beginner's Guide to Christian Mysticism*

"*Metta Valley Gospel* can and should be read by everyone—especially by those who shy away from religion—if only to remind us of the power that can be wielded by those who are inclined to wield it."
—*The Historical Novel Society*

"This is the Jesus story reclaimed from empire. Subversive, nonviolent, and dangerously hopeful, Zach Helton offers a gospel for activists, advocates, and anyone who still believes love can dismantle power. A gospel for those living under strongmen and refusing to surrender their humanity."
—**Cody Deese, author of** *Discovering Your Internal Universe: The Good News About Anxiety, Panic, and Fear*

# Metta Valley Gospel

## Book I
### Zachary Helton

Spark & Scroll

Published by Spark & Scroll
St. Petersburg, FL

ISBN (paperback): 979-8-9928649-0-8
ISBN (hardback): 979-8-9928649-4-6
ISBN (eBook): 979-8-9928649-1-5
Library of Congress Control Number: 2025904841

Metta Valley Gospel™ is a trademark of Spark & Scroll LLC. All rights reserved.

This is a work of historical fiction. While it is inspired by real historical settings, figures, and traditions, the events, dialogue, and characterizations have been fictionalized for storytelling purposes. The novel takes creative liberties in exploring historical, religious, and philosophical themes. Any interpretations presented are solely those of the author and should not be taken as historical fact.

This book engages with ancient religious and philosophical traditions, including first-century Judaism and Buddhism, in a speculative and imaginative manner. The author has made every effort to treat these traditions with respect, but interpretations may differ from historical or theological perspectives.

Biblical passages have been paraphrased rather than quoted directly from any specific translation.

The opinions expressed in this book are those of the author. Any references to real persons, institutions, or organizations are for illustrative purposes only and do not constitute an endorsement.

This book was written entirely by the author, without the use of generative artificial intelligence tools for content creation. AI tools were utilized exclusively as research aids and for grammar and spelling checks, under the direct supervision of the author.

For more information, visit: https://zhelton.com/

First Edition: 2025

I.

# 1

## *Kashi.*

THE MORNING SUN LIT up the auburn spires and domed roofs of Kashi. On the banks of the Ganges, worshippers made their way down for morning washing. In the southeast market, vendors set up booths while children ran between stalls. And in a narrow alleyway just out of sight, Jesus of Nazareth struck his opponent across the jaw, sending him staggering backward.

Jesus tried to run, but the jackfruit vendor grabbed his shoulder and spun him around, hitting him so hard his vision blurred. It was at that point—as he grappled for a wall to keep himself from falling—that Jesus finally admitted this day might be getting away from him. He'd woken up so determined things would be different—so determined to keep his head down and avoid trouble—but that had worked out about as well as it usually did.

Jesus only had time to spit blood out of his mouth before the next blow sent him sprawling. He narrowly avoided landing in a pile of cow dung.

As he lay there for a moment, trying to get his breath back, Jesus felt like David against Goliath, only without the benefit of a slingshot and little hope of divine intervention. He decided it was time for a different approach. "All right, all right," he said, raising his palms in what he hoped was a universal gesture of surrender. His *Magadhi Prakrit* was far from perfect, but he'd learned enough to survive. Almost. "If I apologized, would it help?"

Jesus's accuser—a man he'd only met a moment ago—paused as two men circled behind Jesus, cutting off any chance of his escape. The accuser narrowed his eyes. "Perhaps," he said. "Why don't you try it?"

Jesus forced himself to his feet slowly, swallowing his contempt. He conjured the most sincere expression he could muster. "All right," he said. "I am sorry I stole—"

*"Tried* to steal," his accuser corrected.

Jesus paused, now working twice as hard to hide his disdain.

*"Tried* to steal a jackfruit from your booth," he finished. "How was that?"

"And for trying to run?"

"And... for trying to run."

Thoughtfully, the vendor nodded, then he said something to the men behind Jesus that Jesus didn't understand. They laughed, which Jesus took as a bad sign.

"Pity," the vendor said. "It seems an apology didn't help after all."

Without warning, he hit Jesus hard in the stomach, and Jesus doubled over as pain shot through his gut. He heard the men behind him laugh harder, and despite everything, Jesus wanted to laugh with them. It was so absurd at this point—this lifelong fight he could never seem to win. How was it that his mere presence had always been enough to make people so angry? He was Yeshua the *mamzer...* Yeshua the bastard... Yeshua the vagrant... How dare he scrape by and survive?

"Would you like to try again?" the vendor asked.

"Not really," Jesus gasped in Aramaic, forgetting for a moment where he was.

The vendor frowned, suspicious.

"No," Jesus repeated in the vendor's native language. "I don't."

"That is a shame," the vendor said. "Perhaps it would have worked this time."

The vendor signaled to his friends, who grabbed Jesus, pulling him up and pinning his arms behind him. As he stood there, struggling in vain, a familiar, bitter voice rose in his mind.

*Thou shalt not steal, young Yeshua. Even one as imprudent as you should know that.*

Jesus tensed at the mere memory of the rabbi's voice. "People don't despise a thief who fills a starving stomach," he muttered. "Proverbs."

"What did you say?" the vendor demanded.

"Nothing," Jesus answered. "I said nothing."

As the vendor started talking to his friends—presumably discussing what to do with Jesus—Jesus began ticking through options. There weren't many. Escape was off the table, as was winning this fight. His only hope seemed to be to wait this out—to take his beating until the vendor felt like he'd balanced the scales. Then, he would never return to this market again. It wasn't ideal, but it would have to do. Under normal circumstances, Jesus might've been a good match for these men, but in his current state, his strength was all but gone—a casualty of surviving the streets of Kashi. This was no excuse, though. If he couldn't be stronger, he'd just have to be smarter.

A sobering thought occurred to him, though, as he sorted through plans. He wouldn't be sad to leave this market—it was too loud, anyway, and the smell of cardamom always seemed too strong—but in that moment, he realized this was the last market in the city he hadn't been exiled from. If he had to abandon this one, it would mean having to leave Kashi altogether, and if that happened, where could he go next? The thought of having to set back out on the road, especially in his state, threatened to drain Jesus of what little energy he had left, leaving him feeling more husk than human. Still, he tried to stay focused. One problem at a time.

All at once, Jesus realized the vendor was talking to him, and he shook himself out of his daze.

"—one more reminder," his opponent was saying. "One more reminder that we do not tolerate thieves in this city."

Jesus wasn't sure what this meant, but he didn't like the sound of it. Before he could ask, the vendor plucked a knife from his belt and brandished it in front of Jesus's face.

Jesus realized his plan to wait things out may have taken a turn for the impractical.

"You not only steal from me," the vendor told him. "You steal from my children, and *this* is a crime for which I am less forgiving." He gestured with the knife. "May this be a lasting lesson in justice, my foreign friend."

As the vendor advanced, something in Jesus finally snapped. A laugh escaped from him, and he didn't bother to hold it back.

His opponent stopped short, confused. "This is humorous to you?"

"I guess it is," Jesus said, shaking his head. "It's only... the way you use that word. 'Justice?' The man with a knife and a full belly is going to take a pound of flesh from an unarmed, starving man, and he calls it 'justice?' Do you think I *want* to be here? Do you think I *want* to be stealing from you or your kids? So, yes, I think calling any of this 'justice' is pretty humorous, don't you?"

It took the vendor a moment to understand, but when he did, he grinned. "You think you are very clever," he said. "I can tell. Let's see how clever you are when this blade touches your skin, shall we?"

The men tightened their grip, and Jesus reached for a miracle. He thought quickly, reviewing everything that had happened that morning—searching for anything that might point to a way out. Any little detail might be the key to—

Suddenly, a bell tolled in a nearby temple. In an instant, Jesus saw his chance.

"The man at the black pepper booth," he said quickly. "The, um... *ah,* what's the word?"

The vendor kept coming. Jesus willed his brain to work faster.

"The, um... *the priest!*" Jesus exclaimed. *"The priest* at the black pepper booth!"

At the word *priest,* the vendor hesitated. This was what Jesus had counted on. In all his travels, he'd learned that no matter what country you were in—no matter what city you were passing through—there was one thing you could always count on to make people nervous.

"What about him?" the vendor demanded.

"Well, you are a faithful man, yes?" Jesus asked.

The vendor narrowed his eyes. "What's your point?"

Jesus had been observing the vendor's stall for days. He had seen how the vendor reacted when a priest came through with his white dhoti and the thread and beads decorating his chest. The vendor had never failed to ask for a blessing, bowing in deference as the priest marked his booth with sandalwood paste. He also knew that this vendor kept a small, wooden shrine in his booth, where he would make fruit offerings to one god or another. *Lakshmi? Vishnu?* Jesus couldn't remember. This place had more gods than he could ever keep straight.

"My point is," Jesus said, "that plenty of witnesses saw you chase me into this alley. If someone finds my body here, they'll have a pretty good idea who it was that killed me, don't you think? I don't know how your priests here feel about killing, but back in my country, it's frowned upon."

Jesus had no way of knowing if this would work. For all he knew, the priests in this city didn't care at all whether fruit vendors killed vagrants in narrow alleyways, but it was all he had. He observed the vendor's face, looking for the slightest twinge of doubt.

Instead of doubt, however, the vendor's mouth turned up into another grin. "You assume I wish to kill you," the vendor said. "I have no plans to kill you. Merely, as I said, to leave you with a reminder."

He advanced again.

"Will you listen to yourself?" Jesus demanded. "You can see the bones under my skin! Do you think I'd survive anything you could do with that knife? Whatever 'reminder' you have in mind will leave me bleeding out in minutes."

At this, the vendor hesitated again, and Jesus saw the doubt on his face. He seized his chance. "And when you begin carving and I don't survive," he pressed, "what will your priest have to say about that? Do you really think the blessings will keep coming? And what will that mean for your children once their father's cursed booth fails? Who's stealing from them now?"

Jesus knew the bit about the children might have been unnecessary, but he was taking no chances.

"Look, if you let me go," Jesus said, "you have my word that you will never see my face again. I will leave the marketplace. I'll leave the city. I'll never come back."

The vendor looked over Jesus's shoulder to his friends for guidance, and whatever he saw there must have convinced him. After a tense moment, the knife went back into its sheath. Jesus started breathing again.

"Listen closely," the vendor said, getting close to Jesus's face. "Should I *ever* see you in this market again—and I do not care how noble your reasons—I will bring you back to this place and I will give you a beating you will never forget. Do you understand?"

Jesus wanted to point out he wasn't likely to forget *this* beating, but he deemed this unwise. "Understood," he said.

The vendor hit Jesus once more for good measure, knocking the wind out of him. The men let go, and Jesus dropped to the dust, clutching his stomach. This time, he didn't miss the cow dung.

By the time he could look back up, his opponents were gone.

Jesus sat still, catching his breath, before crawling to a nearby wall and slumping against it. He shook his sleeve as clean as he could, and as he did, he sent up a silent prayer that someone had stolen the vendor's entire stock while he'd been gone. He knew this prayer would go unanswered, though. God had never deigned to answer one of his prayers before—why should this time be any different?

Slowly, using the wall for support, Jesus rose to his feet. One of his sandals had broken while he was running, and he tried to angle his foot so the sandal wouldn't fall off. It would be harder to travel with one shoe, but this wasn't his most pressing concern at the moment.

Checking to be sure no one was watching, Jesus reached careful-ly into his bag and his fingers brushed the skin of four small mangoes—the ones the vendor *hadn't* seen him steal. They were undamaged. He felt a stab of satisfaction. The jackfruit had been a reach, but these were all that really mattered, and the beating had been a small price to pay to get them where they needed to go.

"You can keep your jackfruit," he muttered as he hobbled away, trying to balance his sandal so he wouldn't lose it. "I have an appointment to keep."

# 2

## *Judea, twenty months before.*

THE NIGHT BEFORE HE'D left Nazareth for good, Jesus had been sitting on a bench at the inn, sharing wine with a group of lively textile merchants. When he'd found them, they'd been debating the virtues of wool versus linen for surviving the desert, and Jesus had cheerfully joined the fray, arguing passionately for wool. In truth, Jesus knew little about either wool or the desert, but he did know quite a bit about winning arguments. It was how he relaxed at the end of a long day. "And that's why linen might keep you cool," he brought his case to a close, "but wool will keep you *alive,* which, as I understand it, is the preferable option."

Jesus looked to John—his best friend since childhood—who gave him an approving nod. Jesus grinned, taking this to mean he'd won.

The other merchants laughed as one trader got up to buy a round of diluted wine—his penance for losing. "It's a shame you don't get paid to argue," John said, speaking over the volume of the busy courtyard. "You could earn more than we'll ever make in carpentry."

"I get paid in wine and pride," Jesus pointed out. "I'll take that over silver any day."

This was how Jesus and John spent most of their evenings—huddled around a smoky fire in the crowded courtyard of the inn, meeting travelers and trading stories. Jesus found there was never a shortage of interesting people at the inn, nor interesting stories from outside of Nazareth. John was usually more interested in listening than engaging, but it didn't matter. Jesus enjoyed it enough for the both of them.

No doubt when John's younger brother—James—grew older, he'd be right there along with them.

Jesus surveyed the inn as they waited for their drinks. He spotted other textile merchants with various dyes staining their clothes. He saw regional traders bragging about papyrus from Egypt. As he looked around, he also noticed two Roman soldiers pass the entrance of the inn—their bronze armor catching the firelight and their uniform sandals grinding against the dirt. He frowned. Romans rarely made it as far out as Nazareth—backwoods town that it was—but on the occasion they did, the sight always put a bitter taste in his mouth.

"Look," John said next to him, pointing across the courtyard. "There's Joseph."

"Is it, now?" Jesus asked, the soldiers forgotten in light of this new information. "Well, what do you say we go say hello?"

"I say, why don't you leave that old man alone?" John answered. "Is it not enough he took you on as an apprentice? Did he not earn some reprieve?"

"He did not," Jesus said. "Besides, it's up to you and me to keep things interesting in this hopeless town. You know Joseph enjoys our company, deep down."

"He doesn't," John said. "I promise you, he doesn't."

Jesus accepted his drink from the trader and rose from the bench. "Come on," he said, patting John's shoulder. "Let's at least find out about the job tomorrow. Then we'll leave him alone."

"Yeshua, this won't—"

"Come on!" Jesus urged, already halfway there.

Reluctantly, grabbing his own drink, John followed.

Joseph was a carpenter, and he had taken Jesus and John under his wing when they'd been young. Both Jesus and John had grown up without fathers, and although Joseph would never admit it, Jesus always suspected he'd stepped into their lives as an act of mercy. This had earned him Jesus's respect, though he had an odd way of showing it.

Joseph saw the two approach, and his face fell. "Can you not give me one moment's peace?" he growled. "Is it not enough that we have to spend the daylight hours together? You have to ruin my evenings, too?"

"Good evening, Joseph," Jesus greeted pleasantly, settling onto the bench across from him.

John also took his seat, preparing to watch the show.

"Don't you 'good evening Joseph' me," Joseph said. "You two can just take yourselves and—"

"As much as we hate to interrupt what I'm sure was a satisfying evening of brooding and solitude," Jesus interrupted, "we only wanted to ask about the job tomorrow. As you have thus far kept the information to yourself, it would be nice if—"

"It pays," Joseph grunted. "That's all you need to know. Now go mind your own business."

"Come on, Joseph," Jesus pressed. "You don't think this *is* our business? Just a little?"

Joseph didn't answer, and Jesus didn't let up. "Don't we at least need to know where to show up tomorrow?" he asked. "I mean, do you want us wandering the streets of Nazareth, calling your name? Utterly helpless?"

John tried to hide a laugh.

"Show up at the shop," Joseph said. "We'll go from there. Goodbye, now."

Jesus hesitated, exchanging a wary look with John. They were used to Joseph keeping to himself, but a flat-out refusal to tell them about a job was different.

"Why do I feel you're avoiding telling us until it's too late to say no?" Jesus asked, now a little concerned.

"Because I *am* avoiding telling you until it's too late to say no."

John chimed in. "It can't be that bad, can it? We're not working in the stables again?"

Joseph's face gave them nothing.

"Joseph," Jesus said, "don't you think you owe us at least—"

"I owe you nothing," Joseph said, giving him a hard look. "In fact, I have half a mind to—"

"It's not another job for Samuel, is it?" Jesus went on. "You remember the last time—"

"Drop it, kid."

"Is it the west gate? I swear, if we fix that gate one more time—"

"Enough."

"Then again, if it's the *east* gate—"

"Fine!" Joseph said, bringing his cup down on the table so hard wine sloshed out. "If I tell you, will you leave me be?"

Satisfied, Jesus sat up straight. "On my honor," he said.

John chuckled again. "What honor?"

After another swig of wine, Joseph considered the best way to break the news, increasing Jesus's worry ever so slightly. What could be so bad that Joseph felt like he couldn't tell them until the last minute?

Finally, Joseph just came out and said it. "Synagogue," he said. "The eave supports need reinforcing all around the building. I know it's usually community work, but they're getting bad, and the rabbi needed someone with skill."

*The rabbi.* Jesus's body tensed. John's expression darkened.

"The synagogue..." Jesus repeated, trying to sound casual. "Well, all right. Was that so difficult?"

"See?" Joseph snapped. "*This* is why I didn't want to tell you. You start in with all this self-righteous nonsense! It's money, isn't it? And what's more, it's an important job for this town, not that *you'd* understand that."

Jesus let this go as Joseph calmed himself. "Listen," Joseph said, "I know you've had your trouble with the rabbi, but tomorrow, I expect you to put it aside, show up, and do your job."

"*I'm* not the problem," Jesus protested. "You know how that old hypocrite is."

"That's why *you* are going to control *yourself*, you understand?" Joseph warned. "You're gonna be like water, kid, do you hear me? He throws something at you, and you let it pass through without a word."

Jesus scoffed. "You expect me to just say nothing?"

"Only if you want to get paid."

Jesus sat back, actually wondering if that would be enough. This was a bad idea. He had a lot of things he wanted to say, but he knew how much respect the rabbi commanded in the community, so he was used to watching what he said around others. The truth was that the rabbi made him feel small in ways he hated. The rabbi always had a way of doing that, even during the years when Jesus was in the synagogue every week. Since they'd broken ties, they tried to stay out of each other's way. When they didn't, things had a way of getting heated.

But then there was his mother to consider. If he refused this job, it was the difference between eating and fasting for the next few days. *You have responsibilities here, Yeshua,* his mother had said to him a hundred times. *Sometimes you must swallow your pride and fulfill your obligations.*

"Fine," Jesus answered, "but as soon as he sees me coming, you know he's going to have something to say about it. As far as he's concerned, these hands are unclean, and you know as well as I do he doesn't want them anywhere near his precious synagogue."

"He'll have no problem if he wants the job done," Joseph said, "but it won't matter, will it? Because what are you going to do if he tries to stir up trouble?"

*"When,"* Jesus corrected. *"When* he tries to stir up trouble."

"And what are you going to do?"

Jesus stared at his cup. "I'm going to be water," he mumbled.

"What's that?"

"I'm gonna be water!"

"That's right," Joseph said, triumphant. He regarded Jesus for a moment, shaking his head. "You think you two are so different. It's no wonder you can't stand each other."

"What's that supposed to mean?" Jesus demanded.

"It means you're both arrogant know-it-alls with vanities too fragile for my patience," Joseph said. "Now, if memory serves, we had a deal."

Jesus hesitated, then nodded at John, cutting his losses. Maybe they would've been better off staying with the textile merchants.

"Listen," Jesus said as he stood, "when this all goes to hell, don't say I didn't warn you."

"It won't go to hell, will it?" Joseph asked confidently. "Because you're gonna be water."

"Sure. I'll be water. You be a surly old man."

"Finally, we understand one another."

Jesus had just started back towards the textile traders when he remembered something. He stopped and pulled a coin from the pouch on his belt, flipping it so it landed by Joseph's drink. "The next drink's on me," he said.

"You—" Joseph started. "Come take this back! I will owe you nothing!"

Jesus smiled and walked away. Over years of perfecting his craft, he'd learned the most effective way to get under Joseph's skin was to do something kind. *If your enemy is thirsty, give him a drink. In so doing, you heap burning coals onto his head.*

"Get back here!" Joseph called, but they were too far away.

"The man can't make up his mind," Jesus muttered to John. "Go away... come back... what does he want from us?"

"Why do you have to antagonize him?" John asked. "Is it not enough to keep your head down? To do the work and say thank you?"

"No," Jesus said simply, "and honestly, I'll never understand how it's enough for you."

They made it back to the textile traders, who were now a round ahead of them, and Jesus intended to catch up. He didn't want to think about the synagogue. He hadn't been back in so long—not since his falling out with the rabbi—and the thought of going back now made his pulse quicken. It wasn't the building, of course. It was everything the building had once meant to him, and everything it meant to him now.

"Just keep a handle on yourself tomorrow, all right?" John warned. "I think the rabbi has only gotten worse with age."

"Don't worry about me," Jesus said. "I'm water, remember?"

John gave up, and Jesus jumped back into his conversation with the merchants, which had now developed into a debate about goatskin versus clay jars for keeping wine fresh. Again, Jesus knew very little about either, but leaped in all the same, trying to forget what tomorrow would surely bring.

# 3

## *Kashi.*

JESUS HOBBLED DOWN A few alleyways, making his way until he found what he was looking for: the courtyard of a city gate. Kashi had several gates, and this one was by far the simplest. That might've been why he liked it so much. Time had chipped away at the vines and lotus flowers carved in the sandstone archway, smoothing their edges beyond recognition. Mud and straw had built up in the corners, left behind by farmers passing through with their carts. The gate, as well as the courtyard that opened up before it, was plain and practical—somewhere Jesus could disappear.

He paused as he entered the courtyard, carefully scanning the landscape. The people he was looking for—the ones for whom he'd stolen the mangoes in the first place—were easy to miss and skilled at staying invisible. Today, however, Jesus found them at once. Amid bundles of millet, rice, and sugarcane were four children gleefully playing a game in the dust. Jesus couldn't help but smile when he saw them. Their resilience was one of the few sparks of inspiration he'd found since arriving in this city.

Jesus stayed close to the perimeter, walking past laborers waiting to find work and past old men debating about something he didn't understand. The smell of the cow dung made it harder to go unnoticed, and he ignored the stares and rude gestures as he passed. Finally, he crouched down next to the children. "What are you playing?" he asked.

"Issa!" one child cried out, excited to see him. "Where have you been? We haven't—"

The child's eyes went wide when she saw the bruise on Jesus's face. "Did they catch you? Did they hurt you bad?"

"What? You mean this?" Jesus asked, gesturing to his face. "It's nothing. You should have seen *them.*"

"Did you bring anything for us?" another child asked eagerly, the game forgotten.

Jesus feigned shock. "Did I bring anything for you?" he repeated in mock disbelief. "In all the time you've known me, when have I *not* brought you something?"

He stood and tossed each of them a mango, grinning as their faces lit up. They tore into the fruit eagerly, wiping their hands on their grubby tunics. "I tried to get a jackfruit," Jesus said, "but—"

"Never try to steal a jackfruit," the oldest child—Leela—interrupted. Leela was their unofficial leader, and it was a position she had earned with boldness and practicality. "It is too big."

"Thank you for that sage advice," Jesus said. "I'll keep it in mind."

"But they caught you, Issa!" another child pointed out, wiping juice from his face. "There are no more safe markets for you! Does that mean you're leaving?"

Jesus tried not to look discouraged. "It does look that way," he said. "I'm afraid you may have to manage by yourselves for a while."

"We got along fine before!" Leela declared, flexing a nonexistent muscle. "We are strong."

Jesus pretended to admire her imaginary bicep. "Well," he said, "with muscles like that, you have nothing to worry about."

They talked as the kids took their time eating. This was where Jesus got most of his language practice, as they spoke on about the same level. When the children were finished, they thanked Jesus and the smaller ones started to run off. "Goodbye, Issa!" Leela called as she ran after them. "Be well!"

"Look after yourselves!" Jesus called back, but when she finally disappeared behind a corner, his face fell. They wouldn't be able to look after themselves, and he wouldn't be well. For a moment, everything about the city seemed bleak.

Jesus found a shady corner and sank to the ground, trying to form a plan. He knew he needed to stay focused—to keep moving—or he might lose what remained of his fragile will to press on. He could already feel it crumbling. *One's own folly leads to their ruin,* Jesus remembered his Rabbi saying, *yet still their heart will rage against the Almighty. Do you see the price of your folly, young Yeshua?*

He tried to push the voice away.

*A lack of discipline has brought you here. An abundance of arrogance. When calamity overtakes you like a storm and disaster engulfs you like a whirlwind—when you are overwhelmed by distress and burdened by trouble—you will look to God's face and he will not answer. You will look for salvation, but find none.*

Closing his eyes, he tried to block everything out. He didn't want to think about the vendor. He didn't want to think about the kids. He didn't want to think about the rabbi or Nazareth or Joseph, any of the things that threatened to drag him under. He was suddenly exhausted and his bruised body ached more by the second. He knew he needed to move, but his whole body rebelled against him.

*Only a few minutes,* he thought. *I'll rest for only a few minutes.*

Then he would set out again. Rallying what strength he had, he would push himself further off the edge of the map and into oblivion.

# 4

## *Judea, twenty months before.*

JOSEPH HADN'T BEEN AT his shop, so Jesus assumed he and John had already gone ahead to the synagogue. This was just as well. Jesus wanted some time alone.

He walked slowly to the village center, which was still deserted in the pale light of dawn. It felt strange to Jesus, being out here this early—before the stalls had opened or crowds surrounded the well. This place was the heart of Nazareth, and it was unnerving for it to be so quiet. The sun would be up soon, though, and with it, everyone who would bring this place to life.

*Sustain us at dawn with your unfailing love, that we may sing with delight and be glad all our days...*

Jesus pushed the lyrics out of his head. He hadn't sung a psalm in years—they brought more pain than comfort these days—yet they were all still there. They were like embers, waiting for a gust of wind to stir them back to life.

The clatter of Joseph laying out his tools resounded loudly through the village center. He examined the chisels and mallets and pegs, looking up at the sound of Jesus's approach. "Well, look who showed up," he said, going back to his inspection. "I thought you were going to leave us shorthanded."

*I nearly did,* Jesus wanted to say. Instead, he regarded the familiar building before him. It had been a while.

The modest building was built of hewn stone and sycamore fig wood. Its narrow, unadorned windows felt like eyes, looking down at him in disapproval of this reunion. One look at the synagogue brought back memories of neatly swept, packed dirt floors... the rough texture of the wooden benches, arranged in neat rows... countless Sabbaths spent chanting psalms and listening to readings from their limited selection of scrolls... Their collection was decent for a small town, but far from complete. All of it evoked a bittersweet mixture of nostalgia and apprehension.

It was clear to Jesus why the rabbi had called. The wooden beams that made up the roof extended out over the walls to divert water, but they had splintered badly in several places. If the decay continued further in, the entire roof could go. It wasn't hopeless yet, but if the rabbi had delayed any longer in calling them, it might've been.

Jesus approached John, who was inspecting the three ladders they'd need that day. "Decent of you to come," John said.

"Joseph already used that one," Jesus said, "but good try. Any sign of the physician?"

"Not yet," John said, distracted. "Only us so far."

"The physician" was a nickname Jesus and John used for the rabbi. It had come from a teacher who was passing through the inn one night. The conversation had turned to the rabbi, and when Jesus had described him, the teacher had shaken his head. He'd asked, "What good is a physician who can't heal himself?" and Jesus had never heard it put so perfectly.

John abandoned the ladders, satisfied they wouldn't break their necks. "I know this isn't easy," he said.

"It's nothing," Jesus dismissed.

"Yes, I know, but if you need a break, let me know. I can cover for you."

Jesus hesitated. "Thank you," he said, "but really, it will be all right. What's the worst he can do?"

"Well, just keep in mind, if you make him mad enough, none of us gets paid."

"Thanks, *Joseph*," Jesus said. "I'm supposed to be like water, right?"

"That's the idea."

They stood there for another moment, and just when Joseph was about to tell them to get to work, the synagogue doors finally swung open. There, on cue, was the rabbi, surveying his domain.

"All right," Jesus muttered. "Brace yourself."

To most of Nazareth, the rabbi was beyond reproach. His name—Rabbi Matityahu—literally meant "Gift from God," and he carried himself as if his title had been bestowed by the heavens. He was a Pharisee from the House of Shammai—a group known for its rigid, legalistic adherence to the law—and he had come to Nazareth when Jesus was only learning to walk. The rabbi couldn't have been older than thirty when he'd come, but to Jesus, as he sat next to his mother in the assembly, the rabbi might as well have been the Ancient of Days.

As far as the town was concerned, the rabbi was everything they respected. Upright. Unwavering. Willing to speak the hard words no one else had the courage to say... To Jesus, however, he was a play actor. Legalistic. Self-important. Quick to use the name of God to intimidate anyone into submission... There were many in the town who used tefillin in times of private prayer—leather straps meant to bind scripture to your arms—but the rabbi wore his in plain view of everyone. He said it was to "set an example," but Jesus knew better. It was men like Rabbi Matityahu that Nazareth respected, and it was men like him who made Jesus's life so difficult.

"Joseph," the rabbi called, fixing Jesus with an unwavering stare as he descended the stone steps of the synagogue. "I didn't realize you'd be bringing help."

"Well, I couldn't get the job done on my own, now, could I?" Joseph answered. Jesus admired the way he so casually pushed past the rabbi's judgment. "Is that going to be a problem?"

The rabbi came to a stop before Jesus and John. "I suppose that remains to be seen."

Jesus forced a smile. "Rabbi," he greeted. "Peace be with you."

"And with you be peace," the rabbi replied. To anyone else, it would have sounded sincere. Again, Jesus knew better.

Behind the rabbi's back, Joseph was mouthing something, and it took Jesus a moment to understand.

*Water! You will be water!*

*We'll see,* Jesus thought.

"I heard you were off at the inn again last night," the rabbi began. "Your mother must worry."

Jesus's smile didn't waver. "Without ceasing," he answered, "but she endures."

The rabbi gave a look of exaggerated concern. "I would think you would remember the proverb," he said. "Wine mocks, strong drink leads to brawls, and whoever is led astray by them is a fool. You don't want to be a fool, do you, Yeshua?"

Jesus didn't hesitate in his response. "Well, I would think *you* would remember the psalm, 'God makes grass to grow for the cattle, plants for farming, and wine to gladden the heart of humankind.' You wouldn't want to mock the blessings of God, would you, Rabbi?"

At this, John coughed hard into his hand, trying to suppress a laugh, and Joseph gave Jesus a hard look. The rabbi, by contrast, remained unperturbed. "How about we stick to carpentry and leave the scriptures to those who know how to use them, shall we?"

"Of course," Jesus answered. "If I see someone like that, I will."

Jesus considered this a victory.

As Joseph launched into an apology, Jesus only wanted to turn around and call it a day. It hadn't always been this way between Jesus and the rabbi, but they'd been doing this dance now for years. There had been a time when Jesus had admired the rabbi more than anyone else in the world, and his mother had brought him up going to the synagogue every Sabbath. She'd taught him to believe wholeheartedly in whatever the rabbi said, which mostly included reminders that God was in charge, a list of behaviors that pleased God, and a list of behaviors for which God would wipe cities from the earth. Jesus quickly learned that if God grew angry enough, he was prone to do things like turn women into pillars of salt, so he tried to abide by the behaviors that were meant to please God. He got so good at it, in fact, that by the time he was eleven, he could recite the law better than anyone in town.

By the time he was twelve, his mother had taken to calling him her "little rabbi."

By the time he was thirteen, the rabbi had taken notice, and had taken Jesus under his wing. This training became Jesus's entire reason for being.

The rabbi would spend hours each week quizzing Jesus on the law, teaching him about the traditions, and ensuring that he prayed and practiced well. He was strict, temperamental, and slow to forgive, but Jesus only took this as motivation to work harder. As far as he was concerned, the rabbi's approval was God's approval.

By fifteen, Jesus had the chance to teach in the synagogue, which made his mother glow with pride. She showered him with praise—and Jesus remembered feeling like he was exactly where he was supposed to be. Then, the trouble started.

The fundamental problem was that Jesus liked to ask questions. He couldn't help himself. Where he saw a gap in the law or an inconsistency in the stories, he wanted to explore it. He'd heard that many rabbis welcomed questions—it was how they learned—but Rabbi Matityahu, he soon found, was *not* one of these rabbis. "Where were the children during the great flood?" he asked one Sabbath in the synagogue after everyone had sat down to discuss the week's scripture. "The children, the babies... did God let them drown? Had they sinned, too?"

He felt it was important to nail down exactly what counted as "sin," as he was eager to avoid being killed by a flood.

"God had his reasons, young Yeshua," the rabbi had answered. "Now, if we—"

"Right, but what *were* the reasons?" Jesus had pressed, causing the rabbi's eyes to narrow. He did not like being interrupted.

"Yeshua, you must trust God and lean not on your own under-standing."

"Yes, but—"

"God's ways are higher than your ways," the rabbi had said, his tone sharp, "and often beyond your ability to comprehend."

And that had been the end of it. Jesus had felt slightly embar-rassed at having been chastised in front of the congregation, but that was nothing compared to how difficult it would become over the following months.

Jesus started asking other, more troubling questions:

When he prayed to God, why did God never answer?

When he tried to push his doubts away, why did they keep coming back?

Why did the rabbi make him feel so guilty when he brought these things up?

"If God is just," he asked one Sabbath, "why does he allow the wicked to prosper?"

"God's ways are higher than our ways, young Yeshua," the rabbi had answered again, in what was quickly becoming one of Jesus's least favorite phrases. "You must—"

"Yes, but can God really be just if the innocent suffer while—"

"Yeshua," the rabbi had interrupted in a tone so harsh it made some in the assembly jump. "You must trust in God and lean not on your own understanding. Know your place."

This time, though, Jesus hadn't been willing to let it go. He'd held onto the question until later that afternoon, when he brought it to the rabbi in private, and things hadn't gone well. "I will not tolerate this level of disrespect from you," the rabbi had insisted. "I am the teacher and you are the student. You will do well to remember that."

"But why is it that every time I ask a question, it's disrespectful?" Jesus had demanded, losing patience. "Should a deeper under-standing of God not be our—"

"The fear of God is the beginning of wisdom!" the rabbi had corrected, his face growing a dangerous shade of crimson. "I am hearing much arrogance from you, and very little fear. You are not asking because you wish to find the answers. You are asking because you wish to sound wise, and a boastful heart is *not* a behavior I will tolerate from a student of mine!"

The rabbi was highly skilled at turning things around—making Jesus feel like *he* was the problem rather than the actual problem—and for a moment he'd felt guilty. Maybe the rabbi was right. But soon, the guilt gave way to anger. "Maybe I *do* want to sound wise," Jesus had shot back. "Is that a sin? To take something seriously enough to want to know what you're talking about?"

"Are you suggesting I do not know what I am talking about?"

The fight had gone until the rabbi had thrown Jesus out, and Jesus had been so angry and shaken that he'd stayed home the following Sabbath. When his mother returned from the synagogue, however, her face had been pale. Humiliated, she'd informed Jesus that the rabbi had announced to the assembly that Jesus was fostering "a spirit of disunity and contempt," and he would not have it spreading through the congregation. He had talked about Jesus like he was a disease. Like he was contagious. He had announced that Jesus was not welcome back in the assembly until he had repented of his sin and sought forgiveness, and then he had continued with the service like nothing had happened.

Technically, the rabbi did not have the authority to do this. The synagogue belonged to the community, not to him, but it was a testament to the power he wielded that no one challenged him on this. For most of them, it affirmed something they had suspected all along. Jesus was a troublemaker. A problem—not to be associated with.

Jesus had been so shocked that he had hardly heard any of his mother's lecture about how ashamed he should feel and how he should apologize at once. As his mother went on, however, Jesus's shock had turned to anger. He was sure the rabbi had meant it as a teaching moment—that Jesus would soon return and fall in line and continue with his training—but it wouldn't work. Not this time. Jesus was finished. The rest of Nazareth could let themselves be enchanted by the rabbi's spell, but not him. *Like a snarling lion or a charging bear is a corrupt leader over a helpless people.* Jesus would have no more part in it.

He hadn't been back to the synagogue since. Until now.

Joseph was still trying to apologize for his insubordinate apprentice when the rabbi waved it off. "It is no problem, Joseph," he said. "It is simply his nature, being who he is. Believe me, I have put up with far worse from the all-knowing Yeshua, son of Mary."

At this, Jesus's smile tightened, and his hands balled into fists. In Judea, it was common to refer to someone by their father's name. Jacob, son of Isaac, Solomon, son of David, and so on. If someone's father was unknown, however—as was the case for Jesus—it was only decent to avoid the address altogether. The rabbi, however, had a talent for sounding decent without actual decency. To call someone by their mother's name was a backhanded slight.

"What's the matter, my boy?" the rabbi asked. "Something you wish to say?"

Jesus thought of a hundred things he wished to say, but Joseph glared at him with a thousand unspoken threats. "No," he answered. "Nothing."

"I thought not," the rabbi said. "Whoever keeps his tongue keeps himself out of trouble. Doubtless, you still remember at least some scriptures I taught you."

*When the corrupt rule, the people mourn,* Jesus wanted to say. He remembered all of them.

No one said anything for a moment, and eventually, the rabbi nodded to the other two carpenters. "The town appreciates your service to the synagogue, gentlemen," he said. "Now, the day isn't getting any cooler. I suggest you get to work. *Shalom.*"

"*Shalom,*" Jesus muttered. He was sure the rabbi wished him many things, but *Shalom*—peace—was not one of them.

As soon as the rabbi was gone, Joseph rounded on Jesus. "You—" he started.

"I know, I know," Jesus said before the lecture could get underway. "Like water. I understand. Just let me get working and it won't be a problem again."

"Won't be a problem again..." Joseph echoed skeptically, shaking his head. "Get over there and set up your ladder. This is going to be a bigger job than we thought. The rot goes solid through."

"I don't doubt it."

Joseph shot him one last look of warning, and Jesus held up his palms in surrender.

"I'll be on the other side," John said, taking up his ladder. "Joseph has you on the front, near the door, but I'm serious. If you need a break, say something."

"I'm fine," Jesus repeated. "I'm water, remember?"

John gave a quiet laugh. "Right."

Jesus took his rickety ladder to the front, by the entryway, and Joseph and John took theirs to the side walls. "I'm water," Jesus muttered to himself. He was mostly making fun of Joseph, but the more he thought about it, the more he liked it.

Water splashed back at you when you threw something too heavy into it.

Water could sink boats.

Water could carve stone.

Water engulfed anyone who failed to respect it.

*Save me from the waters, O God,* the psalm rang in his head. *They have risen to my neck and I sink, mired in the depths...*

As he started to work—knocking down sizeable pieces of rotten wood, he smiled.

"I am water."

# 5

## *Kashi.*

JESUS HAD JUST CLOSED his eyes when he felt a shadow pass over him. His body tensed. He had barely recovered from his last fight and had no strength for another. Maybe if he kept perfectly still, whoever it was would move on and leave him be.

"Pardon me, son," the stranger said. "I don't mean to disturb you, but I saw what you did back there."

Jesus sighed. It had been worth a try.

Curious, he risked opening an eye and saw a broad-shouldered old man standing over him, watching him with interest. He had an imposing presence, with thick patches of gray, curling hair sticking out from beneath his cap, matching the gray of his thick, curling beard, which reached down to his tunic. By the state of his clothes, Jesus judged this was a man of some means—a merchant, maybe, or a landowner—but with none of the usual air of condescension. Instead, his gaze held a curiosity he rarely encountered. Something about him felt familiar—unsettlingly so—but Jesus couldn't place why.

"And what is it, exactly, that you thought you saw?" Jesus asked hesitantly.

The old man gave Jesus a wry smile. "He admits to nothing," he said. "Very wise."

Jesus opened both eyes now. The man was definitely familiar.

"Whatever else it is you have done, though," the man said, "I'm talking about what you did for those children."

"It was nothing," Jesus said, cautiously, wondering why this old man was bothering him.

"Oh, it was *not* nothing," the man corrected, his voice firm. "It was *kind*. There isn't enough kindness in this city, that's why I make a practice of naming it when I see it. As a token of my appreciation, I would like to offer you an opportunity, if you're so inclined."

Jesus shifted, trying in vain to find a position that didn't hurt. "An opportunity?" he asked. "What kind of opportunity?"

"One that might benefit someone such as yourself—a long way from home and having a hard time."

Jesus paused. "How did you know I'm far from home and having a hard time?"

Jesus could see a distant calculation going on behind the man's eyes, but when he spoke, it was sincere. "I have spent much of my life here," he said, "and I don't recall seeing you before. Besides—and I hope you don't take this the wrong way, son—but you look a bit worse for wear."

Jesus tried not to be insulted.

"I own a vineyard," the old man finally told him. "I come here looking for laborers who might help with the harvest. I offer a day's work for a day's pay."

"You want me to work in your fields?" Jesus asked. "Have you seen me? What makes you think I'd survive the first hour?"

The old man gave him the same smile. "You'll do what you can," he said. "Don't overstrain yourself, of course. As I said, I only wished to express my gratitude."

Jesus studied the man's face, searching for the deception. "It's a full day's wage?" he asked.

"It is."

"And I'd be harvesting grapes?"

"One of the easiest fruits to harvest!"

Jesus considered the man's offer. A day's wage would go a long way on the road once he got out of the city, but part of him still felt cautious. Unease gnawed at him, though he still couldn't say why. After another moment, however, he decided the benefits outweighed the risk. "All right," he said. "A day's work for a day's wage. I'll do it."

"Excellent!" the old man said, satisfied, and he offered a hand to pull Jesus up. Jesus expected to pull the man off balance, but either he'd grown thinner than he realized he was or the old man was remarkably strong for his age. Either way, he was soon on his feet.

"Now," the old man said, "my cart is just outside the gate here. The others should be waiting."

"Others?"

"Oh yes. I recruit as many as I can. As they say, the harvest is plenty, but the workers are few!"

Jesus had never heard anyone say this, but he knew better than to correct the man who had just employed him.

They made their way across the courtyard—Jesus trying to stay steady on his feet while navigating the uneven tile. His stomach was sore where the vendor had punched him, but he tried to walk tall, not letting the old man see how badly he was hurt.

"Aren't you in the wrong part of the world for vineyards?" he asked as they walked.

"Perceptive," the man answered. "It is primarily a mango farm, true, but we do have a sizeable grape harvest, and we keep a small press. Some of the city officials here find wine a novelty, you see. They keep us in business."

Jesus imagined the city officials paying handsomely for this man's exotic wine while jackfruit vendors tried to stab starving people in alleyways. Something about that made Jesus like this man a little less.

The old man smiled at a passerby he recognized. He greeted them cheerfully, and once again, Jesus had the impression he knew this man.

"Have we met before?" Jesus asked. "You seem very familiar."

The old man considered this. "Perhaps you have seen me in the markets," he said. "Though we certainly have not been formally introduced."

"Are you sure?"

"Oh, I would remember," the old man chuckled. "I may be getting up in years, but I have an excellent memory for faces, and yours, if you don't mind me saying, stands out. As I said, you are clearly far from home."

Jesus wasn't sure if this was good or bad, but he let the matter rest as they passed through the gate and into the sun. As long as he'd been here, Jesus had kept to crowded markets and tight alleyways, focusing only on survival. As a result, he rarely made it outside the city, and he'd forgotten about the view that had enraptured him when he'd first arrived.

The mountains were reflected in the river that ran alongside the road, and from across the sugarcane fields, the smell of jasmine was almost enough to offer a bit of renewed hope. Maybe he would survive this city after all.

"Abraham!" a voice called out, and they both turned. From inside the gate, a tall man in dark robes was hurrying to catch up. "Abraham! A word, if I might?"

The old man bowed slightly in reverence. Jesus wondered if this was one of the "city officials" he had mentioned who found wine so novel.

"Would you mind going on ahead?" the old man asked Jesus, winking. "I need to set this gentleman straight on a few things, but it shouldn't take long."

"Of course," Jesus said. "It's just up here?"

"Just up there," Abraham answered. "The one with the small crowd milling around. You can't miss it."

Jesus nodded and left the old man to his conversation. He passed cart after cart, each hitched to oxen lazily searching the dust for straw. It was nice being out in the open again, though he wasn't sure he looked forward to a day in the open harvesting produce. He was still so sore and lightheaded from his morning that he knew it would be a stretch to make it to the cart, much less to the end of a workday. His body ached for rest—to go back to his corner and hide amid the bundles of rice—but the real world called. He would find another place to rest tomorrow, before he got on the road. By then, he'd have a day's wage under his belt and some borrowed grapes in his stomach, and he'd feel better.

*The fool's wealth shall leave him,* the rabbi's voice warned, *and the undisciplined shall come to poverty and shame.*

Jesus felt some energy drain from his hope, and he tried to push the rabbi's voice away. It had been like this most of his life, but the harder he pushed these days, the more the voice seemed to force its way through. It had gotten especially cumbersome since he'd left Judea.

Jesus paused and laughed at himself for thinking of his journey in those terms. "Left" would imply he'd been given a choice. "Exile" might be a better word. He thought of the rabbi—of the synagogue job that had pushed him out of his hometown and, ultimately, his home country—and the memory left him bitter. He didn't want to think about that anymore. It hung around him like a ghost.

He decided, instead, to focus on the mystery of the old man. Why did he look so familiar? He'd said they hadn't met, but Jesus had gotten the impression he might not have been telling the whole truth. The old man certainly *seemed* kind enough—he hadn't woken him up with the kick or the shouts he'd grown used to—but then again, Jesus had known men to *seem* kind enough before, only to find them showing their true faces much later.

Jesus sighed. He was back to thinking about the rabbi. Full circle.

A small group of people were gathered up ahead, and Jesus assumed this must be the cart he was looking for. It was long, with benches running down either side. A few laborers were already in the cart, sitting on the benches and talking idly to one another, but Jesus wasn't in the mood for chatter. Instead, he set about inspecting the cart, looking for faults he might leverage into further work. That was how he'd earned his way to Kashi, after all—keeping traders' carts in good condition. To his disappointment, the cart was in fine repair—nothing loose or broken. The wheels were relatively new, and the axles were sturdy—the benches were in good repair, and the timber running along the side was smooth and well maintained. He was just giving up when something finally caught his eye. It seemed like nothing at first, but when he bent down to investigate, his eyes went wide and he took an involuntary step backward.

Carved on the side of the old man's cart was an image of a dove, and even though graven images were still something he was getting used to on this side of the world, it wasn't the dove that shocked him. Written under the image was a single word—not in the script of this land, but in a language that had no place in Kashi.

The inscription was in Hebrew.

*Shalom.*

"Something the matter?" a voice asked, and Jesus jumped at the sound of the old man's voice.

"This is..." Jesus started, gesturing at the carving. "This is Hebrew."

A bemused expression lit up the old man's face.

"It is," he said. "Fitting, don't you think? For a Judean far from home?"

# 6

## *Judea, twenty months before.*

THE HOURS PASSED AS the three carpenters chipped away at their work. Joseph had been right. The beams were badly rotted—deeper than had been visible at first glance, especially out over the eaves. The wood should have been replaced years ago, and the lintel over the door was dangerously soft, but little by little, they made progress.

Even with plenty to do, Jesus couldn't shake his unease. He tried to focus on the rotting wood splintering under his hammer—the earthy scent of decay that came from each new piece falling to the ground—but proximity to the synagogue brought back a flood of memories, each trying to compete for his attention. They were nostalgic memories, mostly. Things like where he used to sit with his mother... the psalms they used to sing... or the feeling of pride when he heard the rabbi teach... Permeating those memories, though, was an undercurrent of fear. The fear of being publicly cut down when he'd say something wrong... The feeling of anxiously wondering if he really was on God's good side... The suspicion that, even as hard as he tried, he didn't belong...

Standing so near the synagogue was bittersweet. He wanted to go inside nearly as much as he never wanted to go inside again.

Lost in thought, Jesus didn't hear the rabbi approach.

"Idle hands make for poverty, but diligent hands bring wealth."

Jesus blinked, snapping back to the present. He looked down to find the rabbi next to his ladder. "What?"

The rabbi gave him a condescending smile, as if Jesus's inattention was only to be expected. "I only meant it's good to see you doing something respectable," the rabbi said, gesturing towards the eaves with his staff. "Your mother must be proud to know you're contributing to the upkeep of our synagogue."

"Yes, well," Jesus said, turning his attention back to the wood, "it's a shame it got so bad to begin with, isn't it? What does the proverb say? Through laziness, the rafters sag, and because of idle hands, the house leaks?"

He dropped an eave support to the ground, making the rabbi jump back. Jesus hid his grin.

"As much I have missed our little talks," the rabbi said through clenched teeth, "I'm afraid the door will not close correctly. I will need you to fix it. Now."

"You need to talk to Joseph," Jesus said. "His instructions were—"

"Young Yeshua," the rabbi said, "as skilled as you have doubtless become at manual labor, do you genuinely believe I would first come to you without consulting the professional I *actually* hired?"

Jesus found himself wishing he had aimed better with the wood.

"So," the rabbi said, "unless you report to someone else with whom I am not familiar, perhaps it would be advantageous for you to stop trying to sound clever, and come do as I have instructed."

*Be water...* Jesus repeated to himself as he climbed down the ladder. *Be water... Be water...*

Following the rabbi, Jesus made his way over to the door and inspected it begrudgingly. The rabbi was right—the frame had shifted slightly when Jesus was working on the lintel, and now one door hung slightly crooked. The result was a sliver of space at the top of the doors and a slight overlap near the bottom. "Well, we can fix it," Jesus pointed out, "but we'll have to re-hang those hinges. It'll take about—"

"I need it done *now*, young Yeshua," the rabbi interrupted impatiently, "not whenever it suits you."

"Well, it cannot be done *now*, Rabbi," Jesus answered, keeping his most professional tone. "Even if we started now, it would take time."

"And what do you suggest I do in the meantime?" the rabbi demanded. "Throw a blanket over the door for privacy?"

"I suggest you reconsider whatever it is you need so much privacy to do to begin with," Jesus said, and the rabbi glared at him.

"There is a reckoning coming for you, young Yeshua," he warned. "A fool's mouth is his downfall, and his lips are a snare to his soul."

"Will there be anything else I can do?" Jesus asked, not wanting to get dragged in so deeply that he said something else stupid. "Shall I stop my work and focus on the door instead?"

"Won't be necessary," the rabbi brushed past him. "I have a meeting now. I do not wish to be disturbed. Return to your work."

Without looking back, the rabbi slammed the crooked door shut behind him, and Jesus swallowed about a dozen comebacks. It amazed him how the rabbi could be so mild one moment, then so harsh the next. He could do it at such a speed that it left those around him wondering what had been real. It was a tool the rabbi had used often to convince Jesus that he had simply misunderstood some outburst or another—that the rabbi was the reasonable one, and it was unwise for Jesus to "lean on his own understanding." It had been painfully effective.

As Jesus returned to his ladder, taking up his hammer and continuing to knock aging wood apart, he wondered what had been so urgent that the rabbi had been preoccupied by the door. He knew villagers often came to the rabbi for "wise counsel" and he needed privacy to carry on those talks, but something about this felt different. The rabbi almost seemed nervous, and he didn't get nervous about ordinary villagers. Why would he? They were beneath him. No, the rabbi grew nervous when teachers came to visit or elders came to check in—any time he wasn't certain his authority would go unquestioned. It was possible that's what was happening today—simply a former colleague passing through—and the rabbi didn't want to be interrupted. Maybe it was nothing.

Or maybe it was something else.

Jesus hesitated, stopping his hammer mid-swing. What if the rabbi *was* hiding something? Jesus had made his joke about the rabbi reconsidering what he was doing in private, but that had only been to get under the rabbi's skin. What if he had stumbled onto something real? What if the rabbi was taking a bribe or committing blackmail? Wouldn't that be something—to catch the rabbi in an act of unrighteousness, however small? Something Jesus could use the next time he and the rabbi went toe-to-toe? Maybe he should move closer to the door, just to be sure.

Jesus entertained the idea for a moment, but ultimately, he let it go. He was being childish, and he knew it. Spying on someone to get an advantage felt like the manner of thing the rabbi would fantasize about, not him. Jesus was only here to finish this job and go home—back to his mother, away from this place, and never think about it again.

Then again, the rabbi *had* wanted them to fix the door, hadn't he? If Jesus were to just set his ladder up next to the entryway and work on the hinges for a while, well... he couldn't help it if that put him eye-level with the crack at the top of the doors, could he? And if he *were* to overhear something... well, that wasn't on him, was it? He was just doing his job.

The longer Jesus thought about this, the more reasonable it seemed—the more it just made good sense—until he found himself checking over his shoulder to be sure Joseph was still on the other side of the building.

Quietly, he crept down and brought his ladder closer to the door.

When he got the ladder situated, Jesus took his tools and climbed carefully, quietly back up. Setting to work inspecting the hinges, he found himself perfectly eye-level with the sliver of space over the doors. Jesus could see clearly to the back of the synagogue—the familiar arrangement of benches and the few rugs that covered the packed earth floor. He saw the platform from which the rabbi would speak each week and the ark against the back wall where they kept the scrolls shaded behind its protective veil. He could see the rabbi, pacing up and down the center aisle, too preoccupied with whatever was on his mind to notice Jesus watching through the crack. The pacing made Jesus realize the rabbi was even more nervous than he'd thought. In all the time they'd studied together, he'd never seen him quite like this.

Jesus tensed when he heard a knock at the synagogue's back entrance. The rabbi jumped too, then quickly composed himself and straightened his cloak. Confidently, he strode to the back of the sanctuary and opened the door.

"I instructed you to wait until night," he hissed, and Jesus could tell he was trying to keep his voice steady. "You were to meet me *outside* of the city, not here."

"I waited as long as was feasible," the newcomer dismissed. The newcomer sounded young, and there was no apology in his voice. This was no elder or visiting teacher, and even if it were, no one spoke to the rabbi that way.

Jesus strained to get a better look, but the newcomer was just out of sight and the crack was too narrow.

"You could have been seen," the rabbi said, his voice rigid.

"I will not justify my actions to you," the newcomer said. "Will you sell, or won't you?"

The rabbi hesitated, and to Jesus's surprise, he looked afraid. "Do you... have the payment?" he asked.

"Two hundred and twenty-five denarii," the stranger threw out, and Jesus saw the rabbi catch a small bag of coins.

"We agreed on two hundred and fifty," the rabbi said.

"That was before I remembered I carry a sword, old man, and you do not."

Jesus gripped his ladder. This was hardly a villager coming to the rabbi for sage advice. Whoever this newcomer was, he was dangerous.

"You have the crate, I assume?" the rabbi asked, trying to remain dignified in the face of the newcomer's threat.

"They're no good to me in pieces, are they?" the newcomer spat.

The stranger threw a narrow wooden box to the ground, filled with wood shavings, which spilled out onto the floor. Padding, he assumed, for transport. But for what?

"Quiet!" the rabbi snapped, swooping down to gather the wood shavings. "Someone will hear you!"

The rabbi looked to the windows, and Jesus ducked just as his eyes passed over the door. When he looked back up, the rabbi was standing at the ark at the back wall. The veil was drawn back. Carefully, the rabbi opened the cabinet and withdrew the *Vayikra* scroll—the scroll of the law. His hands were shaking.

"This is one of our most sacred texts," he said as he carried the scroll to the box. "You will assure me it will be handled with the utmost—"

"The moment you accepted that money," the stranger said, "what happened to this scroll became none of your concern." He pushed the rabbi out of the way and kneeled over the box. He inspected the scroll, then replaced the lid. As he did, the stranger turned slightly, and Jesus got a good look at his face for the first time. He gasped. What he saw made him grip his hammer until his knuckles turned white.

Kneeling by the box was a clean-shaven man with short hair. He dressed like he was from the village, but he was no Nazorean. A decorated sword handle stuck out through his robes, his military posture was unmistakable, and Jesus would recognize the style of his sandals anywhere. The stranger was a Roman soldier—a Roman soldier who was taking their scroll.

Jesus had heard rumors of this happening—of occupying Roman forces paying for artifacts from various corners of the Empire, then bringing them back home as souvenirs. They were considered exotic and fascinating, and people would pay to study them or display them as decoration. In so doing, they got to feel a little better about the subjects they were suffocating from afar. Jesus's face flushed with rage.

"Is everything in order?" the rabbi asked, clearly eager to be rid of the visitor.

"It appears so," the Roman answered, standing and picking up his new prize.

"Good," the rabbi said. "Now you will kindly take your box and leave this place."

The soldier gave the rabbi an amused smile. "Feeling guilty, are we?" he asked. "Be disgusted with me all you want, but we both know the actual object of your disgust."

The rabbi's face was stone.

"I should be passing this way again in three months' time," the soldier said. "You know where we stay. Send word if you wish to meet again." He then made his way back to the back door, pausing to cover his face. He even slouched a bit, which Jesus would have taken as an insult if it hadn't worked so well to make him look like one of them—like someone bent under the weight of Roman rule.

"Until then," the soldier said, then left, leaving the rabbi visibly shaken. For a moment, Jesus only stared, watching as the rabbi melted into a defeated and haggard posture Jesus had never seen. It made him sad. He almost felt sorry for the rabbi. Then he remembered.

Slowly, Jesus climbed down from his ladder. He'd known the rabbi was a hypocrite, but never would he have imagined him capable of something like this. The scriptures were beyond precious, and to mistreat them was sacrilege. To sell them to a Gentile? Especially a Roman? This was treachery for which the rabbi would be lucky to escape stoning.

The rabbi didn't notice as Jesus slipped through the doors and stepped inside. He didn't hear Jesus pull the door closed behind him, nor did he hear him advancing up the aisle, hammer in his hand. When Jesus was just a few feet away, he finally spoke. "God will call every deed into judgment..." he said, making the rabbi jump.

"...every secret thing will be revealed," Jesus continued, "whether good or evil. You taught me that one, Rabbi. Remember?"

"Yeshua," the rabbi repeated, a wide, false smile spreading over his face, "I'm not sure what you think you saw, but—"

"I *know* what I saw," Jesus interrupted. He gestured with the hammer and circled around the rabbi. "How many sermons have I endured about the 'dogs and the Gentiles' and their uncleanness? How many warnings about the wrath to come?"

"You have it all wrong, of course," the rabbi assured him. The smile remained, and he spoke calmly, but Jesus saw he was sweating. "You have always been so quick to see corruption and unrighteousness where there is none," he said reasonably. "You must see this in yourself. It keeps you from seeing the truth."

"The truth?" Jesus laughed. "You're going to lecture me on the truth? Now?"

"The scriptures must be maintained," the rabbi explained earnestly. "The lettering fades and the handles loosen over time—you remember this, from when you used to care about the scriptures? I sent them away for repair. That's all. Don't make this—"

*"He* paid *you,"* Jesus corrected, holding his ground. "He paid you two hundred and twenty-five days' wages."

"No, no, young Yeshua," the rabbi said. "Come now. *I* paid *him!* It's no inexpensive thing to have a scroll repaired, you know."

"Let's go after him, then," Jesus said. "Show me my mistake. We'll go together."

The rabbi stiffened. "Your eyes have never been reliable, my boy," he reasoned. "You harbor suspicion in your heart, and you see unrighteousness and injustice everywhere you look. This has always been your struggle. If you search your heart, I'm sure you will see—"

"Enough!" Jesus barked, angry at how much he wanted to believe the rabbi, even now. "Everyone in this town is about to see the truth, Rabbi. Everyone. You can't maneuver your way out of this."

"Yeshua, come now—"

"They will see you as the weak, fearful man you are," Jesus went on, years of unexpressed anger finally coming through. "They'll see how afraid you are of losing what little power you have, and their respect will vanish. They will pity you, like they pity a child who can't have his way."

The rabbi's face grew red. "How *dare* you?" he demanded, his tone changing instantly.

"What's the money even for?" Jesus went on, emboldened. "Does it go straight into your purse? Or are you going to say it's somehow God's purse, so you're clean of wrongdoing?"

"Don't you *dare* take the name of God in vain in this place," the rabbi commanded, taking a step forward.

Jesus laughed in his face. "What do you call *this?*" he asked. "What is it you call what you've been doing all this time if not taking the name of God in vain?"

Jesus could see the rabbi thinking quickly, angrily, calculating his next move. "See reason," he insisted. "You've seen this place—the disrepair into which it has fallen. The community cannot afford to fix it, not with Roman taxes. You know this. If this roof goes, we can scarcely afford to rebuild."

"How noble," Jesus answered. "What a sacrifice you make."

"Perhaps one day you will understand, there are some things that—"

"Oh, I understand," Jesus interrupted. "And as a matter of fact, soon *everyone* will understand. They'll all see what you really are. That scares you, doesn't it?"

The rabbi stood up straighter.

"Good," Jesus said. "It should scare you. Finally, you'll know how the rest of us feel."

Jesus let his arm drop, and the hammer hung by his side. He turned and walked toward the door, and as he did, the rabbi started talking quickly.

"You want to talk about the truth?" he demanded. "You are a blaspheming fool, and you always have been! How's that for truth? All you have ever craved from this place is attention, and that is what you seek still!"

"Baiting me won't work, Rabbi," Jesus said. "You're desperate."

"And what would your mother say?" the rabbi called, as though proving Jesus's point. "Can you imagine her shame? Her *shame*, Yeshua, at what you are about to do?"

Jesus didn't stop. He had what he needed. He reached up, prepared to push open the door and be done with this.

"And then there is the matter of your *father,*" the rabbi said.

Jesus froze.

For a moment, they were both still, neither speaking. "Oh, I'm sorry," the rabbi said, the satisfaction clear in his voice, "did that strike a nerve, my boy?"

Jesus told himself to let it go. He told himself it wasn't worth it. All he had to do was open the door and—

"Since we're discussing truth," the rabbi went on, "allow me to clarify the reason I cast you out all those years ago. It is because of your father, young Yeshua. Because of your father, you will never belong, despite your childish attempts to make up for what you are."

Jesus tightened his grip on his hammer. *Just leave,* he told himself. *Just go tell them all—*

"Your mother sees it every time she looks at you," the rabbi said, "you know that."

*Just leave...*

"So what do you do?" the rabbi asked, now strolling towards Jesus. "You search in vain for someone to please or someone to fight—all to prove to yourself that you're not what you are—that you're good and righteous. But you know what you are, don't you? Son of Mary..."

Jesus held his breath. His grip was slipping.

"Son of *Pantera.*"

Jesus lunged before he could stop himself. Hardly aware of what he was doing, Jesus sent the rabbi stumbling back over a bench, and the rabbi cried out for help. Jesus dropped to his knees and seized the rabbi by the cloak. "You conniving, self-righteous hypocrite!" Jesus yelled.

The rabbi cried out for help again, and some part of Jesus tried to warn him what was happening. Still, he couldn't stop. He only held on tighter. They would finish this now, once and for all.

"What are you *doing?*" a woman shouted, and Jesus came abruptly back to his senses.

He turned to see a woman in the doorway—shock written all over her face. He also looked down to see his hand gripping the hammer, and suddenly, he felt sick.

"It's... it's not what it looks like," Jesus said, hating how much he sounded like the rabbi. It didn't matter, though. The woman was already running back outside, screaming for help.

Jesus dropped the hammer and scrambled to his feet. Slowly, the rabbi heaved himself up, leaning on a bench for support. He brushed off his robes, glowing with triumph. "Well, Yeshua," the rabbi said, satisfied, "what will the people see now? Which of us do you think will carry the crowd's sympathies?"

Jesus tried to call up a plan, but his mind was frozen in panic. He heard shouts outside.

"Better run, son of Mary," the rabbi said. "Run far and run swift. Your time here is done."

"What's this about?" a different voice demanded from the entryway. It was Joseph. "Yeshua. What's going on here? Why aren't you outside?"

Jesus didn't know what to say. In that moment, he wanted to tell Joseph everything—to explain what had happened from beginning to end—but he knew that time had passed. It had passed the moment he'd lost control.

"Joseph, thank heavens," the rabbi said, making himself sound winded. "Yeshua... he tried to attack me... Please, you must help..."

Joseph looked at Jesus in confusion, and Jesus suddenly understood he had one chance, and one chance only. The rabbi was right. He had to run.

"I'm sorry," Jesus breathed, turning from Joseph and sprinting for the back door.

"Yeshua, wait—"

Jesus slammed the door closed behind him, pushing over a heap of baskets, blocking the way. He knew he had to go—to get away from the synagogue and out of the city. Out of the region.

He heard someone coming around the side, and his heart raced. Before he did anything else, though, he knew there was one thing he had to do first. He took off down a back road, hoping no one noticed which way he went.

He had to flee. He had to talk to his mother.

# 7

## *Kashi.*

AT FIRST, JESUS DIDN'T understand. Then, suddenly, the pieces fell into place. He realized in a flash why the old man looked so familiar. It wasn't because Jesus knew him. It was because he knew his features. He knew his accent. He'd been too exhausted to notice before, but now it was clear. "You're Judean," Jesus said, his mind still struggling to catch up. "You're Judean, and you said nothing."

"Well, to be fair, I didn't think I would need to," the old man answered. He now spoke Aramaic, making the moment even more surreal. "But then it became something of a game, I suppose, like Joseph, when his brothers found him in Egypt! I wanted to see how long it would take. After all, how many men in this city do you think bear the name Abraham? And I didn't think *this* was all too subtle, either."

Abraham pulled up his sleeve, revealing his arm wrapped in leather straps—tefillin, just like the rabbi's.

*Pay attention, you dullest of people,* the rabbi said. *When will the foolish open their eyes?*

The old man chuckled as he replaced his sleeve. "I picked *you* out at once, of course," he said, "weeks ago, when I first saw you in the market. You were always busy with something or another, though. I waited for you to notice, but today, when I saw you with those children, I decided enough was enough. It was time to extend some hospitality."

"You've been watching me?" Jesus asked, his stomach tightening as his mind caught up. He felt a surge of anger, though he wasn't sure why.

The man noted the change in his tone and eased off. "I have," he admitted, "though I can see how that must sound. I apologize if—"

"And today," Jesus went on, "when you approached me, that was just... to amuse yourself?"

"Why no, of course not," the man said. "As I said, I only wished to—"

"This was a mistake," Jesus interrupted. "Thank you for the opportunity, but I'm leaving. Play your games with someone else."

"Come now, son," Abraham protested. "Don't—"

"Don't overreact?" Jesus finished for him. "You see me starving in a market, do nothing, and when I turn down your gracious offer of employment, *I'm* the one showing disrespect by leaving, right?"

"No," Abraham said calmly. "I was going to say, don't let the foolishness of an old man cost you a decent wage."

"How I make my wages is my business," Jesus said, "but thank you for your hospitable concern."

He wheeled around and walked away, leaving the laborers to watch in confusion. His pulse pounded in his ears as he marched back towards the gate.

"I'm not sure who I remind you of," Abraham called after him, "but it sounds as though they caused you more than your share of pain. I'm sorry for that."

Jesus hesitated, surprised. His face hardened again. "They did," he said, then continued on, leaving Abraham and his cart behind. Was it too much to ask for just a glimmer of justice? Did the same burdens have to follow him, even to the other side of the world?

*Where can you go to hide from God's presence? Where can you flee from God's sight?*

Jesus kicked the ground, sending up a cloud of dust. A passing woman gave him a troubled look before hurriedly crossing the road, but Jesus didn't care. Let them think he was insane. What difference did it make? He'd rather be insane than be stuck on that cart with that old man, submitting himself to a day in back-breaking fields. His plan now was to go back to the courtyard, hide behind some bundles of rice, and let his body sleep until it couldn't sleep anymore. Then, when he was ready, he would rally himself. He would finally make a plan and leave this city behind to—

Jesus stopped short, his heart plummeting when he saw the courtyard. He'd thought the morning couldn't get worse. Clearly, he'd been mistaken.

*His sin returns on his own head, and on his own skull his foolishness descends...*

Just inside the gate, the vendor and his friends were accosting bystanders and searching around carts and bundles. "You say you saw him in here?" the vendor demanded. "And he had four of my mangoes? *Four?*"

His pursuers started towards the gate, and on instinct, Jesus dove behind a basket of overripe fruit. Black flies buzzed relentlessly around his head, but he dared not wave them away. The men hadn't seen him, but he knew he didn't have long.

Keeping his head, he ticked through options.

He could run... but he wouldn't get far.

Hide... but for how long?

Swim across the river... but he lacked the strength.

Slip back through the gate... but to what end?

He could—

Jesus looked back toward Abraham's cart.

"No," he muttered. "Out of the question."

"I'm going to *kill* him this time!" the vendor growled, his voice almost on top of Jesus.

Behind him, Jesus heard Abraham's cart lurch out onto the road.

"I'm going to break every one of his fingers. Let's see him try to steal my produce after that!"

The vendor's knife was sharper than anything the old man could throw at him. Better the old man than the knife. Jesus pounded the ground, his choice made.

He sprang forward, keeping low. The vendor and his friends were looking the other way, so they didn't see him as he sprinted towards the cart.

*He digs a pit,* the rabbi's voice echoed, *and falls into the hole he has made.*

Jesus put his full strength into catching up with the cart. Then, with the little energy he had left, he launched himself forward, landing ungracefully at the feet of the harvesters. He sent them a silent plea to keep quiet, and they seemed to understand. One of them even nodded in solidarity and tossed his cloak over Jesus, keeping him concealed.

*Thank you,* Jesus mouthed, glancing back one last time.

The cart rounded a corner, and the vendor and his friends disappeared behind the trees.

Jesus knew he was safe, but looking up at the old man at the reins, he still didn't feel it.

# 8

## *Judea, twenty months before.*

JESUS TORE THROUGH TOWN—DODGING houses and pushing past bewildered townspeople, their shouts lost behind him. It didn't matter. He couldn't slow down. He didn't have time. He needed to get to his mother.

As he ran, the rabbi's unrelenting voice echoed in his head.

*You will never belong, despite your childish attempts to make up for what you are...*

He tried to block it out, but it came through anyway, louder and more accusing.

*You search in vain for someone to please or someone to fight—trying to prove that you're not what you are.*

*But you know what you are.*

"Stop it," Jesus demanded through clenched teeth.

*Son of Mary...* the voice kept coming.

*Son of Pantera...*

"Enough!" Jesus yelled.

Jesus knew little about the man called Pantera, but he knew enough.

He knew Pantera's full name: Tiberius Julias Abdes Pantera.

He knew Pantera was from a region in Judea infamous for its citizens joining the ranks of the Roman military—an act seen as treason.

He knew Pantera had been a standard bearer and an archer for Rome.

He knew that no one, in any of the few times he'd heard Pantera mentioned, used his name fondly.

Jesus had first heard of Pantera when he was seven, from a jeering boy his age. "My father says I shouldn't talk to you," the boy had taunted. "You're a *mamzer* and your father was a Gentile pig."

The boy's mother had smacked him, but his words had planted a seed of curiosity in Jesus's mind. That night, he asked his mother about these unfamiliar words—*Pantera* and *mamzer*. Instead of giving him answers, though, she had only started crying and sent him away. Ashamed, he never asked again.

From that point, the scant list of things he knew about Pantera intertwined with the scant list of things he knew about his mother. She had always been silent about her past, leaving her son to imagine her as a mystery—more of a force of nature than a fellow human.

He knew she'd been the daughter of a wealthy family from Jerusalem.

He knew that, at a young age, she'd been orphaned and left with relatives in Nazareth.

He knew that she'd been engaged to a Nazorean man for a time.

He knew that sometime later, Pantera's dispatch had marched through Nazareth, drinking too much and leaving a trail of disarray in their wake.

He knew that shortly after, his mother had found out she was pregnant, and that the Nazorean man she was engaged to had dismissed her quietly.

He knew that he'd been born nine months later, in a stable because his mother had nowhere else to go.

Jesus recounted the list as he ran. He only knew two more things for sure:

He knew Pantera had died at the end of an archer's arrow.

And he knew Pantera wasn't mourned in Galilee.

Strangely, reciting these facts helped focus Jesus's thoughts. At least something felt like it was in order. Predictable pain was preferable to the unpredictable chaos around him.

Jesus was almost there. One more corner, and he'd be home. He'd never wanted to be there more in his life. As he took the last turn, however, he crashed into someone, sending them both sprawling to the ground.

Jesus jumped up, arms in front of him, ready to fight.

"Wait!" John said, still on the ground, holding out his palms. "Easy! It's me!"

Jesus let his fists fall, deflating in relief. "You shouldn't have followed me," he said, offering John a hand up. "It's not safe."

"Not safe?" John asked, taking Jesus's hand and hauling himself back to his feet. "Yeshua, what's going on? What happened back there? Those people are—"

"Listen," Jesus interrupted. "I'm sorry, but I don't have time to explain. I need to go."

He tried to step around John, but John blocked his way, holding out a hand to stop him. "Make time," he insisted. "You just took off back there. That's not like you. You owe me an explanation."

Jesus sighed, torn between gratitude and impatience. Finally, with one more glance over his shoulder, he told John about what he'd seen. About the rabbi. The Roman. The scroll. When he finished, John looked amazed. "Wow," he said. "We knew he was bad, but not *that* bad. What you're describing is treason. It's blasphemy. But why are *you* running? What happened?"

"I attacked him," Jesus said. "He baited me, and I walked right into it. Someone saw, which was exactly what he wanted, and now they think I tried to kill him."

"Kill him?" John's eyes widened. "What in the world did he say to you?"

Jesus shook his head. "It's nothing. John, I've got to—"

"What did he say?"

Jesus hesitated. For a second, he couldn't meet John's eye. "It was stupid," he said. "He called me... He called me a son of Pantera, all right? I lost control."

John looked at him in disbelief. *"That's* all it took?" he demanded, angry at how quickly his friend had thrown his life away.
"Yeshua, when are you going to get a hold of yourself? All it ever
takes is one little—"

"You think I don't know that?" Jesus demanded. "You think I
don't know how much I'm about to pay for this?"

"But *why?"* John demanded. "Help me understand! What it is
about that name that—"

"You don't know what it's like, all right?" Jesus yelled. "At least
you knew your father before he died! At least he had some respect!
Everyone loved him! 'Sons of Thunder,' they call you. And me?
You know what they call me?"

John didn't answer. He'd heard all the names over the years.
"You can still get out of this," he insisted, trying to be reasonable.
"You can still—"

"I don't want to get out of this," Jesus said. "I want to get out of
*here.* If I stay, even without those people after me, it will kill me,
John. We both know it. I was never going to stay in this place. I
can't survive here."

"What you're saying is madness," John protested.

"No," Jesus said, "staying would be madness. I'm not like you,
John. I can't just stand by and do nothing while people like the
rabbi use us like footstools."

John gave a defensive look Jesus rarely ever saw. "Someone has
to keep things running," he said. "I have to take care of my family.
I can't just go around starting fires like you, consequences be
damned. Are you not thinking about your responsibilities here?
About your mother? What's she going to do if you just run off?"

Shame twisted in Jesus's stomach. "I'm not 'running off,'" he
said. "I have to go."

"Because of one person's half-testimony?" John demanded.
"They can't do anything with that!"

"They can and they will," Jesus said, "but it's more than that, and you know it."

They heard someone shout a short distance away, back up the road. They were coming.

"Look, I need time," Jesus said. "Just a few minutes. Can you distract them?"

"No!" John said. "We can sort through this. You know we can."

"John," Jesus said, gripping his friend's shoulders, forcing him to meet his eyes. It tore at his heart how much John wanted to help him, but it was time to move. "I know you don't understand, but I need you to trust me. Please."

John hesitated.

"I need to speak to my mother," Jesus said. "Can you give me that? Can you buy me just a little time?"

John took a deep breath, looking doubtfully at his friend. "A few minutes," he said. "I'll tell them I saw you go west, toward the inn. They'll think you're going for one last drink. You know they'll believe it."

Jesus couldn't help but smile. "Thank you," he said, and he pulled John into an embrace. "Take care of her for me, will you?" Jesus asked. "You and James? As much as you can?"

"Of course we will," John said, his voice muffled into Jesus's shoulder. "You be careful out there. They're not all as nice as I am."

Jesus laughed. "I will," he said, letting go.

He took another moment, then stepped away. "Goodbye, John," he said, then turned and started off again down the road.

He looked over his shoulder briefly to see John running back toward the crowd, preparing to send them in the opposite direction. It wouldn't buy him long, but it was something, and he was grateful. Of all the pain this place had caused him, John had always helped it seem more bearable. He would miss him more than he could say.

Now, though, he had to explain all this to his mother, and he was almost home.

# 9

## *Kashi.*

THE CART ROLLED PAST fields and sparse, mud-brick houses. Jesus sat with his legs hanging off the back, watching rocks and weeds blur beneath him as he considered his situation. He'd made it out of the city—that was something—but now he was on this cart, headed for who-knew-where to harvest grapes. He thought about jumping off. The only thing keeping him from doing that, though, was the infuriating pull of curiosity. He'd solved the mystery of why the old man seemed so familiar, but this had only opened the door to even bigger mysteries. He now had more questions, weighing him to the cart, feeling heavier the further they moved down the road.

At last, Jesus decided it was time to speak to Abraham again. He would keep his guard up. He would stay only long enough to find more answers. Then, when he was ready, he would take to the road and never look back.

Jesus jostled his way to the front, trying unsuccessfully not to step on his co-workers' toes. When he finally made it, catching hold of the front rail for stability, he found Abraham sitting alone on the driver's bench, singing quietly to himself.

*"Praise to the Lord, who grows grass for the cattle, who grows plants for farming and food from the earth. Wine to gladden hearts of despair, oil for faces, and bread to sustain..."*

Jesus listened for a moment, noting how strange it felt to hear those words chanted in this part of the world. After a moment, though, he remembered why he was there. "Who are you?" he interrupted.

Abraham stopped and glanced back. He looked surprised to see Jesus, but also pleased. "I take it you decided to join us after all," he said.

"I had little choice."

"Oh, you always have a choice," Abraham corrected. "I'll pull over right now, if you like."

He held up the reins, as though to bring the oxen to a stop, but Jesus didn't answer.

"Suit yourself, then," Abraham said. "In the meantime, I will say I am glad you're here. I was hoping to see you again. I owe you an apology after skulking around like a thief this past week. Should've spoken to you right off. My apologies."

Instead of reassuring him, this apology only unsettled Jesus further. He still wasn't convinced this wasn't some kind of trick. "What are you doing in Kashi?" he asked.

If Abraham was bothered by Jesus's bluntness, he didn't show it. "Good question," he said, eyes on the road. "I've always appreciated someone who insists upon getting to the heart of what matters. As far as who I am—my name is Abraham, son of Jacob, of Kerioth, south of Jerusalem. And you?"

Jesus hesitated. He didn't want to give this man any power over him—not even his name—but if it got him some answers, so be it.

"Jesus," he said.

"Ah, Yeshua," Abraham echoed. "The Lord Saves! A strong name. Our father Moshe's chosen heir."

"No," Jesus corrected. "It's Jesus. Just Jesus."

He'd stopped using his Hebrew name when he'd left Judea. Latin was easier on the road.

Abraham didn't press the subject. "Understood," he said. "And that would be Jesus of...?"

Again, Jesus didn't answer.

"Oh, come now," Abraham said. "I told you I was from Kerioth, did I not? Does that not earn some good will? Truth for truth?"

"How do I know you weren't lying?" Jesus asked.

Abraham chuckled at this. "To what end?"

That was hard to argue with.

"Nazareth," he answered. "I'm from Nazareth."

Abraham whistled. "You're a long way from Nazareth, son."

"You're a long way from Kerioth."

Abraham nodded. "This is true."

"Are you in trouble?" Jesus asked, determined to get at least one actual answer. "Is that why you're out here? Are you hiding from someone?"

"Am I in trouble?" Abraham echoed. "What a question. I suppose we all run into trouble from time to time, don't we? Why should I be an exception?"

"You're avoiding the question."

"I am," Abraham answered, "but only because to answer it would be to tell you the very long and very impressive story of my life, and as it is, I'm afraid we've nearly arrived."

"Already?" Jesus asked, looking ahead of the cart. "Your farm is this close to the city?"

"It's better for distribution," Abraham explained. "The closer you are, the faster you get to the market."

"It's also better for thieves," Jesus pointed out.

"Oh, is that so?" Abraham asked, glancing at his passenger. "And how might you know that?"

Jesus didn't answer.

Abraham smiled and went back to his driving. "I am joking, of course," he said. "What some call 'thievery,' I'm inclined to call 'justice.' Harvesting your land's produce, you shall not harvest to the edges. You must leave some for the poor and the immigrant, thus says the law."

Jesus recognized the verse, though he'd never heard it recited in Abraham's tone. "You still keep to the law?" he asked. "All the way out here?"

"Well, when you keep it long enough, it has a way of keeping you."

Jesus did not know what that meant, but he let it go. He was just about to ask another question—to try again to learn *something* about the old man—but Abraham interrupted.

"Ah!" he exclaimed, giving the reins a quick shake. "It appears we have arrived."

# 10

## *Judea, twenty months before.*

JESUS ROUNDED THE LAST corner and skidded to a stop in front of their house. One room. Crooked. Mud bricks and cracking clay insulation. It wasn't much, but it was theirs, and his mother would be inside.

Jesus took a moment to get himself under control before he faced his mother. He at least wanted to get his breath back so as not to make her panic the moment he walked in. He wasn't sure how she'd react, but he knew it wouldn't be pleasant. She'd never been very patient with his habit of testing boundaries, but the thought of having to explain to her what had just happened left Jesus's stomach in knots.

How was he going to tell his mother that he had to leave the city? That he had to leave her?

Jesus gripped the gate, wanting more time to calm down, but that was a luxury he didn't have. He pushed the gate open, forcing himself to keep moving toward the house. He passed their ancient goat, oblivious as always, and gave it his customary, absentminded pat on the head. His mother had always talked about taking the goat to Jerusalem for Passover, but it had been years since they'd been able to take that pilgrimage. Jesus strongly suspected the goat had outlived its ability to make the trip. This thought brought another wave of sadness. If they did ever make the trip, he wouldn't be around to see it.

"Amma?" Jesus called as he pushed through the door. "Amma, are you home?"

He closed the door behind him, letting himself pretend for a moment that he was safe. No one answered, and he realized with a mixture of relief and frustration that his mother must be out drawing water. He didn't have time to wait, but her absence would give him a chance to pack without her over his shoulder. He set to work.

Most women drew water earlier in the day—before the sun's full heat—but his mother was not most women. Even though she never said it out loud, she'd long ago decided she'd rather put up with the heat of the sun than the heat of other women's glances, whispering about rumors that she would never outlive. There were two wells in town—one in the village center, by the synagogue, and the other just outside town, near their home. His mother preferred to go to the latter, which meant it wasn't a long trek. She'd be back soon.

As Jesus sorted through his things, the rabbi's words continued echoing in his head. *Son of Mary...* he said. *Son of Pantera...* The words burned hotter each time. Maybe he *should* have hit the rabbi when he'd had the chance. He was facing exile anyway, so he might as well have done the crime they would accuse him of.

*If there is harm, you shall pay eye for eye, tooth for tooth, wound for wound...*

Jesus pushed those thoughts aside. It wasn't how he needed to be thinking. He tried to focus instead on what he'd told John—that he needed to get out of this town one way or another. Something like this was bound to happen eventually.

"What's this?" a voice asked from the doorway. Jesus whirled around, dropping the waterskin he'd been packing.

His mother just stood there, water jug on her hip, watching with suspicion. "I thought you were doing a job with Joseph," she said.

"I was," Jesus started, "but I..." He trailed off, not knowing how to tell her.

"Well then, what are you doing home?" she demanded, setting the water jug down and pulling the door closed behind her. "You aren't in trouble, I assume?" That was when Mary saw the bag in his hand, and let her eyes drift to Jesus's corner, now empty save for his mat. "Yeshua," she said, "what are you doing?"

For a moment, Jesus felt like a child again, small and uncertain beneath his mother's gaze. "Listen, amma," he said. "It's... it's time for me to go."

"Go?" she asked, as though he was talking nonsense. "Go where?"

"Away," Jesus said, knowing already that this would not go well.

"Did something happen?"

Jesus hesitated for another moment, then, steeling himself, he gave the shortest account he could manage. It ended with his lunging at the rabbi—with the woman seeing the hammer in his hand. He wanted to say it was entirely a misunderstanding—that he hadn't planned to do any harm—but he wasn't confident that was true.

When he finished, his mother's face was white—it had been since he'd mentioned Pantera's name. They stood in silence for a moment, but eventually, it was his mother who spoke. "Well then," she said, collecting herself. "It sounds like you know what you need to do."

Jesus felt a flood of unexpected relief. She understood. For once, she understood.

"You need to go back and apologize," she said.

"What?"

"No arguing," his mother ordered, marching over and picking some dried spices off the wall. "It's not too late. Take him these. They're not much, but they're a token of your repentance. You can promise to put things right by taking on the rest of the synagogue work for no charge, then promising to do whatever else must be done to set things right. Really, this is a good thing if you think about it. You have needed to make things right with the rabbi for years. As of right now, there's no damage you can't repair. You must only explain—"

"It's done, amma," Jesus said. "The damage is done."

"Not yet," his mother insisted. "There's still a good chance the rabbi will forgive you and you can—"

"Are you listening?" Jesus demanded. "I caught him selling scriptures to a *Roman!* Does that not make you angry? Does he have *that* much power over you?"

"This is a misunderstanding," his mother said with the utmost confidence. "Clearly, you did *not* see what you thought you saw. There must be an explanation."

"There *is* an explanation," Jesus said. "He's a criminal. He's been deceiving and manipulating everyone for years and you all let him get away with it. You all assume you can't speak out because he's 'God's righteous servant.' *That's* the explanation."

Mary shook her head. "Yeshua," she said, softening her tone. She took his face in her hands, searching his eyes. "You are confused. You will figure things out eventually, but until then, you must trust in the—"

"*Someone's* confused," Jesus said, gently removing her hands from his face, "but it's not me."

He went back to packing.

"Yeshua, enough," his mother snapped. "Things are hard enough without you making them harder. Whatever you *think* you saw, we do not have a choice in this matter."

"Of course we do!" Jesus shot back. "We always have a choice, and this is mine. Don't pretend you're trapped here. You could come with me. Get out of this place."

"This is foolishness."

"*I'm* not the fool here," Jesus said, throwing his last few belongings into the bag and slinging it over his shoulder. "You keep playing his game if you want to. You keep groveling and pandering in the hope he'll toss you some scrap of dignity, but I'm not doing that. Not anymore."

Part of Jesus knew he wasn't being fair—that he could never really understand what she'd been through—but right now, that part felt small and far away. Right now, all he could see was his own anger.

"Do you think you are above this place?" his mother demanded. "Above *me*? I may have little dignity, as you say, but just look at where your pride and self-righteousness have gotten *you!*"

"Well, maybe I am too proud!" Jesus insisted. "Proud enough to stop putting up with this! *Yeshua, son of Mary... Yeshua, son of Pantera...* I won't hear it anymore, amma. If I leave here, I'm free. For once in my life, I get to be Yeshua, son of no one!"

He stopped short as he realized what he'd said.

"I'm sorry—" he started. "I didn't mean—"

His mother put up her hand to silence him. He knew he'd crossed a line, and he wished he could take it back, especially if this really was goodbye.

"Amma—" he tried again.

"You will listen to me," his mother interrupted, working hard to keep her voice controlled. "I have done my best to protect you. I have done all I could to shield you from the worst of what they think of me. Of us."

"I know, amma, and I—"

*"Hush!"* she insisted. "When you were a child, I tried to create a safe world for you. Maybe it wasn't luxurious, but it was the best I could do. But hear me now, Yeshua. It is time to leave the garden. You are out here with the rest of us, now—with the wild beasts—where you only eat by the sweat of your brow. The rabbi calls you these names because it is *who you are*, and the sooner you accept that and learn to live with your lot, the better off you will be."

Jesus had heard this speech before—variations of it, at least—and he grew tense as he heard it again. It was what she said when Jesus got too close to something she didn't want him to see. It was her way of batting him back into his place, but this time, it wouldn't work.

"No," he said. "I'm not going to ignore the truth. I'm not like everyone else here who will just stand back and let him do what he wants."

"I *am* telling you the truth," his mother insisted, "it's you who is playing the fool."

"Amma—" Jesus started, but there was a shout from outside—too close for comfort. He needed to move.

"I'm sorry, amma," he said. It wasn't enough, but it was the best he could do. He took a small pouch of denarii from his bag and held it out to her. She stared at it for a moment but didn't take it.

"You think money will make up for this?" she asked.

Jesus pleaded with her, but she stood firm. "No," she said. "Do what you will, but do not expect my blessing. Go forth and be 'son of no one,' as you've always wanted."

Without another word, she turned and stormed outside, slamming the door behind her and leaving Jesus alone. Jesus wanted to follow, but the shouts were closer now, and he knew he couldn't afford to be spotted.

He grabbed his bag, throwing in the last of what he'd need.

"Step aside," he heard someone demand, making him freeze. They weren't down the road. They were here, and they were talking to his mother.

Silently, he moved towards the back window.

"He's not here," he heard his mother say bitterly. "He has abandoned me and taken leave of his senses. I tried to stop him, but he is beyond reason."

It took a moment for Jesus to realize what was happening. She was lying to protect him—giving him a chance, as John had. Realizing this sent a pain through his heart.

He hauled himself up to the window and dropped silently behind their house. As soon as he did, he heard the front door open.

He remained still for a moment to be sure they hadn't seen him, and when no one appeared at the window, he took off as quietly as he could.

To everything, there was a season. The rabbi had taught him that. Now, it was the season to run.

# 11

## *Kashi.*

ABRAHAM STEERED THE CART through a break in the foliage—through an old gate that hung open, crooked and falling apart with age. Although it had faded, the same Hebrew lettering was carved into it that Jesus had seen on the cart.

*Shalom.*

Once they were through the gate, Jesus got his first look at the vineyard.

Neatly lined rows of fruit trees and plants spread out everywhere. Further up, there was a sloping hill with rows of vines, heavy with grapes. A group of laborers was already up there, gathering and putting their harvest in bags slung over their shoulders.

To his left stood a few simple structures: a wooden shelter for livestock, and another, Jesus judged to be a covered winepress. Next to that was a small building that must have been the old man's home.

Despite his suspicion, Jesus couldn't help feeling impressed. Abraham must've seen it in his expression. "It's a miracle, isn't it?" he asked. "Mundane, but miraculous."

"What is?"

"All of this," Abraham gestured. "We water the ground. The ground turns to fruit. The fruit turns to wine. The wine to joy. With God's help, we transform water into wine each day and don't think twice about it."

Jesus wanted to argue, but couldn't. The old man was right. It *was* a miracle.

The cart came to a stop in front of the main house. Up close, Jesus could see that the building was modest, but compared to his childhood home, it was a palace. On every stone wall was a decorative panel carved with elephants and humans and gods, painted in vivid hues, each telling a different story. On the front door, the artist had carved a flock of doves taking flight. Jesus had never seen a home decorated with such care.

*You shall not make a graven image in the form of anything in the heavens above or the earth beneath,* the rabbi's voice lectured.

Jesus pushed it away. "Leave it to you to find beauty and call it sin."

He climbed down from the cart with the others, and Abraham came down from his seat with a quick jump. "Thank you all," Abraham called to his crew. "Thank you and welcome. Now, if you would step just over here... yes, thank you. Deva?" He called toward the house. "A hand, if you would?"

After a moment, a tall, muscular man appeared from around the corner. He was slightly older than Jesus. He carried himself with the same authority as Abraham, but with none of the warmth—clearly the old man's son.

As the son approached, he inspected the latest batch of laborers with the cool scrutiny of someone appraising cattle. "These are the best you could do?" he asked.

"This is my son, Deva," Abraham introduced. "He will be giving you some instruction. He will keep a civil tongue as he does so, and if he cannot manage, he will be joining you in the fields."

Jesus leaned against the driver's seat and crossed his arms. This would be entertaining.

Deva, meanwhile, ignored his father. "First of all, my name is Deva-datta," he started. "The first one of you to call me Deva will be escorted from the property, empty-handed. Second, the work is simple enough, if you're not a fool. Over there on that wall are sacks which you will fill with grapes. The first crew is already out in the field. You will join them. You will pick grapes. You will put them in the sacks. You will bring them back and you will get paid. Any questions?"

"Do more grapes mean more pay?" asked a hefty man next to Jesus.

"No," Deva said, not even bothering to look at the man. "Come back with a half-full bag, though, and *that* may make a difference. Any more stupid questions?"

The rest of the group stayed quiet, and it looked like Deva was about to send them out, but he paused when he noticed Jesus leaning against the cart. "You there," he called, "are you planning to go to work or just nap on the cart all morning?"

Jesus glanced around, then realized Deva was talking to him. "Oh, I'm sorry," he said, "was napping on the cart an option? If that gets me a day's wage, then yes, that's the job I'd like to request. Thank you."

Some in the group laughed, which Deva clearly didn't appreciate. He turned to his father and said something Jesus didn't quite understand. He caught the words "thin," "unwise," and "starved dogs," but the rest was a mystery.

"He will do what he can," Abraham answered quietly, holding his ground, "and I will remind you what I instructed about keeping a civil tongue."

Deva looked Jesus over, then appeared to decide it wasn't worth the fight. "Fine," he said. Then, to Jesus, "Have one of the other laborers drag you in when you collapse in the field, would you? Save me a trip."

He grabbed a sack from its peg and tossed it to Jesus. "More questions?" he asked. When no one spoke, he gave a curt nod. "Good. On your way, then," and the group started ambling towards the hillside to join the others.

Abraham patted his son on the back, then made his way back to the cart, hauling himself onto the driver's seat.

"Your son is a model of hospitality," Jesus said, switching gladly back to Aramaic. It felt good to speak a language he felt confident speaking.

Abraham gave a humorless smile. "I'd warn you to watch yourself," he said, "but I get the impression you would only ignore it."

Something about Abraham's words gave Jesus a brief and unexpected sense of satisfaction.

"Try not to ignore this, however," Abraham said. "Don't push yourself too hard today. As I said, do what you can, and that will be enough."

"Are you leaving?" Jesus asked, surprised. "Some important landowner business?"

Abraham chuckled. "Quite," he said. "I am going back to the city. There are plenty of people there who need work, and I've got plenty of work to be done."

"The harvest is plenty, but the workers are few, right?" Jesus repeated, and Abraham smiled.

"Wisely put," he said, then, with a flick of the reins, he was off again, back down the path toward the gate. As the cart rolled on, Jesus noticed one of the wheels wobble a bit and wondered if he could talk the old man into paying him to fix it. Any job he could do while sitting felt preferable.

"So he likes to sound clever before a crowd," Deva said, approaching Jesus from behind, "but when the time comes to work, he stands around watching the oxen. I should've guessed."

"I suppose there's no one around to be sure you keep a 'civil tongue' now, is there?" Jesus asked, still watching the cart.

"There is not," Deva answered, "and unless you want to see just how un-civil it can get, I suggest you get moving. Assuming you can make it up the hill without toppling over."

Jesus felt a flare of defiance, and he adjusted his bag on his shoulder. "You worry about your work," he said. "I'll worry about mine."

Then, with Deva watching, he strode after the others.

# 12

## *Judea, twenty months before.*

JESUS FLED NAZARETH, RUNNING as far and as fast as his legs allowed before they gave out, forcing him to stumble to a stop beside the road. It was nearly nightfall, and Sepphoris was just ahead.

Jesus stumbled to a cluster of trees and collapsed at their base. He would take a moment, then carry on. What choice did he have? It felt like his pursuers were just behind him, coming to drag him back to judgment. Would he feel that way for the rest of his life?

At this thought, his anger burned hotter. That lying, blasphemous, two-faced snake would get to stay, gloating in Nazareth while Jesus had to run like a dog.

*Spend enough time among the dogs and Gentiles, young Yeshua,* he remembered the rabbi warning him once, *and that's what you will become.*

The rabbi had won. After all these years at each other's throats, he'd finally gotten exactly what he'd wanted. And it was all Jesus's fault.

A rustling behind him made him spin around, but it was only a rabbit. He told himself to come to his senses. In all likelihood, his pursuers hadn't chased him past the borders of Nazareth. Why would they? The rabbi wouldn't want to risk him saying something. He'd just want Jesus gone, never to return. Stalemate. That was where they found themselves. This was his life now—fleeing to anywhere but Nazareth—anywhere but back to his mother.

This thought sent a wave of shame crashing through his chest. Would that be the last conversation they ever had?

Jesus gave himself another moment before standing up and brushing himself off, shouldering his bag once more. He'd started off towards Sepphoris on instinct, but now that he thought about getting back on the road, he wondered if that was really where he wanted to go. He'd never laid eyes on a proper map, so he had no real idea what waited outside of Nazareth. Sure, he knew stories and fragments of politics from the inn, but that was hardly a substitute for concrete knowledge of where to go or how to survive. He realized there were only four things he knew for sure: North led to Rome. South to Jerusalem. West to the sea. He had no interest in any of these.

That left east. So east it was. For the time being, anyway.

Rallying himself, he got back on his way.

———

JESUS SPENT THAT FIRST night out of Nazareth in the common area at the center of Sepphoris. Usually, travelers could find hospitality if they were still there around sundown, but Jesus looked so haggard and weary, no one wanted to approach him. There was also the fact that he kept muttering to himself, which gave many the impression he was demon possessed. *They aren't far off,* Jesus thought to himself, almost smiling for the first time since leaving.

The next morning, he felt better, but not much. He bought some rations for himself and kept pressing east. By mid-day, he'd made it to Tiberias, and thought about stopping, but his feet wouldn't obey. They wanted to keep moving, and by early evening, he found himself on the bank of the Jordan, where he finally stopped and fell to his knees. On the other side waited the Decapolis, a bigger city where he could look for a convoy of traders or a caravan to travel with. He didn't really care where they were going, only that it was far from Nazareth. He might even be able to barter his services as a carpenter for passage out of the country.

This thought made him pause. Was that what he wanted? To leave the country? To start over entirely?

As he considered this, he watched the water meander by and remembered the stories of the first Israelites to cross this river. Joshua—Jesus's legendary namesake—had stood in the river and commanded the water to stop so the newly liberated tribes could pass through into the Promised Land. It was a story about victory. About hope. The last time he'd thought about the story, he'd been in the synagogue. It had been close to the end of his time there, not that he'd known it then. "But it wasn't *their* land, was it?" he'd asked the rabbi. "Other tribes had been there for generations. The Israelites just came in and... took it."

"No, Yeshua," the rabbi had corrected him. "They trusted God to remove the foreigners from the land, and God delivered it to them as their inheritance. That is, until the idolatry of their descendants drove them into Babylon."

"As their 'right?'" Jesus had asked. "Why would God give us the 'right' to destroy a nation and steal their land? Isn't that exactly what Babylon did to us?"

"That's enough," the rabbi had said, and Jesus had let it go.

The memory made Jesus angry again, and in his anger, he felt some clarity.

Yes, he *was* ready to leave.

He *was* ready to start over.

Once he crossed this river, he'd be seeking his own Promised Land.

Suddenly, he wasn't angry anymore. Suddenly, he felt hopeful. Excited, even.

*Can a leopard change his spots?* the rabbi's voice challenged.

Jesus ignored him. Deliberately, he rose and waded into the water.

He would keep running. He would run farther than anyone he'd ever met at the inn. He would find a place where he could finally be who he wanted to be. He'd find wisdom that was better and more real than anything his rabbi had ever tried to offer him, and if it meant making his home among the 'dogs and Gentiles,' so be it.

He let the water rush over his body and when he emerged on the other side; he felt rejuvenated. Eager.

Dropping onto the far bank, he tossed his bag to the side and laid out in the afternoon sun to dry. He was free.

# 13

## *Kashi.*

WHEN ABRAHAM ARRIVED AGAIN with his third cart of laborers, Jesus took notice. By the fourth, he was puzzled. By the fifth, he suspected something was amiss.

He leaned against a vine support, observing as the cart pulled through the gate once more, stopping in front of the main house to let out the latest collection of harvesters. It was now well past the sixth hour, and there weren't many hours left to work. That meant these latest harvesters would have little time to earn anything. It was barely worth the trip out. Jesus wondered just how desperate the old man was to turn a profit to bring laborers out so late in the day.

Watching the scene, Jesus felt foolish. He'd stayed for answers, but why had he assumed he would find out anything new from the field? Even if the old man wasn't going back and forth to the city all day, he wouldn't be spending his time out here. At this rate, Jesus would leave with a decent wage, but no more answers than he'd come with. It surprised him he wasn't sure which he wanted more.

"And he continues to watch the oxen," Jesus heard Deva's voice behind him. "Was my father not clear that we are paying you to work, not meditate?"

Jesus turned to face him, gripping a vine brace for support. He'd felt unsteady for hours. "You're looking pale," Deva observed. "I hope you're not planning to faint on us. If you think I'm carrying your idle body down from this hillside, you're woefully mistaken."

Jesus regained his balance and stood straight. "You don't like me very much, do you?" he asked. He'd met men like Deva before, and didn't intend to let him keep the upper hand.

Deva scoffed. "I like those willing to work. So, no. You are not high on my list of respected people."

"Ah. So you think I'm a beggar?"

"I don't think you're here to work, if that's what you're asking," Deva said. "I think you're here to skirt by and cadge from those of us who actually earned our keep."

"I have a bag full of grapes here to prove otherwise," Jesus said, unbothered. "So, what is your complaint?"

"My complaint?" Deva asked. "You arrive two hours after the work-day starts, spend half of your time staring at the landscape, yet still expect a full day's wage? You're entitled and undeserving. *That* is my complaint."

"Well, if you don't like my work," Jesus shrugged, "dock my pay."

Deva's face darkened, and from the intensity of his reaction, Jesus wondered if he'd made a mistake in his translation. Deva took a step forward. "You watch yourself," he growled. "The old fool may have brought you here, but now that you're here, you're my responsibility, and he doesn't see everything that goes on in these fields."

"Take care," Jesus warned. "Honor your father and mother and your days will be long upon the earth."

"Watch your tongue or your days on this earth will be quite short." Deva looked around at the other workers. "The work day's almost over," he said. "Try to make yourself useful and keep from fainting until then, will you?"

Jesus didn't answer, so Deva turned around and marched back down the hill.

As soon as he was out of sight, Jesus leaned again on the vine support. He wasn't sure how much longer he'd stay, but he knew Deva would be trouble.

# 14

## *Judea, twenty months before.*

AFTER CROSSING THE JORDAN, Jesus reached the Decapolis, where his fortunes finally changed. First, he found a kind family willing to give him shelter, and he stayed there for a few nights, getting his bearings. It was a chance to let his shaken mind settle. Then, after scouring the markets and inns—far more numerous than in Nazareth—he finally met a group of textile traders heading east. Maybe it was the fact that they were several drinks in (which Jesus had generously purchased) or maybe it was that they needed a master carpenter (which Jesus may have led them to believe he was) but before the night was over, they had enthusiastically invited Jesus along. The next morning he was on a cart, rolling along the bumpy eastern road. When they'd asked his name, he hadn't hesitated. He was ready to be someone new. "Jesus," he said, "son of no one."

They traveled for weeks, and though Jesus wasn't sure exactly when they crossed from the Roman Empire to the Parthian Empire, he soon felt it. It was like stepping out from under a shadow. In a city called Hatra, he finally noticed the iron eagles and carved wolves were replaced by different, wild, and fascinating images. People's clothes changed. Languages changed. Jesus discovered he thrived on learning unfamiliar words and new phrases.

Jesus met new people, tasted exotic spices, and heard stories unlike any he'd known. One meeting at a time, his view of the world expanded. He heard tales of other gods and heroes—villains and tragedies. There were many differences between their sacred stories and his own, but, to his surprise, there were also many similarities. Though he

would have once condemned the idea as blasphemy, he now wondered if some ideas and stories he took for granted had been traded
into Judea right along with the spices and textiles. This theory
would scandalize the rabbi, of course—not to mention his mother—which only made Jesus more eager to explore it.

They moved on from Hatra, and as they traveled, the blasphemous "dogs and Gentiles" the rabbi had warned Jesus about took
on actual names and faces. They became his friends, showing him
more hospitality than he'd ever known in Judea. Soon, Jesus decided if these people were "abhorrent," as the rabbi had called them,
then he was content to be "abhorrent" right along with them.

Jesus and his caravan moved from one city to the next, and
the days became weeks, which then became months. At first, his
journey was effortless. Then, his fortunes changed.

It began slowly. As Jesus moved further beyond the edges of his
world, hospitality stretched thin. People became stingier with their
stories and more guarded with their resources. Fewer new acquain-
tances would give him the time of day, much less opportunities to
work. Soon, Jesus's excitement soured. He asked the traders about
this, and they speculated it was because he was a foreigner—becoming more foreign the further away from Judea they traveled.

As things grew harder around him, things grew more difficult
inside as well. Memories of his mother and her disappointment
began fluttering around in his head, refusing to give him a moment's respite. Thoughts of how the rabbi was going to get away
with his treason knocked at the door of his attention each day. The
thought of John and Joseph working without him, or John sitting
alone at the inn, flooded him with guilt. More and more, the rabbi's
voice would creep in to remind him of something or criticize his
unrighteous conduct, and soon, Jesus became bitter, angry, and
tired from fighting it. He kept trying to remind himself that this
was what he wanted—a new start and a new life—but the story felt
more like a lie each day.

After a year, the caravan reached Kashi—far beyond any city Jesus had even heard of—and that was where they chose to disband. It started as a fight between two of their company that eventually became a dispute between everyone but Jesus, and the traders soon agreed it would be best if they went their separate ways. This was common practice for them, but for Jesus, who had never been outside of Judea, this was a disaster. He had the money he'd saved, but that was all, and it was hardly enough to sustain him in this place that might as well have been a different world. Despite his protests and attempts to reconcile them, however, the caravan had made its choice. They sold the last of their wares, their carts, and their animals, and set off home—a different place for each of them. Jesus found himself alone at a city gate. Stranded.

Work proved impossible to find. His clothes grew tattered, and his strength dwindled. His money dried up, and he traded the last of what he had. Soon, he had nothing. Eyeing the mangoes and the jackfruit in the marketplace one day, hunger gnawed at him. He wondered how long he could hold out before resorting to something drastic.

# 15

*Kashi.*

THE SUSTAINED BLAST OF a nearby horn alerted the laborers that the workday had ended, and Jesus exhaled, relieved. He stood straight, stretching his aching back, then had to catch himself as the weight of his bag shifted. That was the last thing he needed—to lose his harvest at the last minute and give Deva a reason to shortchange him.

Jesus was bone-tired and glad to fall in step with the other harvesters on their trek back to the house. Deva hadn't instructed them on what to do with their harvest, but Jesus followed the laborers on their path to the press, where they emptied their bags and rinsed them in a trough alongside the wall. A short distance away, Abraham was setting up a table in front of the main house, placing a small money box beside a wooden tablet.

Jesus studied the old man as he waited to return his bag to its peg. He looked around for Deva, but it appeared he had left for the night. That was fine with him.

"Yes, thank you," Abraham directed as they finished with their bags and approached the table. "If you could, form a line here in front of this table. We will get you paid, and my driver here will return you to the city as quickly as we can. Thank you."

Jesus followed the instructions, still searching for a way to delay his departure. He took a place in the back of the line to give himself time to think.

"Ah, yes, I apologize," Abraham added when the laborers were nearly finished forming the line. "For the sake of keeping things straight, would you please arrange yourselves according to the order in which you arrived? Those who arrived nearer the *end* of the day, please stand nearer the front of the line. Yes, thank you."

Jesus wondered why this was necessary as the line re-formed itself. Some laborers grumbled while others—the ones who had clearly been here before—kept their places. Jesus stayed near the back. He'd been in the second group to arrive.

Abraham got settled behind his table, making a few marks on his tablet with a reed pen. Then, when he was ready, warmly called the first worker forward.

Jesus barely registered the process as he considered his next move. His plan so far was to tell Abraham he was a carpenter, then he might convince the old man to keep him around to work on the gate or on the cart. That would give Jesus a little more time to ask some questions, but on his terms, and for more wages. Some part of him was still wary from that morning, but he decided if he grew suspicious, he could always leave.

*Leave?* he asked himself. *And go where?*

His spirits fell a bit as he considered this. It wasn't safe to go back to the city, even for the night. There was nowhere he could fall asleep that he wouldn't have to keep one eye open for the jackfruit vendor and his knife. The woods were an option, although he'd spent all of his time since leaving Judea near trade routes or in cities. He wasn't sure what dangers waited for him out there.

*You make darkness, and it is night. The beasts of the wood creep from their places—lions stalking their prey, seeking their portion from God.*

He tried to push the psalm from his mind. As he did, though, a minor commotion at the front of the line pulled him from his thoughts, and he peered around to see what was going on.

It was an older woman, and she was in some kind of disagreement with Abraham. She repeatedly tried to put the money back in his hand, protesting in words Jesus didn't quite understand. Each time she protested, Abraham only shook his head and answered in a low voice, closing her hand back over the wages. "I assure you, there is no mistake," he insisted.

Jesus tried to listen more closely. As the woman protested, the only word he could pick up—and he was only marginally confident about that one—was "fair."

Immediately, Jesus stiffened. Was the old man cheating his workers out of their wages? Was all that talk on the cart about 'justice' just a ploy? Another deception to get Jesus's guard down? The tefillin on Abraham's wrist stood out to Jesus as he tried to offer the woman her wage. He remembered the tefillin on the rabbi's wrist as he'd lowered the scroll into the Roman's box.

The scene repeated until the woman gave up the fight—tears in her eyes—and retreated to the cart. "Next, please!" Abraham called cheerfully, inviting the next laborer forward.

None of the other laborers seemed suspicious, which Jesus didn't understand. Did they not see what was happening? Suspicion and the need to get out slowly replaced his curiosity about the old man.

Fewer and fewer people remained as the line thinned. Finally, after most of the line had received their wage and gone on their way, Jesus was close enough to hear what was going on. He didn't trust himself to understand every word, but he listened carefully. "And you there," Abraham said, gesturing for the next in line, "if you could step forward, please."

A man stepped up—a few years younger than Jesus.

"You were in the third group to come in, I believe?" Abraham asked.

The laborer answered in the affirmative, and Abraham made a mark. "Very good. Here you are, then." He held out the man's wage. Two marked copper coins.

Jesus hesitated, wondering if he was misunderstanding. Two copper coins were a full day's wage, and a generous one at that.

"I'm sorry," the laborer said, glancing over his shoulder as the woman had done. "I was not here for the full day. I only—"

"Some of us are able to rise at the break of day," Abraham inter-rupted, "others cannot. I see no reason that should stand in the way of earning wages enough to live. Here you are, son."

The young man took a moment to understand, then, with several expressions of gratitude, he accepted the coins and hurried over to the cart. The line moved on.

Meanwhile, Jesus struggled to understand what he'd seen. It wasn't what he'd thought at all. In fact, it appeared the old man was *over-*paying the labor, which couldn't be correct. Was *that* what had caused the commotion earlier? The crying woman he'd seen—had those been tears of gratitude? That made no sense. Then, Jesus remembered what Deva had said in the fields. *My complaint? You arrived here two hours after the workday started, and you spend much of your time staring at the landscape, yet you still enjoy the benefit of a full day's wage? You're entitled and undeserving.* That *is my complaint.*

This was what Deva had meant. He knew what his father was doing. He didn't approve, but he knew, and he assumed Jesus had come to take advantage of it. No wonder he'd been frustrated. Jesus would've been too. As he looked around at the people he'd been working with, however, and thought about the difference a full day's wage would make, he felt surprisingly moved. He wondered if Leela's parents were out here, among the workers. He felt a wave of respect for the old man—something he wouldn't have thought possible just a few hours ago.

"Next, please!" Abraham called out, and the man in front of Jesus stepped forward.

"Here you are," Abraham said, offering two copper coins—the same wage he'd offered the last harvester. It confirmed for Jesus that he hadn't misunderstood. Abraham truly was paying all of them a full day's wage. This man, however, just looked at the coins.

"This is it?" he asked.

Abraham looked like he'd had this conversation before, and he kept his tone measured. "Do you find this insufficient?"

"*He* got two coins," the man answered, nodding towards the young man on the cart. "I worked a full two hours longer, didn't I? Is this the manner of business you run?"

"It is, indeed," Abraham said. "Now, if you would—"

Rather than take his coins, the man banged a fist on the table, and Jesus felt his body tense, preparing for another fight.

"Some of these people only worked an hour," the man said, his tone sharpening. "They brought in hardly anything, and *they* get two coins? *We* bore the burden of this day, and we deserve our due!"

Abraham continued to smile, unfazed. "Son," he said calmly, "perhaps if you take a moment to consider—"

"Don't explain it away," the man insisted. "I'm owed more!"

Jesus had reached his limit. He was exhausted, and he couldn't believe he was about to do this, but it was necessary. "You're owed less," he interrupted.

For a moment, there was silence, then the man turned to see who had spoken. He found Jesus and regarded him for a moment in disbelief. "Excuse me?"

"I said you're owed less," Jesus repeated. "We both are. We came in mid-morning, didn't we? The group behind us—*they* are owed a full day's wage. You and I are owed less. So, unless you want the old man here to start thinking clearly and subtract from both of our wages, I suggest you say 'thank you', take your coins, and get on the damned cart."

The man only stared, looking like he wanted to either protest or hit Jesus, but in the end, he did neither. After a tense moment, he turned to face Abraham again. Without speaking, he snatched the coins and stormed off to the cart.

Abraham and Jesus both watched him walk away. "He didn't say 'thank you,'" Jesus muttered.

"That is the second act of courage I've seen from you today," Abraham observed. "Whether we could call it *kind* is up for debate, but it was right, and I am grateful."

"Do people often thank you by demanding more money?" Jesus asked.

"Poverty gives birth to hatred and anger," Abraham said, "perpetuating a cycle of suffering. It is the unfortunate way of things."

Jesus looked confused. "Scripture?" he asked.

"Yes," Abraham said, "but not Hebrew scripture."

Abraham's cryptic tone pressed at the edge of Jesus's exhaustion. He still didn't understand any of what was happening here, and with the weight of the day bearing down on him, he realized all he wanted were some answers and some rest. "Listen," he said, "you can keep the day's wage. Just tell me what's going on here, and we'll call it even. Who are you? Why are you doing this?"

"Hold on there, son," Abraham chuckled, "no need to give up your wages so easily. I can assure you that I have just as many questions about you as you do about me. From the first time I saw you in that marketplace, I've wondered how it was that someone such as yourself made it to this corner of the world, and what manner of fire must burn in your heart to keep you fighting as hard as you do. So, before you go trading your livelihood away, how about I make a counteroffer?"

Jesus waited, listening.

"Join me for Sabbath dinner tonight," Abraham said. "Then we can have a more equitable exchange. Truth for truth."

"What do you mean?" Jesus asked.

"I mean, I will tell you how I came to be here, and you can tell me about yourself. After that, you can even stay in the shed. It's just over there. It's no palace, but it's dry. Tomorrow, if you wish, you can be on your way. No one will hold you captive."

Jesus hesitated. He had forgotten tomorrow was the Sabbath, and he looked again at the tefillin on the old man's wrist. Something in him resisted, but it was like the old man had said. No one was holding him captive. He could always leave if he was so inclined. Still, before he chose, there was one thing he needed to know.

"One question," Jesus said. "Just one, and then I'll decide."

"Go on, then," Abraham invited.

Jesus examined the old man's face for one more moment—searching again for honesty or deception. "Why are you doing this?" he asked. "The wages... the shed... Why?"

Abraham considered this, then smiled. He reached into his money box and pulled out two copper coins, offering them to Jesus. "Why did you give those children the mangoes?"

Jesus stared at the coins, thinking of everything that had happened that day. As he did, something in him surrendered, and he shook his head. "All right," he said, taking the coins. "You win."

"Hoped I might," Abraham said, pleased. He gestured over his shoulder to the main house. "Feel free to wait inside while I finish up here. I shouldn't be long."

"You want me to wait inside your house?" Jesus asked. "How do you know I won't rob you?"

"Such is the risk of hospitality."

Not quite believing this was happening, Jesus stepped to the side, letting the next person step up to collect their wage. For a moment, he only stood before the house, watching the inside lamps flicker against the fading light of evening—inspecting the carvings around the doors and windows.

Then, ready to put the day behind him, he started forward, headed toward the warm light of the house.

II.

# 16

THE MOMENT HE WAS alone—the door closed behind him—Jesus exhaled, tension unfurling in his chest. *Don't get too comfortable,* he reminded himself. *You still don't know what you've gotten involved in.*

Jesus wasn't sure what he'd imagined the inside of Abraham's house to look like, but he was not disappointed. It was cozy and familiar. The main room was maybe twenty paces from side to side. Oil lamps hung on each wall, casting shadows that flickered in the evening light. Like the outside, the old man had decorated the windows and doors with bright colors against walls plastered smooth and washed in a soft shade of orange. A collection of tapestries hung around the room, swaying gently, their texture adding to the warmth.

At the opposite end of the room was a table, and next to the table was a door surrounded by shelves. They held what looked like a lifetime's worth of clay pots, woven baskets, herbs, grains, preserves, and some things Jesus didn't even recognize. Abraham could survive for a month inside this house without running short of provisions.

Then, between Jesus and the table, there was a living area with two comfortable chairs and a couch draped in heavy blankets. Immediately, all Jesus wanted to do was lie down and close his eyes, but he decided against it, both because it would be rude and it would leave him too vulnerable.

The last thing he noticed was a small table pushed up against the longest wall. Inspecting it, he decided it must be an altar, albeit a strange one. There was a pile of pillows next to it, a pile of scrolls beneath it, and the objects on top were enough to make Jesus wonder yet again just who his host was. A menorah stood on one end, old and tarnished, next to an incense tray. In the center was a bronze bowl beside a thick wooden stick, and on the other end, there sat an idol made of black basalt. Jesus picked the statue up, perplexed by an altar that would offer space to both a menorah and an idol.

It was an idol of a man—maybe eight inches tall—with crossed legs and a serene half-smile. Jesus stared, and as he did, let out a short, astonished laugh. For all his time away from Judea, he didn't think he would ever get used to the number of graven images he'd seen in and around Kashi. On top of that, if anyone had ever told him he would one day be holding a basalt idol while a guest in a Judean's home in a foreign country, he would've confidently bet against it.

*You shall not revere other gods,* he heard the rabbi's warning. *For your God is a jealous God—lest the anger of God be kindled against you and he destroy—*

"Enough," Jesus muttered. He let his fingers run over the smooth, cold surface of the statue.

"It won't talk back," a voice spoke from behind him, and Jesus dropped the statue, springing to his feet. Deva leaned against the back door frame, arms crossed. Jesus wondered how long he'd been standing there.

Deva was clearly pleased by the effect of his words. "Calm yourself," he said. "You think I came to pick a fight with you? Where's the challenge?" He turned his back on Jesus and began rummaging through the shelves of cookware around the door.

"You should be careful who you sneak up on," Jesus said, trying to calm down.

Deva laughed. "Somehow, I'm not intimidated."

After a few moments, Deva found what he was looking for—a pot, which he tucked under his arm as he turned attention back to Jesus. "I assume he invited you in for dinner?" he asked. "Throwing my inheritance away on charity cases?"

"He does seem to love throwing money away."

Deva scoffed. "If only you knew."

Jesus heard the bitterness in Deva's voice and wondered again about the tension between him and the old man. Had they always been like this? Had something happened?

"So," Deva said, changing the subject, "you're a Judean."

"How did you guess?" Jesus asked.

"It wasn't difficult. Few in this city speak Aramaic. In fact, between you and my father, I would guess there are two." He regarded Jesus for a moment. "So," he asked, "what is your aim? Steal what you can, then burn the place down?"

"Well," Jesus said, "that *wasn't* my plan, though now that you mention it..."

"Strange, isn't it?" Deva interrupted. "What are the odds that in all of Kashi, you would find your way to us? It makes one wonder."

"*I* am suspicious?" Jesus asked. "*I* am not the one creeping up behind people or throwing money away on strangers."

Deva's face grew darker. "Do *not* lump me in with him," he said. "I have no part in what that old fool is doing here."

"It didn't look that way this morning."

Deva took a step closer. "You know what?" he said. "Go ahead and burn it down. But do me a favor. Put the ledger aside. Maybe with him gone, I can finally turn a profit with this place."

Again, Jesus felt a surprising nudge of defensiveness for the old man.

"Don't be tempted to feel special," Deva said, backing down and heading for the door. "He's always picking up strays. You're just the latest sad case he feels sorry for."

"I am once again impressed by your hospitality," Jesus called after him as he left. "Thank you for that."

When Deva was gone, Jesus started breathing again. It was no wonder Abraham wanted company if *that* was his dinner companion each night.

He returned to the small table, picking up the statue and returning it to where it belonged.

As he waited for Abraham's return, Jesus decided to walk the perimeter of the room, inspecting the decorations more carefully. Every few paces, there was a wooden carving. Most were patterns or a script he couldn't read, but a few featured animals or humans. He paused at one in particular—a carving of a woman sitting outside a house while a man played with two children.

Jesus looked more closely. There was something familiar about the scene he couldn't place. He wasn't sure how long he stared, but he was still looking at the carving when Abraham hurried through the front door. "Sorry to keep you," the old man said.

"You gave me a day's wage, a bed, and a meal," Jesus answered. "I don't think an apology is necessary."

Abraham chuckled. "Let's not over-glorify the bed," he said. "It's more of a bench, really. Here," he offered Jesus a cloth bag. "Set that on the table, if you would. I'm going to change out of these dusty clothes."

Abraham walked to one of the tapestries and pulled it back to reveal an arched doorway. He stepped through, letting the tapestry fall back into place behind him. Jesus opened the bag to find fresh bread.

"When was the last time you had an actual Sabbath meal?" Abraham called from the other room.

"A long time," Jesus answered, setting the bread on the table. "I'd go through the motions with my mother, but I don't think I've cared much for the Sabbath since I was nine."

Abraham reappeared in a dust-free robe. "Nine is an early age to stop caring about the Sabbath. Did something happen?"

"Our rabbi caught me trying to play with a lizard," Jesus answered. "He knocked me on my back with his staff, then lectured me about 'trapping on the Sabbath.' Knocking children over on the Sabbath, though... God called that righteous."

Even though Jesus had resolved not to reveal anything about himself that he didn't have to, this story felt gratifying to share.

Abraham shook his head angrily. "Some people are like dogs in a cattle manger," he said. "They won't eat, but they won't let the cattle eat either. Your rabbi was a Pharisee, I take it? Of the House of Shammai?"

This took Jesus by surprise. "How could you tell?"

"I recognize the spirit," Abraham answered. "Used to have one, as a matter of fact, having lived as a Pharisee for quite some time. Now, let's get that bread on the table so we can eat, shall we?"

Jesus gawked. "You're a Pharisee?" he asked.

"I once was," Abraham corrected, "though I doubt very much that they would still claim me."

"Once were..." Jesus started. "How did you manage that?"

Abraham fetched bowls and cups from the shelves. He took a wine-skin from a higher shelf and set it on the table. On the side, Jesus noticed it said *Shalom*. "Well," Abraham said as he worked, "it's no small feat, but it turns out that if you call your teacher a fraud to his face, tip over the temple coffer before God and Jerusalem, then refuse to apologize for it... that will just about do it. Stew?"

"You did *what?*" Jesus asked, shocked, but Abraham had already disappeared through the back door. He returned a moment later with two steaming bowls of stew and gestured for Jesus to sit.

"You don't seem like one for lengthy prayers," Abraham said, taking his own seat, "so let's keep this brief. If God, who has infinite things to do, can take a day for rest, then what excuse have we? Amen."

Abraham started into his stew, but Jesus could only stare. "I'm guessing you weren't a very good Pharisee," he said.

"Oh, quite the contrary," Abraham laughed. "I was a *very* good Pharisee, as far as the House of Shammai was concerned. Perhaps not a very good person, but an excellent Pharisee. Pass the bread?"

Jesus handed him the bread, and Abraham tore off a piece. "Something the matter with the stew?" he asked.

Jesus realized he hadn't even thought about the stew, as hungry as he was. Abraham's story had taken precedent. He started in, his body thanking him. They ate in silence for a few minutes before Abraham spoke again. "So," he said, "truth for truth. That was our deal, was it not?"

"It was," Jesus said, mouth full, "but I hope you don't think what you just told me counts for a full story."

Abraham smiled. "It was true, wasn't it?"

"It was, but if you want information from me, you'll have to give me more than that."

Jesus hadn't known Abraham long, but he'd known him long enough to get a sense of when Abraham was teasing. "Very well," Abraham said. "I suppose a half-truth can be more dangerous than no truth at all."

"How about you finish your story," Jesus suggested, "then I'll share as much of mine as seems fair." He drained the rest of his bowl, wiping his mouth with the back of his hand.

Abraham, also finished with his stew, settled back and laced his fingers over his belly. "Are you sure you want to pass your evening hearing the ramblings of an old man?"

"The same old man who just said he tipped over the Temple coffer and called his master a fraud?" Jesus asked. "Yes, I'm sure."

Abraham smiled again, and Jesus got the impression he was enjoying this. Given Deva's disposition, he doubted the old man got to share this story often with anyone who might understand. "All right," he said. "Well then, where to begin?" He considered this for a moment. "There are different manners of Pharisee, you know. Different schools with different teachers."

"I did know," Jesus said, "though I know little about them. All I ever learned about other Pharisees from our rabbi was that they were sadly and irreconcilably wrong."

"Of course you did," Abraham said. "I was the same. Only one kind ever made it out in the direction of Kerioth—that I ever knew, anyway—but the truth is, many are quite gracious and open-minded. The House of Hillel, for instance, has produced some truly remarkable and kindhearted teachers. One cannot put them all in the same basket, which is how it is with every tradition and every people."

"So you were one of these Pharisees, then?" Jesus asked. "From the House of Hillel?"

Abraham laughed. "Oh goodness, no. I followed in the footsteps of my father and his father before him. Joyless. Cold. Nothing, though, if not dedicated. I will give them that. That's why, when I came along, you would've been hard-pressed to find a better student in all of Judea. I knew the law backward, forwards, and sideways—written and spoken alike. Neither scribe nor scholar stood a chance against me."

Abraham looked both proud and sad as he told his story.

"When I was old enough, I went to Jerusalem for proper schooling—as I was always expected to do—and that's where the problems began. You see, I'd spent my life studying the law—every letter of every law, and every letter of every law *about* the law. I could recite commandments at the drop of a hat. The prophets, however—*those* I had given little thought to."

Jesus remembered the few readings he'd heard in the synagogue from the prophets. They had been rare, and the ones the rabbi used often involved some threat or another—reminders of what happens when you don't follow the law. *I will destroy the city with my plagues and everyone who passes by will shake their head in pity.* That had been one of the rabbi's favorites.

"We only had Jeremiah in Nazareth," Jesus said. "Some of Jeremiah, anyway. We couldn't afford a complete set of scriptures, and the prophets were never really a priority for our teacher."

*Nor were any of them, it turned out,* Jesus thought bitterly, remembering the Roman with his box.

"You're from Nazareth, correct?" Abraham asked, "That makes sense. Few have a complete collection of scriptures, and most teachers only focus on a small selection anyway, whether or not they are aware that's what they're doing. It was the same with my father. He wasn't too fond of the prophets, so they weren't a significant part of my education. When I found them in Jerusalem, however, I saw another opportunity for greatness. I *had* to master them, just as I'd mastered the other scriptures. I thought perhaps knowing them as well as I knew the law might even set me apart from my peers. So, I got to reading, and what I found there..."

Abraham trailed off for a moment, looking distant.

"It changed me."

"What do you mean?" Jesus asked.

Getting excited, Abraham leaned in. "Tell me, son, did your rabbi ever read from the words of Amos?"

"Amos?" Jesus asked. "No. Why?"

Abraham looked delighted. "Well then, prepare yourself."

He rose and made his way to the altar, rifling through the scrolls underneath.

"Are those scriptures?" Jesus asked, surprised. He'd never seen a private collection before. He caught glimpses of some names and titles as Abraham set them aside.

"Mostly," Abraham called back. "I've had the hardest time tracking down the Scroll of Judges, not that I've lost much sleep over it. Bloodshed and conquering... Ah, here we are."

Abraham pulled a scroll from the stack and brought it to the table, pushing empty bowls away. "When I left," he said, "my father warned me I needed to hold fast to my faith and obedience. He warned that there would be influences in Jerusalem that might cause me to doubt and stumble, and that these were a test of my faith. I didn't think that was possible, but then, I found these."

Searching the scroll, Abraham found his place. "Listen," he said. "The words of the prophet Amos to the people of Israel. 'I hate, I despise your festivals. Your assemblies are a thing of disgust to me! Your burned offerings are unacceptable before my sight! The songs you sing are the sounds of clashing symbols and clanging gongs—'"

"I understand," Jesus interrupted. "We have fallen short. God is angry. We need to do better. I've heard this sermon before."

"Oh, no you haven't!" Abraham corrected. "Listen closely. 'My children, I say to you, I do not want sacrifices, but *justice!* I want *justice* rolling down with the power of a mighty river! Righteousness flowing like a never-failing spring!'"

He paused and watched for Jesus's reaction. "Don't you see? God's not angry because they are trapping lizards on the Sabbath. He's angry because the people are suffering, and the worshipers care more about their assemblies and offerings than helping God's children." He tapped the scroll passionately. "I don't know about your rabbi, but *this* was not the message I received in my training."

"Let me see that," Jesus said, stepping in for a closer look.

*You reject the one who dissents,* he read, *and abhor those who speak the truth.*

*You trample the poor and build wealth on their misfortune...*

"These are scriptures?" Jesus asked. "Hebrew scriptures?"

"Exactly!" Abraham said proudly. "That's what I thought as well! These are not words written from seats of power or behind veils of self-righteousness. *These* are words written from the ground! From people suffering under generations of oppression at the hands of proud teachers and corrupt governments."

Jesus wasn't sure what to do with this. These words weren't written by people like the rabbi. They were written by people like him. His mind reeled.

"What does your God require of you?" Abraham read on. "'What is good in God's sight? Do justice, love kindness, and walk in humility before God!' The words of the prophet Micah."

An image flashed across Jesus's mind. All his life, he'd imagined God looking down from his throne in judgment, but for just a moment, he imagined God among the people. God in the dirt. God who cared about justice and kindness and humility rather than obedience or sacrifice. "This must be an exception or a mistake," he said. "That, or we're reading them wrong."

"That's what I thought as well," Abraham answered. "I kept in mind what my father warned me about, and I wanted more than anything to find a way *out* of what I'd discovered. My answer was to study them from every angle and with every commentary—even the ones my teachers discouraged—but I continued arriving at the same conclusion. Something was wrong."

"So, what did you do?" Jesus asked, imagining what would have happened if he'd brought something like this to the rabbi.

"Well, I panicked," Abraham said honestly. "I mean, imagine what it's like, after a lifetime of practice, to suddenly suspect you hardly knew God at all, much less what God wanted. To suspect you may have missed the point your entire life! It's almost enough to make you deny the whole thing, put away the scrolls, and pretend you'd never found them in the first place, which is what I'm confident some of my teachers had done. That, or come up with remarkably creative ways to explain them away."

Jesus unrolled the scroll further, letting his eyes move down the lines. After a moment, though, his eagerness startled him. He hadn't felt this way since childhood, and that alone made him wary. He took his hands off the scroll.

"So, there I was," Abraham continued. "In one ear, I heard my teachers explain how to rightly present myself while fasting, while in the other, I heard the prophets. 'Is this not the fast I choose: to loosen the bonds of injustice and undo the straps of the yoke? To share your bread with the hungry and bring the homeless into your house?' That one is Isaiah, by the way. The prophets said our 'light would break forth like the dawn,' but I wasn't seeing much light breaking forth from my teachers, I'll tell you that. That's where it all unraveled for me. I no longer wanted to be as my teachers were. When I looked at my peers, all I saw were self-justifying actors, puffed up so full of hot air that there was little room for anything else. It was like the blind leading the blind. I knew if I kept following, we'd both wind up in a ditch."

"Right," Jesus said, remembering. "I know the feeling."

"My colleagues and teachers," Abraham went on, "they'd focus half their attention on the scriptures that suited them, and the other half on the sins of everyone else. 'The faults of others are easier to see than one's own. The cheater hides their shortcomings by accusing the dice of his opponent.'"

"Another prophet?" Jesus asked.

"Another sutra," Abraham corrected. "The words of the Buddha."

"The Buddha?" Jesus said, surprised again. "So, you tipped over the coffer and became an idolater?"

Abraham laughed. "An idolater," he repeated. "It's been a while since I've heard that one. That's certainly what they'd call me, yes. They'd think me an abomination for what I've become. That's all right. The truth is, I realized *they* were the idolaters. We would make an idol of the law, worshiping *it* rather than the Living God. We were white-washed tombs—impressive and ornate on the outside, stark dead on the inside. We were like cups someone had only washed on the outside, leaving the inside to mold. I tried to deny it for a while, but in the end it was no good. My colleagues took to calling me a 'zealot.' A 'radical.' A 'blasphemer.' Anything, I suppose, to make *me* the problem and not themselves."

Abraham paused, a sad expression on his face. He re-rolled the scroll and returned it to its place. "So, there I am," he said, "coming to terms with all this, when what festival should roll around but the Passover? Have you ever been to Jerusalem for the Passover?"

Fuzzy images flashed through Jesus's mind. A flurry of people. Apprehension. His mother snapping at him. "A few times," he answered. "I was young. Few wanted us in their caravan, and we could never really afford the trip or the sacrifice." He thought of his ancient goat and the last time he'd patted him on the head.

"That sounds right," Abraham said. "They do their best to bleed the people dry right along with the animals. Let me tell you this, though, to adults, Jerusalem during Passover is quite tense. A single spark can set the city alight. The priests, Pharisees, and Romans alike are coiled tighter than angry vipers. They're worried about the people getting riled up... worried about Romans getting spooked and killing someone... worried about appearances... tempers are short."

"Hardly the time to tip over a Temple coffer," Jesus said.

"Indeed," Abraham said, smiling. "At the height of the commotion, my teacher decides to make his offering. He'd withhold his offering, you see, for the better part of a year, waiting to have the Passover crowd as a witness. There would be pilgrims from all over Judea there to behold his noble act of charity. He'd claim it would 'inspire generosity,' and would make a big show of pouring coins into the bronze coffer. It would make a tremendous racket. Absurd, of course, but to tell you the truth, I think I could've stomached that. It was what came *after* that pushed me too far."

"What did he do?" Jesus asked, enraptured.

"Not him," Abraham shook his head. "It was an old woman. A widow. No one noticed her but me, but she didn't care. While everyone was busy praising my teacher, this woman comes along and deposits two small coins. Mites. Leptons! It's nothing, but by looking at her, I can tell it's all she has. That, my friend, is what pushed me over the edge. It's the Temple's divinely ordained job, you see, to take care of widows and the orphans—to care for the poor and the vulnerable—and what do they do? They take the last penny from a poor widow while the rich drink in the applause." Abraham shook his head. "*That's* when I couldn't take it anymore," he said. "As I saw it, it was the *people's* money, not the Temple's, so I didn't think twice about it. I let loose preaching from Isaiah and Jeremiah, going on and on about justice and righteousness and corruption! 'I will bring the people to my holy mountain! I will bring them joy in my house, which is meant to be a house of prayer! The offerings and the sacrifices of all will be accepted on my holy altar, for my house shall be called a house of prayer for all people!'"

Abraham grew increasingly lively as he recounted the story, but at this, his spirit died down. "*That's* when I turned the coffer on its side.

The Temple guard dragged me off to a cell. It was awful, but as I sat there, I realized I'd been in a cell for a long time. My teacher came in two days later to let me know he'd sent word to my father. A short time after that, on my father's orders, I was instructed never to show my face in Jerusalem again. That was it. I never saw them again after that."

There was a moment of silence. Jesus could imagine, on a smaller scale, how that must've felt, and he regarded the old man with respect. He remembered how hard it had been to fight back against the rabbi. How much harder would it have been if he'd reached the level Abraham had reached? "I'm sorry," he said. "It sounds like they lost a good student."

Through Abraham's wistfulness, a smile broke through. "That they did," he agreed. "I spent a long time being angry about it before I made my peace. A long time."

"Your peace?" Jesus asked. "How do you make peace with something like that?"

"By realizing all I could do was listen well, testify to the truth, then let go of what I could not control," Abraham said. "It had nothing to do with me, after all. It was about their fear, not my failure. They couldn't see what I saw, nor could I make them."

Abraham rose and retrieved a pipe from a shelf, making his way to a chair by the couch. Jesus followed him to the other. "And what was that?" Jesus asked. "What did you see?"

"That much of what passes for 'God' in this world is not 'God' at all," Abraham answered, lighting his pipe. "It is nothing more than fear and fragile pride. Build it a temple, hide it behind a veil... that's all it is. It is the hubris of humankind, gilded in gold."

"So, you don't believe in God?"

*Only fools say in their heart, "there is no God..."* the rabbi's voice scolded, but Jesus ignored it.

"Oh, I never said that," Abraham corrected. "I believe in the *Living* God. It was the fragile god of my teachers I left behind."

"What's the difference?"

"The difference?" Abraham echoed. "My, my, what a question. How to phrase it? The Living God is like... well, it is like a lamp that shines from beneath the bushel of human life. It may be dampened beneath fear, greed and delusion, but it dwells in the temple of our hearts, and our work is to let it shine. The Living God is Life. It is *Being* itself—the great and unnamable *I am.*"

Jesus recognized the story Abraham referred to. When Moses had asked God for his name, his response had been *I am that I am,* which Jesus had always taken as God being impatient. It sounded like the equivalent of, *I've said what I've said, now cease your questions or I will smite you with a pillar of fire.* The way Abraham said it, however, made Jesus think twice.

"The laws we become obsessed with—" Abraham continued, "I believe they were always meant to point us to something deeper. Something more real. It is like a man trying to get a dog to look at the moon. He points, but all the dog looks at is the man's finger, missing the moon entirely. We were obsessed with the pointing—with keeping the law and offering our worship. We missed the moon—the Living God. *That,* son, is the difference."

Jesus mostly understood what Abraham was saying, but he was having an increasingly difficult time following. The particularity of Abraham's story had been compelling enough to keep him alert for most of the evening, but between the late hour and the stew settling in his stomach, the day's exhaustion was pressing in. Abraham noticed and smiled.

"It would seem I have dominated our time tonight and robbed myself of hearing your story before sleep takes you."

"No, it's all right," Jesus tried to say. He was eager to continue their talk, but a yawn betrayed him.

"How about this?" Abraham interrupted before Jesus could protest further. "What if we re-negotiate the terms of our agreement? You must still hold up your end of the deal, of course, but as a penalty for my vanity, I will offer another night's stay and another meal. You can tell me your story then, after the benefit of a good night's sleep and a full Sabbath's rest."

Despite everything he'd seen so far, Jesus was still surprised. "Really?" he asked. "You would put me up for another night?"

"If it means the benefit of a good story, it seems a small price to pay."

"Well, I won't say no, but I don't know how good of a story it is."

"You underestimate yourself, I'm sure."

Abraham stood and took a blanket from the couch, tossing it to Jesus. Jesus also stood. "So, you really still observe the Sabbath?" Jesus asked. "All the way out here? You know no one in Kashi is going to stone you for working an extra day."

"Far be it from me to refuse a day off," Abraham answered, walking him to the door. "The Sabbath is a reminder that I am more than the fruit I grow or the wine I sell. The Sabbath was made for humanity, not humanity for the Sabbath. You can tell your rabbi I said that."

"I will. The next time I see him."

Abraham opened the door and pointed toward the shed built off of the ox pen. "Are you all right to go on your own?"

"Of course," Jesus said with more confidence than he felt. "I can make it."

Abraham took a lamp from the wall. "Here," he said. "Take some light with you. Careful though. Knock it over, and you'll wake up to a warm shed."

"Understood," Jesus said, taking the lamp.

"Meet me back here for breakfast, if you wish," Abraham invited. "I'll leave you be for the day, but tomorrow night, I expect you to hold up your end of the deal."

"Of course," Jesus agreed, then paused. "Thank you," he said. "For all of this."

Abraham patted him on the shoulder. "Freely I have received, and freely I shall give. Now, I bid you a good evening, and I will see you in the morning."

He stepped back and pushed the door closed, leaving Jesus to take a moment to enjoy the night's calm before heading over to his shed. It was quiet except for the buzzing of the insects.

Jesus's feet and back ached, and he longed to close his eyes, but he also noticed a spark of something he hadn't felt in a long time. He thought of the eagerness he'd felt standing over the scroll of the prophet—the way his sight felt clearer and his mind felt sharper as Abraham read the prophet's words about justice. How many more scrolls were there under that altar? How many that he'd never seen? Voices he'd never heard? He hadn't felt this kind of inspiration since he was younger, learning about the law at the rabbi's feet. It was something he'd missed and grieved—something he never thought he'd experience again. With this thought, though, also came a creeping sense of caution. The old man had quickly earned his trust—his respect, even—but Jesus had to remind himself that Abraham was still a relative stranger. He didn't know him—not really—and for all he knew, he could be just as devious as the rabbi. Jesus thought again about the tefillin, wrapped steadfastly around Abraham's wrist.

His arm was starting to ache from holding the heavy, oil-filled lamp, so he made himself move toward the shed. The sooner he got there, the sooner he could sleep.

As he walked, he began to think practically about the next day. What would he tell Abraham about what he was doing here? How would he tell the story about where he'd come from—about the rabbi or the Roman or the exile? He felt a pang of shame as he thought about lunging at the rabbi—about gripping that hammer. How much did Abraham really need to know?

Even given what the old man had trusted him with, Jesus still felt guarded in sharing his story. He didn't want to give away more leverage over himself than he absolutely had to. In this case, though, it was the price he'd have to pay for more of Abraham's story—and he was absolutely sure there *was* more to the story. He had so many questions, and had he not been so exhausted, he would've asked them tonight. For instance, of all the places he could've gone, why had Abraham come to Kashi? How had he come to do so well as to own a vineyard while Jesus wound up in an alley? Perhaps most interesting to him, though, was the question of how Abraham had gone from a Pharisee-in-training to a man who spouted teachings about the "Living God" or cited a sutra as quickly as he cited the psalms.

There were many holes in the old man's story, and Jesus intended to see them filled.

He arrived at the shed, remembering not to get ahead of himself. Tonight, he intended to sleep, and with a roof over his head and a door between him and the outside world, he intended to sleep well.

# 17

JESUS WOKE TO THE sound of shouting. He'd been dreaming that he was ten, and kids were chasing him—calling him a *mamzer* and throwing rocks. He'd been pulling at the synagogue doors, but they were locked. *"No mamzer shall enter the assembly of God,"* the rabbi's voice called from inside. *"Even to the tenth generation, none of his descendants shall be worthy to enter."*

The last thing he remembered was the stones hitting him in the back as children yelled.

As he sat up and rubbed his eyes, it sounded like the yelling had followed him out of his dream. It was coming from outside, but outside of where? Where was he?

It took him a moment to get his bearings. He looked around at the table and stools, shelves, and rugs, and remembered that he was in what the old man had incorrectly referred to as a "shed." Last night when he'd arrived, he'd discovered the "shed" was actually a full guest house, complete with a platform to lay a mat on. The word "shed" made Jesus think of a cramped storage space, but he'd never had this much space to himself, not even in Nazareth.

The yelling continued, indiscernible from inside. "All right," Jesus muttered, scratching his head and stretching his aching back. He brushed messy, tangled hair out of his eyes.

"We cannot afford this!" he heard as he stepped into the warm morning sunlight. How late was it? Later than he'd slept in a long time—that much he knew. "Don't tell *me* to be reasonable!" the shout came again. "We are sinking!"

It was coming from the direction of Abraham's house. It took him a moment to recognize the voice. Deva.

He knew that whatever was happening was not his business, but he thought it was worth investigating further, just to be sure the old man was all right.

The shouting continued as Jesus stumbled over to the house, his grogginess clearing as he went. When he reached the house, he waited just behind a corner, listening to see what he was walking into. "If your aim is to put every other farm out of business," Abraham said, "then yes, we are doing a woefully poor job. If the goal is to sustain ourselves and aid others, then we are doing quite well."

"You are throwing away the profits we could invest in—"

"We are *investing* in the stomachs of the poor," Abraham interrupted. "We are investing in the well-being of our neighbors. That has always been enough and it will continue to be—"

"It is not wise to pay laborers for work they did not do, father, or to give food and lodging to vagrants that may well rob you in the night."

This cleared Jesus's head. They were talking about him.

"It is *wise* to act justly toward our neighbors," Abraham argued. "To do for them as we would want them to do for us if we were in their position. This is a treasure that no thief can steal, and no moth can eat—a treasure which neither rusts nor passes away."

"Enough with your platitudes! This is not the time!"

"Quite right," Abraham agreed. "Now is the time for breakfast. Here, I've prepared you a bowl."

Jesus heard something shatter. Deva had knocked the bowl out of Abraham's hand. Abraham spoke again.

"Now you tell me what good it does complaining about waste when you're going to smash bowls in my courtyard."

"I *will* make something of this place," Deva pressed, ignoring his father. "Just because you've taken leave of your senses doesn't mean I'm going to let you run this place into the ground. Mother would've—"

"Your mother would've done no different from I am doing now, son," Abraham said gently. "I wish you could see that."

There was silence, then Jesus heard Deva march away. The fight over, Jesus realized he hadn't meant to stand there eavesdropping as long as he had, and he backed away quietly. "You can reveal yourself now," Abraham stopped him. "He's gone."

Jesus cringed, then came out from behind his corner. "I'm sorry," he started. "I didn't mean to—"

"It's all right," Abraham said. "It's me who should be sorry for waking you with our arguing."

Abraham scooped up the shattered pieces of a bowl and tossed them into the fire. They charred and cracked as Abraham watched. "I practice to be like fire," he recited, "which consumes all things—beautiful or ugly—free of attachment or aversion. I practice to be like the earth, which receives all things and transforms all things. Even the foulest thing becomes food for the flowers."

"More scriptures?" Jesus asked.

"In a way," Abraham answered. "Breakfast?"

Jesus sat across from Abraham on one of four benches that had been built around the cooking fire. "I know it's none of my business," he started, "but it sounded like your son meant what he said."

"Oh, he most certainly did," Abraham answered, picking up a clean bowl and filling it from the pot suspended over the fire. "He's nothing if not prone to extremes. He has been since he was a boy." Abraham smiled sadly. "I suppose I still see him as that boy. That may be part of our problem."

He offered the bowl to Jesus, who looked at it with curiosity and caution.

"Stewed figs," Abraham said. "We grow them on the south property. The meat is a salted pork belly. Not everyone in this area partakes, of course, but it's something I've picked up in my travels."

"Unbelievable," Jesus said, taking the bowl. "You've gone full Gentile."

Abraham chuckled. "You will love it, I assure you. Unless of course you're concerned with being smote by brimstone and fire, in which case, perhaps you should limit yourself to figs."

"I'll take my chances."

Jesus tried it. It was exquisite.

"You know," Abraham reflected, stoking the fire, "it has long been a mystery to me, our prohibition against pork. Since leaving, I've come to understand many of our commandments in new ways. Don't murder, don't steal, don't bear false witness... these things keep the people safe... but pork? Mixed fabrics?"

"I was taught we weren't supposed to ask those questions," Jesus said, swallowing a bite. "Trust in God and don't lean on your own understanding."

"Hmm," Abraham nodded, "and you were satisfied with this response?"

Jesus didn't answer.

"Tell me," Abraham said after a moment, "do you know the parable of the law and the orchard?"

"No," Jesus said. "I've never cared much for parables."

"Really?" Abraham asked, surprised. "And why is that?"

"Intelligent men use them to make themselves sound more intelligent, then shame the rest of us for not understanding. That's why."

"Ah," Abraham nodded. "In that case, I daresay you have heard them used poorly. In the right hands, they make simple the over-complicated and complicate the over-simplified. If I might offer one that seems appropriate?"

"Go ahead."

Abraham cleared his throat. "There was once a land in which fruit trees were sparse," he began, "so they enacted a law that each citizen was to pick only one piece of fruit a day. One. To do otherwise was considered a grievous sin, punishable by beating. For generations they abided by this law, only taking one piece a day, until one spring, the farmers realized how to care for their orchards more effectively, and suddenly the desert transformed into a paradise. Fruit abounded. Still, however, even as fruit rotted on the ground, the people held to the ancient law: One piece a day. None of them could see the spirit of the law, or that waste was the deeper sin. So it goes with any who value a dead law over the Living God. The true law is not written on tablets of lifeless stone, but on the hearts and minds of humankind."

Jesus listened carefully. When Abraham finished, Jesus couldn't help but laugh. "My rabbi would loathe you."

Abraham smiled. "I do not doubt that a bit."

For a moment, they were quiet, enjoying their breakfast. Then Abraham spoke again. "Harvesting figs was always my son's favorite task, you know," he mused. "He loved when the harvest came in and we could make this stew."

"Really?" Jesus asked. "He didn't seem all that excited when he shattered your bowl."

Abraham looked confused, then comprehension dawned. "Ah, forgive me," he said. "No, I'm afraid Deva was always a bit harder to please. I'm talking about my youngest."

"You have another son?"

"Oh yes. Ananda. It used to be the four of us out here—Deva, Ananda, me, and my wife, Radha."

As Abraham spoke, Jesus remembered the art on the wall inside—the two boys playing with their father while a woman watched from the porch. "The drawings inside," he said. "They're of your family?"

Abraham smiled. "The drawings were Radha's," he said. "Incredibly talented. She and I started this place together. It had always been a dream of hers."

"Starting a vineyard?"

"No, not a vineyard exactly. It was more what this place meant. She and I met in the city, you see, near the same courtyard where I found you. I was aiding a farmer in moving his product to the market, and I saw her. We began talking. It was quite the scandal. Her parents didn't exactly trust a foreigner with no references and no family. Still, we weren't deterred. She inspired me. She had vision and faith in a way of life that I found absolutely marvelous, and the more we spoke about it, the more I began to see her vision as akin to the vision of the prophets—for a way of justice and restoration and peace..."

"*Shalom,*" Jesus said.

Abraham nodded, pleased. "*Shalom,*" he echoed. "That was what we wanted this place to embody. The best years of my life were my years building this place by her side. It began as a simple farm, but after leaving Judea, I'd spent a good bit of time on a trading ship carrying wine all over the Empire, and winemaking was something I'd wanted to try my hand in. Everything was only made sweeter with the birth of our sons."

"What happened?" Jesus asked, then regretted it almost immediately. "I'm sorry," he said. "You don't have to—"

"It's all right," Abraham said, but his smile had faded. "Radha grew ill. The boys were grown by then, but only just. She held on for a long time—longer than most would—but when she finally died, it hurt us all. You believe yourself to be prepared for something like the death of someone you love, but..." he trailed off. "Deva became so bitter I hardly recognized him. Every day it was, 'If only we'd been richer... if only we'd given her better care... if only we'd offered more sacrifices...' He needed someone to blame, I think, and I was closest. Ananda, meanwhile, turned inward. It was difficult to get him to talk to anyone, let alone me. Who knows what sort of story he was telling himself about what happened? Deva began resenting him. He resented all of us, I think. By the time I realized something needed to be done, however, it was too late. Ananda had disappeared."

"Disappeared?" Jesus asked. "What do you mean?"

"One night, as we slept, he took what he felt was his rightful share of our savings and left without a word. We haven't seen him since."

"He robbed you?" Jesus asked, feeling suddenly angry.

"Nearly ruined us," Abraham continued. "We almost lost the vineyard. Ananda always was short-sighted that way. More than that, however, I think he took with him any chance of Deva healing from his grief. He became trapped by it, wounded more deeply than he'd allow anyone to see. He became obsessed with 'restoring the farm' and 'getting things back the way they were.' I told him he could make this farm the most profitable on all the earth, but it wouldn't bring his mother or his brother back, but at that point, he'd become deaf to my voice. I fear it will take us years to heal from the wounds we sustained in that season. A lifetime. More than that, I fear what might happen if Ananda ever decided to return."

Jesus scoffed. "You say that like you *want* him to return."

"Well, of course I want him to return," Abraham answered, surprised. "He's my son, is he not? My love for him has no conditions."

Jesus felt confused. "Even after what he did to you?" he asked. "You aren't angry?"

"Of course I was angry!" Abraham laughed. "I was angry for a good long while. But I also know that the truth is bigger than my anger, and it was in that truth I had to trust."

"You mean to say you could forgive him?"

Abraham waved this off. "We speak too often of forgiveness," he said. "I *understood* him. It took time, but I came to see the story of grief and pain that ensnared him, and if one can understand, forgiveness naturally follows. To force them out of order is quite impossible. In the early days, when I'd get upset, Radha would say to me, 'Abraham, why get angry with a grapevine? They grow the only way they can.' I have never forgotten that."

"A grapevine?" Jesus asked. He wanted to be respectful of Abraham's late wife, but this also struck him as absurd. "Do you really believe that's the same? Grapevines only grow. People have choices."

"Perhaps," Abraham said, "but consider this. A grapevine withers because its leaves cannot reach the sun, or it is being attacked by an insect. It wilts when its roots can't find water. In the same way, will a person not wither from lack of love? Will they not lash out if assaulted by fear, if that's the only way they've known? Will they not wilt if they can't find inspiration? A person may have choices, but they grow the only way they *can* grow, and those choices are the result. It does no good to blame them, then, any more than it does good to blame a grapevine. All we can do is understand what is happening, accept it for what it is, and—if we can—try to intervene so the vine can grow stronger moving forward. Forgiveness is only a natural part of the process."

"And what stops them from trampling over you while you spend all your time accepting them?" Jesus asked. "How many times do you forgive them before you see your blame is justified? Six times? Seven?"

"More like seventy times seven," Abraham said, "but you imply that acceptance means doing nothing. What I said was that we *understand* and *intervene*. Resist and draw lines if you must, but 'hatred doesn't cease in this world by hating, nor does fire cease by fire. Fire ceases by water and hatred by love. Overcome the miser by giving, and the liar by truth.' That is simply the truth of how healthy change occurs."

"Another sutra?" Jesus asked.

"That it is," Abraham answered. "'If anyone should deal a blow with their hand, a stick, or a knife, then one should abandon all desires for revenge and utter no evil words.' Holding fast to resentment and anger... this only breeds pain. If you wish to do something that truly makes a difference, then show your understanding. Water the seeds of goodness in others. If you love your enemies, give them food and water—"

"I think I've reached my limit on foreign scriptures for the day," Jesus cut Abraham off. "Thank you."

Abraham grinned. "Proverbs, actually," he corrected. "If your enemy is hungry, give them food to eat; if they are thirsty, give them water to drink. In doing this, you will heap burning coals on their head."

Jesus stopped short, embarrassed.

"I spent a great deal of my life thinking of ways to defeat my enemies," Abraham said, "and it very nearly killed me. Freedom only found me when I realized my aim should be to *awaken* them, not overpower them. There are none alive whom I would not be exactly like if I'd been born in their place. I dare not judge them, lest I judge myself."

"And this has worked for you?" Jesus asked skeptically. "This is how you overcome your enemies?"

Abraham shrugged. "Perhaps we have a different understanding of 'overcome.'"

Jesus shook his head, exasperated.

"My friend," Abraham said gently, "I am sensing that we have left my story behind, and may be speaking of something else entirely."

Jesus looked away. Abraham was probably right, but he didn't want to talk about it.

"I think, perhaps, I have nearly broken my word," Abraham said, standing and collecting Jesus's empty bowl. "I assured you I would leave you be for the day so that you might rest, and here I am inundating you with stories and asking you about yourself. Very clever, by the way, tricking me into sharing more of my own story out of turn. Don't think this absolves you of your end of the bargain."

Jesus gave a soft laugh, grateful to Abraham for a way out. "I know, I know," he said. "Although I'll say again, you may be disappointed. It's not that much of a story."

"And I will say again, you underestimate yourself, I'm sure."

Abraham took the empty bowls over to a narrow washing trough by the house.

"So, what am I supposed to do all day?" Jesus asked. "Like I said, I haven't really kept the Sabbath in a long time."

"That is a fruit you must chew for yourself," Abraham answered, washing the bowls. "Take a nap! Walk the property! What restores your soul is between you and God. Despite what your rabbi might say, the Sabbath *is*, in fact, for chasing lizards and lying around. It is not for sitting in a room listening to proud men impress themselves with words. Although," he looked back over his shoulder, "that is a service I'm happy to provide."

Jesus smiled. "That won't be necessary."

He rose and started his way back to his "shed," deciding he'd figure out what to do from there. He would've preferred to just stay and hear the rest of the old man's story—to finally get the full answers to his questions—but he knew that wouldn't happen until he'd shared his own story, and he was glad to delay that for as long as possible.

He still wasn't sure what he was going to say or how much he really trusted Abraham, but apparently, he had an entire day to figure it out.

# 18

JESUS MEANDERED ALONG A short stone wall marking a boundary of the property. He kept the wall to his right and the grapevines to his left. He'd used approximately an hour, which meant only nine more to go until he met Abraham again.

As he walked, he thought about another Sabbath a long time ago, around the time of the lizard incident. He'd been about seven, alone, outside of his home. He'd spent the afternoon sculpting an entire world out of mud, and his kingdom sprawled out in front of him. He'd been quite proud. He was putting the finishing touches on a dove when someone cast a shadow over him.

"And what is this, Yeshua?" a voice asked, deceptively calm. "Are these graven images?"

Jesus had stared at the rabbi, frozen in place. Saying anything felt like it would only make things worse.

"You will speak when I ask you a question, Yeshua," the rabbi had warned.

Jesus had only nodded.

"Do you know what we do to graven images, young Yeshua?" the rabbi had asked, and Jesus was about to answer when the rabbi brought his heel down onto the dove, hard. Thick mud spattered Jesus's face.

"We *smash* them," the rabbi had scolded. "Now do away with this at once, before your poor mother sees."

Obediently, Jesus had flattened his creation. He'd held his breath until the rabbi had walked away, not wanting to let the rabbi see him cry.

As he walked, Jesus tried to push the memory from his mind. That probably hadn't been what Abraham had meant when he'd told him to find what "restored his soul." Dragging up old memories of the rabbi was essentially the opposite. Trying to distract himself, he began kicking a stone absentmindedly along the path, making a game of keeping it in front of him. It was just starting to work when he heard a snapping noise from among the vines, and paused, watching for the culprit. He expected to see a small animal, or perhaps nothing at all. Instead, he saw a familiar tangle of dark hair disappear behind a row of vines.

Delighted, Jesus broke into a wide smile. "If you're here to steal grapes," he called, "I don't think you need to hide. The owner of this place would just as easily give them away for free."

Jesus saw the tangle of hair again, then a grimy face.

"Issa?"

"Leela," Jesus bowed slightly. "Did those mangoes not fill you up?"

The girl scrambled over the vines, knocking clusters of grapes loose as she ran up to tug at the edges of his clothes. "I thought you were leaving!" she said. "What are you doing here?"

"Well, I'm not entirely sure," Jesus said. "Finding information? Resting? The owner let me stay in his shed for the night."

"Really?" the girl tilted her head. "He let you stay?"

"He did. As a matter of fact, you could probably tell the others this place would be a safe place to come if you're in trouble. You might also try asking for work here. The owner will hire anyone, I think."

Leela shot him a skeptical look.

"I don't think there's a trick," Jesus clarified. "He seems to genuinely want to help."

"If you say so," Leela said thoughtfully, "but if he does not let you leave or makes you work to pay him back, then we will know for sure that there is a trick."

"That's true," Jesus nodded seriously. "If that happens, maybe you should stay away."

Leela looked back to the fields, clearly still hungry. "But you say he will let us eat his fruit?" she asked.

"Help yourself," Jesus told her. "In fact, you go enjoy. I'm going to continue on my walk. You stay safe, all right?"

"I will!" Leela called. "Thank you, Issa!" She grinned and dove back into the cluster of vines. She was usually so serious that it always surprised Jesus to see her act like the child she was. He carried on, leaving her to her plunder.

He hadn't walked far when he realized he'd left his kicking stone behind and started looking for a suitable replacement. He tried a couple, but whether it was him or the stones, they kept getting away from him, bouncing off the path and under the vines. Inevitably, the memory of the rabbi and the mud crept back into his mind, and he sighed as he kept walking. How was it that even this far away, the rabbi still felt like he was there, watching over his shoulder?

*Where can you flee from my Spirit? Where can you hide from my presence? If you take the wings of the morning and fly even to the uttermost parts of the sea, I am there...*

"You reject the one who dissents," Jesus muttered, remembering the prophet's words from the night before, "and abhor those who speak the truth. You trample the poor and build wealth on their misfortune."

The rabbi's voice went quiet, and Jesus was grateful for the reprieve. He wondered if the rabbi had encountered the words of the prophets and if they bothered him as they had bothered Abraham. What had the rabbi done to justify his way out of their rebukes and their challenges? As he imagined the rabbi coming up with some verbose argument out of the prophet's call, Jesus wondered what else was written on those scrolls under Abraham's small altar—what other wisdom and demands for justice?

As Jesus thought about it, he felt that same eagerness he'd felt the night before—that familiar inspiration and call forward that he hadn't felt since he was younger, learning at the feet of the rabbi. He'd had a purpose, then. Hope for the future. A sense of his place. As much pain as the synagogue had brought him, it had also brought him that. Now, he felt like he had none of those things. He wondered if there was anything he could offer to trade or repair that could convince Abraham to let him see the scrolls again—to explore what was written in these odd new scriptures. They called him like a smoldering fire on a night that was too dark and too cold. There was a flame there. It just needed attention.

Jesus was so absorbed in his thoughts that he almost missed the figure approaching him on the path. He heard muttering and looked up to see Deva walking purposefully in his direction, his eyes on the ground.

Jesus hesitated. His first instinct was just to turn around and walk the other way, but as he turned, he remembered Leela. He hadn't warned her about Deva, and while he was confident Abraham wouldn't mind Leela gleaning from his fields, he was just as confident Deva would. He would need to distract him—to start a small argument so that Leela would notice and disappear. It would be no trouble. In fact, arguing might just be the thing that "restored his soul."

As Deva approached, his muttering became clearer, and Jesus realized he was counting something.

"One hundred thirty-seven," he said, eyes still on his feet, "one hundred thirty-eight, one hundred thirty-nine—"

"Good morning, Deva," Jesus said pleasantly, and Deva nearly ran into him. Deva jumped back, surprised. It took him a moment to remember who Jesus was.

"Deva*datta*," he corrected, his surprise settling into disapproval. "I see you're still here."

"Perceptive," Jesus answered. "And I see you pass your Sabbath counting your own footsteps?"

Deva tried to step around him, but Jesus moved into his way. Leela needed more time. "Counting to measure, maybe?" Jesus asked. "Surely you're not measuring to buy or sell? You are aware this land doesn't belong to you, yes?"

Deva gave him a bemused look. "Tell me," he said, "has my father's hospitality tricked you into the delusion that you are somehow entitled to an opinion? That you have some kind of standing here?"

Jesus didn't answer.

"If so," Deva went on, "your ability to deceive yourself is truly remarkable."

"Not as remarkable as yours," Jesus said, knowing he was pushing it. "You think you're going to convince him to exchange his vision for this place for a profit?"

"Oh, I see. He's been feeding you his *Shalom* nonsense, hasn't he? He's convinced you of the righteousness of his cause."

"You're not convinced?"

Deva scoffed. "Are you asking if I'm persuaded that overpaying beggars is going to heal the world? I am no more convinced of that than I am convinced tossing a pebble into the Ganges each morning would cause a dam."

Jesus nodded in mock consideration. "Even so," he said, "I still don't see how that gives you the right to make decisions about buying land without talking to your father."

"Surely, this is a joke," Deva laughed. "My father put you up to this?"

Again, Jesus didn't answer, and Deva took a step closer. "How about you let me deal with my father, and you deal with yours, all right? Wherever he is, I'm sure he's very proud of the man you've become."

Jesus stiffened, and a sharp heat filled his chest. Deva didn't know what he was saying, of course—he couldn't—but that didn't mean his words didn't cut deep.

Deva made to step around Jesus once more, but again, Jesus blocked his way. His face was dark. This wasn't about Leela anymore.

"So you're going to wait until your father isn't paying attention," Jesus asked, "then creep in and steal what you think you're entitled to? You're a lot alike, aren't you? You and your brother?"

Immediatly, Deva grabbed Jesus roughly by his cloak and pulled him in close. "Don't," he said in a low growl. "Don't you dare."

He pushed Jesus away from him so hard that Jesus nearly fell.

"My father sees that fire in your eyes and thinks it's courage," Deva said, "but you know it's not. It's desperation. Desperation to come across as more than the vagabond you are."

Jesus clenched his fists. *You search in vain for someone to please or someone to fight,* Jesus heard the rabbi's voice, *all to try to prove to yourself that you're not what you are.*

"I think it's safe to say you've nearly worn out your welcome," Deva said. "Try not to get too comfortable."

After a moment, Deva moved on, picking up his counting where he'd left off.

Jesus stood rooted, not trusting himself to move until Deva was well down the path. When Jesus judged him to be a safe distance away, he turned, scanning the field for Leela. To his relief, she was gone.

Straightening his clothes and forcing himself to breathe, Jesus started off back to his shed. He needed to be alone.

# 19

THE SUN WAS SETTING as Jesus ambled from the shed back to the main house. Since his run-in with Deva, he'd spent most of his time in his shed, thinking. He'd also discovered that the stool in the shed had a slight wobble, and he did his best to fix it using improvised tools. He figured it was the least he could do in exchange for two nights' stay, three meals, and atonement for picking a fight with Deva.

As he approached the main house, Jesus heard singing—a welcome change from the shouting he'd woken up to that morning.

*"Refrain from your anger and turn from your wrath,"* Abraham sang, *"for to fret only leads to despair. The wicked shall fade, no more shall be found, and the meek will inherit the earth..."*

"When you sing it like that," Jesus said, coming around the side of the house, "it almost sounds bearable."

"Yes, well," Abraham said, tending the fire, "one might use a pot to scald or to nourish. The hand determines its purpose. I was singing when I found this place, I was singing when my sons were born and as I grieved my wife, and God willing, I'll be singing on the way to my grave."

Jesus took a seat on his bench. "What could you possibly want to sing on the way to your grave?" he asked.

"I've thought about that a great deal," Abraham said, lifting the lid of his pot to check on dinner. "If I had the chance, I'd start with *'My God, my God, why have you forsaken me?'* haunting as it is, and then I would carry on singing as many as I could until I breathed my last. It seems a fitting container for the sorrow I might have surrounding my death."

Jesus considered this. He found it morbidly beautiful.

"I am a believer that there is a psalm for every occasion," Abraham said, ladling out a bowl of stew, "and an occasion for every psalm."

He offered Jesus the bowl, and Jesus took it gratefully. "More figs and pork belly?" Jesus asked.

"Not tonight," Abraham said. He served his own bowl and took his seat. "Did your mother never make this for you? It was a staple in our home."

Jesus smiled, remembering his mother's cooking. "I know she tried her best," he said, "but my mother was good at making exactly one kind of stew, and it was mostly salty water."

"Ah," Abraham nodded. "And what of your father? His family never made something like this?"

Jesus paused, the question taking him off guard. He felt a familiar tightening in his chest. "I, um..." he started. "I wouldn't know. I never had a father. He was gone before I was born."

"I'm sorry," Abraham said. "He died?"

Jesus thought about trying to explain, but decided not to get into it. "Worse," he said. "I was a sinner when my mother conceived me. Let's leave it at that."

"That sounds like your rabbi talking," Abraham said. "Surely someone like you is smart enough to know that their value is not limited by the circumstances of their birth."

Jesus just stirred his soup. "I have a lifetime of experience that might say otherwise."

A moment passed with neither of them saying anything. Jesus knew Abraham was waiting for him to say more. It was his turn to share his story, after all. That's why they were there. Still, that didn't mean he wanted to. He tried to think of ways to avoid it, but came up short. After a while, he sighed. "All right," he said. "It's my turn, isn't it? Truth for truth."

Abraham shrugged. He seemed to be perfectly comfortable with the silence. "If you are willing," he said. "But I hope you know me well enough by now to know I leave that up to you."

"I don't suppose we could renegotiate again?" Jesus asked. "There's no way I could say I'm too tired and draw this out for one more night?"

Abraham only smiled.

"Fine," Jesus said, putting his bowl down next to him. He watched the flames dance for a few seconds as he decided where to begin. He'd given it a lot of thought that day, but hadn't come to any firm conclusions. "I'm here because I had to leave," he started. "I did something foolish, but for that to make any sense, I have to start further back. With the rabbi."

Bracing himself, Jesus dove into the story as Abraham listened. He told him about the time he'd spent studying with the rabbi—about his mother and how well he'd done. He told Abraham about their eventual falling out, and how he'd been cast out of the assembly. He told Abraham about Joseph taking him and John under his wing, and how that had eventually led to the synagogue job and his witnessing the rabbi and the Roman, and how that had led to their fight where he'd lost control. Jesus tried to avoid talking about the taunts that had sent him over the edge, but the more he told his story and saw Abraham's understanding, the more he wanted to tell the old man everything. He told him things he'd never wanted to share with anyone, not even John.

Abraham nodded along and asked the appropriate questions as Jesus talked about the rumors he'd heard when he was a boy—about Pantera and about his mother. He made the appropriate faces of outrage as Jesus talked about how it had felt to have the town's judgment on him every moment of his life—atoning constantly for a sin that wasn't his. He listened carefully as Jesus talked about how he'd felt when the rabbi had taunted him and why he'd felt like he had to run, about meeting up with the caravan of traders and about what Jesus told himself about making a new life as a *Son of No One*. Jesus's soup lay forgotten beside him, now stone cold.

The story slowed down as Jesus talked about how he'd gotten stranded in Kashi, leading to the morning he'd met Abraham at the city gate. It felt like a great weight had been lifted from his chest. He didn't realize how heavily his untold story had weighed on him.

"I know I had no choice," Jesus said, "but I tried to convince myself that leaving was for the best." He paused. "It hasn't worked out that way, though. Maybe I was too late, or maybe there was never a point. Maybe new starts are for people braver and smarter than I am."

Abraham, who had been engaged and curious for the duration of the story, suddenly drew back as though Jesus had said something outrageous. "Braver and smarter than you?" he asked. "You aren't serious."

Jesus laughed bitterly. "Need I remind you," he asked, "that when you found me, I was bleeding in the dirt, having just tried to steal a jackfruit?"

"And need I remind *you*," Abraham answered, "that you did so to procure food enough for four hungry children?"

Jesus looked away.

"Don't sell yourself short," Abraham continued. "That's what your rabbi taught you to do. He may have handed you that nonsense when you were too young to know better, but you're no child anymore. You can hand it right back."

Jesus shook his head. "It's more complicated than that," he dismissed.

At this, Abraham set down his bowl and looked suddenly serious. "Now, you listen," he said. "As both a father and a former rabbi-in-training, I take it as my solemn duty to tell you this. Someone needs to, and frankly, your rabbi and your mother did a poor job of it."

"Tell me what?" Jesus asked, surprised by the old man's intensity.

"Yeshua of Nazareth," Abraham pronounced, "there is a very simple reason your rabbi did not like you, and it is precisely because you *were* the smartest and bravest one in the room."

Jesus tried to wave this off, but Abraham wouldn't have it. "No," he said firmly. "As one who has spent a great deal of time thinking about how these things work, allow me to share a little observation. People like your rabbi—they are afraid. There is a hole of insufficiency within them, and rather than accept themselves as they are, they seek projects that can help them fill this hole. In his case, he tried to fill it with the illusion of righteousness and certainty and order. People will buy and sell scriptures and ideals like commodities in the service of this project."

"Listen—" Jesus started, but Abraham pressed on.

"But here is the truth," he said. "Being built on illusion, such projects are fragile. They are threatened easily, as darkness is threatened by light. That is why anyone bold or clever enough to ask questions or suggest alternatives is labeled a threat, and to them, threats must be dealt with by any means necessary, be it ostracism or crucifixion."

"Where is all this coming from?" Jesus asked.

"Decades of relentless introspection," Abraham answered. "*I* used to be the one doing the ostracizing, and so it is my curse forever to notice and expose it in others. The point is, son, your rabbi didn't hate you because there was anything wrong with you. Your parentage was merely the easiest excuse he had. He was a small man who employed charm and shame as weapons—who disguised manipulation as care and called it righteous. To keep you small, he had to convince you that you were a child of disgrace, that your curiosity was offensive to God, and that it was only by appeasing him you would find a blessing. This was a lie. The truth is far more generous."

"Is that so?"

"Oh, it is," Abraham insisted. "Here is the truth: you are as brave and clever as they come, son. You frighten weak men because weak men fear the truth, while you are satisfied with nothing less. You are *not* a child of disgrace. You are *not* a child of shame. You are a child of the Living God, beloved, just as you are. The next time you tell your story, you would do well to remember that."

Abraham sat back and crossed his arms. "Smarter and braver..." he muttered, shaking his head. "Of all the foolishness..."

For a moment, Jesus wasn't sure what to say. "Well, now you're just blaspheming," he said. "I've got a whole village back in Judea that would testify to the opposite."

"A village of fools, perhaps," Abraham argued. "You're not ready to see it yet, but rest assured, son, the day will come when you are, and when that day comes..." he gave a low whistle. "When that day comes, you will unleash something into this world the likes of which it has never seen. Mark my words."

Jesus only smiled patiently. "Marked," he said. He still felt the relief of having shared his story, but Abraham was overreacting, and he wished he would stop. He appreciated the solidarity, but there was no need to embellish. There was just too much the old man couldn't understand. "All right," he said, hoping to change the subject, "now it's your turn."

"My turn?" Abraham asked.

"Yes, your turn," Jesus repeated, "to finish your story."

Abraham laughed, willing to let Jesus's story go for the time being. "What more could you possibly wish to know?" Abraham asked. "I told you how I came to leave Judea."

"You did," Jesus agreed, "but not how you came to arrive in Kashi—a vineyard owner citing sutras as easily as scriptures."

"Ah yes," Abraham said, reaching beneath his bench and extracting a wineskin. "That." He drew out two cups and set them on his bench, filling them generously. In the fire's light, Jesus saw *Shalom* on the side of the wineskin. Rising and making his way to Jesus, Abraham offered him a cup. "You want to hear about Metta Valley," Abraham said.

"What valley?" Jesus asked, accepting the drink.

"Metta Valley," Abraham repeated, returning to his bench. "It's the piece of the story I believe you're looking for. How I got from there to here."

Jesus leaned forward, listening intently. This was what he'd been waiting for.

Abraham took his time, considering where he wanted to pick up. "When I left Judea," he started, "I began a maritime life. Like you, I joined with traders so that I might travel. Unlike you, I remained with them for several years. Long enough to save up quite a bit. It wasn't the money that kept me on, though. The truth was, I had no desire to be still. I was angry. Bitter. Whatever passion the prophets had ignited in me had turned to a smoldering resentment toward all matters of faith. Where you had the openness to hear new stories, I had only impatience and distrust. I was a nightmare to be around, to be sure, and I stayed like that for quite a long time. I thought I might die that way. Would've been content to."

"And what happened?" Jesus asked.

"Well," Abraham said, "I grew weary of life on a ship. By that time, I'd traded in enough wine to know a great deal about it, and for some time I suspected I might be quite good at actually making it, if given the chance. I disembarked in Tamralipti, bought a horse, and began riding all over the countryside, learning what I could of the land, the harvest, the ways of trade... I lived off of my savings, supplemented by what I made helping and learning on this farm or that. One day, however, I was between farms, and I was riding out between villages when a snake spooked my horse. She threw me and ran off, leaving me stranded with a broken leg and nowhere to crawl."

"What did you do?" Jesus asked, enthralled. He'd never known anyone thrown from a horse, but he'd heard an injury like that could be fatal.

"Not much I *could* do, was there?" Abraham continued. "There I was on the side of the road, not knowing which way to drag myself, when who should happen upon me but two monks in yellow robes?

Buddha followers, headed back to their community. They asked if I needed help and offered to take me with them. Naturally, I told them I'd rather die on the side of the road than be taken prisoner in their temple."

"But they convinced you?"

"Of course not!" Abraham said. "They merely assumed I was delirious with pain and took me anyway!"

Jesus laughed out loud at this, imagining these two poor monks dragging an angry Abraham, cursing and flailing, back to their home.

"I'm glad you're amused," Abraham said. "I tell you, I must have passed out at some point, because when I awoke, I thought perhaps I had died and was glimpsing the world beyond. I was being carried through a wide gateway, into a magnificent place built between the sheer walls of a mountain. The monks informed me, however, that I had not, in fact, died, but was being brought into their community. 'Metta Valley,' they called it."

"And you stayed?"

"Well, what choice did I have? Eventually, they got me inside and waited for me to stop cursing each of them and each of their mothers, and then the monk in charge told me they planned to care for me until I could walk out myself." Abraham shook his head, still grinning. "That was the beginning of a long road to recovery."

"So, you were stuck there?" Jesus asked.

"Oh, I was free to go," Abraham said. "I just couldn't. I was quite useless, yet they cared for me. They assigned a novice to see to my well-being and, despite my initial displeasure, we became friends. I learned that these residents of Metta Valley weren't what I expected. They were kind. Soft-spoken. They genuinely wanted to help me heal, and after a while—a *long* while, mind you—I trusted them. Couldn't help it. At my prodding, the novice began telling me about their practices and their scriptures. At first, I wanted only to question the novice on everything they told me, but soon I was fascinated."

"Why?" Jesus asked. "How was it different from what you'd learned in Jerusalem?"

Abraham drank some of his wine, considering how to explain. "Well," he said, "it was as though dogma or obligation were secondary. They valued genuine transformation above all else. They cared about practice that might water seeds of kindness and justice in the soul. They cared about teachings that would make someone the manner of person who would naturally wish to stop and help a struggling man on the side of the road. To them, faith meant very little if it didn't lead to a firsthand experience of... well..." Abraham trailed off.

"Of what?" Jesus asked eagerly.

Abraham smiled. "It is difficult to put into words."

"Try," Jesus said.

Abraham hesitated for another moment, looking at Jesus as though he knew Jesus wouldn't understand. Still, he pressed on anyway.

"Of God," he finished. "A firsthand experience of the Living God."

For a few moments, an awkward silence hung between them. Jesus felt confident he'd misunderstood.

"I told you," Abraham said, "I know it sounds—"

"You are saying that you met God—" Jesus started.

"I realize—"

"At a Gentile temple?"

"Not 'God' in the way you understand 'God,'" Abraham explained. "As I said last night, The *Living* God is not like an object or being—"

"No one can see God's face and survive," Jesus teased. "That's in the Scroll of Names. Everyone knows that one."

"Son," Abraham said, holding out a palm to stop him. "I will not try to explain to you or convince you of anything. It is just as much a mystery to me as it is to you. I will only say what I *do* know. The more time I spent cultivating my awareness of the Living God, the more I watched my former self slip away. You are correct in saying no one can see God's face and survive, and I am no exception. That bitter, angry, rigid man I had been started to die, and in his place was a new creation—something truer, though long covered over by fear and delusion. In his place was someone who looked on the world with love and joy—with peace and patience. It was someone from whom justice grew like fruit from a well-nourished tree. It is a great paradox of wisdom, I'm afraid, that one must be willing to lose their life in order to find it. That, my friend, is what I did."

Jesus nodded along, telling himself that what Abraham was saying made no sense, but the truth was, something about Abraham's story made his heart quicken.

"At day's end," Abraham said, "it is something you must experience for yourself. Words are a poor substitute. I am only a man pointing to the moon."

"But you didn't stay," Jesus observed. "You wound up here, singing Hebrew psalms with tefillin on your arm."

"This is true," Abraham said. "The thing about Metta Valley is that, after a year of practice, they send you on what they call 'an errand.' It is usually to do some service in some part of the world, but really, I think it's more about learning to integrate what you've learned. It's easy to practice wisdom behind the community's walls, but your wisdom means little if it cannot stand against the storms and crashing waves of life in the real world. At the end of your errand, you have the choice to either return as a monk or stay where you are to embody the Way in whatever way is best for you."

"The Way?" Jesus asked.

"It's what they call their practice."

"So, they don't require you to come back," Jesus observed. "And you chose not to?"

"Well... I chose Radha," Abraham corrected, smiling as he said her name. "I'd been on errand at a farm near here—still taking every chance to learn about agriculture and so forth. I was helping the farm owner get his produce to the city when Radha and I met and began to share ideas. We envisioned this place together and... well, you know the rest. As far as the tefillin on my arm," Abraham held up his wrist.

His sleeve dropped down, revealing the leather straps. "In many ways, exploring another path helped me become more fully a child of Israel. They are not exclusive practices, as I had been taught. They enrich one another. I learned more from listening to the Buddha and Moses converse than I might ever have learned from either on their own. They helped me see treasures in the traditions of our people that I didn't have ears to hear from my old teachers."

"And wouldn't your teachers be proud of you now?" Jesus asked with a smirk.

"Oh, I'm sure they would," Abraham said.

They were quiet for another moment. They watched the fire burn, and Jesus felt the wine warm him, loosening his aching muscles. After a while, Abraham spoke. "Well, there you have it," he said. "We now know how one another arrived at this place. You now know my every secret, including that of Metta Valley."

"Which is apparently the true Temple of the Living God," Jesus joked.

Abraham laughed. "Oh, no," he said. "No, no. If you wish to see the true Temple of the Living God, you need merely walk over to that trough and look at your reflection. It was into humankind that God breathed God's Spirit at the dawn of time, and it is in humankind that it dwells today. Beware anyone who tells you otherwise. Metta Valley only gave me eyes to see."

"Did you ever go back?" Jesus asked. "To Metta Valley?"

"Oh, yes, from time to time. It is more difficult for me now, but I used to travel back as often as I could. It was helpful for times of renewal and remembering. There are worse places to spend a season, if you're looking for somewhere to go from here."

Jesus laughed. "If you think I would thrive in a community like that, you haven't been listening very well."

"Oh, I don't know about that," Abraham said. "I've been listening quite well, and what I hear is the story of a young man aching for something more real than his rabbi could ever offer—someone who is, even now, growing weary of running from Mara's voice whispering in his ear. Am I close?"

Jesus hesitated, not trusting himself to meet Abraham's eye. "Who's Mara?" he asked, hoping to change the subject.

"In Metta Valley, Mara is the name they give to the voice always speaking in your head," Abraham said, "the voice always urging you to judge or reject or pursue—the one making promises it can never seem to fulfill. You're familiar with this voice, I assume?"

Jesus didn't answer.

"My friend," Abraham offered, "for what it's worth, I believe there are times when others can hear our stories more clearly than we can ourselves. This has certainly been the case for me—embarrassingly so, at times. I wonder if, perhaps, this is one of those moments. When you hear your story, I sense you hear the story of one who must remain at odds with the world—one who is unclean or unrighteous, perhaps hopelessly so. When *I* hear your tale, I hear the story of one who is remarkably capable, who is growing exhausted from fighting the voice of Mara so relentlessly in himself and others, and one longing for a way to practice justice that really is justice, and truth that really is truth."

"I'm not you," Jesus said.

"No, you are not," Abraham admitted, "but I can say you are certainly more like me than is flattering for either of us."

For a moment, they were both silent, staring at the fire. Jesus wasn't sure what he was feeling besides a vague sense that he should find an excuse to thank Abraham for dinner and go back to his shed. He was grateful, then, when Abraham spoke again.

"I am under no illusion that you will go, of course," Abraham admitted. "I was merely fulfilling my duty."

"Is that so?" Jesus asked. "And what duty is that?"

"My duty to listen well, testify to the truth, and let go of what I could not control," Abraham said. "This is the sacred duty of us all."

"Well, consider your duty fulfilled."

Abraham nodded solemnly, then dropped the subject. For that, Jesus was grateful. His drive to leave faded.

"As it is," Abraham said, "my duty being fulfilled, perhaps it would be appropriate for me to make an alternate proposition."

"Does this one have to do with running off and joining the Buddha followers?"

"Far less dramatic," Abraham laughed. "Stay here—for a time, anyway."

This took Jesus off guard. It took a moment for Abraham's words to sink in. "Really?" he asked. "You'd let me stay?"

"Of course!" Abraham said. "Help us with the vineyard. Save up some money and get your strength back. I could offer nightly meals and a day's wage for each day worked."

"For how long?"

"That would be up to you."

Jesus considered this. "Your son wouldn't approve," he pointed out.

Abraham shook his head. "Perhaps not," he said, "but if I began filling tablets with things that displeased my son, I would have to fell every tree in Kashi."

Even after everything that had happened over the last two days, Jesus was still hesitant. He wanted to say yes, but it felt too good to be true.

"All right," Abraham said, noting his hesitation, "you drive a hard bargain. In addition to housing, food, and wages, I will also grant unfettered access to my collection of scrolls—assuming you show them the proper care, of course."

Jesus kept a straight face, but his heart leaped. This had sealed it. He spoke carefully, not wanting to appear too desperate. "I think," he started, "that I might consider that."

Abraham smiled. "Excellent to hear," he said. "Let us settle the terms tomorrow."

"Agreed."

Neither said anything for a while. Even though he'd spent the day resting, Jesus was feeling as exhausted as he had the night before. After a few minutes, Abraham sang quietly to himself. It took Jesus a few moments to place it. *"Sing to our God, let all praise his name. He rides on the clouds, and great is his name. Defender of widows, home for the lonely, father to fatherless ones..."*

A psalm for every occasion.

"I should go," Jesus said, brushing himself off and rising.

"Wise," Abraham said. "Praise not excessive wakefulness, nor excessive sleep. A life of balance is a life of well-being. I will also be turning in shortly."

"Right," Jesus said, assuming this, too, was some scripture he didn't know. He was too tired to ask.

Jesus started to leave, but lingered for another moment. "I only want to say thank you. For everything."

Abraham only nodded. *"Shalom,* son. It's good that you're here."

*"Shalom."*

Jesus walked away from the fire, pulling his robes close against the cool night air. He heard Abraham continue to sing to himself as he sat by the fire.

It wasn't until he was halfway back to the shed that Jesus realized that he'd started humming along.

# 20

THE FIRST THING HE noticed was the smell of smoke. Half-asleep, he dismissed it. Through the fog of slumber, the smell reminded Jesus of a parable Abraham had told him once about a man who'd burned a wooden idol to stay alive in the cold, and a priest who had condemned it as an act of irreverence. *It takes a poor priest indeed,* Abraham had concluded, *to value a dead statue over a living man.*

Jesus smiled. In the three months he had worked the vineyard, Abraham had shared more parables than he could count. It had become Jesus's job to take the cart into town to find workers, giving him a great deal of time on the road to turn the parables over in his mind. He did the same while walking the grounds, doing his best to avoid Deva. The two hadn't become friends, but neither were they at one another's throats as openly. They'd reached an uneasy and fragile stalemate. As Deva had said the morning after Jesus decided to stay, *You stay of my way, I'll stay out of yours.*

"*Issa!*" someone called out, but the voice was half-lost in dreams. "*Issa, are you here?*"

Jesus only rolled over, trying to get comfortable again. Naps were part of his new Sabbath routine—a practice he now wouldn't trade for the world—and he wanted to steal just a few more minutes before it was time to join Abraham for dinner. After they ate, they'd return to the scrolls, as had become their custom. Jesus had almost made his way through all of them, and he was eager for the rest. They were brilliant, and he'd come to relish the way they danced and clashed with the scriptures he knew well. He loved the way the prophets dressed down the traditions he knew, stripping them of pretense and giving the ancient stories new textures and tones. The voice of Hosea pushed back against the strictness of the law, while the embrace of Jonah undermined the brutality of Joshua. The doubt of Job and the Kohelet stood in tension with the certitude of the psalms and the proverbs. Together, they felt sharper and more alive than any of them had on their own. For the first time since he was a child, he found himself growing excited to study them. Studying under Abraham, he came to see scriptures less like a set of rules and more like an instrument. They didn't demand obedience. They invited him to join an ancient dance. An ancient rhythm that called for creativity and improvisation.

As he read and re-read, gaining a deeper appreciation for Abraham's "Living God," the irritable, ever-watchful God of his rabbi began to lose his teeth. In his place was a deep, alluring rhythm, calling Jesus to move with justice and understanding.

*"Issa!"* the voice called again, closer this time, and Jesus opened one eye. As he was about to settle back in, the voice cut through again—sharp and urgent. *"Issa!"*

He sat up, suddenly recognizing the voice. Something was wrong.

"Leela?" he asked, still groggy.

That was when he really noticed the smell of smoke.

Leela threw open the door to his shed. When she saw him, she beckoned frantically. "Come on!" she cried. "I've been trying to find you! The house! It's burning!"

Fully alert now, Jesus threw off the blanket and bolted past Leela towards the open door. When he saw the house, he stopped, frozen. The house was almost entirely engulfed in flames. Tongues of fire leaped ten feet in the air. Jesus could see the designs over the doors and windows charring to lifeless black. "Get Deva!" he barked as he took off towards the house.

"But Issa—"

"Get Deva!"

*"Devadatta was in the house!"*

Jesus slipped to a stop. "What?"

"I was in the field picking grapes, like you said," Leela explained frantically, "and I heard shouting! I came closer and saw Devadatta running from the house and smoke coming from the windows."

For a moment, Jesus didn't understand.

"That's when I called for you!" Leela said. "It happened so fast!"

"What about Abraham?" Jesus demanded

"I don't know!" Leela cried. "I haven't seen him!"

Jesus turned back around, facing the inferno. He knew Abraham might be in there. There was no time to wait or ask more questions. "Go into town and find help," he commanded. "Go as fast as you can." He took off towards the house.

Without checking to see if Leela obeyed, Jesus sprinted toward the burning house. He hardly registered the heat on his skin. Without hesitating, he ran forward until he felt the front door splinter apart against his shoulder, and from somewhere, a faint voice in his head told him that would hurt tomorrow. He didn't have time to think about that now. He had to find Abraham.

"Abraham!" he shouted. He couldn't see anything through the smoke. He inhaled to call again, but suddenly, his lungs were on fire. Instinctively, he dropped to his hands and knees, finding a pocket of clean air. His eyes watered, and he struggled to keep them open. "Abraham!" he called again, now coughing painfully. He knew he couldn't survive long in here, but he also knew he couldn't let the old man die like this. This was not how it was going to end. He wouldn't let it.

Jesus started to crawl, urgently feeling his way around the floor. From behind him, he heard a crash. He hurried forward, his hand knocking against something solid. The couch. Now at least he knew where he was.

"Abraham!" he called again, grabbing a blanket from the couch and throwing it over himself. It helped, but only a little. The crackling and popping became more muted, and in the sudden quiet, the rabbi's voice rose to the surface.

*Let God rain coals of fire on the wicked,* he chanted. *Fire and sulfur and a scorching wind will be their portion and their inheritance...*

"Not now," Jesus said, still feeling his way around. He was feeling lightheaded. He didn't have long.

*You will set them ablaze like a burning oven. God will swallow them in his wrath and they will be consumed by fire...*

"Enough!"

Stars floated in the corners of his vision. He moved faster. In a few moments, he, too, would be trapped. He didn't even know if Abraham was in the house, but he couldn't leave until he was sure. That was when he heard the cough.

"Abraham?" he called, listening.

It had sounded close, and he took off in that direction. Soon, his hand came up against something else solid. A sandal. A foot. It was Abraham sprawled out on the ground, unconscious. "I've got you!" Jesus cried, triumphant.

He pulled the old man's body towards him and threw the blanket over them both.

Jesus didn't have time to stop and see if the old man was alive. He only started dragging Abraham toward the front door, hoping they had enough time. On his way, there was another crack—louder this time—and something heavy thudded to the ground in front of them. Jesus risked a look from under the blanket to see their way blocked by an enormous piece of the roof. "All right," he said. "Back door."

As he moved, Jesus couldn't stop coughing. His insides felt as seared as his outsides. With his hands hooked under Abraham's arms, Jesus dragged him past the couch, then the table. Mercifully, the back door was open, and he felt the temperature around him drop as he passed through. The blanket snagged on the doorframe and fell off as Jesus pulled Abraham backwards into the light. Jesus took in another lungful of smoke. He coughed and sputtered, but he didn't stop. He wouldn't stop until they were a safe distance from the house.

When they were finally out of reach of the heat and the smoke, Jesus collapsed in a fit of coughing. Tears welled in his stinging eyes as he tried to catch his breath. It felt like every part of him was on fire.

His vision blurred as he tried to attend to Abraham, who was still unconscious.

"There they are!" someone shouted. "Behind the house!"

Leela. Bless her.

Someone else answered, but Jesus didn't recognize the voice. He heard footsteps pounding toward them, but didn't look up. "Is he breathing?" the second voice asked. "Is he alive? Abba?"

*Abba?* Jesus thought. That was Aramaic. "Father." And the only one who would call Abraham *abba* would be—

Immediately, Jesus lunged, grabbing Deva's robe and knocking him to the ground. When Jesus finally got a good look at him, though, he was confused. It wasn't Deva at all. It looked like him, to be sure, but it wasn't him. This man was thinner, and he had an anxious, confused expression that Jesus could never imagine on Deva's face. At the moment, though, Jesus didn't care who he was. "Water," he commanded. "Get water."

It took a moment for the man to understand, but then he turned to Leela and nodded. She took off.

Jesus released the stranger and crawled back to Abraham. "Come on," he whispered, looking him over for injuries. He had a lump on his head and burns in several places, but he was still breathing.

Leela returned and dropped a bucket of water next to them. Jesus snatched it up and poured part of it over Abraham's face, and immediately Abraham's eyes opened, bringing a fit of coughing and shaking. He tried to sit up, then collapsed again.

Jesus was so relieved he laughed out loud. He let himself fall to the ground. They were both alive. Jesus had long since stopped believing in miracles, but he thought maybe this was a good time to restart.

There was another crash from the house, and Jesus looked just in time to see the roof collapse in an explosion of flame and sparks. The house was gone.

He turned back to Abraham, Leela, and the stranger. Jesus tried to stay alert, but his vision became more blurred, darkening at the edges. He tried to ask for more water, but no words came. "Issa?" Leela said, noticing his condition. "Issa, are you okay?"

That was the last thing he heard before the world went black.

# 21

WHEN JESUS FINALLY WOKE, the blue sky had been replaced by a cracked, mud-plastered ceiling. He took this to mean that he was not, in fact, dead, though he wasn't sure yet whether this was a good thing. He tried to move, but a violent cough seized him before he could sit up. A dull pain radiated through his chest, and his head ached. His shoulder throbbed, and his lungs felt dry and heavy. As he tried to get his coughing under control, an older, unfamiliar face appeared above him, and he stopped coughing in surprise. "Well, good afternoon," the stranger said. "Welcome back to the land of the living."

The first thing he noticed was that he was on a mat. He was in a wide, well-lit room, along with several others lying on their own mats around the perimeter. Steam rose from clay pots of simmering herbs around his mat, their smells thick in the air. The steam soothed his chest, if only a little. Jesus tried to speak, but had to swallow several times to coat his dry throat. "Where am I?" he finally managed in a low croak, hardly recognizing his voice. His thoughts were as fuzzy and jumbled as his words.

"You, my valiant friend," the man answered, "are at my home in the city. You took in a great deal of smoke, it appears. I am a healer, and I have started you on a few remedies that should soothe your lungs. It will be uncomfortable for a bit, I'm afraid, but should improve with time."

"How long have I been here?"

"I have been looking after you since this good fellow brought you in for care," the healer answered, then gestured towards the foot of

Jesus's mat. Painfully, Jesus propped himself up to look at his rescuer. He recognized the stranger he'd seen at Abraham's home—the man Leela had brought back. Again, it struck Jesus how much this man looked like Deva, set apart only by a thinner, more nervous face. As he tried to make sense of what he was seeing, something clicked into place. "Ananda?" he asked.

The stranger nodded awkwardly. "And you are Yeshua," he said. "I'm glad to meet you—properly, this time."

"Your father..." Jesus started. Suddenly, the rest of his memories tumbled into place, and he tried to sit up. "Is he alive?" he demanded.

The healer put a hand on his shoulder. "You must rest. Please. Your body needs time. Abraham is alive."

Ananda stood and moved closer. "You saved his life," he said. "But he... he doesn't have long."

Jesus stopped trying to get up. "Doesn't have long? What does that mean?"

"It means he... well..." Ananda faltered, looking to the healer.

"It is morning now," the healer said. "By the time the sun rises tomorrow, his body will have given out."

It took a moment for the healer's words to sink in, then Jesus's thoughts collapsed into a jumble. "That's not... that can't be right. I saw him. I dragged him out! He was awake—breathing, speaking—he was..."

*My ineptitude overshadows me. Like a heavy burden, it weighs me down...*

"I'll give you two a moment," the healer said to Ananda. He patted Jesus on the shoulder, making him wince, then moved across the room to another patient.

"Yeshua—" Ananda began haltingly.

"It's Jesus," Jesus corrected automatically.

Ananda nodded. "Jesus. They tell me my father was badly burned, and he took in a lot of smoke. His lungs..." Ananda trailed off, clearly more affected by the news than he'd first let on. "It also appears he sustained an injury to his head before the fire started—"

"Deva," Jesus said urgently. "A witness saw him running from the fire. Leela—"

"Yes," Ananda interrupted. "I was returning from the city when she met me on the road. That is how I reached you so quickly. They have my brother in custody. The city's elders will decide his fate."

"Returning from the city?" Jesus asked. Every time Ananda spoke, he felt like things became less clear. It was only now that it occurred to Jesus that Ananda shouldn't be here at all. He was supposed to be in some far-off country with his stolen inheritance. "When did you return?" Jesus asked.

"Today," Ananda said, wilting. "I wanted to make amends. I thought perhaps if I worked for my father without pay, then I might..." he trailed off.

"But Deva saw you," Jesus guessed. "Deva wouldn't allow that to happen."

"In a way," Ananda answered. "I met my father first. I tried to apologize—to tell him that I would make it right—but he only embraced me. He... he welcomed me home." Ananda blinked back tears as he spoke. "We spoke for a while, then he sent me into the city to buy supplies for a feast. He said... he said he'd speak to Deva in my absence."

"But that didn't go well," Jesus said.

Ananda shook his head. He wiped his face self-consciously.

Jesus felt a wave of resentment rise in him towards Ananda. Jesus resented him for leaving in the first place. He resented him for daring to come back. He resented him for putting his father in this position. *Cursed is the one who dishonors his father and mother,* he thought. *Their blood is surely upon them...* He opened his mouth to say all this, but then, something else came out.

"It's not your fault," Jesus said.

Ananda looked at him, surprised. Jesus, too, was surprised, but he also knew where it had come from. It was what Abraham would've wanted him to say. *Why judge a grapevine?*

"Thank you," Ananda said, "but it is. It very much is. I should've died on that road."

"That's not true," Jesus said, coughing. "Your father wouldn't say that, and neither should you."

Ananda tried to protest, but Jesus interrupted. "Why are you here with me?" Jesus asked. "Why aren't you with your father?"

"They're changing his bandages," Ananda explained. "He asked me to come see to you until they were done. They're probably finishing up any moment now."

"All right," Jesus said. He wanted to talk to Ananda more—to find out more about what had happened—but he also knew there were more pressing things to attend to. Painstakingly, he lifted himself off the mat. "I need to talk to him."

"I don't think you're supposed to," Ananda said, nervous. "The healer just said—"

"The healer can say what he wants," Jesus interrupted. "If your father might not make it to morning, I'm going now. Thank you for checking on me, and I don't mean to sound ungrateful, but you can either help me or get out of my way."

Ananda hesitated, then nodded. He helped Jesus up. "All right," he said. "He's in a private room, across the courtyard. Come on, before the healer sees."

# 22

JESUS LEANED ON ANANDA for support, avoiding the healer's eye and trying not to cough too loudly. After a few tense moments, they finally hobbled out into the sunlight. Jesus blinked as his eyes adjusted.

The courtyard was larger than the room inside. Benches and flowering plants decorated every corner. A few patients strolled around, taking in the air, and Jesus marveled for a moment at the courtyard's beauty. "He's this way," Ananda said, pulling him gently to the left.

They shuffled toward Abraham's room. They passed two carpenters busy replacing shutters—their tools laid out in a row along the wall. Jesus tried not to bring attention to himself as he coughed and ambled past. When they were nearly there, Jesus noticed two names etched into the stone wall in decorative script. "Wait," he said, pulling Ananda to a stop. He stepped closer so he could make out the words. "Are these your parents' names?"

Ananda followed his gaze, and his expression moved from concern to admiration. "They are," he said. "When I was young, my parents paid for much of this place to be built. The healer wouldn't have this much space without their help. Traces of their generosity are scattered all over the city, if you know where to look."

Jesus nodded, lingering a moment on the inscription. "I'm sure they are," he said.

When they entered Abraham's room, he was sitting up on his mat, his tefillin now replaced by cloth bandages wrapped tightly around his arms and legs. Another bandage spread across his head, looking like a bloodstained mockery of a phylactery. The parts of Abraham that Jesus *could* see were covered in blisters and soot, and his lips and fingertips were a disconcerting shade of blue. His breath came in rattling gasps. When Abraham heard them, he opened his bloodshot eyes and smiled. "Sing praise!" he said tiredly, his voice hoarse and low. "Behold! The rock of my salvation!"

Jesus tried to look encouraging, but the sight of Abraham settled on him like a boulder. "Do you really want to be blaspheming?" he asked. "Now?"

"The dying can do as they like," Abraham said before his words faded into a painful fit of coughs.

With Ananda's help, Jesus got seated next to Abraham's mat. Jesus groaned as he sat. Every muscle ached.

"Most young men your age don't make sounds like that," Abraham said.

"Most young men my age don't drag old men out of burning buildings," Jesus answered.

Abraham gave a weak smile. "That's fair."

Ananda hovered for a moment, unsure of his place. "I'll give you a few moments, all right?" he said. "I'll be outside."

"Thank you, son," Abraham said, nodding appreciatively.

When Ananda left, Abraham turned to Jesus. "I see you met my son," he said. Even in this condition, Abraham glowed. "I never thought I'd see him again. It hardly feels real."

"Maybe that's all the smoke you inhaled," Jesus said.

"Possibly," Abraham smiled, but then his tone became serious. "Thank you," he said. "What you did was incredibly brave."

"I had little choice," Jesus dismissed. "When a building is burning, you do what you must."

Abraham used a bandage-wrapped finger to point at Jesus. "There you go again," he said, struggling to get enough air to speak. "You underestimate yourself. Listen to me, son. There is no greater act of love than to lay down one's life for one's friends. You could have died."

Jesus was unsure what to say, as he always was when Abraham started talking to him like this. He looked down at his feet and tried to change the subject. "How did I know it would end up like this?" he asked. "How did I know your stubborn grace was going to be the thing that killed you?"

Abraham gave Jesus's arm a weak squeeze. "I can think of worse things to die for than an act of stubborn grace," he said.

There was a knock at the door, and Ananda poked his head in. "I'm sorry, abba," he said. "Rajendra is here. He says you asked to see him?"

"I did," Abraham nodded. "Please tell him to come in." Abraham tried to sit up straighter, which looked like it took great effort. Jesus did the same. After a moment, a remarkably old man came in. He supported himself on a staff, and his clothes were made of a dark fabric with decorative borders. Jesus recognized him from the day he'd first met Abraham—from the square by the gate. "Rajendra," Abraham said.

"Abraham," the man answered, pressing his hands together in greeting.

"Forgive me for not standing," Abraham said, his breathing shallow. "They tell me I'm dying, which I'm finding increasingly inconvenient."

The man was clearly used to Abraham's humor. "Quite," he said. "And here I was thinking you would outlive us all."

"I'll step out," Jesus said and began to stand.

"No, no," Abraham signaled for him to sit. "Stay, please. It's good to have a witness for things like this. I'd like you to meet Rajendra, an elder of the city."

"Pleased to meet you," the man again pressed his hands together. "A friend of Abraham is a friend of mine."

Jesus wondered if he would've said that if he'd met him a few months ago as he was scavenging for scraps in alleyways.

The elder turned his attention back to Abraham. "How are you feeling?" he asked.

"I've been worse," Abraham said, and the elder smiled.

"Somehow, that is difficult to believe. I am glad you were well enough to call, however. Horrible business about Devadatta. I knew the loss of his mother left him bitter, but I never would've thought him capable of—"

"Any of us are capable of anything," Abraham said. "We only need the right circumstances."

"Well, as I'm sure you know, there is little I can do," the elder said. "Even for a friend, I am bound by the law. The boy's crime is attempted murder."

"The boy's crime is *grief,*" Abraham answered calmly. "It is pain and delusion, and these are wounds which can be healed."

"The law demands atonement."

"And there is more than one way to atone. Our job is to restore, not destroy. You know this."

"Wait," Jesus said. "You're not suggesting they let him go?"

*If someone lies in wait for their neighbor and tries to kill them,* Jesus heard the rabbi's voice, *the killer shall be brought back and handed over to the avenger of blood to die.*

"Hatred doesn't cease by hating," Abraham answered, "nor fire by fire."

Rajendra called them back to business. "Justice must be served," he said, "one way or the other. What are you suggesting?"

"I suggest that we serve the *truest* meaning of justice," Abraham rasped. "The rain falls on everyone, whether their mind is good or ill..."

The elder finished for him. "The sun shines on both those who stand high and those who stand low," he said. "I know the sutra."

"Then let the rain fall," Abraham went on. "Water the seeds of healing in him. Send for the aid of Metta Valley."

The elder looked unsurprised. "How might I have guessed?" he said. "Your solution to all things is Metta Valley. Reform a prisoner? Metta Valley. Sprained ankle? Metta Valley..."

"When it stops being effective, I'll stop suggesting it," Abraham said firmly. "They can send a student ready for their errand. They could also attend to other prisoners while they're here, which would be a service to the city. They'll do it if I ask. You know they will. If, at the end of the season, there has been no change, then do what you will. I only ask for a chance."

The elder looked skeptical. "Abraham, justice—"

"Justice *restores,*" Abraham finished, stifling a cough. "It does not destroy."

The elder took his time considering this, rubbing the bridge of his nose.

"Rajendra, please..." Abraham said, and for the first time since Jesus had known him, Abraham sounded truly vulnerable.

At this, the elder sighed deeply. "If it were anyone else requesting this," he said, "the city would not allow it. As it is, however, Kashi owes you a great debt, and I shall take this under advisement."

"That's all I can ask," Abraham said, exhaling with relief.

Jesus was stunned. He wanted to interrupt—to tell the elder that Abraham was obviously not thinking clearly and Deva undoubtedly deserved the fullest possible punishment—but the elder spoke first. "Of course," he said, "there is also the unusual matter of your property. If you recall, we formed our contingency on the assumption that Ananda might never return—"

"The choice goes to Ananda," Abraham said, the confidence returning to his voice. "If he will renounce his claim, then proceed as discussed."

The elder nodded. "Understood. I shall see to it at once." He pressed his hands together once again. "Abraham, my friend, it has been an honor."

Abraham gave a small nod in return—the best he could manage from the mat. "Likewise," he said. "You have been kinder to me than I've deserved."

"I have, haven't I?" the elder said.

"Sentimental as a thorn bush, that one," Abraham said after the elder had left. "Always has been."

Jesus, however, barely heard him. His outrage overshadowed his capacity for humor. "He tried to *kill* you!" he said so loudly it burned his throat and sent him into a fit of coughing. "He burned your home to the ground!" he continued through his coughs. "He wants to dismantle your legacy, and you're still giving him another chance?"

Jesus felt like Abraham wasn't nearly angry enough, so he felt twice the indignation to compensate. Instead of matching his anger, however, Abraham only gave a half-smile, like the Buddha on his altar. When Jesus finally stopped talking, Abraham spoke gently. "I'm only doing what I've been doing for the last three and a half decades," he said patiently. "It is my duty."

"What does that mean?" Jesus asked. "What's your duty?"

"To listen well, testify to the truth, and let go of what I cannot control," Abraham answered, as he had three months ago. "I am putting my faith in a story larger than my own."

"But look at where your 'duty' has gotten you!" Jesus objected. "All your so-called 'truth' and 'grace' and 'justice'... it's all led you *here*, and you're still holding to it? You lie there, speaking like you've achieved victory, but the fight is over! Greed won! Hatred won! It's over!"

"Perhaps," Abraham said. "Then again, perhaps it is only a matter of re-defining victory."

Jesus deflated back into his chair, astonished. All this talking was clearly costing Abraham the little energy he had, and Jesus thought it best to let it be. "What was all that about the estate?" he forced himself to ask. "What you said to the elder?"

"Ah," Abraham whispered. "Yes, that. It is a plan Rajendra and I have had for some time. It was Radha's idea. In the event of our death, the property would go to our sons, of course, but if they would be willing, it would pass instead to the workers. I have records of those who work the land most often. It would become cooperatively owned and maintained. After all, why should anyone have to pass their days working for rich old fools like me?" Another round of coughs racked his body. "The choice would've been Deva's," he said when the coughing had subsided. "It now passes to Ananda, which, perhaps, is a blessing."

"And you trust these harvesters?" Jesus asked. "With your legacy?"

"My story is ended," Abraham said. "We all must surrender our legacy, eventually. I can only listen well, testify to the truth, and—"

"Let go of what you can't control," Jesus finished. "Yes, you've said."

"And I shall keep saying," Abraham insisted. They sat silently for a moment, Abraham closing his eyes, and Jesus trying to sort through the feelings rising in his chest. There was another question weighing on him—one he didn't want to ask, but didn't think he'd get another chance to. "Are you afraid?" he finally let himself ask. "Afraid to die?"

"Oh, what is death?" Abraham returned, eyes still closed. "Clouds come together, they come apart... It is only change, son. Life doesn't end. It just... changes."

"That's a pretty big change," Jesus said.

"It's all change," Abraham answered. "It always has been. Always will be. Learn to trust it. The work of the spirit is the work of dying, after all. To die before you die... this is the only way to live free."

"The paradox of wisdom," Jesus quoted. "You have to lose your life to find it."

"Well, look who's been paying attention."

After a moment, he squeezed Jesus's hand. "Son," he said. "I'm afraid there's one last thing I need to ask of you."

"Of course," Jesus said. "What is it? I'll do what I can."

"Rajendra. He's going to need a messenger to Metta Valley."

Jesus hesitated. "Oh," he started, "I... I don't think—"

"You may stay at the vineyard, of course," Abraham said. "You may join in what it will become. Or you could leave the city and move along to whatever is next. However, if you are willing and if you are able, I would very much like that messenger to be you."

Jesus still resisted the idea. This wasn't the first time the old man had nudged him into going since the first night he'd brought it up, and each time Jesus had found a way out of talking about it. He wasn't sure what it was, exactly, but the thought of traveling to Metta Valley—of trusting himself to their Way—sent a contorting feeling through his gut. There was something appealing about it—to be sure—but also something deeply frightening. "Why?" Jesus asked. "Why are you so insistent on me going to that place?"

"Because you're good enough!" Abraham said with a determination that took Jesus off guard. "And you're smart enough! And it's time you learned it! They can teach you. You don't want to spend your whole life in a losing battle with a voice in your head!"

Abraham paused, squeezing Jesus's hand again. His tone softened. "I want you to go because you, Yeshua of Nazareth, are a child of God, and you *must* learn to see it if you are going to become what you are called to be."

"How do you know what I'm called to be?" Jesus asked.

"Because I see you more clearly than you see yourself," Abraham insisted. "There's a spark in you that needs fostering. The prophets are a start, but you must keep going. You are a prophet of the Living God, son, and with practice, you can become the teacher you've always needed."

You *are the teacher I've always needed,* Jesus wanted to say, *and now you're dying.* Instead, he turned away. "I'm no prophet," he said.

"Would that all God's people were prophets," Abraham answered, and Jesus recognized the words of Moses. Still, Jesus couldn't meet his eyes. He wasn't sure he could give Abraham what he was asking. Abraham must've sensed this, because after a moment, he squeezed Jesus's hand once more. "Don't let the frightened and insecure men of this world keep you from trusting what you are," he insisted. "May you be free, and may you liberate others with your freedom. May you bring good news to the poor, freedom to the prisoners, and sight to the blind. May you surrender every half-true story, embrace truth, and know yourself a beloved child of the Living God."

Jesus wanted to protest—to tell the old man he'd overestimated him once more—but he couldn't. He couldn't bring himself to say anything.

"Take the time you need," Abraham said, closing his eyes. Jesus noticed just how exhausted he sounded. "But if you don't mind, I'd like to speak... to my son... one last time."

Jesus nodded, grateful for the moment's escape. "All right," he said. "I'll get him."

Abraham didn't answer.

With effort, Jesus stood and hobbled toward the door. Just as he was about to leave, he heard something and paused. Turning back, he realized Abraham was singing quietly to himself, as he had been the first time Jesus had met him.

*"My God, my God, why have you forsaken me? I cry, but your ears are deaf to my groans. Yet it was you who drew me from the womb, and you who fed me at the breast. On you I was cast from the day I was born, and not once have you drawn away. Be not far from me now that this trouble is near, none can love me as you do..."*

A psalm for every occasion. This, more than anything, made Jesus realize that this would be the last time he'd see the old man, and he felt a tightness in his throat. This had been Abraham's plan all along—to sing until he breathed his last. Now he wanted his son to join him.

Jesus forced himself to step out, where Ananda was waiting. "He wants to talk to you," Jesus said, swallowing back tears. "He's in and out."

"Thank you," Ananda said.

"Of course."

"Do you need help to get back?" Ananda asked. "Are you in pain?"

"No," Jesus lied. "I'm fine. Go. Be with your father."

Ananda nodded and thanked him again, then he entered Abraham's room, leaving Jesus alone.

With considerable effort, Jesus made his way over to one of the benches in the center of the courtyard. He collapsed down onto it, grateful to be alone, if only for a moment. He wiped his face, not wanting anyone to see his tears and come to ask if he was all right.

Through everything, Abraham's request continued to echo through his head. *I would very much like that messenger to be you.*

He didn't want to go to Metta Valley. He had submitted himself to a teacher before—to a way that promised him so much—and the result had been only pain. The thought of doing it again, even in a tradition that felt so different, made him want to writhe and hide away. Still, the feeling he'd rediscovered poring over scrolls with Abraham these last few months was undeniable, and part of him wanted nothing more than to pursue that feeling with everything he had. It had reawakened something in him and brought him to life in a way he hadn't felt alive in years. There was a significant difference, though, between informal study with Abraham—study he could leave whenever he chose—and submitting himself to the precepts and rules of a place like Metta Valley. He didn't know those people. Didn't trust them. All he had was Abraham's story and his word. In the end, he supposed it came down to one question:

Could he trust Abraham?

The answer to this question came to him quickly. He trusted Abraham with everything. Within that answer, Jesus realized he'd found the answer to his other question.

"All right," he muttered to himself. "I'll do it. I'll go to Metta Valley."

# 23

IT WAS EARLY AFTERNOON as Jesus wandered through the charred remains of what had once been Abraham's house. He kicked at various pieces of rubble, causing them to fall apart or collapse into ash. His lungs were better, but he still hadn't fully recovered, so he drew his cloak up over his face against the dust. He would depart for Metta Valley the next morning. He wanted to see the vineyard one last time.

Jesus sang quietly to himself as he surveyed the ruins. *"Our people shall tell your story,"* he mumbled. *"We shall sing your song to those yet unborn..."* He never thought he'd find himself singing psalms on his own again, but here he was. He'd been singing a lot since Abraham's funeral ten days before. It had been a crowded and chaotic affair, but it had been beautiful in a way Abraham would've appreciated. It had been eclectic, like Abraham.

The morning after Abraham had died, Ananda found Jesus on his mat, still at the healer's home. He'd told Jesus that the procession would be later that day and asked Jesus to say a few words. Since neither Ananda nor Deva had ever taken much of an interest in Abraham's Judean lineage and traditions, Ananda believed Jesus was in the best position to offer something that honored that part of their father's life. After some resistance, Jesus had agreed.

Later, moving carefully, Jesus had accompanied Ananda and Abraham's body from the healer's home down to the street where the procession awaited. When Jesus first saw it, he again felt moved to tears. If anyone had doubted Abraham's legacy, the sight of that crowd would've put it to an immediate end. There were laborers who had worked the vineyard, city officials, children, merchants... even the man from Jesus's first day on the vineyard—the one he'd thought might fight him over wages. Together, they had all set off from the house, accompanying Abraham on one last journey across the city with chants and final farewells.

When they'd finally reached the pyre, on the bank of the Ganges, Ananda recited a story he remembered his father telling him about the Buddha speaking to his own dying father. "Father," he said with difficulty, "look at me through clear eyes. Look at the leaves, lush on the branches beyond your window. Life goes on, and as life goes on, so do you. You live on in me and my kin. You live on in all people. The elements came together to form you, Father, and now they disband to form something new in the cycle of eternal life. Do not believe, Father, that because your body has died, death holds you captive. It does not. Your true body is no less than the entire cosmos. These words are true. May it be so."

Soon, it was Jesus's turn, and although he hadn't planned out what he'd say, he trusted something would come. As he stood there, what rose to the surface were the words of Isaiah. The fire had reduced the scrolls to ash, but like Abraham had said, the truest words were those written on human hearts. "Who has believed?" he recited, "and to whom has the truth of God been revealed? He grew up before God a tender plant, as a live root from dry ground. The world saw him, but he was rejected and despised, a man of sorrows, acquainted with suffering. Surely he has borne our grief and carried our sorrows. He was wounded for our transgressions, bruised for our iniquities, yet by his pain, we have been healed."

As he recited, Jesus noticed guards had brought Deva to stand by Ananda. He had bindings on his wrists and ankles, which seemed redundant. Anyone could tell from Deva's face that he wasn't in any condition to run. At first, Jesus felt an overwhelming rush of rage, but it was short-lived. It was soon replaced by sorrow. Abraham had loved him, even in the end. Who was Jesus to say he was deserving of anything less?

"He was oppressed and afflicted," Jesus continued, "yet he did not open his mouth in anger or strike out for revenge. His life was an offering to redeem us from our greed and fear, and when we see the truth, then the seeds of his life shall prosper. By knowledge of himself has God's holy servant justified many, and therefore he shall be divided as a portion among the great and the strong. Amen."

With that, he looked at Abraham's body once more on its decorated pyre, touched his feet reverently, and stepped down to join the crowd. His part was finished—a single, small mark on the scroll of Abraham's life.

After a few more rituals and chants, Ananda held a torch to the dry sandalwood, and in seconds, the entire pyre was ablaze.

In hours, Abraham was gone.

The next ten days had passed quickly. In Kashi, mourning lasted ten days, just as in Judea, it lasted seven. Jesus had spent most of those days on his mat recovering, coughing less and breathing easier each day. Ananda would come visit daily, and the two would talk. Jesus soon learned Ananda was as clever as his father, though more reserved and prone to turning inward, as Abraham had said. Ananda was pragmatic, loyal, and soft-spoken, but when he broke, the break was intense. Jesus knew this because it would happen anytime he'd mention Ananda's time away, or when Ananda would remember that his father wouldn't be at home, waiting for him. His face would contort in pain, then, just as quickly as he'd fallen into it, Ananda would steady himself and wipe his face. "I apologize," he'd say. "There I go again when you've got your own healing to worry about."

Rajendra had come by a few times to sort through legal details and help Jesus plan his upcoming trip to Metta Valley. The elder insisted on paying for all the preparations since Jesus would travel as his messenger, and he heard no complaints from Jesus. By the end of the ten days, they had taken care of most of the preparations, leaving nothing for Jesus to do but collect his supplies and say goodbye to what was left of the vineyard.

Now, Jesus walked through the rubble, pushing things aside carefully with his foot and inspecting the charred remains of one unsalvageable item after another. He wasn't sure if it was right to say he felt eager for his journey to Metta Valley, but now that he'd committed, he found himself restless to get going. He was careful with his hope, but couldn't help recite Abraham's words to himself each time he thought about it.

*I will not try to explain to you or convince you of anything. It is just as much a mystery to me as it is to you. I will only say what I do know. The more time I spent cultivating my awareness of the Living God, the more I watched my former self slip away. You are correct in saying no one can see God's face and survive, and I am no exception.*

Jesus found something about this sentiment deeply appealing. Maybe Abraham was right. Maybe he would actually find the Living God in this Gentile temple.

As he wandered through the ash, Jesus stopped as he felt something under his foot. He stepped back, then bent to investigate the fragmented pieces of something black in the soot. It took him a moment to realize it was what remained of Abraham's altar. There was the menorah—mangled and warped from heat, then the bowl—a misshapen mass of metal. Next to those was what remained of the small basalt Buddha. It had cracked into pieces from the heat.

Jesus inspected the pieces of the idol. He saw its base and the pieces of its chest, broken diagonally through the torso. Then he found the head, now a small black stone about the size of a coin. Its gentle smile had survived, still etched deeply into the stone, though the rest of its features were barely recognizable. Without giving it much thought, he dug a small hole in the ash, then placed every piece but the head into the small grave and covered it gently. The smiling stone he put into the pouch on his belt.

The shed was exactly as he'd left it, untouched by the fire. He'd accumulated precious few possessions over the last three months, and he was packing them up when he heard a knock on the doorframe.

"Ananda," Jesus greeted, returning to his work. "Came out to say goodbye?"

"Something like that," Ananda said, shifting uncomfortably. "The others are on their way from the city now."

"I know," Jesus said. He folded the blanket Abraham had given him on the first night and put it in his bag. "I'm trying to leave before they arrive. I don't want them to show up at their new home to find an intruder lingering in their shed."

Jesus had gotten a brief look at the list of people selected to be put in charge of the farm as their work began. He recognized several of them as people he'd taken back and forth from the city. He'd gone out of his way to ensure Leela and her friends would have a place here as well.

"Do you need help?" Ananda asked.

"No," Jesus said. "I can manage. Not much here to pack. Most of the supplies are ready to go at Rajendra's house. I'm leaving at first light, which is good, because I think he's ready to be rid of me."

Ananda smiled self-consciously, watching Jesus tidy up. Jesus could see something was clearly on his mind. "Did you really come out here for one last look?" he asked.

"Not exactly," Ananda said. He hesitated. "I... wanted to speak with you about something."

"And what's that?" Jesus asked.

Again, Ananda paused. "What would you say if I traveled with you?" he asked at length. "To Metta Valley?"

Jesus looked at him in surprise. "You want to go to Metta Valley?"

"Not if you don't want company, of course," Ananda said quickly. "I'd understand if you wanted to go on your own. I just thought since you were going and it is better to travel with companions, then—"

"Wait," Jesus interrupted. "I'm not saying no. I'm only wondering why now. We've been talking for days, and you haven't mentioned this."

Ananda shuffled his feet. "Yes, well," he started, "it was my father's idea, actually."

"Your father?"

"The night he died," Ananda explained, "after we'd decided about the vineyard, he told me what he'd asked you to do. He advised that—if I felt I needed a new start—I might consider going with you."

Jesus smiled at this, remembering what the elder had said. *Your solution to all things is Metta Valley. Reform a prisoner, Metta Valley. Sprained ankle, Metta Valley...* He could now add *find a new start for his son* to the list.

"I could never find a good time," Ananda continued, "and then it felt like an imposition, and now—"

"Now is your last chance," Jesus finished.

"Well, yes."

Jesus thought about what Ananda was proposing. He wanted to say yes, but something gave him pause. "You've endured a lot," he said. "I know the ten days are over, but are you sure you want to do this now? You don't want to take some time to settle or maybe speak to your brother?"

"No," Ananda answered quickly, standing straighter as he did. "There is no need to dwell on the past. The best thing I can do now is honor my father's legacy and do my best to walk in his footsteps."

Jesus didn't quite believe him. "And that means going to Metta Valley?" he asked.

Ananda's awkwardness returned. "Yes," he said. "If you would have me, of course."

Jesus considered this for another moment. "Look, Ananda," he started, "you and I have gotten to know one another pretty well over the last ten days, and I hope you don't mind me saying, but I'm not sure if your father knew how hard you would—"

"This was his idea," Ananda repeated. "I spent too long doubting my father. I owe him at least this much."

Jesus nodded. Whatever his reservations were, he knew this was Ananda's choice. He knew what was best for him. Besides, part of him was deeply relieved to have the company. The thought of traveling on his own had been daunting, to say the least. "Well then," he said, extending an arm, "it's decided. We're traveling companions."

Ananda broke into a wide grin, his awkwardness fading in the light of his excitement. He grasped Jesus's wrist to seal the agreement. "Excellent," he said. "Very good, yes. I'll start making arrangements at once."

Jesus slung his bag over his shoulder and started back toward the cart. Ananda followed. "I'm leaving at sunrise," Jesus said. "Did I mention that?"

Ananda nodded eagerly. "I will be ready. I'll meet you at Rajendra's stables."

They both took a seat on the bench on the front of the cart, and Jesus picked up the reins. A second later, they were rolling forward, away from the ashes that had been their home. "I needed this, you know," Ananda said as they left the vineyard. "My father was right. I needed a way to start over."

"Well," Jesus answered, "I hope we both find what we need."

They rode on in silence for a moment. "Perhaps I should change my name," Ananda mused, "as you did."

"Well, I didn't exactly change my name," Jesus laughed. "I only began going by my Latin name. It was easier for people outside of Judea to pronounce."

"Do you know the Latin counterpart of Ananda?"

"I don't. Sorry."

"I suppose I could pick a new name," Ananda continued. "Or I could use my Hebrew name..."

"You have a Hebrew name?" Jesus asked in surprise. He wasn't sure why he was surprised. It made sense that Abraham would give his sons Hebrew names.

"Oh yes," Ananda said thoughtfully. "Deva and I both. Although our father only used them when he was angry. 'Noach! Get out of that wine press!'"

Jesus laughed. "Your name's Noach, then? That one's easy. It'd just be 'Noah.'"

"No, no," Ananda corrected. "'Noach' was what he called Deva."

"What was yours, then?" Jesus asked.

"Yehudah."

"Yehudah," Jesus repeated. "That one's also easy. That would be Judas."

"Judas," Ananda repeated, testing the sound of it. "That settles it then. Once we leave this city, I will be Judas. And my father was from Kerioth originally. Does that make a difference? How would you say Judas of Kerioth, on the road?"

Jesus considered this. "Well, you'd say Judas," he answered eventually. "Judas Iscariot."

III.

# 24

THE ENORMOUS WOODEN DOORS loomed in front of them, so heavy that Jesus wondered if they even worked. They looked like they could just as easily be for decoration. Judas inspected a thick, braided rope hanging beside the doors, still damp from the rain. He looked back at Jesus for approval.

"No use waiting," Jesus answered. The canyon walls around them would soon block out what little sunlight remained.

Obediently, Judas took hold of the rope and pulled. It didn't pull easily, but after a moment, it gave, and a heavy bell rang beyond the wall. Judas released the rope, startled.

They listened as the deep tones faded into nothing, leaving only a chorus of bugs.

"I hope they aren't sleeping," Judas said.

"If they were, they're not anymore."

The two waited for something to happen, and Jesus hoped it would happen soon. He felt isolated and claustrophobic between the two sheer rock faces on either side of them. The massive wall before them stretched from one rock face to the other, which meant if someone were to approach from behind, there was nowhere to escape. "Metta Valley" suddenly felt like too generous a name. "Metta Gorge" might be more fitting. Or "Metta Tomb." Jesus wondered, not for the first time, if this had been a mistake.

They'd been trying to get here for three weeks, even though neither Jesus nor Judas had any actual idea what waited for them on the other side. For all they knew, the Metta Valley Abraham knew was long gone, and the people on the other side of this wall would knock them unconscious and sell them, like Joseph in the scriptures.

*Rescue and deliver me from the hands of foreigners!* Jesus heard the rabbi's voice. *Their words are lies, and their right hands carry deceit!*

Jesus tried to push the voice away and thought instead about the road that had taken them there. It had been fraught, to say the least, and there had been times when Jesus thought they'd be better off trying their luck back in Kashi. The road curved so often that they could never see what was coming, and there was a constant stream of sounds from wild animals just off the path and out of sight, just waiting for their chance to devour unsuspecting travelers. At various junctures, the road was so narrow and overgrown that it wasn't clear whether it was a road at all, or if they'd wandered into the woods by mistake. To make matters worse, they were so far from civilization that, should they get lost, they would be on their own.

Just before leaving Kashi, Judas had the idea of buying donkeys to carry their gear. This might've been a great plan, if not for the fact that these donkeys proved to be the laziest and most difficult beasts in the region. Jesus was certain that by the end, the donkeys had wound up costing them a week's travel time. The *bnei beliya'al*, Jesus called them—*Sons of Iniquity*—and there were days when even this felt too kind.

On one occasion, the donkeys had very nearly gotten them killed.

It had been the day the first rains fell. As the first drop hit Judas on the shoulder, he'd become tense. "The rains are early," he'd said, looking up at the sky. "We need to find shelter. Now." Sure enough, they'd only just gotten their donkeys off the road and under some trees when the skies opened, drenching them in an instant. Judas tried to tie the donkeys to a tree while Jesus dug through their packs for anything that might keep them dry.

"What are you doing?" Judas called.

"Building an ark!"

"A what?"

"Don't worry about it!"

Jesus scanned the area. "There!" he called, pointing at a nearby overhang of rock. "Let's head over there!"

When Judas finished with the donkeys, they ran to the makeshift shelter, unable to see anything beyond the wall of water pouring in front of them. They were soaked. "Don't worry," Judas said, shaking himself off. "It'll be heavy for a while, but then there will be a break. There always is. We need to keep moving, though. This will start happening more and more."

They waited until the break in the storm Judas had predicted. It came, finally, but when they ventured back out, the donkeys were nowhere to be seen. Jesus scowled at the broken rope. He'd lost count of how many bindings they'd chewed through. "Damn it all!" he growled. "Those stubborn, stiff-necked—"

"They probably went off in search of higher ground," Judas reasoned. "Can you really blame them?" He had a tender spot for animals, which had been endearing at first, but Jesus was starting to find it irritating.

"I can, and I do," Jesus said, "because they took our supplies with them. We need to track them down. All we've got left are our mats."

"We can't track them down now," Judas protested. "It's almost dark."

Judas was right. It would be easy to get lost in these woods, especially after dark. In fact, Jesus could hardly tell where they were now. It'd been pouring down rain when they'd left the road, and he'd completely lost his bearings. He did a quick survey, trying to see which direction they'd come from. When he couldn't, he asked Judas, who also realized he didn't know. "We can't panic," Jesus said. "We just need to make camp for the night, and tomorrow, we'll try to find the road."

"What about the donkeys?"

"May they go in peace."

As it grew darker, and as they tried to get comfortable under their rocky overhang, they noticed a light flickering not too far off—through the trees. This surprised them both because, to their knowledge, they were nowhere near any kind of village or populated area at all. "Perhaps we should talk to them," Judas had suggested.

Jesus shook his head. "They could be bandits."

"Or they could be kind people. Maybe they could help us find the road."

Jesus suppressed an impatient look. Along with his over-the-top tenderness for animals, Judas was also relentlessly optimistic. Most days, it was encouraging. That night, it was not.

After a brief argument, they'd decided to investigate. "Fine," Jesus said. "The worst thing that could happen is that the stranger kills us, and then this whole thing would be over."

"That's the spirit."

Carefully, they'd moved towards the light and found themselves at a modest campsite. Jesus had slowed as he'd noticed a single figure sat, hooded and silent, beside the crackling fire.

"Um... excuse us," Judas said, pressing his palms together as they approached. "Good evening. We're sorry to come up on you like this."

The stranger remained silent.

"We're traveling to... Metta Valley?" Judas tried again. "Perhaps you know it? We've lost our things, and we've gotten a bit turned around. We only wondered if we could share your fire for a while."

Still, the stranger didn't speak, and Jesus felt more uneasy. He was about to back away when a hand emerged from the stranger's robes and gestured toward the fire in invitation. "Thank you," Judas exhaled, moving toward the fire. Reluctantly, Jesus followed.

They sat there for a while, letting the fire chase away the damp. Jesus couldn't see the stranger's full face, but every so often, when the fire flickered just right, he glimpsed a crescent-shaped scar around the stranger's left eye. He resolved to keep awake as long as they were at the campsite, but after a few hours, he made the mistake of leaning against a tree trunk, and before he knew it, it was morning.

Jesus woke to a tickling sensation on the back of his neck and opened his eyes to find a bright green snake slithering its way over his shoulder. He yelled and jumped up—the snake falling indifferently to the ground.

"What? What is it?" Judas cried, waking suddenly. He saw Jesus frantically swatting at his clothes, then noticed the snake. Gradually, he started laughing.

"I'm glad you find this amusing," Jesus snapped, giving his cloak one final shake.

"It's only a cat snake," Judas said.

"It eats cats?"

"No," Judas laughed harder. "Its eyes—vertical pupils, like a cat. They—" but he stopped short. "Wait," he said, "where is our host?"

Jesus looked around, and all that remained of the campsite was a mound of embers and a small pile of fruit. As Jesus kneeled to examine the fruit, he also saw that the stranger had drawn an arrow in the dirt.

"Where does that lead?" Judas asked.

"I don't know," Jesus said, following the arrow with his eyes. "Let's find out."

After packing the fruit, they'd followed the arrow and soon found the road. Relieved, they'd resumed their journey—now, mercifully, without donkeys.

Two nights later, they'd reached the massive wooden doors.

"Should we try again?" Judas asked, taking up the rope again after a long silence.

"I suppose," Jesus said. "But if they didn't hear it the first time—"

"Hello," an unfamiliar voice called from nearby, making them both jump.

A bald monk with a calm smile approached with a lantern. He was quite old, and clad in saffron robes that stood out against the darkening landscape. The monk gestured to the great doors. "That gate is for large deliveries," he said. "Livestock, oxen, and the like. You aren't delivering an elephant, are you?"

"No," Jesus answered. "Are you expecting one?"

"No," the monk said, and for a moment, they only studied one another curiously.

Jesus wasn't sure if the monk was testing them or if it was only his own unease, but either way, his patience was thin. "We're sorry for the late hour," he said, "but we've been traveling for a long time, and we've come with a message."

"Messengers?" the old monk asked, raising his eyebrows with interest. "Oh, how exciting! By all means, come in! Come in!"

He turned and slipped through a small door that they hadn't noticed before, leaving it open behind him.

Judas and Jesus exchanged wary glances. Then, with no other choice, they followed the monk inside.

# 25

JESUS AND JUDAS FOUND themselves in a warm reception room. A row of clay lamps flickered from niches in the walls, casting shifting shadows across the room. A small brazier glowed near one wall, warming a teapot over its embers. The furniture consisted of simple wooden stools lining the far wall beneath windows covered by woven screens, and cloth cushions stacked near the brazier's hearth. The blithe monk latched the door and shuffled to the pile of cushions. There, he set one near the fire and descended into a cross-legged position that boggled Jesus's mind.

"Have a seat, please," he invited.

Jesus nodded. "Thank you." He un-shouldered his satchel and took another cushion from the stack, trying and failing to mirror the monk's pose.

Judas fell into the pose without effort.

"You've done this before?" Jesus asked.

"My father taught us," Judas explained. "He had a few cushions like this. Made them himself."

"The cloth cushion is beneficial for any practitioner," the monk said. "Your father is a student of the Way?"

"He is," Judas said, then hesitated. "He was."

"He has died, then," the monk said. "I am sorry. My name is the Venerable Moggallana. I am second in stewardship of Metta Valley. Please, friends, whom do I have the honor of addressing?"

Jesus thought of how Leela and her friends had always said his name, and this seemed like as good a chance as ever to start over once more. "Issa," he answered. "I come from Nazareth, in Judea."

"Judea?" Moggallana asked, impressed. "My, my, Brother Issa has traveled some distance to find us."

"You know Judea?" Jesus asked, surprised.

"I've heard its name," Moggallana answered, "though little else, I'm afraid. It is an honor to meet you." He turned his attention to Judas. "And you?"

"Judas," he said, "son of Abraham, of Kerioth."

"Abraham?" Moggallana's face lit up again. "Might I assume you mean Brother Abraham, who has spent so much time here? You must be Ananda."

"Yes, sir," Judas said, surprised. "Although, I am going by Judas, for the time being, if you please."

"Brother Judas," Moggallana affirmed. "Well then, might I assume it is a message from your father that you bring?"

Jesus and Judas exchanged a glance. Moggallana's smile faded. "Ah," he said. "I see."

"The message is from Abraham, yes," Jesus told the monk, "but I'm afraid he gave it just before he died. He and his son—Devadatta—had a fight. Devadatta tried to kill him. I'm here because Abraham asked me to come on his behalf and request that you send a student on an errand to..." Jesus paused. Even now, it was difficult to pass on Abraham's request. "To... help Devadatta. To help him find his way. He mentioned you might help other prisoners in Kashi as well."

Moggallana closed his eyes, taking in the weight of this news. "This is difficult indeed," he said. "Many here will be deeply grieved." He opened his eyes once more. "I thank you for delivering this message, Brother Issa. Per Brother Abraham's wishes, we will indeed dispatch a novice on an errand to the city. Brother Judas," again, the monk turned his attention to Judas, "I am sorry for your loss."

Judas looked at the ground. "Thank you, sir," he said.

"You two must be exhausted, of course," the monk said. "I will certainly not delay in offering you food and lodging for the evening. If there remains nothing to discuss, then in the morning, we shall—"

"Actually," Jesus said, "I have one more thing to discuss, if you don't mind."

Moggallana's eyebrows lifted, then he settled back. He gestured for Jesus to continue.

"Well," Jesus said, looking at Judas for support. "If it's all right, we'd like to stay for a while. I think both of us are curious about this place and about your Way."

"Stay?" Moggallana asked, surprised again. "In what capacity, I wonder?"

"As students," Jesus said. "We've both heard a great deal about this place from Abraham, and we wanted to learn."

"As novices," Judas cut in. "That's the phrase I heard my father use. We'd like to come on as novices, for as long as that can last."

"Novices," Moggallana echoed. "I see. Well, that does change things, doesn't it?"

Jesus and Judas exchanged a glance. "Does it?"

"Oh, quite," Moggallana said. "To live among us, even for a short time, is no easy task. Ultimately, the yoke of our practice is easy, and its burden light. In another way, however, it is quite challenging, especially at first. For that reason, we must ask any aspirant one important question to ensure that they are, in fact, prepared."

"All right," Jesus said. "Ask. We're ready."

Moggallana paused, looking from one of them to the other. "Why?"

Jesus hesitated. "What do you mean?" he asked. "Why what?"

"*Why* have you come?" Moggallana asked. "*Why* have you seen fit to leave the life you know and go without material comforts or rich foods, just to become a student of the Way? What do you seek in this place?"

Jesus hadn't anticipated this. He looked to Judas, but Judas clearly hoped Jesus would answer first.

"Well," Jesus started, "it's not as though I had much of a life to leave behind. I don't really have anywhere else to go."

"Indeed," Moggallana said, nodding. "And you, Brother Judas?"

"I am here to learn the Way my father learned," Judas answered without hesitation. "I wish to honor his legacy."

Jesus felt jealous. That was a better answer.

"I see," Moggallana said, regarding them both. After a moment, he stood from his cushion. "Follow me, if you would," he beckoned, and with Jesus and Judas following, the old monk stepped back through the door they'd entered. "Friends," Moggallana said, leading them into the open air, "do you see the stars above us?"

Jesus looked up to find a black sky. "No," he said. "There are too many clouds."

"Precisely," Moggallana said. "The stars are there, to be sure, but they are obscured. To see them, the clouds must first be removed. The same is true, I believe, of your intention for being here. What must be done, my friends, is to thin the clouds of confusion before the light of intention can shine through and serve its purpose. Therefore, unfortunately, while it is our practice to offer hospitality to travelers and messengers, one wishing to come on as an aspirant invokes a different custom. Our common rule, I'm afraid, prevents us offering lodging to an aspiring novice until they are able to uncover those stars of intention, and it is to that work you must now turn. Until then, my friends, I bid you good night."

Jesus realized what was happening one moment too late. He looked away from the sky just in time to see the monk pull the door closed and hear a latch fall into place. "Wait!" Jesus yelled, following and pounding at the door. "You can't just leave us out here! I changed my mind! I'm just a messenger!"

No response.

He tried a few more times, but after a while, he just let his head fall against the door. "Your father had a broken leg," Jesus said. "That's why they let him in. He didn't come asking to be a novice."

"Are you suggesting one of us should break our leg?"

Jesus ignored him. He couldn't believe the old monk had locked them out. They should've kept quiet. They should've let the monks offer them hospitality, give them a bed, maybe offer breakfast, *then* brought up becoming a novice. Abraham could have given them some warning.

A few feet away, Judas began unrolling his mat.

"What are you doing?" Jesus asked.

"Making camp. He made it sound like we'd have another chance tomorrow. Tonight, I doubt he'll be letting us back in."

"I don't know," Jesus said, looking around for the braided rope. "Maybe we should keep ringing the bell."

"We will think more clearly with rested minds," Judas argued. "Why not get what sleep we can?"

Jesus let his head fall against the door one more time. "Fine," he conceded, then peeled himself away and set to unrolling his own mat directly in front of the door. Judas gave him a puzzled look. "If he comes out again," Jesus explained, "I don't want to be surprised."

"No," Judas said. "Only stepped on."

Jesus got comfortable on his own mat, and Judas dragged his mat closer.

"I think your father may have oversold the hospitality of this place," Jesus said, yawning.

"Have faith," Judas answered. "They are only doing what they have to."

"What they have to do," Jesus scoffed. Weeks they had traveled to get here, and when they finally arrived, they were cast out.

Part of Jesus took this as confirmation that his fears about this place were true—that what waited for him beyond this wall were only more Pharisees, bound to their legalistic ways at the expense of any kind of hospitality or justice. After all, was this not exactly what the rabbi would do if someone in his home were found to be unclean? *The place of the unclean is outside of the camp, Yeshua,* he remembered the rabbi warning once during one of their lessons. *Is that what you want? To be cast out of the camp?*

It was a tactic the rabbi had used often—leveraging the fear of being cast out to bend someone into conformity—and Jesus wasn't interested in the least in taking up with another teacher who would use the same tools. Still, he knew he had to trust Abraham. Abraham wouldn't have sent them here if these teachers were the same as the ones he'd fled in Judea. Would he?

He rolled over, uncomfortable as the stones pressed into his back. He knew this would be a long night. Judas was right, though. They would think better after a night's rest. Tomorrow, they would figure out what they needed to say to be allowed in.

Tomorrow, they would answer the question.

# 26

JESUS ROLLED OVER AND felt something press against his nose. Slowly, his eyes opened to see a bowl of porridge.

"Good morning, Brother Issa!" a voice greeted cheerfully. Jesus squinted into the morning sun and found Moggallana seated patiently beside Judas.

"How..." Jesus started, glancing at the door. How had the old monk stepped over him without him noticing?

"I thought you might like some breakfast," Moggallana said, "and I wanted to ask if you had reconsidered."

"Reconsidered?" Jesus echoed, still groggy.

"The question," Judas said, tucking into his porridge. "He wants to know if we've thought more about why we want to stay."

Jesus rubbed a hand across his face. Morning was not the time for riddles. "And when exactly was I meant to be reconsidering? In my dreams?"

Moggallana nodded and stood. "Perhaps you are right," he said, moving back towards the door. "Tomorrow, then."

"Tomorrow?" Jesus said, suddenly more alert. "No, wait—"

"That should give you plenty of time to reconsider."

"If you just—"

"Find those stars, Brother Issa!"

Before Jesus could protest again, the monk slipped past him and pulled the door closed. "Wait!" Jesus called, but the only response was the sound of the latch falling back into place. "So, he'll offer us food, but he won't let us in?"

"It won't be tomorrow," Judas said. "Don't worry. He told me we could try again this afternoon. He's testing us, I think."

Again, Jesus tried not to think too deeply about this. Angrily, he took up his own porridge.

"I like him," Judas said.

"Of course you do."

Jesus finished his porridge in just a few bites, then rose to stretch and inspect their surroundings. The darkness had concealed the landscape the night before, but now Jesus saw the road widening into a clearing, ending at the great wall and towering doors. Just as Abraham had described, Metta Valley was nestled between sheer rock faces. In the daylight, Jesus could see that the doors were decorated with Brahmi scripts alongside carved wheels, lotus flowers, and footprints. As he walked, Jesus noticed a carved figure in the same pose Moggallana had assumed the night before, and a few feet away, a carving of an unnerving figure with a shadowy presence and many hands. His form seemed to shift in a trick of the light, and it made Jesus's hair stand on end. He couldn't take his eyes off it. "Mara," read the script beneath the figure. The name tugged at his memory, but he couldn't place it. With a shiver, he made himself walk away.

After the doors, Jesus went on with his inspection, feeling like an Israelite about to storm Jericho. As best he could tell, the wall had three openings. There was Moggallana's small door, the "elephant doors," and one small drain in the bottom left corner, through which ran a little stream. Bars framed this last one, and Jesus couldn't find a good angle to see through to the other side.

Eventually, he found a shady place in the corner of the gorge—next to a small tree growing in front of the wall—and sat. Leaning against the tree's trunk, he considered the question. Why had he come to Metta Valley? What was it that had led him to take the risk of coming to a place like this? To trust Abraham?

Reaching into his robes, he took out the basalt Buddha stone and began rolling it over in his hand as he thought. It helped him concentrate. He'd offered the stone to Judas on the road—reasoning it was rightly Judas's—but he'd told Jesus to keep it. Now, Jesus felt the smoothly curved line that had once been the Buddha's smile and considered Moggallana's question. He was here because of Abraham—that much was clear—but how could he explain that?

"Because... he was different," Jesus muttered to the smiling stone. "Because he was kind and just... because he was free."

That much was true, he knew, but that didn't really answer the question.

"Because I want to be like him," Jesus concluded. "The spirit he found... I want to know it for myself."

He knew this was the truest answer he could give. It was because meeting Abraham with his scriptures and practices had reignited a hope and purpose that Jesus hadn't felt in a long time, and it drew Jesus forward like fire would draw a cold traveler. Pursuing that flame was worth anything they could throw at him—whatever fasts, laws, or trials they demanded. If he tried hard enough, then maybe he could live up to at least a fraction of who Abraham had been. That was enough for him. It would have to be enough for Moggallana, too.

A while later, after Jesus had spent probably too long figuring out exactly how he'd phrase his answer to Moggallana, he returned to the small door where Judas waited. Jesus sat with his back against the door, next to his traveling companion, and for a moment, neither said anything.

"Are you imagining another bowl of porridge, too?" Jesus asked.

"How did you guess?"

"A hunch."

Judas smiled. "I've been thinking," he said. "Maybe an imposed fast is part of the discernment process. You know, like to be sure we really want to be here?"

"You're probably right. That, or the old monk is just toying with us. Maybe he'll make us wait out here for three more days, just for fun."

"No," Judas said. "I'm certain he'll return soon."

"Well," Jesus said, "I'll tell you one thing. When I see him again, I won't let him leave without—"

Before he could finish, the door opened. Jesus and Judas both suddenly found themselves falling flat on their backs, looking up at Moggallana's smiling face.

"Yes, Brother Issa?" he asked curiously. "Without what?"

Jesus scrambled to his feet and whirled around to face the old monk. He stopped short when he realized Moggallana wasn't alone. Next to him was a woman. She was slender, her sharp gaze studying him, and her head was shaved like Moggallana's. She wore the same saffron robe, and Jesus guessed she might be about the same age as his mother. He also noticed her left eye. Around it was a scar in the shape of a crescent moon. "I remember you," he started. "You're the one from the road. You helped us."

"Brother Issa," the woman greeted in a steady, contralto voice. "Brother Judas. I understand you are friends of our late Brother Abraham. I also understand that you wish to join us for a season as aspirants. Is this true?"

Jesus was too surprised to speak, so Judas stepped in. "Yes, it is," he said. "It's true."

"Very good," the woman said. "Well, what shall we say, Brother Moggallana? Shall we allow them another chance?"

Brother Moggallana smiled. "I don't see why not."

The woman stepped aside, gesturing for them to enter. "In that case," she said. "Please join us."

Jesus gave Judas another wry look. Then, for the second time, they entered the receiving room.

# 27

THE RECEIVING ROOM FELT more spacious than it had the night before. Someone had removed the woven screens from the windows on the far wall, allowing natural sunlight to illuminate the room. Jesus craned his neck, hoping to glimpse what waited beyond the wall, but from his position on the cushion he could see nothing.

Moggallana sat across from Jesus and Judas on his own cushion—his legs folded again into that impossible shape—while the woman took her time over the brazier, preparing an herbal drink Jesus didn't recognize. Jesus watched her work, wondering who she was. Had she been following them? She was tall—taller than Jesus or Judas by a hand width—and although she wore the same smile as Moggallana, it sat more subtly on her calm, sharp face. Her every movement was deliberate and precise.

When she finished, the woman handed each of them a cup. "I am sure you can understand the importance of knowing one's motivation," she said. "Intention, after all, can greatly influence experience."

"Of course," Jesus said.

The woman lowered herself onto a cushion.

"I'm sorry," Jesus said, "but who are you? We saw you that night on the road, didn't we? It was you."

The surprise on Moggallana's face made Jesus wonder if he'd spoken out of turn. The stranger, however, didn't blink. "Indeed," she said. "Please forgive me. I imagine this must be confusing. My name is Master Gotami. I am the Head Teacher of Metta Valley."

"Head Teacher?" Jesus asked.

"I lead this community and provide instruction," she clarified. Then, noting the look on Jesus's face, she asked, "Is something the matter, Brother Issa? You seem more confused still."

"Oh, no," Jesus said. "It's just... I've never seen a woman lead or teach, is all. In Judea, it's only ever the men."

"Well, this may come as a surprise to you, Brother Issa," Master Gotami said, "but I find I use my genitals very little in teaching, and if your teachers were using theirs, I daresay they are doing it incorrectly."

Judas snorted into his drink, causing it to splash out onto his lap, and Jesus felt his face go red. "I'm sorry," he said. "I shouldn't have said anything."

"Oh, it's quite all right," Master Gotami said as Judas cleaned himself up. "Always better to ask questions than to let them fester. It only serves powers of oppression not to question one's assumptions. Here, we encourage our students to investigate every assumption and ask every question. Should you join us, you will soon find that we put our trust in our own experience, not in an unquestionable tradition. Regarding my being a woman, it is our understanding that we perceive the truth more fully when we give everyone a voice to share their experience, particularly those whose voices are so often silenced by the powers that be. This practice may be rare in our tradition, but you'll find that we do many things differently at Metta Valley. Wisdom favors neither men nor women, only those who would seek it."

"Well," Jesus said, trying to recover, "thank you for what you did for us the other night. We would probably still be out there if it weren't for you, as lost as our donkeys."

"You are quite welcome," Master Gotami said. "Ah, and on that subject. Your donkeys were found wandering the woods near here shortly after our encounter. They have been brought to our stables and seen to."

"Oh, good!" Judas said, looking at Jesus gratefully.

"Yes," Jesus forced himself to say. "Thank goodness."

"Now, please," Master Gotami said, "I would very much like to return to the question at hand. As Brother Moggallana explained yesterday evening, this question of one's intention is of utmost importance. For this reason, I shall ask again. Why is it that you wish to stay among us here at Metta Valley?"

For a moment, none of them spoke.

"Brother Issa," Master Gotami prompted, "would you like to begin?"

Jesus took a deep breath. "All right," he said. "I assume Brother Moggallana told you about our message?"

"He did," Master Gotami said. "I was sorry to hear of Brother Abraham's passing. He and Radha were much beloved here."

"You knew my father as well?" Judas asked.

"I did. I was only a novice when he arrived. As part of my novitiate work, I was given the task of tending to his wounds. We spent many hours speaking of the texts and practices of our respective ways—that is, after he stopped cursing me every time I walked through the door."

"That was you?" Jesus said. "He told me about you. He said you helped him a great deal."

"I found him a curious and wise man," Master Gotami said. "Hurt and bitter at times, yes, but wise. I might have known you were his son, Ananda. I have not seen you since you were quite young."

"Thank you," Judas said, "but it's Judas now. I left Ananda behind for a time."

Master Gotami smiled. "If only it were so simple. Now, Brother Issa, you were saying?"

"Yes," Jesus said, remembering what he'd prepared earlier. "I am here because of Abraham. He followed a Way I want to understand. He was alive, and he was free, and made others feel the same. He lived with justice, kindness, and mercy, and I want to do that, too. I'm sure it came from a lifetime of experiences and practice, but he said an important part of it was what he learned here. He encouraged me to come, and although I resisted at first, I think he was right. So here I am. I want to learn how it was that he was able to find such truth and life."

Master Gotami listened carefully until he finished. "Thank you, Brother Issa," she said, pressing her hands together. "I believe what you have said will serve you well here. All the same, I must warn you that, in this place, 'to learn' means more than mere memorization and compliance. To thrive in Metta Valley, you will find that you must move into deeper, less comfortable places than intellectual investigation."

Jesus pressed his hands together in return. "Thank you, Master Gotami."

Master Gotami then turned her attention to Judas, who seemed to become smaller under her gaze. "And you, Brother Judas?" she asked. "If you please, what has brought you here, seeking to learn our practice?"

Judas glanced nervously at Jesus, as though expecting his help to answer. "I'm here because I want to honor my father," he said after a moment. "It's what he would want, and I want to do right by him. If you knew him, then you know what I... you know what happened between us. I have made mistakes. I wish to make peace."

Jesus listened carefully. It was the first time he'd heard Judas actually acknowledge the incident since Abraham died.

Master Gotami looked as though she was sorting through a puzzle. Quietly, she plumbed the unspoken depths of Judas's answer. "Your grief weighs heavily on you, Brother Judas," she concluded.

Judas shifted on his cushion. "I just want to do what's right."

"Indeed, you do," Master Gotami agreed, "and no doubt your desire to honor your father would see you through whatever your practice here may have in store, but I would issue you a word of warning. While love and the desire to learn a better Way are fine motivators, shame and the desire to work off a debt will rarely take you where you wish to go. These feed a hunger that will never be satisfied, and will breed only resentment for yourself and others. It was the neglect of grief following the death of your mother which, if I understand correctly, led to the mistakes of which you speak."

Judas only stared at the ground. Master Gotami's bold honesty shocked Jesus, but it differed from the harsh reprimands he was used to hearing from the rabbi. This was honesty interwoven with compassion. There was no judgment in her words.

"If you wish to work with your shame and grief during your time at Metta Valley," she continued, "then I daresay your work may be quite fruitful. Should you continue to look away from these things, however, taking refuge in that which is easier to face, then I am afraid what awaits you will be heartache, and perhaps more mistakes you may later regret. Suffering is the first noble truth, Brother Judas. It is only by facing it that it can be dealt with."

"Of course," Judas said. "Does that mean... you'll permit me to stay?"

Master Gotami studied Judas for another moment, then Jesus. "Yes," she said, and Jesus exhaled with relief. "The intentions you have stated are clear enough to serve their purpose, and I bid you keep them in mind over the next few weeks, as you begin the more demanding requirements of our practice."

"Thank you, Master Gotami," Judas breathed. Jesus wondered what she meant by *demanding*.

"Brother Moggallana will see that you are both provided with robes, bowls, and basic instruction before he shows you to your quarters," Master Gotami said. "Part of our requirement is that you surrender any physical possessions you bring with you before entering. The robes and bowls will be your only possessions as long as you are here. Do you object?"

"No," Jesus and Judas said in unison.

"Even the donkeys?" Jesus asked.

"Indeed," Master Gotami said. "They will be well cared for in our stables, should you wish to give them to the community. Otherwise, you may take the time you need to make other arrangements."

Jesus sighed with relief. "They're all yours."

"Very well," Master Gotami said. "Your time at Metta Valley will begin with a one-week trial. If, after a week of living among us and following our practice, your wish to stay persists, then you may stay on as an aspirant. Should you choose to leave, we will send you off with goodwill. Questions?"

"We didn't travel this far only to leave after a week," Jesus said.

Master Gotami gave him a knowing smile. "Let us see how you feel seven days from now."

"What happens after that week?" Judas asked. "If we decide to stay, I mean?"

"The aspirant stage will last one year," Master Gotami answered, "or until one has demonstrated appropriate maturity to continue to the next stage of their training. At the end of that time, should you choose to stay on, then you will engage in a rite of initiation and be assigned an errand. Following your errand, should you choose to return, you may begin your training as a novitiate."

"What is the rite of initiation?" Judas asked.

"A tradition of our order," she said. "A forty-day sojourn into the wilderness."

Jesus paused. "Forty days?" he echoed. "Alone?"

"Forty days," Master Gotami repeated, "for meditation and solitude. You understand now, I think, why the clarity of one's intention is vital. Our training is not for the faint of heart."

*Clearly,* Jesus thought.

Master Gotami stood, and the other three followed. "Unless there are further questions," she said, "your training shall begin tomorrow at sunrise. I shall oversee the task myself. A word of instruction as you begin your journey, however. Over the next year, you may find yourself greatly troubled, but may you never cease from seeking until you find that what you seek is already yours. It is said that only the one who allows themselves to become troubled can hope to become awakened.

Only then can they transcend all things. Have you understood these things?"

"No," Jesus said, "but I suppose we will soon."

Master Gotami smiled and pressed her hands together again. Jesus and Judas returned the gesture. "Very well, friends," she said. "All that is left is to say welcome to Metta Valley, and we are deeply honored you are here. Brother Moggallana, I leave them in your charge."

Moggallana gave a respectful nod, and Master Gotami left through the door that led into Metta Valley.

"Well," Jesus said, picking up his bag, "where do we begin?"

Moggallana grinned. "Eager to get started, are we?"

"We are," Jesus said. "We've come a long way."

"Indeed, you have," Moggallana said. "First, you will follow me. There is much to see."

With that, he led them through the door and into Metta Valley.

## 28

*YOU WILL NEVER BELONG, despite your childish attempts to make up for what you are. Your mother sees it every time she looks at you, you know that.*

*That's enough!* Jesus shouted, shaking the rabbi by the cloak, but the rabbi pressed on.

*You search in vain for someone to please or someone to fight—all to try to prove to yourself that you're not what you are—that you're good and righteous. But you know what you are, don't you? Son of Mary...*

*Enough!*

*Son of Pantera...*

*I said enough!*

Jesus raised his hammer to strike, but couldn't. He tried again, but he felt frozen in place. People were pouring in—watching him, hearing the rabbi, but they did nothing. They only watched. Finally, just as Jesus forced his arm to move, a wave of sound reverberated through his room, yanking him violently from the dream.

"Whawasat?" he asked, sitting bolt upright. Judas did the same.

He and Jesus searched the dark, wondering what had just rattled them from sleep. After a moment, another wave pummeled through the room, and Jesus kneaded the sleep out of his eyes. As the sound faded, they heard shuffling outside their room. "I'll see what's going on," Jesus muttered, tossing his thin cover aside and stumbling to the door. His scalp tingled in the cold, early morning air. He felt exposed without his hair.

When he got to the door, he opened it to see a line of bleary-eyed students streaming towards the stairs. There was another wave of sound, making Jesus jump and clutch the doorframe, but this time he could see it was a bell—the one they'd sounded outside of the front wall. It was even louder on this side, and he felt slightly guilty for ringing it that first night.

He tried to get the attention of a passing resident. "Excuse me," he said. "What's happening?"

One resident stepped out of the stream of the crowd. "It is the bell," he replied, then stared at Jesus blankly.

"Obviously," Jesus said. "What does the bell *mean?* Is the building on fire? Are we under attack?"

"You must be new," the resident said, pressing his palms together. "Welcome. My name is Upali."

"Issa," Jesus said, impatient. "Now, the bell? Is there somewhere we need to be going?"

"Is there a problem?" another resident asked, also stepping out of the stream.

"New aspirants," Upali explained, nodding towards Jesus. "They were asking about the bell."

"Oh!" the student said, pressing her palms together. "Welcome! How exciting—to hear the bell for the first—"

"Can one of you just tell me what it means?" Jesus interrupted. "Please?"

"Of course," Upali explained, as though Jesus's outburst was entirely reasonable. "We invite the bell to call us to mindfulness and to set a rhythm for our day. We are currently going to the meditation hall."

"Do *we* need to go to the meditation hall, Upali?" Jesus asked.

"I do not know," Upali admitted. "Although, if Master Gotami has not yet given you instruction, then I would enjoy my sleep. She will likely instruct you on what to do tomorrow."

"All right," Jesus muttered. His ears were still ringing. "Enjoy my sleep. Right."

"I suspect someone will come to collect you at daybreak," the other monk said. "Enjoy your first day of instruction!"

"I'm sure we will," Jesus said, closing the door before they could respond.

Judas was already asleep again. Jesus laid back down, but his mind was now wide awake, thinking about what Moggallana had shown them the day before—wondering what they'd talk about today.

———

THE PREVIOUS AFTERNOON, AFTER Master Gotami had left them with Brother Moggallana, the old monk had walked them down a narrow hallway to a door. "Are you prepared, *samaneras?*" he'd asked.

"*Samaneras?*" Jesus had echoed.

"Forgive me," Moggallana said. "This is our word for a resident of your status."

"Ah," Jesus had said. "Well then, lead the way."

Moggallana smiled. "Welcome to Metta Valley."

He opened the door, and it took Jesus several seconds of blinking before his eyes adjusted. Even in the afternoon, the contrast between the dark room and the open courtyard was blinding. When he could finally see, he stood in awe of the scene in front of him.

The first thing Jesus noticed was the sweet, earthy scent that emanated from the courtyard. Pink, bell-shaped flowers clustered around the edges of the grounds, which Jesus recognized as muskroot—the plant used to distill the perfume they called spikenard back home.

The second thing he noticed was the height of the walls, towering as high as the Temple in Jerusalem. As he'd seen from the outside, the two sheer mountain faces made two walls on either end, but what he couldn't have seen from outside were the huge, mesmerizing patterns of shapes and symbols carved into the stone surfaces. On the far rock face, anchoring the sprawling pattern, Jesus could make out a great eight-spoked wheel.

The man-made wall on the far side of the courtyard had four levels. The first jutted out further than the others, with three doors spaced out evenly across it. On the upper levels, though, were rows of wooden doors, connected by an exterior corridor with a sturdy railing. On either side, spiral staircases wound upward like vines, framing the wall like a great work of art.

"Come," Moggallana beckoned. "Let us keep moving."

Jesus and Judas followed the monk further into the courtyard, and Jesus turned to see the "elephant doors" in the center of the front wall. There were rooms built on either side. One was the room they'd just come from, but atop the room on the far side was a platform accessible only by a rickety ladder that had seen better days. On the platform was a strong wooden frame supporting a colossal bell, with a great beam suspended next to it. It was like a battering ram, prepared to let loose and wake the bell from its slumber.

A stream ran from one corner of the courtyard to another—the modest creek he'd seen from the outside. It came in through one barred opening in the far wall, flowed across the courtyard, and went out through the other opening in the front, and Jesus could tell that whoever had designed this place had graded the ground slightly downwards so that rain could drain into the stream. Given the downpour they'd witnessed on the road, Jesus imagined this was necessary to prevent the courtyard from becoming a marsh. Two small arched bridges crossed the stream in different places, connecting a series of gravel walkways that led around the courtyard. Other residents in saffron robes—the first monks Jesus had seen besides Moggallana and Master Gotami—walked steadily along the path, absorbed in each step.

Then, at the very center of the courtyard, beside the stream, stood the largest fig tree Jesus had ever seen. *Happy are those who meditate day and night,* Jesus heard Abraham singing in his mind, *for they are like trees, rooted by streams of water, bearing their fruit in due season...* It was incredible. Its trunk of aerial roots reached up toward the sky, and heart-shaped leaves waved from its branches, greeting the newcomers.

Its roots, Jesus imagined, must undergird the very foundation of the monastery and drink constantly from the flowing stream.

"Just through here," Moggallana said.

Jesus and Judas followed, walking beyond the elephant doors toward the room at the far end, beneath the bell. This turned out to be a storage room housing countless robes and bowls, which Moggallana busied himself rifling through. "Each resident," he explained—his voice muffled by robes—"is allowed two robes and a bowl. The villagers bring them as an offering, but we often have too many. We give the surplus away, but all the same... Ah! Here we are." Emerging from the robes, he presented them with two robes each, then he picked up two bowls. "Care for these well," he instructed. "While you are here, they shall be your only possessions. Even then, we cannot say that we truly possess them. We are but stewards for a time."

"Understood," Jesus said. "Thank you."

Moggallana then took their satchels and stowed them away for safekeeping. Jesus kept the smiling Buddha stone, hiding it in his palm as they changed.

"During your time here," Brother Moggallana continued, "there are five precepts you must follow. These are the most basic laws we follow both for the training of our minds and for the harmony of our common life. Are you prepared to hear them?"

"Of course," Jesus said.

"The first is that you will not kill," Moggallana said. "You will refrain from taking the life of any living being while you are here. The second is that you shall not steal. You will refrain from taking anything which is not given."

"These sound familiar," Jesus said. "The next is on adultery, correct?"

"You've heard these before," Brother Moggallana said. "Most impressive. The third is that you shall not engage in sexual misconduct. You will refrain from sensual pleasure in any way that causes harm to yourself, others, or the community. The fourth is that you shall not engage in false speech. You will refrain from any speech that is dishonest, slandering, or harmful in any way."

"Easy enough," Jesus said. "And the fifth?"

"You shall not indulge in the consumption of any form of intoxicant."

Jesus hesitated. "Say that again?"

"You will refrain from consuming alcohol in order to protect the clarity of your mind."

"The clarity of our..." Jesus trailed off. "You're joking. Abraham ran a *vineyard*. You can't be asking us to—"

"I can," Brother Moggallana said calmly, "and I am."

Jesus looked at Judas, who merely shrugged. "Fine," Jesus conceded. "No wine. No alcohol. Is that all?"

"Quite," Moggallana said, looking pleased.

"Do you still observe the reconciliation ritual?" Judas asked. "My father made that a staple in our house whenever my brother and I would fight."

"Indeed, we do," Moggallana said.

Jesus looked confused. "What's the reconciliation ritual?"

"Whenever two members of our community have a falling out," Moggallana explained, "then it is our tradition that the two parties shall separate, allow themselves to calm, then come back together to work through their issue, sometimes with the aid of a mediator. When all is said and done, the parties bow, kiss one another on the cheek, and they recite the words, 'Wrongdoing arises from the mind. If the mind is made clear, no wrongdoing remains.'"

"A kiss?" Jesus asked. "Is that necessary?"

"Does Brother Issa have a problem with kissing on the cheek?"

"No," Jesus said. "It's just so... intimate."

Kissing on the cheek was an awkward concept for Jesus. It wasn't that they didn't kiss on the cheek in Judea—he saw it all the time—it was just that he had never done it himself. His own mother didn't even kiss him on the cheek. The thought of having his face that close to a stranger made him want to cringe.

"No exceptions," Moggallana said. "Do you feel you can abide by these precepts?"

"I do, Brother Moggallana," Judas answered without reservation.

They looked at Jesus, who shifted uncomfortably. "All right, fine," he said. "Yes, I will do it."

"Very good!" Moggallana said joyfully. "Well then, let's see to shaving those heads!"

---

JESUS HAD BARELY DRIFTED off when a knock jolted him awake. He didn't know how much time had passed, but slivers of sunlight shone through the door's edges. He heard Judas stir on the other side of the small room. "S'your turn," Jesus muttered, "and if it's a monk named Upali, tell him to go away."

Judas groaned, pushing himself upright and stumbling towards the door. After a moment, Jesus heard him again, awake and alert. "Master Gotami!" he said.

Jesus jerked upright and sprang from his mat.

"Good morning," Master Gotami said. "I trust you rested well."

"Well enough," Jesus lied. "Is it time to begin?"

"Brother Issa is eager," Master Gotami observed, "but I'm afraid he will have to wait a bit longer yet. I came to inform you that breakfast is being served downstairs in the dining hall. After you have eaten, I shall wait in the meditation hall. I trust Brother Moggallana acquainted you with the grounds?"

"Yes," Judas said. "He gave us a tour yesterday. We'll be there."

Master Gotami pressed her palms together in farewell and glided away.

After changing from one set of robes to another, Jesus and Judas went downstairs and ate quickly, nearly finishing their meager portions in seconds. A few of the other residents stared, and Jesus hesitated as he noticed their slow, mindful bites. He nudged Judas, and they both slowed down. When they were finished, they hurried off toward the meditation hall.

Master Gotami waited, sitting in that impossible position that Jesus now knew was called a "lotus pose." Moggallana had explained it the day before on their tour. "I could tell you a story of its noble origins," he'd said, "but the truth is, it is the only position in which you can fall asleep without falling over. This comes in handy!"

Master Gotami opened her eyes as they walked in. "Friends," she greeted, "welcome to the meditation hall."

"We're sorry to keep you waiting," Jesus apologized.

"No matter," Master Gotami said. "Only those bound to expectation grow impatient. Please, sit. Prior to your first lesson, I should like to hear more about where you have come from. You have shared your intention for being here, but I know nothing of your lives leading to this moment."

Jesus and Judas sat obediently on two of the cushions that Master Gotami had laid out and silently negotiated about who would go first. Judas lost, so he awkwardly began recounting his story first. Master Gotami was already familiar with much of it. When he got to the part about stealing his family's money and running, he was light on the details and hurried to his return, the fire, and his father's death. Once he finished, Jesus began. He might've struggled to tell his story a few months prior, but having told Abraham, he found it easier.

"Very good," Master Gotami said when they finished. "I am deeply grateful for your trust and your stories. We shall discuss them further in the weeks to come, of course, but this brief introduction has given me enough to know how I might best introduce our practice to you today. If you will, please follow me."

With ease, she unfolded her legs and rose, and Jesus wondered if he'd ever be able to do that. It seemed doubtful. She led them out of the meditation hall towards one of the spiral stairways that led up to their quarters. Jesus checked his pace more than once, adjusting to her steady rhythm.

"You seem uneasy, Brother Issa," Master Gotami observed. "What troubles you?"

"I'm fine," Jesus said. "I'm just excited to get started."

"Mmm," Master Gotami mused. "Do you recall what I said yesterday about asking questions rather than letting them fester? I find the same is true for feelings and concerns. That which is unaddressed or unacknowledged is that which has a great, unseen power over you. It is up to you whether you share, of course, but I find airing my concerns to be of great benefit."

Jesus sighed. "I suppose I'm nervous," he admitted. "A part of me can't believe I came here at all."

Master Gotami nodded. "This makes sense," she said.

"It does?"

"Of course," Master Gotami said. "Your body is working to keep you safe. It is a wonderful ally and advocate, after all. It remembers what it felt like to feel betrayed—ostracized, as you shared earlier. If I'm not mistaken, it wishes to save you from the same fate here."

Jesus felt his insides churn. "I suppose that could be true," he said hesitantly.

Master Gotami continued, "I wonder if there is a deeper fear at work as well. After all, not only were you hurt by your teacher, but you trusted him to provide a certain level of meaning and purpose. Losing this hurt you too, did it not?"

Jesus didn't answer.

"Perhaps you are afraid that this place will likewise fail to deliver—that you will again be subjected to the despair of suspecting that there is no meaning. No purpose. Such despair, I imagine, would be even more painful than further ostracism. Such despair may even feel like a kind of death. It is right that you are fearful."

"So, what do you suggest I do about that?" Jesus asked.

"Well, perhaps this may help," Master Gotami said, leading them up the stairs. "Both of these fears are quite valid. I am familiar with the tradition from which Brother Abraham came, as he told me a great many stories. I do not envy the pain you must have felt under their leadership."

The rabbi's voice rang in Jesus's ears. *You will never belong, despite your childish attempts to make up for what you are...*

"And you really believe this place is different?" he asked.

"Oh, goodness me, yes," Master Gotami said. "We have our struggles and blind places, to be sure, but here, we do not tie our worth to our ability to adhere to a set of laws or appease a divine disciplinarian, nor do we shy away from difficult inquiry. We do not rely on willpower to achieve righteousness, nor do we believe that qualities such as justice or righteousness are achievements to be earned at the zenith of a spiritual ladder. Here, our approach is more natural."

They passed the first-floor landing, the wooden steps creaking beneath their feet.

"Natural?" Jesus echoed, uncertain.

"Our practice is more akin to tending a fruit tree," Master Gotami explained. "Fruits, you see, are only borne when a tree's roots have been well nourished. If one wants fruit, one does not focus on the fruit itself, after all, but on the conditions in which fruit may manifest. One focuses on sunlight, water, and care. With these things in place, fruit grows naturally. You wish to bear the fruits Brother Abraham bore in his lifetime, yes?"

"And you're saying it's the same?" Jesus asked. "That they grow naturally under the right conditions?"

"Precisely," Master Gotami said. They passed the second landing. "As with figs, so it is with love, joy, peace, patience, and so on. One does not grit their teeth and simply *be* at peace or act with justice in the same way one does not grit their teeth and simply *be* joyful. These things are not goals; they are side-effects of something deeper. External action without internal transformation leads to suffering. Our practice, then, is to clear the soil of our minds so that these qualities may grow naturally from who we most truly are. Our practice is to provide water and sunlight and compost. In this way, these qualities may grow, first the stalk, then the ear, then the fruit."

They climbed past the third floor, and at last reached the fourth, where Master Gotami stepped off the stairs and led them down the open-air corridor. Halfway down, she stopped and motioned to a small room. Jesus stepped inside, cautious. Judas followed close behind. It looked identical to the other cells except that on the back wall was a heavy door with a bolt.

"So, what does that mean for a person?" Jesus asked. "How do you 'clear the soil' and 'provide sunlight' when you're talking about a person's mind?"

"Excellent question, Brother Issa," Master Gotami said, "and it is the very subject which we strive to teach at Metta Valley, starting with what lies beyond this door."

Master Gotami stepped toward the back door, fingers resting on the bolt. "Are you prepared, *samaneras,* for your first lesson?"

"None of that counted as our first lesson?" Jesus asked.

"Consider it a preamble," Master Gotami said. *"This* is why I brought you here. Prepare yourselves."

With that, she slid back the bolt, and the door flew open.

# 29

Cool air and bright light rushed to fill the room, and Judas took a step back in surprise. The back door didn't lead to another room but opened to the outside, onto a precarious ledge high above the ground. Cautiously, Jesus stepped forward and saw a platform running the length of the monastery's back wall. Wild, spacious mountain-scape stretched out before him.

"For your first training," Master Gotami said, "I would like you to engage in a little exercise. Brother Judas."

Judas stood up straight.

"Would you please describe the road you took to arrive at Metta Valley?"

"Yes…" Judas started, "it was difficult. Dangerous. We were isolated for much of the journey, far from civilization, and worried about wild animals."

He looked to Jesus for affirmation, and Jesus nodded.

"Isolated," Master Gotami echoed. "Far from civilization. Very good. Follow me if you would."

Master Gotami stepped through the door and onto the platform. She didn't acknowledge the aging wood groaning under her feet, but it put Jesus on edge. He followed her out, stepping lightly.

Diagonal beams braced the platform from underneath, offering some support, but not nearly enough. It was older than Jesus, certainly—maybe even older than Master Gotami—but even with the obvious danger, it was worth it for the view.

"Judas," Jesus said, "do you see this?"

Judas didn't answer, his eyes locked on the platform.

"Judas?"

"Can't speak," Judas said, carefully testing the old wooden planks. "Too high."

Amused, Jesus extended an arm for Judas to hold for balance, and Judas latched on.

"This way," Master Gotami called. She had already walked the length of the platform and was ascending another set of stairs that led to what Jesus assumed was the roof of the back wall. At least the roof would be firmer—he hoped.

When they reached her, Master Gotami extended an arm, helping him up—not onto the roof, but onto a narrow path carved into the mountain wall, invisible from the ground. It led all the way to the front wall of the monastery, and Jesus willed himself not to look down as he walked. The great fig tree looked more like a shrub from up here.

They walked the length of the path, and as Jesus stepped onto the wide roof of the front wall, he gave a low whistle. A breathtaking, vivid landscape surrounded them in every direction.

"Now, returning to the subject of the road," Master Gotami said. "Brother Issa, if you could kindly tell me what you see from *this* perspective."

Jesus stepped a little closer to the edge, careful not to look down. He stood directly above the elephant doors. He scanned the area until he found the path they'd come in on, and from this vantage point, it looked entirely different. Gone was the winding, claustrophobic road they'd followed, and in its place was a far more generous path. It wove, to be sure, but only to avoid some of the more difficult inclines and obstacles. He could even see roofs in the distance—small villages and farms just off the road. "Villages?" he asked. "We never saw them. Judas, do you see this?"

Judas only managed a grunt of acknowledgment.

"Indeed," Master Gotami said. "And I must ask, how many of these wild animals actually attacked you along the way?"

"One," Jesus said. "A cat snake."

Master Gotami smiled. "I should hardly call that an 'attack,' Brother Issa. It sounds like, in fact, the danger you feared turned out to be no danger at all."

Jesus looked back down at the road, which was so much less menacing from up here.

"This is your first training in tending the mind," Master Gotami explained. "You see, as real as these things may have seemed in the moment, many of the mind's most basic perceptions are, in fact, illusions. In reality, you never saw the road. What you saw was your *perception* of the road, which is quite different, and your reality unfolded accordingly. This is likewise how we approach the world. You do not see the world. You do not see me. You do not see Metta Valley. As strange as it may sound, you do not even see yourself. What you see instead are your own *perceptions* of these things. You see stories offered by the mind to make sense of what is otherwise a neutral and often gracious reality. Left unbalanced, the mind would have us live in an illusory world of our own fearful perceptions, trapped in the stories we would believe about ourselves, others, and our world. It is not trying to deceive us, of course. It is merely trying to keep us safe, but the result is much suffering."

"Suffering?" Jesus asked. "How?"

"Well, consider this," Master Gotami said. "Imagine a traveler comes across a rope in their path. The rope is harmless, naturally, but if they believe the rope to be a snake, they may become afraid and run. They may tell others of the dangers of snakes on the road. They would never know that their path was, in fact, safe, and that all was well. Their view is obscured by perception. The skillful practitioner, by contrast, learns to investigate their perceptions, and if they are incomplete, to let them go. Often what we see as snakes are merely ropes."

Master Gotami began walking mindfully across the planks of the rooftop, and Jesus and Judas followed, watching their step. "Wherever there is *perception*, there is *deception*," Master Gotami said. *"Deception,* in turn, is the cause of much suffering. This is your first lesson, *samaneras*, and the first step on the Noble Path. It is called Right View, and it is a way of seeing beyond perception."

"So that's how we cultivate the soil of the mind?" Jesus asked, eager to understand. "By seeing past perceptions?"

"It is the first step, yes," Master Gotami answered, "though it is more difficult than it may sound. These perceptions are the lifeblood of many nations and traditions. It is their aim to peddle stories that make them feel strong or secure—as with your former rabbi. Such leaders tell stories of who is *pure* and who is *impure*, what is *right* and what is *wrong*, what is *good* and what is *bad*, and they do not respond kindly to those who would challenge them. These stories, however, exist only in the mind. Despite what we believe, our stories are not Reality."

"But that is not what you do?" Jesus asked.

"In Metta Valley, we do not teach belief," Master Gotami explained. "We teach *awareness*. When you are aware of these stories—the ones we tell and the ones imposed by others—only then do you have choices. You can believe such stories or investigate them—live by them or let them go. With awareness, you may acknowledge perceptions as illusions and move beyond them. The more skillfully you can let these stories go, the more fully you can see what remains when they are gone."

"But what remains?" Jesus asked. "With no stories or perceptions, what's left?"

Master Gotami paused at the end of the roof, turning the other direction and facing Jesus and Judas. "Reality," she answered, "un-fragile and spacious. To live in Reality is a different life indeed. It is a life of freedom. We need not fretfully defend Reality as we might defend beliefs. We need not convince others. We need not justify, manipulate, or shame. We need only be aware, investigate, and see. This is Right View, and from it, Right Action will naturally follow. Reality is the solid ground on which we must learn to walk if we are to thrive. It is the only firm foundation worthy of trust. There, we see ropes where there were once snakes."

Master Gotami began walking in the other direction, past Jesus and Judas. They followed carefully. "Consider the elephant," she taught. "Do you know how it is trained?"

"Large sticks?" Jesus ventured, mindful of his footing.

Master Gotami smiled. "A reasonable guess," she said, "but incorrect."

"Rope," Judas said, taking care not to look down.

"Correct, Brother Judas," Master Gotami said. "While an elephant is still young, a rope is placed around her neck, and the other end is staked to the ground. The young elephant may strain and pull against the rope, but to her, it is unbreakable. Now, as she grows, her trainers will continue to use this same rope to tether her and lead her around as they see fit. Of course, after some time, she could easily snap the rope and be free, yet she does not. Why?"

"Because she believes a story," Jesus answered, realization dawning. "She believes a story that she's not strong enough."

"Precisely," Master Gotami said. "She is ensnared, not by rope, but by perception. Her freedom is only a matter of letting go of this perception. In truth, she is already free. She simply doesn't know it yet. So it is with each of us. The eye is the lamp of the mind. If the eye is covered over by stories and perceptions, then the mind will be clouded and full of darkness. If the eye is clear, then the mind will be full of light."

"So, we are like trained elephants?" Jesus said. "Caught in stories, blind to truth?"

"Precisely," Master Gotami said. "Let us return to the image of the fruit tree. If truth is a tree growing in the soil of our minds, then stories and perceptions are weeds—choking its roots and stealing its light. They are rocks, impeding the tree's growth. The seeds of justice, kindness, and humility are stifled and not allowed to grow. Delusions swoop down like birds and try to snatch the seeds away."

Jesus nodded. "I see what you mean."

Master Gotami had reached the other end of the roof, and again, she paused. "*Samaneras*, it comes to this," she said. "You have been handed stories about yourself and about this world which are, to be frank, simply false. You have been peddled perceptions about who you are and what you can do which do not hold up to investigation. Your teachers imposed these stories. Your rulers frightened you into believing them. Your families gave them to you as an inheritance. Each story is a rope tied around your mind. This, however, is our work at Metta Valley. Here, we seek to help one another see the Reality beneath and beyond all illusions. In this way, we work to uproot suffering and embody the well-being that this world so needs. We no longer see this world as something to be feared. We no longer see ourselves as less than we are. You wish to be free and to free others, Brother Issa? This is the Way. By this practice, we will know the truth, and the truth will set you free."

"And that's what Abraham did?" Jesus asked. "He attained... what did you call it? Right View?"

"Ah," Master Gotami warned. "Now, what have we said about attainment and spiritual ladders? You must remember Right View is not a matter of attainment. It is a matter of letting go and recognizing it is already there—as the elephant recognizes it is already free. Our salvation is not found in grasping at new perceptions, but in relinquishing false ones. This is a process. A journey. With mindfulness, concentration, and diligence, one's view becomes clearer. From Right View grows Right Thinking, and from Right Thinking grows Right Speech, Right Action, and Right Vocation. Seek first Right View and live accordingly, and all these things shall be added to you. *This* is the Noble Path we walk at Metta Valley, and if you wish to bear the fruits of justice, mercy, and humility, then this is the Way, the truth, and the life you must live. And yes," she smiled, "Brother Abraham walked this Way with skill."

"Well, that *sounds* simple enough," Jesus said. He could see how Abraham had lived this way—inspecting stories and perceptions and living above them rather than caught in them. Abraham hadn't bought into his teacher's stories about what should count as righteous, and he hadn't bought into Deva's story that profits were more important than justice. He also hadn't bought into Jesus's story of hopelessness and self-judgment, and the fruit of his practice had been powerful.

"Simple enough to learn, yes," Master Gotami said, "but in practice, far more difficult. One is not healed by the word 'medicine.' As I said, the nations and institutions of our time are built on stories—so too is our sense of self—and we do not take kindly to these stories being questioned. We do not like letting go of who we think we are, even if our self-perception has caused us suffering. You shall soon see."

"And these stories," Jesus said, "you called them the root of suffering?"

"Quite," Master Gotami said. "Consider this, Brother Issa. Why does your rabbi cause such pain to your community? Why did Deva act as he did toward his own father? Why does the Emperor of Rome seek to conquer the world? The soldiers who attacked your mother—what possessed them to act the way they did?"

Jesus hesitated. "Stories," he said. "They were caught in stories."

"Very good," Master Gotami said. "They were caught in perceptions from which they could not escape. This is the cause of every form of suffering. We must learn to see these perceptions clearly if we are to fight and relieve suffering—that of ourselves and others. The antidote, Brother Issa, is truth."

A low rumble of thunder echoed across the valley, and Master Gotami paused. "Come," she said. "We must return to the ground."

Judas, who had turned a pale shade of green, sighed in relief, and Master Gotami started to lead them back to the stone path.

"There's something else that's bothering me," Jesus said.

"Yes?" Master Gotami asked.

"What does any of this have to do with God? Abraham talked about finding the 'Living God' here, but you're talking about perceptions and illusion."

"Ah," Master Gotami said. "A profound question. I think you'll find that the problem with many traditions is that they approach 'God' as something to be defined and believed in. 'God,' then, becomes a distant ruler in the sky, looking down over creation. This, however, is not our Way. If Brother Abraham were here, I imagine he would say 'God' may not be a being, per se, but more of a title."

"A title?" Jesus asked.

"Correct," Master Gotami said, climbing down onto the wooden platform. "Specifically, a title for that which is Ultimate or Absolute—the truest and most powerful entity in one's life. A 'God' is that to which we sacrifice and for which we live. Many fall into the trap of making their 'God' far too small. In truth, however, one might argue that any 'God' which can be so easily defined is not 'God' at all, but merely a story—a perception, wrapped in divine clothing."

*...much of what passes for 'God' in this world is not 'God' at all,* Jesus remembered Abraham saying. *It is nothing more than fear and fragile pride. Build it a temple, hide it behind a veil... that's all it is. It is the hubris of humankind, gilded in gold.*

"I would encourage you," Master Gotami continued, "not to worry about such things until you are further along in your practice. Do not reduce 'God' to merely a story. This, I believe, is the true spirit behind your law's prohibition of idols and graven images. If you wish to practice like Brother Abraham, then allow 'God' to be revealed in time."

Master Gotami reached the door and stepped through, waiting for Jesus and Judas. Jesus stepped inside, relieved by the feeling of solid wood beneath his feet. Judas came in next, and he leaned against the wall for support. When they were all safely inside, Master Gotami swung the door closed, pushing the heavy bolt back into place. "I am sensing, Brother Judas, that you are not fond of heights?" she asked.

"That..." Judas answered, catching his breath, "is an accurate perception."

"Well then," Master Gotami said, smiling, "let us get you back to solid earth."

———

AFTER A TREK BACK down the spiral stairs, they found themselves once again in the courtyard—the sweet smell of spikenard surrounding them. Brother Moggallana waited at the foot of the stairs. "Good first lesson?" he asked, rocking on his heels. "No one died this time, I presume?"

"This time?" Judas echoed, wary.

"Brother Moggallana is fond of jokes," Master Gotami said, taking her place next to him, "even if the only one they amuse is himself."

Moggallana chuckled.

"The first training is complete," Master Gotami said. "Brothers Issa and Judas prove willing and perceptive students. They have been instructed in Right View and walking meditation. I now hand them over to you for their next training."

"Forgive me," Jesus said, "but I don't think you mentioned walking meditation."

"No?" Master Gotami said. "My, my. I apologize. In that case, consider this. There are many ways to walk, Brother Issa. One might walk quickly, as if preoccupied with a destination. One might stroll along, entirely lost in thought. Or should one choose, one might walk slowly and mindfully, immersed in each step, as though one were on an unsteady platform at a great height. There you have it. Walking meditation."

Jesus let out a short laugh—then flinched as a deep toll echoed through the air. Up on the platform, a resident pulled back the great plank of wood suspended by the bell, letting it go three times for three steady tolls. Master Gotami and Moggallana paused to breathe deeply with each toll.

"I shall practice midday meditation in the receiving room," Master Gotami informed them when the last toll had faded. "Friends, thank you, and I wish you a good day."

She pressed her palms together, and they all returned the gesture, then she walked off toward the front wall.

"She has a pure heart," Moggallana said. "The Dharma shines through her, free from obstruction. We are fortunate to call her teacher."

"That's easy to say from the ground," Judas muttered.

Moggallana either didn't hear or ignored him. "Let us proceed," he invited. "This way, to the meditation hall."

"Is it time for our next training already?" Jesus asked.

"Basic sitting," the old monk said. "Right this way."

"Sitting?" Jesus asked, frowning. "And you think we need training for that?"

In front of them, Moggallana chuckled. "I suppose we shall soon see, won't we?"

# 30

By the time they reached the meditation hall, heavy raindrops pounded the ground around them. Still, Moggallana instructed them to stop under a small overhang just outside the door. "It is customary to pause and breathe mindfully," he said, his voice rising above the rain. "One does not enter the hall carelessly."

Obediently, Jesus and Judas waited, trying to avoid the rain, until they had taken a breath deep enough to meet the old monk's standards. "Now," he said, "We shall go in and you can find a place to sit. Then, I shall give a word of basic instruction on the nature of sitting meditation. When I am finished, you yourselves will try it. Afterward, we shall talk about your experience. Doubtless, we will have some... knots to work through."

"Knots?" Jesus asked. "We're only sitting."

Again, Brother Moggallana laughed. "Please," he said, "after you." He gestured towards the door of the meditation hall, and after a wary glance at one another, Jesus and Judas entered.

As Jesus stepped over the threshold, silence pressed in around him. The rain became distant and muted. Tranquility pervaded, and it felt like even the dust was still with reverence. It was as though he had stepped into a world beneath sound and beyond time.

Brother Moggallana gestured to two empty places among those already seated, and Jesus and Judas took cushions from a pile by the door and moved carefully to their places, trying not to disturb the other meditators.

Narrow windows were spaced evenly across the front and back of the room, and between each window were simple frescoes depicting scenes Jesus didn't recognize. Candleholders sprouted from the walls. Moggallana took his seat next to a platform supporting a life-sized statue of the Buddha—dazzling white, in full lotus. All around the figure, candles burned on golden stands. Someone had arranged flowers at his feet, and there was a half-smile on his face, as though delighted by the scene before him.

To the Buddha's right was a slightly lower platform, supporting Moggallana's cushion and a large bronze bowl. To his left was a tall set of shelves, full of what appeared to be bound clusters of small, rectangular strips of something like palm leaves. Jesus strained to see, and even from halfway across the room, he could make out writing. His heart leaped as he realized it was some sort of scroll. The shelves were full of rows and rows of scrolls.

"My friends," Moggallana addressed the room. "Many days, we practice our meditation in silence, but this day will be special. In the spirit of hospitality toward our newest practitioners, let us begin with a word of instruction to guide our awareness."

Jesus tore his attention from the scrolls, trying to listen carefully.

"Now," the old monk said, "can someone tell us why we sit?"

A resident near the front pressed her palms together, and Moggallana nodded toward her.

"Brother Moggallana," she said, "we sit to settle our minds. We sit so that we do not become caught in thoughts, feelings, and perceptions. We sit to clarify our view so that we might clarify our thinking, speech, and actions."

"Very good," Moggallana said, smiling.

Jesus felt a small stab of resentment. The resident's words were helpful, but they also made him feel inferior—behind, somehow. He wished they were receiving this training in private.

"The purpose of our sitting meditation is twofold," Moggallana said. "First, it is to settle our minds. The mind, my friends, is a basin of water, filled with the sediment of thought and feeling—of perception and story and judgment. We sit in order that the mind might become still, for it is only when we become still that the sediment might settle and the water might become clear."

Jesus nodded, following so far.

"Second," Moggallana continued, "we learn to be aware, and to let go. Until we learn to recognize and let go of our thoughts, feelings, and perceptions—to *recognize* rather than *identify* with them—then they will drive our actions like frightened oxen driving a cart."

There was some laughter from the residents, but Jesus had a hard time being amused. The position he sat in was already growing uncomfortable.

"Much of our lives," Moggallana went on, "we believe we *are* our thoughts, feelings, and perceptions, but this is not our true nature. Our *true* nature stands above these things, watching them pass. Our *true* nature is the watcher—the presence beyond thoughts and feelings as they rise and fall. We can take refuge in this—our true nature—for it is the Buddha Spirit within. Questions?"

No one spoke, so Moggallana nodded and reached into the bowl at his side and picked up a small wooden baton. "Now, as I invite the sound of the bell, I likewise invite you to breathe deeply. Then I shall lead us in the full awareness of our breathing. Ready? Let us begin."

He sounded the bell, and at first, Jesus wasn't sure what to do. Everyone straightened and closed their eyes, so he did the same—peeking to see the others as the bell faded. For a moment, there was only silence, then Moggallana spoke.

"Breathing in," he led, "know you are breathing in... breathing out, know you are breathing out..."

Jesus understood and tried to obey—watching his breath move in and out. He shifted slightly to ease the discomfort in his lower back. The cushion was becoming less comfortable by the second.

"Breathing in," Moggallana repeated, "I know I am breathing in... breathing out, I know I am breathing out..."

Jesus caught himself and refocused, remembering what Moggallana had taught. He imagined his mind as a basin of water. The feelings of discomfort swirled in his mind, and he settled his attention on his breath, watching the swirling slow down. His body relaxed. This made sense alongside what Master Gotami taught them that morning—about Right View and how it led to Right Action. If they sat, observing their thoughts and feelings, then perceptions and stories would—

"Breathing in," Moggallana's voice broke in again, "I know I am breathing in... breathing out, I know I am breathing out..."

Jesus shook his head slightly, realizing he'd been distracted yet again. This was supposed to be simple. Why was he having such a hard time?

Again, he settled his attention on his breath and committed to simply watching it as it rose and fell. It wasn't supposed to be difficult, yet it was so foreign to him. He'd never tried simply to watch his thoughts without identifying with them before, and even in the long stretches he'd spent alone as a child, it wasn't like this. He remembered once sitting on his mat when he'd been little, his mother hanging herbs on their wall to dry—

"Breathing in..." Moggallana started again, and Jesus inwardly kicked himself.

He could do this. He furrowed his brow, forcing his attention to follow the in and out of his breathing. He would not get distracted. He would not get lost in thought. He started to sweat from the effort.

"Breathing in, I know I am breathing in..."

As Jesus tried to focus, though, the image of his mother wouldn't leave him. In fact, the more he tried to push it away, the more vivid it grew. The scent of the herbs. The sound of her voice, brittle with rejection. *Do what you will, but do not expect my blessing. Go forth and be 'son of no one,' as you've always wanted.*

He shook his head, trying to shake off the memory.

"Breathing in..."

Jesus squirmed on his cushion. Suddenly, he wanted only to get up and go examine one of the new scrolls. He wanted to talk to Judas. He wanted to find Master Gotami and ask about their next lesson. Anything but continue to sit here with these memories of how he'd left his mother alone and vulnerable.

*You must honor your father and mother,* he heard the rabbi's voice—a warning he'd given early in their lessons. It had made him feel ashamed on two fronts. He had a bad habit of disobeying his mother, and he had no clue what it meant to honor his father. How could he honor someone whose mere memory made his mother break down into tears?

*This is what God has commanded you. Have you honored your mother, young Yeshua? Have you been obedient?*

"...I know I am breathing in..."

Jesus gritted his teeth and bore down. *It is because of your father, young Yeshua,* the rabbi's voice said. *Because of your father, you will never belong, despite your childish attempts to make up for what you are.*

"Breathing out, I know I am breathing out..."

*So what do you do? You search in vain for someone to please or someone to fight—all to try to prove to yourself that you're not what you are—that you're good and righteous. But you know what you are, don't you? Son of Mary... Son of Pantera...*

Jesus breathed deeply. He wanted to start over—to shake off the thoughts that swirled in his mind more violently than they had when he began. He was doing so poorly at this. He wondered what the rabbi would say if he could see him now. *Take care you are not ensnared by the gods and practices of foreign lands,* he'd warn. *You shall not worship God using their ways...*

Then again, the rabbi would probably also criticize the fact that Jesus couldn't even blaspheme correctly. He was trying to practice the Way of these 'dogs and Gentiles,' and he couldn't even manage that correctly. *You miss the mark in every conceivable way, young Yeshua,* he could hear the rabbi say. *It is only a matter of time before these dogs and*

*Gentiles realize, too. They will cast you out, just as I did. You fool yourself if you think you belong here.*

He tried to push the thought away—to come back to his breath—but he couldn't. The voices only grew louder and the memories more vivid as he tried to will them away. His heart pounded, and he felt sweat bead on his forehead. His hands balled into fists.

"Breathing in..."

*Where can you go from my spirit? Where can you flee from my presence?*

"I know I am breathing in..."

*If you go up to the heavens, I am there. If you make your bed in the depths, I am there.*

"Breathing out..."

*If you rise on the wings of the dawn, if you settle on the far side of the sea, even there my hand will guide you, my right hand will hold you fast.*

"...I know I am breathing out..."

It was all too much.

Jesus stood, keeping his gaze low as he made his way to the door. Judas looked up, surprised. "Are you all right?" he whispered, but Jesus couldn't answer. Instead, he tried not to think about the dozens of eyes following him as he hurried from the meditation hall into the courtyard. He didn't say anything to Moggallana. He just left, hardly noticing the rain.

# 31

BY THE TIME THE meditation ended, Jesus was sitting on a smooth rock by the stream, rolling the Buddha stone around in his palm. For twenty minutes, he'd been letting the scent of spikenard and the murmur of the water settle him. The rain had stopped, but the air still felt heavy.

It was remarkable how much could change in a day. The night before, he'd been eager to begin. That morning, he'd hung onto Master Gotami's every word. Now, he was considering reclaiming his things and leaving. The thought was humbling. Maybe he'd been wrong. Maybe he should've refused Abraham's request. Maybe he didn't belong here.

*You don't,* the rabbi's voice whispered.

Behind him, residents filed out of the meditation hall. He felt their gazes, judging him. He put the stone away as Judas approached.

"Are you all right?" Judas asked, sitting next to him.

"I'm fine," Jesus muttered.

"Look," Judas said, "don't be too hard on yourself. Meditation can be difficult. I can only do it because my father brought us up with it."

"Is that so?" Jesus asked. "Tell me, have you ever seen it drive someone out of a room like that?"

"Well... no," Judas admitted. "But I have heard that some start crying?"

Jesus scoffed. Perhaps Master Gotami would let him skip meditation and focus only on the lessons. He said as much to Judas, and Judas shrugged, trying to look supportive. "You could always ask," he said.

"Indeed, you could," another voice came from behind them, "but I doubt she would agree."

Moggallana waited, his hands clasped in front of him.

"Brother Moggallana," Jesus said, standing. "I was only—"

"No need to explain," Moggallana interrupted gently. "It is understandable. If we are not honest about our troubles, then they become impediments to our practice. Ill content, left unacknowledged, will grow into a demon all its own. Let's take a walk, shall we? Brother Judas, would you excuse us?"

"Of course," Judas said. He gave Jesus an encouraging look, then hurried away.

Moggallana led Jesus across the courtyard, unhurried. "Now," he said, "would you like to talk about what happened?"

"No," Jesus said.

Moggallana laughed, unfazed. "I like you," he said. "You have a good humor about you. Humor is not nearly common enough within these walls. Let me rephrase my request. You clearly do *not* want to talk about what happened. Would you be willing to, all the same?"

Jesus sighed. "I'm not sure what happened. I understand what you're saying about the sediment and the water, but that felt like wallowing in the mud."

"Your thoughts remained turbulent?" Moggallana asked.

"Yes."

"Your body was uncomfortable?"

"Like I was trapped in a room full of snakes."

"Thoughts arose you would rather avoid or overcome?"

Jesus stopped and looked at Moggallana. "Is that normal?"

"Oh, quite," Moggallana answered. "This is simply the nature of the practice. However, it does not differ from physical exertion. What exercise is not difficult for a novice who has only begun?"

"Well, I'm not even a novice, am I?" Jesus said. "I'm an aspirant."

"All the more," Moggallana said. "It grows easier as you grow stronger. It is like cultivating a seed. Given the right conditions, it will grow with time. Your seed is still a sprout, fragile and growing."

Jesus shook his head. He'd had his share of plant metaphors for the day. "Listen," he said. "I'm just wondering if it's necessary. I mean, everything Master Gotami taught about stories and perceptions—that makes sense. Is it not enough just to learn?"

Moggallana nodded thoughtfully. "You are not the first to ask this question, and you will not be the last. It is one common pitfall of the Way. Perhaps a parable would help."

"I don't think that's—"

"Once," Moggallana began, "there was a man who built a house on sand. It was a lovely house, to be sure, but when storms came and wind battered its sides, the house crumbled at once. There was a second man, however, who built his house upon rock. When the storms came, the wind battering its sides and the rain pouring down its roof, this man's house remained. Why? Because a house is only as strong as its foundation, Brother Issa! We can offer you wisdom, but unless your wisdom is built on a foundation of *practice* and *experience*, then your ideas, however admirable, will crumble at the first sign of suffering. You must be a *practitioner* of the Way, Brother Issa, not a hearer only."

"And by practice," Jesus said, "you mean meditation?"

They had arrived near the corner of the courtyard, close to one of the wooden bridges arching over the stream. Moggallana sat on a bench, gesturing for Jesus to sit beside him.

"There are other forms of practice," Moggallana admitted. "Living in community is a practice. Being honest about one's thoughts and feelings is a practice. Studying, fasting, working, service, doing what one loves... many are the practices that nourish the seeds of the Buddha Spirit within, helping it to grow strong and resilient. However, if you wish to follow our Way, as Brother Abraham did, then meditation *must* be at the heart of your practice. There are many reasons for this, as you will soon learn, but suffice it to say that without meditation, we will fall prey to any passing thought and feeling. We fall prey to the stories that others thrust upon us because we lack the skill of seeing them and letting them go. With meditation, there is awareness, and with awareness, there is freedom—freedom to choose which stories to indulge and which to investigate. This practice is crucial."

"And without practice—" Jesus started.

"Vanity!" Moggallana finished. "We leave the soil of the mind unattended while we pile things on the surface. Weeds grow rampant. The result is a preoccupation with hollow, external expressions of piety and certitude. Such people follow rules and protect tradition, but the state of their minds goes untouched. Perhaps you know the type?"

Jesus very much knew the type. "I do," he said, "but what am I supposed to do? I mean, *that*—" he gestured toward the meditation hall, "that was torture. Am I supposed to just sit and hope it gets better?"

"Not at all!" Moggallana assured him. "It is a skill we must build with intention, patience, and self-compassion. At the risk of too many parables, have you heard the story of the Buddha and Mara?"

"Mara..." Jesus repeated, frowning. He recognized the name from the engraving outside, but also knew he'd heard it elsewhere—where?

"According to legend," Moggallana explained, "Mara is the tempter of all humanity. He is the accuser, whose voice whispers into the ear of every person who draws breath. His is not a fantasy magic, but the magic of stories and perceptions—of judgments and distraction. He tells us false stories, you see, about who we are—building us up and tearing us down from within. He tells stories about what is possible and what we should fear—of who is worthy of love and who is an enemy. Mara is the master of all delusion, greed, and hatred—the enemy of Right View."

Jesus wanted to make a joke, but suddenly, it hit him where he'd heard the name before. "Abraham said something about Mara," Jesus said, "when I first met him."

*Mara is the name they give to the voice always speaking in your head,* Abraham had told him, *the voice always urging you to judge or reject or pursue—the one making promises it can never seem to fulfill. You're familiar with this voice, I assume?*

"I am sure he did," Moggallana said. "Mara sounds different to everyone, and Brother Abraham certainly had his own struggle with the beast. It is said that on the night of the Buddha's awakening, as the Buddha sat in meditation beneath the Bodhi Tree, Mara appeared to him. As the Buddha tried to concentrate, Mara made him promises of great wealth if only the Buddha would renounce his path and return to a normal life. When he didn't listen, Mara whispered threats about what would happen if he continued. When he didn't listen again, Mara attacked the Buddha's worth—leading the Buddha to question who he was to think he could pursue such wisdom. When the Buddha tried to argue with Mara, Mara would only argue right back. When the Buddha tried to ignore him, he only spoke louder. When the Buddha was tempted to believe Mara, then Mara's lies only gained power."

"So, what did he do?" Jesus asked.

"He realized what was not working," Moggallana explained with a smile. "This was the Buddha's strength, you see. He was diligent in testing and re-testing his practice until he found what brought him to the truth. So, he ceased arguing with Mara. He ceased his attempts to ignore Mara. He ceased believing Mara's stories. Instead, trying a new method, he invited Mara to stay."

"To stay?" Jesus asked, surprised. He had expected some divine clash, like the fiery battle between Elijah and the priests of Jezebel.

"He invited Mara to stay," Moggallana repeated, nodding, "and noted Mara's words with neither aversion nor attachment. He did not fight Mara's stories, you see, nor did he cling to or judge them. He merely observed Mara's storytelling, and in response he said, 'I see you, Mara. I hear you, Mara.'"

"And that worked?" Jesus asked, disbelieving.

"Without the energy of grasping or pushing away," Moggallana explained, "Mara had nothing to grab onto. He told his stories until he would tire himself out, then Mara would simply go on his way. This is how it worked *most* of the time. Other times, when Mara was particularly insistent, the Buddha would have to listen more carefully, becoming curious about the source of Mara's ferocity. The Buddha would become curious as one would become curious about a crying infant—discerning what it needed to help it calm. With enough mindful curiosity, Mara would reveal the source of his trouble, then become tranquil and leave the Buddha alone."

"So that's the trick?" Jesus asked. "To say, 'I see you, Mara, I hear you, Mara?'"

"It is a *practice,*" Moggallana corrected, "not a trick. We offer no magical solutions here, Brother Issa. That is the practice, however, both in meditation and in life. What happens in one is a preparation for acting skillfully in the other. Having learned this lesson, the Buddha saw beyond perceptions and into Reality. He saw the truth beyond all stories. He achieved enlightenment and salvation from all suffering. That night, he became 'The Awakened One'—the one who is free and who offers others a path to freedom. This is what we practice to become."

Jesus rubbed his temples, overwhelmed. "You know, if every day is this difficult, you should consider waiting until after sunrise to ring that bell."

Moggallana laughed and patted Jesus on the back. "Take solace in knowing that what follows is primarily a repetition of this same lesson," he said. "It is a spiral leading deeper into understanding, not a ladder. Do not be discouraged. Skill grows with practice. Keep seeking, and you will find. Keep knocking, and the door shall be opened. The Buddha Spirit is available to all who ask with diligence. It is already within you, as a seed waiting to be watered."

Jesus didn't answer. The weight of it all still pressed in on him.

"You're considering leaving, aren't you?" Moggallana asked after a moment.

Jesus looked at him, surprised. Was he that easy to read?

"The choice is yours, of course," Moggallana said solemnly. "There is no shame either way. However, I see a spark of wisdom in you, Brother Issa, and I do encourage you to stay. You show great promise. I imagine Brother Abraham saw it, too."

Jesus only stared at his feet. He wasn't sure what to say.

"That is all I will say on the matter," Moggallana said, standing and stretching. "For now, let me only say thank you, Brother Issa, for your practice and your willingness to fail so boldly."

"Anytime," Jesus answered, not meeting the old monk's eye.

"Have you given any thought to what you wish to do now?" Moggallana asked. "You have free time for the next hour. You may spend it however you see fit."

Jesus thought seriously about going back to his cell—to sleep, or to leave. Just as he was about to say that, though, he remembered something else. "Those scrolls," he said. "In the meditation hall. Do residents have access to them?"

"Scrolls?" Moggallana asked, confused.

"The written teachings," Jesus clarified. His Magadhi Prakrit was much improved, but he still struggled sometimes with words like this. "Those... bundles of leaves."

"Ah," Moggallana said, suddenly understanding. "The *talapatra.*"

"Right," Jesus said. "Whatever they're called, can residents read them?"

Moggallana smiled. "Of course," he said. "Right this way."

# 32

SOON ENOUGH, THEIR SECOND lesson with Master Gotami was upon them. This time, she'd sent word with Upali to meet her below the great fig tree, and as Jesus descended the stairs with Judas, he felt tense. He was still eager to learn, but that day in the meditation hall had left him shaken. Gone was the confidence he'd felt that first morning on the roof, and in its place was a haunting sense that Abraham had made a mistake sending him here. He worried he lacked something essential to succeed in a place like Metta Valley.

Today was also the last day of their trial week, and some part of Jesus fully expected Master Gotami or Moggallana to take him aside and tell him that he didn't belong—that they couldn't teach him after all. There was something crucial missing, and try as he might to find it, it evaded his grasp.

He'd gotten used to the routine. That part was simple enough. In the mornings, he'd wake with the bell (which seemed earlier every day), practice walking meditation (which was easier than sitting meditation, if only just), eat his meager breakfast (which didn't hold a candle to Abraham's cooking), and perform his morning chores (which meant doing battle with mustard weeds in the garden). In the afternoons, he'd eat lunch *(still* nothing compared to Abraham's food), perform his afternoon chores (mustard weeds became his mortal enemy), and then, with the time he had left, he'd break away to the meditation hall to explore his newfound scriptures. He pored over the palm leaves, reading alone, making sense of the teachings as best he could. They differed from the scriptures he was used to. These were narrower in scope and more explicit in purpose. There were no grand epics of exiles moving through the wilderness—no sermons from prophets crying out for justice. Instead, they consisted mostly of lectures and parables, with the occasional myth or history. On the whole, they struck him as the experience-based, time-tested words of teachers who sought to address the suffering of the world. Jesus quickly realized where Master Gotami, Moggallana, and Abraham picked up their inclination toward illustrations and parables.

Some afternoons, other residents would try to study alongside Jesus, which always put him on edge. He was quick to grow irritable when someone offered him help or tried to engage him about a teaching. Eventually, Moggallana had seen fit to intervene. "We have *discussions* here," the old monk said one day after hearing Jesus's tone. "There is no need to do battle!"

Still, Jesus couldn't help it. The truth was, he suspected his fellow residents were watching him. Sizing him up. Whispering about him behind his back and finding him lacking. With the exception of Judas and his teachers, Jesus felt alone.

Judas, meanwhile, didn't share these struggles. He followed the schedule without complaint and even volunteered for extra chores—something that baffled Jesus until he saw the pattern. Judas always volunteered to deliver surplus supplies to nearby villages, a task remarkably similar to something his father used to do back at the vineyard. "You know," Jesus tried to broach the subject one afternoon, "they won't hold it against you if you ask to rotate chores now and then."

"I don't mind," Judas had answered.

"I'm sure, but—"

"Really," Judas had insisted, an edge in his voice. "This is where I want to be."

Jesus let it go. He knew pushing further would only make Judas go quiet, tense, or change the subject. After several unsuccessful attempts at engaging, Jesus had learned it was best to steer clear.

"Are you all right?" Judas asked as they walked together to meet Master Gotami. "You're taking the stairs two at a time."

Jesus caught himself, slowing his pace. "Didn't notice," he muttered.

"Is something on your mind?"

Jesus hesitated. How could he explain this sense that he didn't belong? How could he say he was afraid this private lesson would end with Master Gotami telling him he had no place, or that he was afraid he'd soon be back on the road, wandering the wilderness?

*The wise set their face toward wisdom,* he heard his Rabbi's voice warn. *The eyes of the fool are always on the horizon.*

He tried to push the voice away. "No," he said finally, resuming his descent. "I'm fine."

They found Master Gotami waiting patiently beneath the fig tree in the center of the courtyard. *"Samaneras,"* she greeted warmly, pressing her palms together. "Please sit."

Jesus and Judas returned the gesture and obediently took their seats. Again, Judas folded himself into the lotus pose with ease. Again, Jesus struggled.

"I have observed your diligence," Master Gotami said. "I know these early days can be challenging. I am pleased by your progress."

"Of course," Jesus muttered, though he wasn't sure if he believed her.

"Shall we continue from where we left off?" she asked.

Judas sat straighter. "On the roof?"

Master Gotami smiled. "I did not mean quite so literally, Brother Judas. Last week, we discussed Right View—the practice of seeing beyond the stories and perceptions that blind us. The stories we believe about the world and ourselves can be driven by fear and greed and often lead us astray. We must learn to engage in what the Greeks refer to as *metanoia*—going above the mind."

"You know Greek?" Jesus asked, impressed.

"I travel, Brother Issa," Master Gotami said simply. "To learn the Way is a lifelong task only deepened by perspective. Now, to engage in this work of seeing beyond stories, it is helpful to note that there are only a handful of stories which most commonly blind us. Two, in fact, which are most difficult. We each have our own unique perceptions, of course, but there are two we all seem to share in common. In becoming aware of these stories, we can learn to see beyond them and, therefore, set ourselves free. Are you prepared to receive this training?"

"We are," Jesus and Judas both answered, and out of his periphery, Jesus noticed a few other residents coming to sit behind them to hear Master Gotami. He felt a twinge of annoyance. Their private lesson wouldn't be so private after all.

"Now, *bhikkhus*," Master Gotami said, "can anyone name the first great illusion?"

"Yes, Master Gotami," said a voice behind Jesus—a young monk seated in full lotus. "The first is the story of permanence. In our fear of change, the mind often imagines things as fixed and unchanging. In Reality, however, nothing is permanent. Everything changes. Always."

"Very good," Master Gotami nodded, and Jesus checked his impulse to say something sharp.

"Let us begin with permanence," Master Gotami said. "Dear ones, our minds would reduce an ungraspable, ever-changing Reality to something changeless and stagnant. We name objects as if they were fixed: 'stream,' 'tree,' 'rock,' 'Master Gotami'…"

A few of the residents laughed softly.

"And while these ideas make it easier for our minds to pin objects down—to make judgments and predict a future—we must remember that permanence is merely an illusion. In Reality, there are no permanent entities."

Already, Jesus was lost. Master Gotami must've seen it on his face.

"Allow me to give an example," she said. "One might call the water moving through the center of our monastery a 'stream,' correct? But what is a 'stream,' really? Is it ever truly the same from one moment to the next? Can one ever step into the same 'stream' twice? How, then, can we call it a fixed or permanent entity? It is *im*permanent."

Jesus followed her gaze to the stream twisting and shimmering through the courtyard, its surface never still. He understood, but he wasn't sure what good it did to give up a story of permanence.

"A 'stream' is not fixed," Master Gotami went on, "but *im*permanent. It is ever-changing, ever new, and here is why that matters a great deal: What is true of streams is true of all things. For instance, you may consider *yourself* a fixed entity, but you, too, are a stream. What is a human if not an ever-changing stream of thoughts, feelings, and perceptions? Your very body changes, albeit very slowly, in every moment. Who you were last year is no more. Who you will be next year is yet to be seen. You, *bhikkhus, are* change."

This reminded Jesus of what Abraham had said when he knew he was dying. *Clouds come together, they come apart... Life doesn't end. It just changes. It's all change.* This must've been why Abraham hadn't been afraid of death—one of the reasons, anyway. He'd been dying and being re-born in every moment for his entire life.

Master Gotami held up her own hand as she continued.

"I am not a 'self,'" she observed, "but a *process*—a pattern—a whirlpool in the flowing stream of the cosmos. In the same way, everything bears this nature of impermanence. Streams, mountains, nations, feelings... they all rise, change, and fall. We may impose a story of permanence, but this story is merely an illusion. Everyone and everything is capable of change, for good or ill. Even the greatest kingdom is impermanent, as mighty as it seems. We can be part of this process if we so choose, shaping the direction of this change. There is something empowering about this, is there not? All is in flux. Always."

At this, Jesus's mind immediately went to Rome or the Temple—the two most solid and unchanging entities he'd ever known. Suddenly, they didn't seem so permanent and unyielding. Master Gotami was right. That *was* an empowering thought.

"Now," Master Gotami continued, "can someone tell us the second most common false story we all so often believe?"

There was a moment of silence, then another resident spoke up behind them. "Yes, Master Gotami," she said. "The second is the story of separation. The mind makes distinctions and judgments. In Reality, however, every form is composed of the same basic elements. We are one."

"Very good," Master Gotami said, and again Jesus tried to hide his annoyance.

"Dear ones, in the same way our minds create stories of permanence, they also create stories of *separation*. As we said earlier, the mind would have us believe that there is 'a stream,' 'a tree,' 'a rock,' and 'a Master Gotami,' and that each has a separate self. However, this too is an illusion. Consider for a moment what we commonly call a 'Bodhi tree.'"

She gestured up at the fig tree, its aerial roots reaching skyward.

"We call this a 'tree,' yes? But I ask you, what is a 'tree,' really? When you look at it deeply, is it not formed entirely from *non*-tree elements? For instance, what is a tree but water absorbed through its roots? What is it but soil from which nutriments are drawn? What is it but the sunlight which coaxes its leaves into growth? If we look deeply enough, we can even see the lineage of this tree's ancestors—the seed from which it sprouted and the intention of those who planted it so long ago. Each of these non-tree elements comes together to create this formation we simply call 'tree.' But at what point, I ask you, does the mind take these non-tree elements and flatten them into one manageable and fixed idea? An idea to which we give the word 'tree?'"

Master Gotami looked back out at the group. "Now, to further complicate matters," she said, "what are each of *us* but these same elements? Do we not also consist of water, soil, heat, air, and intention? Are we not also moving and changing like a stream? What is a 'self' but a conglomeration of *non*-self elements? Where, then, lies the 'self' at all?"

Again, Jesus was having a difficult time following.

"If I might offer another illustration," Master Gotami continued, "it may help to consider the nature of waves on the ocean. Waves rise, they fall, and they crash into the shore. A wave may look at other waves and say, 'I am separate from these waves and I am permanent,' but is this true? No. This is an illusion. Through the eyes of Right View, we see every wave is truly a temporary, ever-changing manifestation of the one, great ocean. The same is true of you and me. I am a wave. You are a wave. This tree is a wave. *Suchness* is the ocean. We are temporary, ever-changing manifestations of the one, great *suchness*, transcending the cycle of birth and death. In the light of this awareness, all stories of prejudice, discrimination, or judgment lose their power."

Suddenly, something about this struck Jesus as familiar. He'd heard this before. Where?

"It is the habit of the mind to take *one* and divide it into *two,*" Master Gotami continued. "With Right View, we make the *two* into *one*. The difference between you, me, and this tree is only one of form, and even then, this difference lasts only for a time. One day, we will return to these elements and become something new. You came from the Source and to that Source you will return."

*From dust you have come and to dust you shall return.*

The recognition gnawed at his attention. Then, in a flash, it came to him. His first night at the vineyard.

*So, you don't believe in God?* he'd asked Abraham.

*Oh, I never said that. I believe in the* Living *God. It was the fragile god of my teachers I left behind.*

*What's the difference?*

*The Living God is like... well, it is like a lamp that shines from beneath the bushel of human life. It may be dampened beneath fear, greed and delusion, but it dwells in the temple of our hearts, and our work is to let it shine. The Living God is Life. It is* Being *itself—the great and unnamable I am.*

"That's it!" Jesus burst out, startling Judas. The *suchness* Master Gotami described—this ever-changing, boundless unity—was what Abraham had meant all those months ago.

"Brother Issa?" Master Gotami said. "Something you wish to say?"

Jesus blinked. There was a lot he'd like to say, but he wasn't sure how to say it. Words fell so short. Something about his realization moved him deeply, and he suddenly felt tearful. He felt expansive—connected with every other person, friend and enemy alike. He felt connected to every tree, animal, and clod of dirt. They were all waves moving across the same ocean of being. This was the truest truth, hiding behind every story. How could he *not* love it all? How could he *not* act with justice?

Then, as quickly as it had come, it was gone—like water slipping through cupped hands. Still, his heart glowed within him. He'd glimpsed it, if only for a moment.

"It's... God," Jesus said, the words clumsy in his mouth. "This is what Abraham meant, isn't it? The Living God."

He realized this must be the "Buddha Spirit" Brother Moggallana spoke of—the "Watcher" that made Right View possible. It made sense with what Abraham said, that it was so often crowded out by stories of fear, greed, and delusion. This was the spirit that Abraham had cultivated with such care. It was what he'd come for, and he'd finally understood.

Master Gotami smiled. "I believe Brother Issa understands," she said. "This 'God' goes by many names, of course. 'Brahman.' 'Dharmakaya.' 'Atman.' 'I Am That I Am.' It is the Ultimate Reality in which we live and move and find our being."

Jesus opened his mouth to say something, but Master Gotami held up a hand in warning.

"Remember, however," she said, "these are not objects or ideas to be grasped. They are not possessions. They are processes in which we find ourselves. These are not words to own, but signs pointing to a mystery greater than themselves. Do not forget this. I believe you have experienced firsthand the suffering that comes from trying to own a mystery."

"I think I understand," Jesus said. But the understanding felt fragile, like a flickering flame. He saw now why Moggallana emphasized practice so heavily. What he had glimpsed for an instant would take a lifetime to cultivate.

"Now, *samaneras,*" Master Gotami said, "we have already covered a great deal, but there is one final teaching which I would like to impart."

Jesus gave her an incredulous look. He wasn't sure he could hold any more in one morning.

"This is not one of the common illusions with which so many struggle," Master Gotami pressed on. "Quite the opposite, in fact, but it is crucial for understanding what we have discussed today. This last teaching helps us understand what remains when we have extinguished all stories and stand in the bold light of Right View. With Right View, we enter a new world, as it were. We enter an Ultimate realm of Reality beyond stories of separation or permanence—beyond judgment or shame. This new world is at hand already, of course. We are already in it, as an elephant bound by a rope is already free. We only lack eyes to see. In our tradition, this realm has a name. Can anyone tell me what it is?"

Master Gotami looked from one resident to another.

"Anyone?"

After a moment, someone answered.

"Nirvana."

Jesus looked around to see who had spoken. To his surprise, he found it was Judas.

"Very good, Brother Judas," Master Gotami said, clearly surprised herself. "Would you care to elaborate?"

Judas looked like he regretted speaking up, but answered all the same. "My father," he started, "he used to tell us this story about a king. His son went mad and ran away."

"Yes," Master Gotami affirmed. "A well-known tale. Continue, please."

"Well," Judas continued, "the son was a prince, of course, but because he'd gone mad, he'd forgotten. He forgot there was a kingdom at all, so he wandered the country under the delusion that he was only a peasant. It took him years to wander back toward the palace, and when the king's guards saw him, they brought him to the king. When the king saw his son, he didn't want to overwhelm him, so instead of telling his son the whole truth, he let him work for him. It took months and months, but slowly, the king would share stories and put the prince back in familiar places, around familiar faces. Eventually, the prince saw through his madness and remembered who he really was. He remembered that the kingdom was his."

Judas hesitated. "My father—he used to tell us that Nirvana was like that kingdom. He told us that we were princes, and the only thing that separated us from that truth was our madness. 'We've all gone mad,' he'd say. He'd tell us God was like the king, calling his children back to the truth."

Master Gotami nodded in approval. "Thank you, Brother Judas. Quite appropriate. Your father would be proud."

Judas blushed.

"The realm of Nirvana may indeed be likened to the kingdom," Master Gotami said. "A kingdom in which truth reigns as king. One might even say, as you have phrased it, Brother Judas and Brother Issa, that *God* reigns as king. As in the story, this Kingdom of God is at hand even now, as the ocean is *at hand* to a wave, though the madness of our delusions keeps us from seeing it. With the practice of Right View, we are set free from falsehoods. We see that in this Kingdom of God, there is no distinction between slave or free, male or female, but all are one. This, dear ones, is the wisdom and the salvation we have to share with the world. It is that this realm of truth is immanent. The Kingdom of God is at hand. We must only let go and enter."

In that moment, the bell-keeper sounded his call, inviting the residents to pause and breathe. Jesus felt jarred from the trance he'd fallen into, listening to Master Gotami, and he made himself take the customary mindful breaths.

"I think that's quite enough for today," Master Gotami said, nodding reverently to them all. "Thank you, dear ones, for your attention and for your diligence. As you go about your work, may you do so in the freedom of impermanence and the knowledge of *oneness*. May you work in the mindfulness that you are each an heir to the Kingdom. Farewell."

One by one, the residents pressed their palms together in gratitude, then began to rise and go back about their schedule. Jesus, however, felt rooted to the spot. He felt like, after a week of seeking, he'd finally found what he'd been looking for.

"Brother Issa?" Master Gotami called. "Brother Judas, a word?"

As everyone else left, Jesus and Judas rose to meet Master Gotami, who also stood to address them.

"Today marks the end of your trial week," she said. "Now, you must decide. Will you stay, or return to the life you left behind?"

This was the moment that Jesus had been dreading, but now that it was here, his doubts felt like they belonged to someone else.

Master Gotami turned to Judas first. "Your decision?"

"I'd like to stay, Master Gotami," Judas said, his voice steady. "I would like to remain until the ritual of initiation."

"Very good," Master Gotami said. "And you, Brother Issa? Have you made your choice?"

Jesus still wasn't sure whether he belonged there, but he was sure it was where he needed to be. He'd glimpsed what Abraham had intended for him to see, and now that he'd done that, he couldn't imagine going anywhere else.

"Yes," Jesus said, his words feeling solid, inevitable. "I'd like to stay."

Master Gotami studied them for a moment, then smiled. "I hear from both of you that your heart is in your desire to learn and awaken," she said. "Where your desire is, there also is your self, for as your desire, so is your will. As is your will, so is your deed. As is your deed, so is your future. It is an honor to have you here, Brothers Judas and Issa, and I look forward to meeting you again next week."

"Thank you, Master Gotami," they said, pressing their palms together. Then they departed.

Jesus was eager to get back to the palm leaf manuscripts in the Meditation Hall, which now seemed to glow with new importance.

IV.

# 33

JESUS MEDITATED BENEATH THE Bodhi tree, his legs folded in full lotus, waiting.

It had been twelve months since the rooftop. Twelve months since his first bout with sitting meditation. Twelve months since the teaching about the Kingdom of God. His first year had included study, discipline, and struggle, and he'd found himself in more than a few reconciliation rituals with his fellow residents. It had been a year of shifts, not least of which had been in his imagination of "God." To him, God was no longer the divine disciplinarian looking over his shoulder. Instead, God was more difficult to define. Transcendent, but also immanent. Outside of himself, but also his deepest essence. Beautiful, but terrible. God was no longer an idea he could hold in his mind, but an experience that held him. His understanding of prayer had shifted—no longer the long, rote recitations of his rabbi, but a practice merging with his growing meditation training. Prayer had become a way to let go of his stories and perceptions and become transparent to something greater—to allow God to live through him. It was a kind of dying, but one that awakened him to deeper life. *It is a great paradox of wisdom,* Abraham had once told him, *that one must be willing to lose their life in order to find it.* Jesus felt like he was only now beginning to understand what that meant.

He felt himself overcoming his madness—like the prince in Judas's story—and opening his eyes to the Kingdom of God around and within him. He was becoming less reactive and more skilled. What had started as a flicker had become a steady flame. Metta Valley had become his home, and the last year had easily been the best of his life.

Judas had also grown, albeit differently. He wasn't as concerned with plumbing the depths of divine mystery, but cared deeply about charity and service, and it wasn't long before Moggallana had put him in charge of Metta Valley's work distributing the surplus to nearby villages. Judas had proven to be naturally talented with numbers, and he used his skill to reimagine their process, working with a ferocity and single-mindedness Jesus hadn't seen in him before.

Jesus rolled the smiling Buddha stone in his palm as he sat. Soon, he felt a shadow pass over him. He grinned, eyes still closed.

"Good morning, Master Gotami."

"My, my," Master Gotami said. "You have arrived early. Perhaps it is now *I* who should apologize for keeping *you* waiting."

Jesus slipped the Buddha stone into his robes and opened his eyes. "Only those bound to expectation grow impatient," he said. "Is it time?"

"Indeed, it is."

About three months prior, Master Gotami had approached Jesus with a new training, teaching *chandala* children—children of the lowest caste—in a nearby abandoned orchard. "If you can teach the Way simply," she'd explained, "as telling stories to a child, then you can teach anyone." Jesus had taken to the task earnestly, falling instantly in love with these overlooked children and accompanying Master Gotami each week back to the orchard. At her urging, he shared parables and stories—even stories he'd learned as a child from his own scriptures. "A teacher of the Way should be like a householder," Master Gotami had said. "They should be able to reach into their storeroom and bring out new treasures as well as old." Jesus had even started making up his own parables, and had discovered, to his surprise, that he had a knack for it. He told stories about a shepherd who'd lost one of his sheep, and a *chandala* who'd saved a dying man while priests wouldn't lift a finger to help. He told stories about a ruler who invited his entire kingdom to a banquet, only to find that none but the poor wanted to come. Some parables worked better than others, and the children were always quick to let him know. Now, Jesus unfolded himself from his lotus pose and stretched, following Master Gotami to the orchard once again.

"Have you talked to Judas this morning?" Jesus asked as they made their way to the receiving room.

"I have," Master Gotami answered.

"He's nervous. I think the rite of initiation has crept up on him."

"That is Brother Judas's fruit to chew, I'm afraid," Master Gotami said, holding the door open for him as they entered the receiving room. "You must let him tread his own path."

"We're meant to leave tomorrow," Jesus said, stepping in. "You're not just a little worried he might not—"

"Brother Issa would do well to focus on his own concerns, would he not?"

Jesus couldn't suppress a smile as they crossed the receiving room to the front door. He didn't have any concerns. Judas saw the rite as a looming, intimidating beast, but Jesus welcomed it. He was ready. After a year of training—not to mention surviving the streets of Kashi—he was sure of his ability to face whatever came his way, and if forty days in the wilderness was what he had to do to move on in his training, it was a small price to pay.

Master Gotami must've seen his expression. "Confident as always," she observed. "Nearly a year of training, yet we have done little to touch upon your vanity."

"Oh, don't say that," he told her. "No one is more skilled than you are at keeping me humble."

"Indeed," Master Gotami said, "and none more skilled than you at transparent flattery."

They stepped back out into the sunlight, Master Gotami closing the door behind them, and set off down the narrow path. They walked until the valley opened up and the grade of the walls became less

severe. "Might it be more fruitful to discuss your errand?" Master
Gotami asked. "Assuming you successfully complete your rite of initiation, have you considered where it is you would prefer to go?"

Jesus feigned offense. "You doubt I'll survive my rite of initiation?"

"Oh, I have little concern regarding your survival. Snakes and wild
animals are the least of your concerns. There are far more dangerous
devils in the desert."

Jesus didn't pursue this. He'd learned better than to ask Master
Gotami to clarify her every cryptic comment.

"I've thought about returning to Kashi for my errand," he said.
"I think it would be good to see the vineyard again, to see how it's
changed, and I'd like to see it as a *bhikkhu* rather than a starving
drifter."

"The difference may be more subtle than you imagine," Master
Gotami said, then paused to regard him. He hated when she did this. It
always felt like she could see right through him. "Do you really think
you're so different?" she asked. "That you are no longer the starving
drifter who sought us out only a year ago?"

"Of course," he said. "You've been watching me. Surely you don't
doubt that."

After a moment, Master Gotami continued down the path. "Again
with the confidence, Brother Issa," she said. "Be wary. The world has
a way of confronting us with the growing edges of our practice."

Over the year he'd been a resident, Jesus had come to respect Master
Gotami deeply. Slowly, whatever reservations he'd had dropped away,
and he trusted her. The depth of her wisdom never failed to astound
him, even when she was cutting him to the quick, and she had a way of
uncovering the practical, embodied truth of nearly any teaching. She
was the opposite of the rabbi in nearly every way, and his trust in her
only became stronger when he saw her respect for the children. *They
freely root themselves in the present,* she'd taught after their first lesson
in the orchard. *They have little consciousness of the self. Is it not to such as
these that the Kingdom of God belongs?* He couldn't help but imagine

that if he'd had someone like her nearby when he was a child, his life might've turned out quite differently.

They turned off onto a barely perceptible trail into the woods, following it through thick vines and undergrowth. Even before they reached the orchard, they could hear the children squealing as they played. "Sounds like at least a dozen today," Jesus said.

"At least," Master Gotami agreed. "I hope you have prepared a good story."

"Master Gotami," he said. "When have I *not* prepared a good story?"

They entered the clearing, and the children caught sight of them at once. "Mama Gotami!" they yelled. "Brother Issa!" Two of the younger children, happily sculpting in the mud, scrambled to their feet and ran over. They grabbed at the hem of their robes, leaving grubby handprints.

Jesus opened his arms in greeting. *"Samaneras!"* he called, tousling hair. "I hope you've been well!"

"Kapu hasn't been well," one of the older children answered him somberly. "He got in trouble today."

"Trouble?" Jesus echoed, seeking Kapu out. He was one of the smaller boys, always barefoot and wearing the threadbare loincloth. "Kapu!" he called, finding him. "What happened? I rarely expect trouble from you."

Kapu had been darting playfully around Master Gotami's feet, but when Jesus called him, he stopped and lowered his gaze. "A farmer threw ash in my eyes," he said. "I saw a water pot outside of his home, and I drank some water. He was angry. He said I defiled it."

The children often brought stories like this, and they never failed to make him angry.

*Whatever an unclean person touches shall be made unclean,* Jesus heard the rabbi's warning. *Anyone who touches that shall themselves become unclean until evening. You don't want to be unclean, do you, young Yeshua?*

Jesus clenched his jaw, and his smile faltered.

*There are plenty who are clean in their own eyes,* he rebutted, *who are not washed of their own filth.*

Master Gotami placed a hand on Kapu's head. "Does water discriminate whose thirst it quenches?" she asked. "It does not. But the ignorance of those mired in judgment causes great suffering."

Jesus again felt a swell of gratitude for Master Gotami. It helped him force his anger down. "That farmer was a fool, Kapu," he said. "He'll never know what he missed by turning you away."

Kapu raised his eyes, the grin returning to his face. "Have you come to tell us more stories?" he asked.

Jesus marveled at how children could move on so quickly. "Of course!" he said. He took one child by the hand and led them to a patch of grass that wasn't as muddy as where they were standing. He sat down at their level, and they fell into place around him. Master Gotami found a seat on a flat rock, and a child instantly leaped into her lap.

"How about the one about the snake in the garden?"

"You told us that one!" Kapu objected, vying for a place next to Jesus.

"Did I?" Jesus feigned thoughtfulness. "How about the one about the three men thrown into the furnace?"

"You told us that one too!"

"Hmm," Jesus said, an idea coming to him. "Well, how about the one with the *chandala* adopted by a royal family?"

The children's eyes went wide. "We don't know that one!" a girl said.

"Tell us!"

"All right, all right," Jesus calmed them. "Everyone settle in. Are you ready? Once, many years ago, there was a kingdom ruled over by a king who feared *chandalas* above anything else. He feared them because of their numbers and great power, and because he was afraid, he decreed that all the *chandala* babies born in his land be thrown into the great river!"

The children gasped.

"Yes," Jesus nodded, "it was terrible, and there was much weeping, but one mother loved her baby so much, she was willing to do anything for him to be safe. So, in secret, she sealed a basket so it would float, then put her baby in and sent him drifting down the river."

"Were there *crocodiles* in the river?" one child asked, concerned.

"Were there *gharials?*"

"Were there *cobras?*"

"There *were* crocodiles," Jesus said, "and gharials, and cobras, and many dangers, *but* the god of that land knew what was happening was not right. He loved all the people deeply, especially the *chandalas*, and he knew something had to be done. So, he came up with a plan. He guided the baby safely past the crocodiles and the gharials and the cobras, and brought him all the way to the *palace,* where the princess was bathing."

The children listened, transfixed by the story.

"When the princess saw him, she did not see a *chandala*. She saw only an innocent child who needed care, so she took him in and raised him as her own. The boy grew up to become a prince of the region."

"A prince?" one boy echoed, astonished. "A *chandala* became a *prince?*"

"That he did," Jesus said, "and he was just as much part of the royal family as anyone. One day, though, when he was grown up enough, he realized that his people were suffering. It tore at him—seeing his royal family hurt his people. It pained him so deeply that one day, when he found a member of the royal guard beating a *chandala* man, he became so filled with rage that he *killed* the guard!"

The children gasped. Jesus noticed Master Gotami listening thoughtfully, still holding a child on her lap. He knew she would leverage this into a lesson for their discussion later. She always did.

"What happened?" a child demanded, calling Jesus back to the story.

"Well, I'll tell you what happened!" Jesus answered dramatically. "He was found out! He was chased from the kingdom and told never to return! He had to live in the wilderness, among strangers, while his people continued to suffer back in the kingdom. There was nothing he could do. But then, one day, the god of that land appeared to him."

"The same god who saved him?"

"The same god," Jesus said. "And that god called the prince to speak for him—to gather others who would become his hands and feet. He asked the prince to go back and tell his people it was time to be free—to rally the people and speak in a way the king could not ignore."

"And did he?"

Jesus nodded. "He did. With the help of the god, the people rose up and became a free people with a land of their own."

The children chanted in amazement, and Jesus relished the look of hope on their faces.

"So, I wonder," he asked, using a trick the Buddha would often use in his own stories, "in a previous life, who were *you* in this story?"

"I was the crocodile!" one child shouted, baring his teeth. "In the river!"

"I was the baby's mama, keeping him safe."

"I was the prince!" Kapu said, shoulders back proudly. "I saved the people!"

Jesus put an arm around the boy's scrawny shoulders. "Yes, you were," he said. "I'm sure of it."

"Will you tell us another story?" one child asked, and several more echoed their request.

"I'm not sure," Jesus said, looking to Master Gotami. "It depends on what Master Gotami says."

All the children looked at her, pouting. "Please! Please, Mama Gotami!"

"Oh, all right," Master Gotami said. "One more."

Jesus grinned. His "one more" turned into three more, then into a wild chase through the orchard, the children shrieking with laughter.

In the end, they were in the orchard for the better part of two hours before Master Gotami finally called out, pointing to the darkening sky. "The rains are coming, my *samaneras,*" she said. "I'm afraid it is time for us to return! We will meet you in this same place next week."

The children protested, but Master Gotami held firm. "Better to leave now than to be caught in the rains!" she said.

"Don't worry," Jesus said, trying to catch his breath after running around the clearing with the children. "I'm sure next week Master Gotami will have whole new stories for you. In the meantime, don't forget to—"

"What is all this?" a harsh voice cut through the children's laughter.

They all froze.

An aging man stood at the orchard's edge, his once-fine robes faded and worn. His hair was well-oiled and in his right hand was a sickle that looked like it had been recently sharpened.

Instinctually, the children shrank behind Jesus.

"Well?" the man demanded. "I asked a question."

He advanced into the clearing, crushing the children's mud sculptures as he went.

Jesus tried to be diplomatic. "We were only teaching these children," he said. "There's no need for trouble."

"Not on my land," the man spat. "I won't have filth like this defiling it."

Jesus squared his shoulders, fists tightening at his sides.

At that moment, Master Gotami stepped forward. "Friend," she said calmly, "I am the Venerable Gotami, Head Teacher of Metta Valley. If we might—"

"I don't care who you are," the landowner interrupted. "You have no right to be here. You need to—" The newcomer's eyes landed on Kapu, and he pointed an accusing finger. "You!" he growled. "I had a feeling I hadn't seen the last of you. Came back to defile more of my property, have you?"

Kapu shrank further away as Jesus realized that this must've been the man to throw ash in his eyes. He extended an arm to block Kapu from the man's view, and he felt fiery flames of rage swell in his chest.

"You think you can crawl around sullying my fruit trees, do you?" the landowner demanded, advancing. "Perhaps you need a sharper reminder."

Jesus heard the rabbi's voice, echoing from the back of his mind. *Folly is bound up in the heart of a child,* he chided, *but the rod of discipline will drive it far away.*

Deliberately, Jesus stepped between them. "Are these your fruit trees?" he asked. "You'll forgive us for assuming this grove was abandoned. Given the state of these trees, I assumed the owner was dead."

The man hesitated, noticing Jesus for the first time. His expression was bitter. "Well, I assure you I am not."

"Clearly," Jesus said. "Just too foolish to know how to mind a field."

The man's eyes widened. "What did you say to me, boy?" he demanded. "Who do you think you are?"

"I'm the one who won't let you insult these children."

The landowner gripped his sickle. "Then perhaps I'm the one to teach you the natural order the gods have set."

Jesus stepped forward, but he suddenly found his path blocked by a flash of saffron robes. "Clearly, there is a misunderstanding," Master Gotami said evenly. The landowner hesitated. "We were under the impression that this clearing was free and that we might use it to provide these children with moral instruction. It is clear now that this is not the case. I assure you that you will not find us on your property again."

The man hesitated. He glanced over Master Gotami's shoulder at Jesus, who was still fuming. "I don't know what passes for 'moral instruction' with you," the man said, "but the gods have entrusted me with this land, and I expect you to keep this filth off of it from now on."

"Filth?" Jesus shot back, trying to step around Master Gotami. Her arm shot out in front of him, holding him back with surprising strength.

"Brother Issa will refrain from unskillful speech," she said evenly.

"You can't be serious," he said. "You can't stand there and let him—"

"Silence," Master Gotami snapped, then turned her attention back to the landowner. "I will dismiss these children now, and you will not see them again. Please accept our apology for this misunderstanding. I apologize also for the naivete of my student. He is early in his practice. He has not yet learned to master his tongue."

The landowner scoffed. "Clearly."

Jesus was too stunned to speak. His breath came quick and shallow.

"Dear ones," Master Gotami turned to address the children, "let us meet this same time next week, but at the grove south of the village. Do you understand?"

"Yes, Mama Gotami," some of them answered. The others remained silent, their eyes on the ground. Jesus wanted to lunge at the landowner—to wrench the sickle out of his hands.

"Very well," Master Gotami said, smiling serenely. "Return home now, and I shall see you then."

Obediently, the children disappeared into the trees.

Master Gotami turned back to the farmer. "Thank you for your patience," she said. "We will be on our way. Come, Brother Issa."

She turned back toward Metta Valley, but Jesus couldn't bring himself to move. He couldn't take his eyes off the landowner.

"Brother Issa," Master Gotami called firmly. "You will follow. Now."

Tearing himself from the spot, Jesus forced himself to follow Master Gotami. He couldn't believe what he'd witnessed. This man had insulted and threatened their children, and Master Gotami had done nothing. Worse, she'd *apologized*. His stomach churned in betrayal and fury.

He stormed after her, through the vines and back onto the path. He needed her to explain. They needed to talk.

# 34

"Do you want to explain why you let that happen back there?" Jesus demanded, pushing vines out of his way and trying to catch up with Master Gotami. "Now we're just going back like that was nothing?"

Master Gotami didn't vary from her steady pace. "And what is it you suggest I do, Brother Issa? You would have me draw a weapon and strike him down in the name of peace? Is this the nature of justice you have learned?"

"No," Jesus answered, "but you could've done more for those kids."

"And I wished to. I might have asserted the dignity of those children with creativity, in a way that made him see their worth."

"Well, why didn't you?"

Master Gotami stopped walking and faced Jesus. "Because you removed that option when you insulted him. You treated him as the worst version of himself, and he became it."

"So, you surrendered?" Jesus shot back, more an accusation than a question. "You let him treat them like filth? They'll remember this. It will stay with them. I thought we trained so that when the time came, we could actually *do* something."

"I treated him with dignity, as I would have him treat us," Master Gotami said, continuing on her way. *"That* is what we train for. The most skillful way to fight evil is to embody a better way. I might've done more, but if you recall, he had a weapon, and you provoked him. My first concern became protecting the children, as yours should have been."

"That's not good enough," Jesus insisted. "What good is any of this if we can't *do* anything?"

To his surprise, Master Gotami rounded on him. He took an instinctive half-step backwards.

"I *am* doing something," she said, a warning in her voice. "Every week, for years, I have come to this place to loosen the fetters on those children's minds. I have come to help them imagine a world in which they are beloved and were not born merely for digging latrines. I daily train students in the practice of awakening so that they may see beyond these ways of injustice. I do everything in the hope that awakened people may one day resist in numbers too large to ignore—to challenge ways of oppression with weapons that cut deeper than knives and swords. But until that day comes, Brother Issa, we will fight with the tools we have. Dignity. Patience. Understanding. Persistence. *This* is the work to which I have dedicated my life. Pick up a sword if you like, but by that same sword you will die—another body in an endless, senseless cycle of violence, and God knows how many lives you will take with you."

"And what if that's still not enough?" Jesus challenged her. "What if it's not enough to sit behind our walls and meditate and tell stories about God and justice while people like that landowner walk all over the weak and vulnerable?"

"It *must* be enough!" Master Gotami returned. "I trust in something greater than myself, Brother Issa. I trust in a truth which existed before me and will exist long after I am gone. I serve the slow work of a greater truth, acting as its hands and feet, watering seeds in a garden of liberation I will likely never see. I can afford patience and grace, Brother Issa, because though I may die or men like that farmer may strike me down, I know *none* can strike down the Reality which I serve. The Spirit which drives me dwells in every tree and root—every rock and mountain—everyone who ever walked this earth, and if I were to remain silent, it would cry out from the very stones beneath our feet. So yes, Brother Issa, my life may not be enough, and neither may yours, but you of all people should know that the truth endures. All we can do is listen well, testify to the truth, and let go of that which we cannot control. Brother Abraham's words. He died believing this, did he not? It is how he was able to live the life he lived."

"He wouldn't have let that farmer talk to them that way," Jesus said, shaking his head. "You sound like my rabbi. 'Trust God and lean not on your own understanding...' Well, I've heard it before, and I'm not interested. Those kids are hungry *now*. People insult them *now*. They can't wait while we contemplate the nature of suffering in the safe shade of the Bodhi Tree. I thought you actually *believed* in the things you taught."

"Then teach me a better way, O Wise One," Master Gotami said. "How does one end the suffering of this world swiftly? How does one bring about instant justice? By returning violence for violence? By answering prejudice with prejudice? What is the way by which we are saved from our ignorance? Do you have the answer? If so, teach me now. I shall be your disciple, and you the master."

Jesus stared at Master Gotami for a long time. His hands were shaking, and he was too angry to form words. He thought of the looks on those children's faces... Of the landowner's words tying themselves around their minds like ropes around baby elephants... He thought of Master Gotami just seeing it all and still having the audacity to apologize and tell Jesus to be patient. Holding it all, he felt only rage.

"I thought not," Master Gotami said. "You would do well to not so easily exchange skillful, effective action for your own self-avenging gratification, Brother Issa. If you do not, then I fear your story may come to a swift and fatal end."

Jesus didn't know what to say. He felt a gulf opening between them. Suspicion replaced all the trust he had built, and he suddenly felt like a fool for letting himself be taken in. Master Gotami was no different from the rabbi, and Metta Valley was no different from Nazareth. He'd been stupid, and this time he had no one to blame but himself.

*You search in vain for someone to please or someone to fight,* he heard the rabbi's voice, *all to try to prove to yourself that you're not what you are—that you're good and righteous.*

*But you know what you are, don't you?*

Jesus felt the first drop of the afternoon storm on his shoulder. "I shouldn't have come here," he said. "I should've known better."

Master Gotami didn't answer. She only held her ground as Jesus stepped around her and hurried back to Metta Valley, alone.

---

JUDAS WAS MEDITATING WHEN Jesus got back to their room. Seeing Jesus's expression, he unfolded his legs and stood. "Are you all right?" he asked. "What's going on?"

"I don't want to talk about it," Jesus muttered, pacing in the small cell. Rain dripped from his clothes as he paced, flinging water with every step.

"Are you sure?" Judas asked. "You seem—"

*"I said I don't want to talk about it,"* Jesus repeated, louder. Some part of him knew this wasn't fair—that Judas was only trying to help—but that part seemed weak and distant. He'd grown angrier with every step and every drop of rain.

"I'm sorry," Judas said, surprised by Jesus's outburst. "Perhaps... if you go speak to Master Gotami, she may be able to help. Whatever it is, perhaps it's not as bad as it seems?"

"Why do you do that?" Jesus demanded, stopping and facing Judas. "Why do you always have to make everything all right? Sometimes, there are things that can't be fixed! You can't smooth over everything and act like it never happened!"

Judas stood straighter. "What is that supposed to mean?"

"You know what it means," Jesus shot back.

"I'm only trying to help."

Jesus laughed. *"To help.* Of course. You're always only trying to help, aren't you? Trying to make everything well because you know it will *never* be well... Trying to stay busy so you never have to face the truth..."

"This isn't about me," Judas insisted. He was growing irritated. Still, Jesus couldn't seem to stop himself.

"It never is, is it?" Jesus said. "It's about everybody *except* for you, because if it *were* about you, even for a moment, you would have to face what happened back in the city, wouldn't you? You would have to talk about your father, or how you betrayed your family."

"That's not fair."

*"Not fair,"* Jesus echoed. "How long are you going to run, Judas? How long are you going to keep trying to put up a joyful front? Exhausting yourself with chores? Trying to make up for what happened?"

"That's enough," Judas said. "You need to stop this."

"Or what?" Jesus asked, calling his bluff. "You're not here because you're honoring your father's legacy, Judas. You're here to *hide behind it."*

Before he could react, Judas struck him across the face, sending him stumbling back toward the wall. He tripped over his mat and landed hard.

Judas flexed his fingers, trying to hide the pain. "Don't speak about my father," he demanded, "and don't talk about what *I'm* feeling. You don't know the first thing about what I'm feeling."

Jesus realized he'd gone too far. He met Judas's eyes and felt a sharp pang of regret. "I'm... I'm sorry," he tried.

"No, you're not," Judas said. "You think you know everything—that you are on this sacred mission—but do you know what? You're selfish. You're selfish and conceited and all you do is multiply suffering. *That's* who you are."

"Judas—" Jesus tried again, but Judas shook his head, on the verge of tears.

"Don't," he said.

Judas stormed out of the room, leaving the door open. Rain pounded outside, mist creeping into the small room.

Jesus felt dizzy, both from Judas's punch and the realization that his world was collapsing around him. Everything he'd built over the last year felt like it had given way in an afternoon, and he didn't know that it could ever be restored. He wasn't even sure he wanted it restored. It was the second time in his life he'd lost his temper and then lost everything.

*Like a dog that returns to his vomit,* he heard the rabbi say, *is a fool who repeats his foolishness.*

That was him. A dog who returned to his vomit—destined to do the same thing forever.

Jesus let himself fall back onto the mat and stare at the ceiling, marveling at his own ineptitude. He was exactly where he'd started in Kashi, before Abraham had found him. He felt exhausted and overwhelmed. Forcing himself to close his eyes, he listened to the sound of the rain and willed himself into the oblivion of sleep.

# 35

Slowly, the bamboo supports above him came into focus. His head ached, his jaw felt tender, and he wasn't sure how long he'd been out. The rain had stopped, and the light filtering through the slats had softened. Late afternoon?

Jesus pushed himself up. He felt calmer now—his anger dulled by his few hours of sleep—but in its place was a lingering shame. Even after all his training—all his practice—he'd lost control so easily. He thought he knew better.

*Can a leopard change its spots?* he heard the rabbi's voice. *You will never belong, despite your childish attempts to make up for what you are. Son of Mary... Son of Pantera...*

The rabbi was right. He could shave his head and don saffron robes, but he was still the same child of shame he'd been when he'd walked into Metta Valley the year prior. Now, he'd burned another bridge. Master Gotami would have him escorted from the grounds before sunset tomorrow, he was sure of it.

The thought sent a pain through his heart. He'd let her down. He'd let Abraham down. Whatever he'd seen in Abraham—whatever spirit had driven him to this place—Jesus had clearly picked up none of it. Despite all his learning, he was an actor, playing the part of a holy man, no better than his rabbi.

The thought made him want to sink into his mat and vanish. What was left for him after this?

Jesus closed his eyes and forced himself to breathe. Whatever happened next, wherever he was going, he knew he needed to find Master

Gotami and at least apologize—to thank her and tell her he would leave willingly. After that, he'd find Judas. Maybe, before he left, he could at least make up for some of the damage he'd done.

---

He made his way to the courtyard and began asking around for Master Gotami. No one had seen her. After asking several residents with no success, he found Brother Moggallana in the meditation hall.

"She is on the roof," he told Jesus. "She goes up there sometimes when she needs space to come back to herself."

"Thank you," Jesus said, pressing his palms together. As he turned to leave, Moggallana's voice stopped him.

"Brother Issa?"

Jesus paused, bracing himself.

"We all make mistakes. Do not judge a grapevine. Tend to it and allow it to grow toward the light."

Jesus lingered in the doorway for a moment, not knowing what to say.

After a moment, Moggallana closed his eyes and returned to his meditation. "If the mind is made clear," he said, "no wrongdoing remains."

Slowly, Jesus made his way to the spiral stairs and ascended to the top floor, to the room Master Gotami had shown them on their first day. He found the door to the platform and stepped through, mindful of his footing on the damp wood. As he made his way across to the front wall, he saw Master Gotami sitting in lotus pose, staring out at the mountains.

She said nothing as he approached and sat next to her. The silence stretched on forever.

"I'm sorry," he said after a moment. "I was out of line. At sunrise, I'll get my things and leave."

For a moment, Master Gotami said nothing. Then, "Do you recall our first lesson here?"

Jesus hesitated. "Yes," he said. "You taught us about Right View. I thought Judas was going to faint."

Master Gotami smiled. "Indeed. I taught you that the stories told by the mind are often incomplete, if not entirely mistaken. Perceptions are not reality. Ropes are not snakes." She paused for a moment. "Brother Issa, did you know that I am a *chandala?*"

"No," Jesus said, realizing, not for the first time, how little he knew about his teacher.

"It is true," Master Gotami said. "My mother swept streets. My father was beaten to death when I was only a child. I, too, was routinely beaten. I carry many scars, not all visible on the flesh."

Jesus looked at the crescent moon scar around her eye, wondering once more where it had come from.

"When my mother died," Master Gotami said, "I found this place quite by chance. There was a monk on errand in my village who took pity on me and brought me back with him. I was quite young. I was also angry. Impulsive. I was determined to outshine my peers, though I only became an obstacle to myself in the process." She gave a half-smile, still gazing out at the mountains. "No one could have imagined that I would one day be called 'Master Gotami.' Certainly not me."

After another moment, she turned to face Jesus. "I understand your anger more than you may know," she told him. "Yet it is from my deepest wounds that I have found wellsprings of the deepest wisdom. I will admit that I have, perhaps, given you slightly more attention than others because I see this potential in you as well."

"Potential?" Jesus asked.

"To find that wisdom," Master Gotami said. "To seize this opportunity. However, you must learn to release the stories that Mara whispers into your ear."

"What do you mean?"

"I mean, you believe your worth depends on the approval of those you respect, and so you live in fear of their rejection. You believe you are only as good as your ferocity in fighting systems of falsehood, and so you live in anger with everyone. You believe you are unworthy of trust, and so you distrust Reality. These are ropes you tie around your mind—madness you spin to keep yourself imprisoned in illusion."

As he often did, Jesus felt exposed under Master Gotami's eye. He'd felt the same way about Abraham.

"You fight only yourself, Brother Issa," Master Gotami continued. "'Though one should conquer a million in battle, they are the noblest who may conquer themselves.' It is you who keeps yourself imprisoned, and you will only know freedom when you let these stories go, seeing who you truly are. That is when you will finally nourish the fruit of love and justice you seek to bear."

"And who am I?" Jesus asked. "Because I keep thinking I know, and I keep being wrong."

Master Gotami sat with this question. "I'm afraid I could tell you," she answered, "but you can only truly understand when you have come to the answer yourself."

"That seems unlikely. I've been here for a year, but I keep making the same mistakes."

"Brother Issa," Master Gotami said, "growing in the Way does not mean that you do not make mistakes, just as meditating does not mean you do not get distracted. Growing in the Way simply means you are learning, with increasing skill, to bring your attention back to the truth. Do you think Brother Abraham was immune to such things? Do you think I am immune?"

Jesus didn't answer.

"I accept your apology," Master Gotami continued, "but what's more, I must tell you I hold you in deepest respect, even after today."

Jesus looked over at her, surprised.

"You do not see it," she continued, "but you are a kind, courageous, compassionate student, and I have learned a great deal from you. We are better from your having chosen to come to Metta Valley."

Jesus hadn't expected this, and he wasn't sure how to respond. Master Gotami's words moved something deep within him, and he turned away so she wouldn't see his tears. Even as he did it, he knew this was futile. She could see right through him.

"You asked how you are supposed to find who you are," Master Gotami continued. "This will come in time, but the next step on your path is clear. It is time for you to complete the rite of initiation, Brother Issa. You must go into the wilderness. There, you will discover what is real."

"My rite of initiation?" Jesus asked. "Are you saying... you're not sending me away?"

"Goodness no," Master Gotami said with a laugh. "If we turned away a student every time they grew angry with their teacher, Metta Valley would've died long ago."

Jesus only gawked. Even after everything, she was letting him stay.

"Wrongdoing arises from the mind," Master Gotami said, invoking the words of reconciliation. After countless fights, Jesus knew them well. He also knew what he was meant to say in return.

"If the mind is made clear," Jesus answered, "no wrongdoing remains."

Master Gotami smiled and put a hand on his shoulder. "Very good," she said. "I know how uncomfortable you find the kiss of reconciliation, so I shall forgo it this once. Do not tell Brother Moggallana."

Jesus felt like he could melt with relief. "I wouldn't dream of it," he said.

Master Gotami let him go, and for a few moments, they went back to watching the sun sink lower. Soon, it was nearly dark.

Master Gotami stood and extended a hand. "Come," she said. "The sun is sinking, and there is work yet to be done. You have your rite of initiation to prepare for, and I imagine you'll want to apologize to Brother Judas before it is time to retire."

Jesus let her pull him to standing. "How'd you know about that?" he asked, surprised.

"Brother Issa, I am the Head Teacher of Metta Valley," she answered. "Not the slightest whisper escapes my attention."

Jesus followed her across the stone path to the back wall.

"Also," she added, "there is a sizeable bruise on your jaw."

Jesus touched his jaw gingerly. "Ah," he said. "That reminds me. Judas's hand may need bandaging. I don't think he's ever thrown a punch before."

"How honored you must be."

Jesus stepped onto the roof of the back wall. "I don't know if he's going to be quite so generous with his forgiveness as you were," he said as they navigated down onto the platform.

"Perhaps not," Master Gotami said, "but all we can do is testify to the truth and let go of what we cannot control."

Jesus hesitated. "What is that?" he asked. "You and Abraham both say it. Is it from a sutra that I haven't found yet?"

Master Gotami paused. "You will not find it in a sutra," she said, facing him. "That is something Brother Abraham and I came up with together. It served as his mantra during his recovery here. It was meant to remind him not to remain caught in fear of being overwhelmed by the future. It helped him to focus on what he *could* do, one moment at a time, and to do it as skillfully as possible, regardless of the outcome. Testify to the truth and let go of what you cannot control."

Master Gotami continued across the platform, through the door. Jesus followed.

"In the end, Brother Abraham came to embody this in everything he did," Master Gotami said. "He let go of stories and half-truths and acted with justice and humility, even with no guarantee of success. As a result, he was free to accomplish some beautiful things, even unto death. It was how he lived, and it was how he died."

Jesus closed the door behind them. He knew Master Gotami was right. He hoped it was a lesson he could one day learn as well.

----

By the time Jesus made it back to the ground, the evening meal had ended, and the courtyard was deserted. He wondered if Judas would still be awake, or if he would even return to their room. He wouldn't blame Judas for wanting to move.

Jesus knocked gingerly on the door of their cell. "Judas? Can we talk?"

Silence.

He knocked again, slightly louder. "Judas—"

The door swung open, and Judas stood before him. "What do you want?"

"I... want to apologize," Jesus said, surprised. "I didn't mean what I said."

"You did mean it," Judas said. "Don't pretend otherwise."

Judas retreated into the room and sat on his mat. He left the door open, which Jesus took as an invitation. He followed Judas inside and pulled the door closed behind him.

"You think I only came here to hide?" Judas demanded. "Do you truly think there is anywhere I could ever hide from what I've done?"

"Judas," Jesus started, "I didn't mean—"

"Forgive me for trying to find some kind of salve," Judas pressed on. "For trying to do *something* to balance the mistakes I made, if only a bit. I know perfectly well what I am."

"Judas," Jesus said again, sitting on his own mat, "what I said earlier wasn't about you. I had a fight with Master Gotami. I was trying to make you as angry as I felt."

"It was true, though," Judas insisted. "What you said. It's not working. There is no balancing what I've done, however much good I do."

"Your father loved you, Judas," Jesus started, but Judas interrupted him.

"Don't tell me about my father," he snapped. "You only knew him for a few weeks. You weren't his son."

Jesus backed down. "I didn't say I was," he said gently. "You're right. You knew him far better than I did. I suppose I only... I wonder what he would say to you now, if he were here."

Judas hesitated, then lowered his gaze. "He would probably tell me to stop feeling sorry for myself," he mumbled, "to move on and get back to what it was I was meant to do."

"And what is it you're meant to do?" Jesus asked.

Judas was quiet for a long moment. "I don't know anymore."

"Listen," Jesus said. "What I said earlier... I'm sorry. I'm very good at tearing other people down—I learned from the best—but it had nothing to do with you."

Judas raised his eyes. "What you said was—"

"Self-serving and half-true," Jesus cut in. "The most dangerous lies are the ones built on half-truths."

After a moment, Judas gave a reluctant nod. He stood, and Jesus thought for a moment he was about to walk out.

Instead, he said, "Wrongdoing arises from the mind."

Jesus realized what he was doing. "You don't have to do this," Jesus said. "What I said was—"

"Do you want to be reconciled or not?" Judas asked.

Jesus smiled. He stood up and put a hand on Judas's shoulder. "If the mind is made clear," he said, "what wrongdoing is left? But we don't have to do the—"

Judas pulled Jesus into an embrace, kissing his cheek as the ritual dictated.

Jesus allowed Judas to embrace him for a moment, then pulled away. "All right, all right," he said. "We are reconciled. Are you happy?"

"I am," Judas said, and Jesus could see it was true. They both returned to their mats. "So, what happened?" Judas asked. "What was the fight you had with Master Gotami?"

Jesus told Judas the story—about the orchard and the landowner... about their fight and conversation on the roof... By the end, Judas's eyes were wide. "It's no wonder you were upset," he said. "I would have been upset as well."

"Thank you," Jesus said.

"And you're still going through with it? The rite of initiation?"

"Apparently so. Are you?"

Judas sighed. "I suppose so."

"Well then, we'd better get some sleep," Jesus said.

"You're right," Judas said. "I'm sorry I hit you. I shouldn't have done that."

"Yes, you should've," Jesus said, lying down on his mat. "I deserved it."

"All the same," Judas insisted, also getting comfortable. "I didn't think I was capable of something like that. I know I've... I've hurt people, but I thought I'd learned."

He hesitated for a moment.

"It's just made me wonder... what if that's just who I am? What if I'm someone who gets too angry and hurts the people close to him?"

"Then you're like me," Jesus said.

"What if I do it again?"

"Then we'll do this again," Jesus said. "We'll do the whole reconciliation ritual, and you'll kiss my cheek, and all will be well. Whoever you are, Judas, you're my friend. That won't change."

Whether this convinced Judas or not, he nodded, putting the subject to bed.

"How's your hand?" Jesus asked.

"It hurts," Judas said, holding it up for inspection. It was swollen. "That's what I deserve, though."

"Not as much as I deserve this bruise on my eye."

"I suppose we're even then."

"We really should get some rest. The bell waits for no one."

Judas reached over and extinguished their oil lamp, and darkness enveloped the room.

"I was talking to some of the other residents tonight about the rite of initiation," Judas said. "Its roots run deep—back to the solitary retreat the Buddha undertook before his enlightenment."

Jesus slipped the smiling Buddha stone out of his pouch, rolling it in his palm in the dark. "Well, who knows? Maybe we'll become enlightened, too."

"Do you think there's anything dangerous out there?"

"Do you think they would send us out there if there were?"

Judas was quiet for a moment. "You're probably right," he said.

As Jesus rolled the Buddha stone around, though, he couldn't help but remember what Master Gotami had told him. He thought it best not to share it with Judas. No need to cause him more worry than he already felt.

*Snakes and wild animals are the least of your concerns,* she'd said. *There are far more dangerous devils in the desert.*

# 36

AT THE BELL'S TOLL the next morning, Jesus rose, ready. As they made their way down to the courtyard with all the other residents, though, Judas was clearly distracted. "I don't think I can survive this," he mumbled, his face drawn.

"Of course you can," Jesus said. "Where's that confidence you had last night?"

"Gone," Judas said. "Stolen in my sleep."

"It's only forty days," Jesus said, and Judas scoffed.

"Think about it," Jesus went on. "If you run into a leopard or a boar, you can always just strike it across the face. You're good at that."

Judas smiled weakly, which Jesus considered a victory. He didn't want to tell Judas that, after yesterday's events, he was having his own hesitations. His loss of control in the orchard had shaken his unshakable certainty in his readiness, creating space for doubt to sneak in and put down roots. Even after Master Gotami's encouragement on the rooftop, he wondered if he was really prepared to face what was ahead. This was his final training, after all, before being sent on his errand. It all came down to this. Every moment since Abraham had found him at that gate had led him to this training.

By the time they stepped into the courtyard with the other residents, Jesus wasn't sure who was more nervous—him or Judas.

Immediately, Jesus saw something was different. Rather than congregating in the meditation hall, Master Gotami and Brother Moggallana directed students to various spaces, congregating around the Bodhi tree as though they were about to receive a teaching.

"What's going on?" he muttered.

Judas only looked around, bewildered. "I have no idea."

"Find a seat, if you please," Master Gotami called. "We shall begin our practice here this morning, for it is a day of significance."

Jesus and Judas began to sit down in the back, but Moggallana caught them. "Oh no, my friends," he said, pulling them back up again. "You two make your way to the front. This is, after all, for your benefit!"

"*Our* benefit?" Jesus asked.

"Of course! It is only customary to send our *samaneras* on their rite of initiation with a bit of fanfare. After all, this may be the last time we see you."

Judas swallowed hard, his breathing shallow, and Jesus took him reassuringly by the arm. *Brother Moggallana is fond of jokes,* Jesus remembered Master Gotami saying on their first day, *even if the only one they amuse is himself.*

They made their way to the front, stepping between the other residents and taking their place beside Master Gotami. Moggallana followed them, and when they were all settled, Master Gotami raised her arms. "Dear ones," she began, and everyone fell silent. "Today, we join Brothers Issa and Judas to prepare for their sojourn in the wilderness as they move to the next stage of their training. Today, we honor a year of diligent practice. We honor a year of growing in skill. Today, we acknowledge that they have practiced with dedication and have nourished the seeds of the Buddha Spirit within them. Now, the time has come for their rite of initiation."

Jesus felt the eye of every resident on him. *The eyes of this community are on men like you and me,* he remembered the rabbi saying to him when he was younger. *We must be always at our best, lest they see us falter and it cause them to stumble.*

He slipped the Buddha stone from his robes and rolled it between his fingers.

"When Siddhartha Gautama sought to find a medicine for the world's suffering," Master Gotami went on, "he traveled into the wilderness and sat beneath the Bodhi Tree for many days and many nights. He sat in full awareness of his mind and body until the seed of understanding sprouted and bloomed, and he saw Reality. He saw the impermanent, interdependent nature of all things. He sought the truth until the truth presented itself to him. Now, Brothers Issa and Judas, we invite you to join in that tradition."

Moggallana picked up two brown satchels and two solid walking sticks, offering them to Jesus and Judas.

"With these supplies," Master Gotami said, "we send you out into the wilderness for forty days of solitude. On your own, you shall learn things that no teacher could ever pass on, and no writing could ever convey. In your bags, you will find a waterskin and the elements to start a fire. This is all. Do you have any further questions?"

"Only one," Judas asked. "Would you say it's safe out there? Are there any wild animals we should be concerned about?"

"You've got your sticks," Moggallana smiled. "Besides, Brother Judas, wild animals should be the very least of your worries."

"What does that mean?" Judas asked, but Moggallana was already clapping his hands together.

"Now!" he said. "This is how we shall begin. We will send you out one at a time, with a half-hour in between your departures. This way, you may make your own way and walk your own path. This is, after all, an exercise in solitude. Brother Issa? Let us begin with you."

Jesus gave Judas one last, desperate look, then Moggallana put a hand on his shoulder and guided him towards the back wall. There, they approached a barred set of double doors that Jesus had never been through. It led into the wilderness beyond Metta Valley, beyond the edges of civilization.

Residents pressed their palms together as they passed. Jesus wasn't sure if it was in solidarity or farewell.

When they reached the doors, Brother Moggallana stopped and patted Jesus on the shoulder. "I make my jokes," he said, his voice low, "but in truth, you will be all right, Brother Issa. I know you are nervous, but you are prepared for this."

"Nervous?" Jesus said, keeping his voice steady. "Don't be ridiculous."

Master Gotami took her place beside them. "There is something we offer each *samanera* before they embark on their rite of initiation," she said. "A teaching. As it was once offered to me, I will now offer it to you if you are prepared to receive it."

"I'm prepared," Jesus said, even though he was feeling anything but.

"Then listen well," Master Gotami said. "If you bring forth what is within you, then what you bring forth may well be your salvation. If you do not, then what you do not bring forth may well be your destruction. Do you understand these things?"

"No," Jesus said, "but I suppose I will soon."

Master Gotami smiled. "Indeed, you will."

Brother Moggallana unbolted the door, and Jesus held his breath. "You told me once that you sought to be free," Master Gotami said, "and to lead others to freedom. Is this still your intention?"

"It is," Jesus said, thinking of Abraham, who must've once stood in this place.

"Well then," Master Gotami said, "it is likely that the freedom you seek waits on the other side of this door, but it will not be easy. You can find what you seek, Brother Issa, but to lead others to freedom, you must first become free yourself. In the wilderness, the mind stretches. At times, it may even break. Things are not what they seem within the confines of our community. Out there, we may see things which are not real, and yet we may also see that which is most real. Take courage. The gift you seek awaits if you dare receive it."

Master Gotami nodded to Moggallana, who pulled the door open. Jesus felt a rush of wind on his face.

"Brother Issa," Master Gotami said, "we will see you in forty days."

# 37

ONCE, IN KASHI, JESUS had gone an entire week without meaningful interaction with another soul. To him, that had felt like an eternity. It was the most isolated he'd ever been. After six days, he'd been ready to pick a fight just to remember what it felt like to talk to someone. In the wilderness, however, Jesus realized a week was no time at all.

After the door to Metta Valley had closed behind him, Jesus took the first path he saw. He hadn't been sure where he was going, but he didn't want to stray too far in case something went wrong. After walking for some time, he'd found a steep path out of the valley, and followed it until the greenery thinned and he found himself walking on dry, reddish-brown rock. He tried to remember every detail for his return.

Jesus continued until he heard the trickle of water and followed the sound to its source. He knew he could survive for months without food, but not without water. Soon, he crested a hill and looked down to find a shallow, forked creek with a flat bank on the far side. It was no Ganges, but it would do. He studied it for a moment. "I suppose this is it," he muttered, then made a note to stop talking to himself before it became a habit.

There was a rocky overhang nearby, and carefully—not wanting to disturb anything—Jesus peered inside to be sure it was unoccupied. It was vacant, so he set down his satchel, claiming it as his shelter. It would work well enough to shelter him against whatever weather or fanged beast would inevitably come along to do him in. So far, he'd only seen a yak and a few marmots, but he was sure the leopards and boars were just over the next crest.

He'd taken up his walking stick and climbed to the highest point he could reach to look over his new home for the next forty days. Even from there, he couldn't see Metta Valley, and with a jolt, he realized just how alone he was. It wasn't like when he and Judas had thought they'd been alone on the road to Metta Valley. This time, it was real. He was truly alone.

"So what do I do now?" he muttered, forgetting his rule about talking to himself.

It was then that he'd felt another unpleasant jolt. The answer was *nothing*. There was *nothing* to do. That was the point.

With that thought, he took a deep, steadying breath.

This was going to be a long forty days.

---

THAT FIRST WEEK, JESUS had spent hours meditating. He sat until his legs ached and walked until his feet blistered. Tally marks began to fill the cave wall, and he fed the fire as he counted and recounted them. He trusted Master Gotami when she said this would be a fruitful exercise, but so far, he was having trouble seeing how.

Often, the rabbi's voice would rush in to fill the void of his thoughts. *You will never belong,* he'd say, *despite your childish attempts to make up for what you are.*

"Enough," Jesus muttered.

*So what do you do? You search in vain for someone to please or someone to fight—all to try to prove to yourself that you're not what you are—that you're good and righteous. But you know what you are, don't you? Son of Mary... Son of Pantera...*

"Enough!"

By the second week, hunger gnawed at his insides. He knew fasting was part of the exercise, but he started noticing every berry he came across. Only his inability to distinguish the edible berries from the poisonous kept him from breaking his fast.

His hunger, however, quickly became the least of his concerns. His biggest concern was the whispers.

He'd tried to ignore them at first, worried that his sanity might be slipping after just two weeks. Soon, however, they had become impossible to ignore. Every night, from the treeline around his camp, he'd hear sounds. Rustling. Whispers. He told himself it was just the wind in the leaves—that spirits and demons were children's stories—but the sounds, along with Master Gotami's warning, eroded his resolve. The story of Saul and the Witch of Endor—a story that had always frightened him as a child—began repeating in his mind.

*I see spirits rise from the ground,* he remembered his rabbi reading, his voice low and dangerous. *It is an old man, wrapped in a robe...*

He'd tried to shake the fears away as the shivers ran down his spine. He tried to tell himself he was losing touch. "I see you, Mara," Jesus had begun muttering to himself, remembering Brother Moggallana's story. "I hear you, Mara..."

As if the hunger and the whispers weren't enough, then came the dreams. He'd started dreaming about his mother sitting alone at her table, weeping and inconsolable. He'd wake up in a panic, unable to banish the image from his mind as he added sticks to the fading fire. Thoughts of his mother had been less of a problem in the monastery, where he had studies and fellow residents to occupy his attention, but out here, with nothing to do, every fear rose to the surface at once. It ate at his mind as the hunger ate at his stomach.

One afternoon, while refilling his waterskin from the stream, he'd slipped and hit his knee on a rock. It wasn't bad, but the pain and frustration were enough to push him over the edge. *"What am I supposed to be doing here?"* he demanded of the sky, as though the sky might answer. *"What is the point of all this? What am I waiting for?"*

He stood there, breathing heavily, but only silence answered. He told himself to trust Master Gotami, but this training was beginning to feel like a cruel joke.

----

MIDWAY THROUGH THE THIRD week, something shifted.

He would've been hard-pressed to explain it, but it was as if his mind had struck a breaking point—an involuntary surrender. It was as though his mind simply stopped fighting and accepted the hunger, the rabbi's voice, the whispers, and the dreams of his mother. In some ways, it felt as though his thoughts were no longer his own—like he was watching himself from a distance. He existed above his thoughts. In the spaces between his feelings. He observed his actions and perceptions like leaves on a stream, especially during meditation, which he now practiced without ceasing. The shift was a blessed relief.

"So this is it, then?" he muttered to himself one day, looking at his reflection in the stream. He felt stronger. Proud. He'd finally discovered the point of the wilderness training. It had taken only three weeks. Of course, this confidence only seemed to provoke the rabbi in his head. *Pride precedes destruction!* the rabbi warned, cutting him down as he always had when he felt Jesus was growing too bold. *A confident spirit goes before the greatest fall!*

As best he could, Jesus let the rabbi's voice pass like a cloud in the sky.

He could finish this. He was sure of it.

----

THE EVENING OF THE thirty-third day found Jesus singing as he gathered grass and sticks for his fire.

*"They wandered in the desert waste, finding no city or town. Their hunger and thirst nearly drove them mad, and their soul became faint on their own..."*

He paused, smiling and wiping sweat from his forehead. A psalm for every occasion.

Jesus plucked up a handful of dried grass and saw a striped snake coiled beneath it. "I'm sorry about that," he said, placing the bundle of grass back over the snake. His apprehension of wildlife had left him weeks ago, but that didn't mean he wasn't still cautious. There was fear, but he wasn't afraid. He wondered if this was how the first man had felt in the garden.

As he stared at the bundle of grass, he thought about that story. It was like his story, but it was also different. That story had ended with the first people being exiled from the garden—with a fiery sword placed between them and their peace. He'd done the opposite. He'd found the garden again and now felt he could live in it forever. Even when he had to go back to Metta Valley—when he had to go out into the world on his errand—he'd take the garden with him. The Kingdom of God was at hand, and he wouldn't lose sight of it.

He continued singing as he finished gathering and returned to his cave. The sun dipped low, setting the sky on fire with orange and crimson.

*"They cried out to their God in their time of trouble, and God delivered them from their distress. He led them on straight paths—led them to a city to settle..."*

Content, he folded his legs into lotus pose and steadily fed the fire—giving it just enough to keep going. As he did, he performed a quick count of the tally marks on the wall across from him. He was in no rush, but he wanted to stay mindful of his time. He finished the count, then made himself count again. Could that be right?

"Thirty," he muttered, "thirty-one, thirty-two, thirty-three..."

It was almost time. His forty days—which had seemed like an eternity a few weeks ago—were nearly finished. He'd done it. He was almost ready for the next phase of his training. Jesus couldn't help but smile as the fire illuminated the cave with renewed light.

The rabbi's voice rose from the back of his mind. *After pride,* he warned, *then comes disgrace.*

"Everyone should take pleasure in their toil," Jesus recited. "This is God's gift."

The sun was nearly gone, leaving the flickering fire as his only source of light. He settled onto his makeshift seat of bundled leaves. The warm glow of accomplishment spread through him. Then, Jesus began to meditate, as he did every night.

He let his eyes close halfway, keeping his gaze on the fire and watching the rise and fall of his breath as Moggallana had taught him.

*In... out...*

He watched until his breathing slowed, and his mind relaxed.

He watched as the shadows grew long, enveloping everything in darkness.

He followed the rhythm of his breath until time slipped away and his legs began to go numb...

Then, his eyes snapped open.

At first, he wasn't sure what it was. He strained his ears, listening to the night sounds creeping in from outside the cave. He was almost ready to let it go, returning to his meditation, when the hair on the back of his neck stood straight.

The whispering. It was getting closer.

As with the snake, there was caution, but he wasn't afraid. He unfolded his legs, rubbing the feeling back into them, aware that he might need to run. At the same time, he wondered if this was futile. There was only one way in and out of the cave. Where would he go?

The whispers grew louder. There were more of them—whatever *they* were.

Slowly, he stood to get a look outside, but he was instantly met with a wave of lightheadedness. He swayed, catching himself against the cave wall. He was used to lightheadedness after weeks of fasting, but this was different. The whispers pressed closer as he closed his eyes, trying to focus his mind. *"Give praise to our God,"* he mumbled, trying to focus on his own voice, *"for all thirst is quenched and the hungry are filled with good things..."*

Had he been poisoned? Had the snake bitten him without his noticing? He doubted it, but what other explanation could there be? Perhaps he was losing his mind, like the king's son in Judas's story. Try as he might, he couldn't clear his head. The cave spun, and he felt nauseous. Then, just as quickly as it had come on, everything stopped.

His head cleared. There was silence.

Steadily, he pushed himself upright and took the Buddha stone from his robes, rolling it in his hand. He gave himself a moment to see if the dizziness would return, but when it didn't, he lowered himself back into a sitting position, gazing into the fire.

"I practice to be like fire," he recited, trying to center himself, "which consumes all things, beautiful or ugly, free of attachment or aversion. I practice to be like the earth, which receives all things and transforms all things. Even the foulest thing is compost for flowers..."

His hands trembled slightly as he held onto the stone.

"I practice to be like fire, which consumes all things, beautiful or ugly, free of attachment or aversion. I practice to be like—"

"Like the earth," another voice cut in, causing Jesus to jump. "Which receives all things and transforms all things..."

The stone nearly slipped from Jesus's grip. There was a hooded figure sitting across the fire, warming his hands—a figure who had appeared without a sound.

"Then again, perhaps fire only burns," the stranger said. "Perhaps beauty doesn't have all that much to do with it after all. Ask your friend Abraham. He would know."

Jesus's staff leaned against the cave wall behind the stranger. As he estimated how quickly he could get to it, the stranger noticed and shook his head. "Don't bother. Your satchel is empty anyway. What would I steal?"

"Who are you?" Jesus demanded. A hood cast deep shadows over the stranger's face.

"You know who I am," the stranger said, and Jesus could make out a smile under the hood. "The question is, Yeshua, who are *you?* They may hesitate to tell you, but I will."

Jesus froze. There was something familiar about his low, gruff voice. "How do you know my name?"

"I have a better question," the stranger answered. "What are you doing here, Yeshua? No one is holding a knife to your throat. There is plenty of bread in the village. You could disguise yourself as a beggar, and the great Mama Gotami will never even know, would she? She probably did it herself during her rite of initiation. Go a day without bread and see how quickly righteousness crumbles."

"Sometimes wisdom is more valuable than bread," Jesus said, still trying to get a look at the man's face. Almost without thinking about it, he quoted the law. "You've been humbled with hunger to understand no one lives on bread alone, but on every word issued from the mouth of God."

The stranger laughed out loud. "The Scroll of Words!" he proclaimed. "Very good. How I've missed playing these games with you. I didn't think I would, but I have. The arrogance! Yeshua of Nazareth, the new Elijah! Yeshua of Nazareth, the new Moses! You do not disappoint—except, of course, when you do."

Jesus thought about kicking sparks in the stranger's direction. That might distract him long enough to escape. "You're going to tell me who you are," Jesus commanded, dropping any pretense of hospitality. "I'm not playing this game."

"Oh, but you are," the stranger said, grinning.

Deliberately, he raised his hands to his hood and pulled it back.

Jesus's breath caught as he saw the stranger's face. He wasn't a stranger at all. Across the fire, looking just as Jesus remembered, was the rabbi.

# 38

"WHAT'S THE MATTER, YOUNG Yeshua?" the rabbi asked. "Aren't you glad to see your old teacher come to rescue you from the dogs and Gentiles?"

Jesus jumped to his feet. "How are you here?" he demanded. "How is this possible?"

The rabbi gave a wide smile, clearly pleased by the effect of his presence. "Maybe I came all this way just to see you," he said. "Maybe I realized you were right all this time, so I finally sought you out to atone for my sins. Then again, maybe the town found out about the scrolls and ran me out, so I came here to kill you because I have nothing left to lose. Maybe, maybe, maybe…"

Jesus closed his eyes, struggling to steady his breath. It came in rapid, shallow bursts. "You're not here," he insisted. "You can't be real."

"I'm as real as you are."

"That's not true."

"Truth," the rabbi scoffed. "What is truth?"

Jesus tried to make sense of what he was seeing. Surely this was a hunger-induced delusion. That, or he really had been bitten by that snake or some other venomous insect. Maybe there was something in the water, or maybe this was the inevitable madness of being alone too long in the wilderness. Some distant part of him wondered if this was a vision or a spirit, but he kept that part at bay.

The rabbi leaned forward. "Let's take a look at you," he said. "Incredible, isn't it? You've taken blasphemy to new heights. 'You shall not shave the hair on your temples—nor mar the edges of your beard…'

'You shall not seek after other gods—the gods of the foreigners around you...' 'You shall have no other gods before me—making no carved images for yourself of any likeness...' How easily you disregard the commandments you once held so dear. Do you not remember the stories of the judges, young Yeshua? Have you ignored the words of those prophets you love so much? 'And the people of Israel did what was evil in God's sight and served false gods...' And you dare call me a hypocrite..."

Jesus glared. "You don't know what you're talking about."

"Don't I? The worst punishments are reserved for those who would mix the God of Israel with the gods of dogs and Gentiles. What have they promised you? Power? Gifts? The ability to divine the future or call up the dead? Show me the power of your new gods, and I'll show you the power of mine. Come now. Let's have it out, like Elijah and the priests of Jezebel. It'll be fun. Climb to the roof of your beloved Metta Valley and jump. Let's see if your new gods save you."

The longer the rabbi talked, the more anger replaced Jesus's fear. "If you'd spent less time selling scrolls and more time reading them, you'd know the scripture, 'You shall not put God to the test.'"

The rabbi grinned. "And here we are again," he said. "This same old song and dance. All this time, and you haven't learned a thing."

Jesus no longer cared whether he was talking to the rabbi or to his own delusion. He knew only the rage he felt—the rage he'd tried to put off for too long. "You think I care what you say?" he challenged. "I know the game you're playing. I see it now. You've never cared about God or truth. You care only about power and control. You've hated me my whole life, not because of anything I've done, but because you're afraid."

"Is that what the old man told you?" the rabbi asked. "Well, tell me, Yeshua, if you care so little about what I think, why are you so upset? Would my words bother you if you weren't afraid they were true?"

Jesus gripped the Buddha stone so tightly it hurt his palm.

"I'll tell you why you're upset," the rabbi said, stoking the fire. "It's because you've learned such big ideas, but you don't believe what you're saying. Not a bit. You know the right words, yes—you've always been good at that. Your beloved Abraham gave you the terms, as did your beloved Master Gotami, but they're not *yours,* are they?"

Jesus opened his mouth to refute him, but hesitated.

"That's what she meant that night on the roof," the rabbi went on. "You don't really know these things for yourself, do you? You have only secondhand truth. Deep down, you know what you really are. You know why I cast you from the assembly. It wasn't because you were 'brave' and it certainly wasn't because you were 'smart.' It was because you were *unclean*, Yeshua. You still are. I cast you out for the simple reason that you had no place with us, and a righteous God could never use or accept someone as unworthy, arrogant, and worthless as you. *That* is the truth."

"You're a liar."

The rabbi shrugged. "Don't take it from me, then."

The way he said this sent a shiver down Jesus's spine, and after a moment, he heard a new voice from deeper within the cave. He knew the voice at once.

"Yeshua?"

He looked back and saw her there, sitting at their old table as she had in his dream, watching him.

"Amma?"

"You left me," she accused. "You betrayed me. You left me alone."

"No, amma, I—" Jesus started, but she wasn't finished.

"I tried to warn you, child," she pressed on. "I told you that things would be difficult enough without you making them worse, but you've gone and done it anyway. It has been hell for me, do you know that? You have tried to fight against something so much bigger than you were, and *I* am the one who has suffered for it."

"You could've come with me," Jesus said. "You had a choice."

"Don't fool yourself."

His mother's disappointment in him was palpable. "I tried to protect you," she went on. "I did all I could to shield you from the worst of what they thought of me. Of us. You were a child, and I tried to keep you safe, but I can see now that I shouldn't have. I should've told you the truth right off, because now you're trapped in a fantasy."

"I know the truth, amma."

"No, child," his mother shook her head. "The rabbi is the only one who tells you the truth, and you're a fool not to see it. There are laws written deeper than you or I could ever touch—God's laws, written into being on the foundations of the earth. He will judge sons for the sins of their fathers, and that is our lot. It is not something you or I can ever escape."

"Yes, it is!" Jesus yelled. "It's not true what they say. There are stories we tell ourselves, and the truth—"

"This is *their* world, Yeshua," his mother insisted. "It's not ours. This life belongs to the rabbis and the Romans and the priests and the kings. It belongs to people like Devadatta and that landowner in the orchard. You can't fight them, no matter what you do. You say God is a title, yes? The truest and most powerful thing in life? Well, tell me, what is more real or powerful than what I am saying to you now? To what other God can this world possibly belong?"

"That's not true."

"It's the *highest* truth! Had you accepted that, things might've been better for us! But you don't care about that, do you? You don't care about me. You don't care about anyone but yourself. Well, I see you've got what you've always wanted. Yeshua, son of no one. I hope you enjoy it."

"Enough!" Jesus said, turning back to the rabbi. "Whatever this is, it's proving nothing except that I love my mother, and it kills me that she chose to stay. I'm not arguing with a phantom. I don't know what this is, but it's over."

"Is it?" the rabbi asked.

Jesus tried to leave, desperate for fresh air, but when he reached the mouth of the cave, he found his path blocked by a snarling leopard—hackles raised and eyes reflecting the firelight. Slowly, Jesus withdrew back into the cave.

"You are mistaken," the rabbi said, calmly stoking the fire. "You say it proves nothing, but it proves you're weak—that you're delicate and easily taken in. It proves that, despite all this 'wisdom' you throw around, you haven't grown a bit."

Jesus looked back at the place where his mother had been, but she was gone. Once again, it was only him and the rabbi.

"All that talk about finding a better way," the rabbi said, "you prove it was worthless, just like you."

"I *did* find a better way," Jesus growled, looking around for a way out. "I found something more real than anything you ever offered. You taught fear and obedience. These people have taught me freedom. They teach justice. Truth."

"Don't confuse a shaved head and a yellow robe for growth, young Yeshua. That's just a new outer layer to make you feel holy. Inside you're the same little bastard, afraid of being walked over... afraid of being trapped and helpless... afraid that everything might really be as meaningless and violent and pointless as it seems... *That's* the truth."

The fire on the cave floor grew hotter and brighter as the rabbi stoked. Smoke billowed and covered the ceiling of the cave, like storm clouds. Jesus continued to grind the Buddha stone into his palm.

"How about this?" the rabbi asked. "Let's have a brief test to see just how much you've grown, shall we? Son of Mary?"

Jesus willed himself to remain silent in the face of the rabbi's taunt, but a satisfied grin spread across the rabbi's face all the same. "You can't hide it from me," the rabbi said. "I see it all. Every thought. Every feeling. Every ounce of anger and fear and weakness, laid bare before my eyes."

Jesus stopped trying to find a way out and met the rabbi's eye. "What are you?"

"What am *I?*" the rabbi echoed. "*I* am the one who sees how small you remain, and *I* am the one who will not let you forget. *I* am the one who sees that you know full well you don't belong here anymore than you belonged back in Nazareth."

"Leave me alone," Jesus commanded.

"*I* am the one who knows you know the truth, however reluctant you are to admit it to yourself. I see it right there in your eyes. You know that God could never approve of one such as yourself."

"Your god is only a story you told us to keep us afraid," Jesus said. "To keep us small."

The rabbi chuckled, and the fire continued to swell. Smoke ran down the walls unnaturally on every side, blocking the mouth of the cave and swirling around them. It was like a slow-moving whirlwind.

"You heard your mother," the rabbi said. "By your own definition, the god I taught you is the most real "god" there can be. What could be more real than that which reminds you just how small you are in this world? Than that which keeps order by threat of judgment, drowning armies in its fury?"

"I'm not listening to this," Jesus said. As always, he hated how much he was tempted to believe the rabbi's words—how much he feared that he really did believe them.

"You could have learned to play the game, you know," the rabbi said. "As much as it pains me to admit, you *are* intelligent. You always have been. You're only foolish about how you use your intelligence. You're stubborn and arrogant and self-righteous. If you'd wanted to, you could've worked your way all the way to the top. You still could if you choose to! You could be running that Metta Valley of yours in only ten years."

Jesus had heard enough. Picking up a rock from the cave floor, he hurled it at the rabbi, hoping to bring an end to this whole nightmare. Instead of striking him, though, the rock only sailed through his shoulder, replacing Jesus's anger with an icy fear. He felt out of his depth.

"You could have run that vineyard, too," the rabbi went on. "With your ties to that blaspheming vineyard owner and his naïve son, you could be running all of Kashi if you'd only stopped being a fool and learned to play some politics. You want freedom? What could offer more freedom than *that*? You hate everyone in power anyway—all the corrupt officials and systems that leave the vulnerable in the dust. Why not *do* something about it? Cut them down! Start your revolution! Unseat the old fools like me and finally make the world the way you think it should be!"

"I don't want that!" Jesus declared, skirting the cave walls and growing angry again.

His anger only seemed to feed the rabbi, whose voice grew stronger until it echoed off the cave walls. It swirled around him from every side, like the smoke from the fire. *"Do not lie to me, Yeshua,"* the rabbi boomed. *"Do not assume that just because I wear this face that I am as small-minded and ignorant as your absurd rabbi. I know you better than you know* yourself, *and you can hide nothing from me! You are capable of all this, and you know it. The strength of the Roman Empire flows in your blood, does it not? It's there, in your parentage."*

"Don't," Jesus said. He could see where this was going, and he wanted no part of it.

*"Perhaps it is time for you to meet the man who gave you life?"*

"No!"

*"Are you prepared, Yeshua, son of Pantera?"*

From the clouds now swirling around him like a violent windstorm, a man stepped out. Jesus had never seen him before, but he knew him instantly. He wore the uniform of a low-ranking Roman soldier, and his hands were stained with blood. The soldier's eyes were hungry, like a wolf.

"He's right, son," the soldier said. "Look at my face. You are capable of all I've done and more."

"I'm *nothing* like you!" Jesus yelled.

"But you are," the soldier insisted. "Listen to yourself. Ambitious. Quick-witted. Willing to do whatever it takes. You can *use* that, you know. You can use it to bring justice. You can raise up the vulnerable and bring the powerful down low. And why not? Why not make us feel the pain we've inflicted on you?"

"Because that's not how justice works," Jesus argued. "All you did was leave a trail of suffering. That's all the Empire ever does. You left a legacy of pain, and no one shed a tear when they cut you down."

The soldier looked disappointed. "Your mother has kept you weak."

Jesus ran at the soldier, but when he reached him, he ran through the soldier like smoke. Jesus collided with a cave wall and felt a searing pain in his shoulder. He fell to the floor, his back against the cave wall, and the Buddha stone fell from his hand, clattering into the smoke.

"There it is..." the soldier said from the other side of the room. "You know what people like me deserve. You know what *everyone* deserves, don't you? And you can give it to them. You want to be free, Yeshua? Truly? You want to set others free? Well, then... do something about it."

Jesus heard something clang at his feet. The soldier had thrown his sword onto the floor.

"Take it. Let's see if all your talk of justice is only empty words."

For a moment, Jesus stared at the sword, tempted to take it up and put an end to all of this. Slowly, he rose to his feet, glaring at the soldier. Then, Jesus kicked the sword across the cave. It disappeared behind the wall of smoke.

*"Perhaps I was wrong,"* the rabbi's voice boomed again, and the soldier disappeared. *"Perhaps you really are only a frightened, powerless little boy, looking for someone to please or someone to fight. Perhaps you are doomed forever to fight a losing battle—trying to make up for what you are."*

"Stop this now!" Jesus commanded.

The rabbi only glared.

*"No."*

Suddenly, the rabbi disappeared, and Jesus found himself alone in the center of a fierce whirlwind. The fire he'd made of brush and twigs now rose into a pillar of flame, illuminating everything with a wild, flickering glow.

*"You have failed, and you have failed again,"* a voice crashed like thunder from the pillar of fire. *"You miss the mark in every conceivable way. You are disappointment made flesh."*

Jesus raged into the storm. "I hate you!" he bellowed. "You twist truth and beauty into weapons! You are a deceiver and a liar!"

Once more, Jesus looked wildly for a way out, but there was nothing. The ground rumbled as rocks and debris broke loose from the walls and churned around him. Ducking quickly, Jesus covered his head to avoid the worst of it.

*"Pitiful,"* the voice boomed, and at that moment, Jesus was assaulted by a flood of memories. He was a child, the rabbi crushing his mud sculptures at the outskirts of town... He was asking his mother about Pantera, watching her cry all night, all because of him... He was humiliated before the assembly, then cast out... The memories came in waves, crashing over him as the rocks tumbled from the walls. He felt ashamed, afraid, and angry.

Trying in vain to shield himself, Jesus curled into a tight ball, bracing himself against the avalanche of memory, stone, and dust. They wore him down. He tried to hold tight to his anger and indignation, but it slipped through his grasp.

*"It is a losing battle, Yeshua,"* the voice issued from the storm. *"Your rabbi... your mother... your God... despite your efforts, there are none whose love you have earned. There are none who bless you. That is the truth of what you are, Yeshua, son of no one."*

Rocks continued to crash against Jesus's back, cutting into his skin. He truly had gone mad in the cave, and now he knew he would not make it back from this. This was where he died. He would never see Metta Valley again. Would never see Master Gotami or Moggallana or Judas. He would never see Nazareth or Judea or his mother.

He closed his eyes, waiting for the end.

# 39

*I*T IS A GREAT *paradox of wisdom that one must be willing to lose their life in order to find it.* Jesus almost laughed as these words echoed through his mind—words Abraham had spoken so long ago around their warm cooking fire. He was sure Abraham never meant for him to take them quite so literally, yet as the rocks and smoke continued to churn around him and the painful memories flooded in, he knew he didn't have much longer.

As he braced himself against the onslaught, a rock wedged itself beneath his knee. Jesus risked a glance from under his arms. It was the Buddha stone, its carved smile unchanged even amid the storm.

Jesus closed his eyes tightly and reached for it—his fingers curling around its smooth surface. He remembered the first time he'd held the Buddha idol in Abraham's home—the way it had rested on his small altar, serene and half-smiling among the sacred pieces. He'd been so suspicious of Abraham—so distrustful of that voice he'd come to trust so deeply.

The other voice continued to echo from the storm and the pillar of fire, and Jesus tried to shut it out.

*"There is nothing left for you, young Yeshua,"* it boomed. *"Nothing but to let go and surrender."*

Jesus covered his face and clung to the stone. If he was going to die, he would die remembering the taste of Abraham's stew—not raging against this storm. He was going to die remembering what Abraham had said when he'd listened to Jesus's story from start to finish. *Here is the truth: you are as brave and clever as they come, son. You frighten*

*weak men because weak men fear the truth, while you are satisfied with*
*nothing less. You are not a child of disgrace. You are not a child of shame.*
*You are a child of the Living God, beloved, just as you are. The next time*
*you tell your story, you would do well to remember that...*

Despite everything, this memory made Jesus smile. He hadn't believed him then, but Jesus had cherished those words all the same. No
one had ever spoken to him like that before. No one had ever seen
him as anything more than the fatherless troublemaker from Nazareth.
Abraham had believed he could be more.

This thought brought an unexpected wave of sadness. What would
Abraham think if he could see him now? If he could see Jesus cowering
in the face of madness? Prisoner of a delusion, drowning under the
weight of memory? And then there was Master Gotami. What would
she say if she could see him now? What would Moggallana say if—

Jesus's eyes snapped open.

That was it.

Moggallana had given him the answer—as had Abraham and Master Gotami—but he hadn't had ears to hear until now. It was so simple,
yet not simple at all. There was only one way to get through this, and it
wasn't to hide beneath his arms. Nor was it to fight. It was clear what
he had to do.

Jesus clenched the stone tightly and unfurled his body, rising to his
full height and standing boldly amid the whirlwind. Slowly, he stepped
forward, facing down the pillar of fire.

*"And now he dares to speak!"* the voice thundered from the flames.
*"Now, in the final hour. Speak, then, young Yeshua. What words of*
*rebuke do you have for me? What barb of wit or wisdom?"*

Jesus didn't flinch. He planted his feet and breathed deeply. He felt
his body relax, accepting what was happening around him. He had no
barbs. No rebukes. There was only one thing to say.

"I see you, Mara," Jesus said calmly. "I hear you."

Immediately, as though Jesus had thrown dry brush on the fire, the
flames roared and billowed outward, driving Jesus back a step. The

voice raged from the whirlwind. *"Do you think I am a villain in one of their parables? Do you believe you can defeat me by playing their little games? You know nothing of the truth, boy, nor do they! I am truth! It was I who laid the foundations of the earth! It was I who made its measurements and set the standards to judge all who live therein!"*

If there had been any doubts before, they evaporated. Deliberately, Jesus moved around the flames to where he had been sitting. There, he lowered himself to the gritty cave floor and watched his breath, mindful of the chaos before him. Stones stung his face and neck, but he didn't waver. "I see you," he repeated. "I hear you."

*"Enough!"* the voice bellowed. *"Rise and face me!"*

But Jesus didn't rise. He remained still. He watched the rise and fall of his breath. He tuned his mind to see the impermanence of the storm. He tuned his eyes to see the Kingdom of God—beyond stories and delusions—and suddenly the voice lost its venom. It was only a voice. Its story was only a story. Beyond them, there was something else—still, quiet, and eternal. Something real.

"I see you," he repeated, his voice stronger now. "I hear you."

The smoke began to thin. The pillar of fire grew dimmer. Jesus saw the outline of the rabbi across the fire, straining frantically to reach him. Some unseen force kept him at a distance. *"Stop this!"* he commanded.

"No," Jesus said, watching the rabbi struggle. He remembered his training—noting without attachment or aversion. With relief, his resentment and fear drained away. Curiosity took their place. Compassion.

"You cannot ignore me, Yeshua!" the rabbi raged, but his voice now came from only one place. "You cannot deny me! Who are you if you are not fighting against me? Who are you without your anger and your indignation?"

Jesus listened to him, then smiled. It was a good question. When he answered, there was no argument in his voice. No defensiveness. The truth needed no defending.

"I am a child of the Living God," he said. "I am a grapevine who will not be judged. An heir to the Kingdom of God. A wave on the ocean of being. I am Yeshua, son of God. That's who I am."

As he said it, he believed for the first time that it was true.

The rabbi roared in frustration. "That woman and the old man have drawn you into madness!" he snarled. "You're only doing this to please them! To win their praise! How long until they see who you really are, Yeshua? How long until they cast you out, just as I did? Just as your mother did?"

"I don't need to please them," Jesus said. The rabbi's words passed him by like leaves on a stream. "They don't accept me because of anything I've done. They accept me because they see the truth, like I do now."

"I am not leaving!" the rabbi shouted.

"And I'm not asking you to," Jesus said. "Stay as an advisor. A guest. But that's all you are now. My days of letting you push me into anger or fear are over."

As he said this, Jesus felt spacious. Radiant. He was part of something far greater than himself—an instrument of transcendent peace and justice. It was like the glimpse of freedom he'd caught under the Bodhi tree, but this time, it was no fleeting glimmer. It was no flickering candle flame. It was as unshakable and bright as the sun. For the first time, he stood on solid ground. For the first time, he felt free.

The smoke thinned, and the cave walls came back into view. The flames had dwindled to a meager fire. "Listen to me," the rabbi shouted desperately, the authority gone from his voice. "Think of what the powers of this world will do to you! That vendor from Kashi! Devadatta! The orchard owner! Do you remember what it was like? Do you remember what happened to Abraham? They'll crush you! Kill you! Injustice will reign supreme, and you will fade into oblivion!"

"That may be," Jesus said, "but it doesn't end with me. All I can do is listen well, testify to the truth, and let go of what I can't control. My teacher once told me that."

The smoke cleared, and Jesus could see outside. The leopard had disappeared, and Jesus could see a cloudless sky, scattered with stars. He felt the rising and falling of all things—the ever-changing dance of the cosmos—and he knew he was part of it. All the universe was a temple. His own heart was a temple. Suddenly, he wanted to bow down in worship and lift his voice in every psalm of praise he knew.

"You'll never make it like this!" a voice cried, but it no longer sounded like the rabbi. It was small. Afraid. "It's not safe! *We're* not safe!"

Jesus looked back, but in the rabbi's place was a child in the rabbi's billowing robes, absurd on his small frame. The child's eyes brimmed with tears.

"What if they hurt us? What if we're scared and all by ourselves?"

Looking at the child, Jesus was filled with compassion. All he wanted to do was comfort this boy—let him know he wasn't alone and that everything would be well. The boy hurried over and leaped into Jesus's lap, and after a moment of surprise, Jesus embraced him. "I've got you," he said, and it felt like something greater was speaking through him. "I see you. I hear you."

Soon, the wind died, and the world went still. The only sounds were the chirps of the cicadas and the murmur of the creek. Even in the stillness, though, Jesus saw the world flowing into a dance. He closed his eyes and joined it, letting it move through him. Without thinking about it, he began to sing.

*"Why do the nations conspire? Why do the people choose chaos? God laughs in the face of their folly, and in time, they will all see the truth. God speaks this eternal decree: Today, my child, I've begotten you—you've become a beloved son of God..."*

He sang to calm the child. He sang to praise the truth. He sang because he couldn't imagine doing anything else.

Jesus sang until the psalm was finished, then he moved on to the next psalm, and the next. At some point, he found himself against the cave wall and drifted to sleep, still mumbling the words of praise.

When he woke up, with the light of morning streaming onto the embers of his fire, the child was gone. He was alone except for the Buddha stone in his hand, smiling up at him, as always.

# V.

# 40

JESUS SAT ON THE ground in the dining hall, a warm cup of thinned porridge before him. He had taken only one bite, but it was plenty. After forty days, his stomach could only take so much.

Moggallana sat across from him, cross-legged, his eyes bright. "Well," he said, "you survived after all."

Jesus cleared his throat. "Did I?" he asked, his voice hoarse from so many days in silence. "I've always wondered if they served porridge in Sheol."

Moggallana laughed. "I see the wilderness was not ferocious enough to sap your sense of humor."

Jesus had returned to Metta Valley earlier that evening, just before sunset. He doubted several times whether he'd make it down into the valley. By the time he arrived, he felt entirely spent, and needed help from residents to make it to the dining hall.

"Where is Judas?" Jesus asked, pushing the porridge aside. "Did he make it back all right?"

Brother Moggallana's smile faltered. "I'm afraid Brother Judas's time in the wilderness was... cut short."

"Cut short?" Jesus echoed. "What does that mean? Is he all right?"

"Oh yes, he's all right," Moggallana said. "Don't worry. I am afraid, however, that Brother Judas returned to us over a week ago. He was unable to complete his rite of initiation."

"What happened?"

"That is not mine to share, I'm afraid. Brother Judas may speak to his own experience, but rest assured, he is all right. For the time being, you must worry about yourself. Eat. Rest."

Jesus knew he needed to talk to Judas. "I'll rest," he said, "but I think the eating part is done."

"Wise. A few spoonfuls are customary following a prolonged fast. When I returned, I made the mistake of eating too much too quickly. I would wish that mistake on no one."

"I am sure Brother Issa could have done without that image," came a voice behind him.

Jesus turned to see Master Gotami standing in the doorway. He smiled, pressing his palms together in greeting. "Master Gotami."

"Welcome home, Brother Issa," Master Gotami said, returning the gesture. "Metta Valley has been far too quiet in your absence."

"I intend to remedy that as quickly as possible."

Moggallana rose. "I will leave you to discuss in private," he said. "It is good to see you again, Brother Issa."

"You too, Brother Moggallana."

Moggallana pressed his palms together and left, and Master Gotami sat across from Jesus. "So, Brother Issa," she began. "Do you have the strength to share what waited for you beyond the walls of Metta Valley, or does such talk need to wait until morning?"

Jesus started to speak, then hesitated. He was unsure of what to say. How could he tell her what had happened to him in the cave? Would she think he had gone mad? "To tell you the truth," he said, "I don't think you would believe me."

Master Gotami joined her hands and leaned forward.

"Let us find out."

After a moment's hesitation, Jesus told his story as best as he could. He told her about the whispers from the dark. He told her about the cave and the rabbi—the flames and the whirlwind. He told her what he'd done—how he'd comforted the child. "I was there for another few days before the tally marks told me it was time to go home," he said, "but that sense of peace never left me. It still hasn't. For the first time in my life, I feel... free."

Master Gotami listened in silence, and when he was finished, Jesus thought she might tell him to go lie down and clear his head. Instead, she gave a subtle nod. "It is as I told you," she said. "There are things the wilderness can teach you that no teacher could convey."

"Is that what happened to you?" Jesus asked.

Master Gotami gave a half-smile. "Strange things happen, Brother Issa, when we are unable to run or hide in distraction. Forty days is a great deal of time to spend in the company of anyone, especially yourself. It opens our eyes to things we might not otherwise see."

"So I didn't lose my mind?"

"Perhaps you merely found a clearer one."

Jesus lowered his gaze, considering this.

"It sounds as though the rite has served its purpose," Master Gotami said. "If you are in agreement, I believe you are ready to move forward in your training."

Jesus met her eye. "The errand."

"Indeed," Master Gotami said. "So, the question becomes, Brother Issa, what will you do with this experience? Where does it call you as you go forth from here? Do you still wish to return to the vineyard?"

Jesus had given this a great deal of thought during his final days in the wilderness. When the idea first came to him, he'd dismissed it, but when it didn't go away, he began to consider it more carefully. Now, the answer felt clear to him.

"Judea," he told Master Gotami. "I want to return to Judea. It's time for me to go home."

Master Gotami raised her eyebrows in surprise. "Is this so? I am curious. What brought you to such a conclusion? Returning to your homeland is not something in which you have ever expressed interest. In fact, you've always seemed quite resistant to the idea."

"I think that's the point," Jesus said. "I don't want to be angry with them anymore. If I can practice this freedom where it's most difficult, that's the only way I'll learn. Besides, there are people there who would benefit from what you've taught me here."

"This is true," Master Gotami said, "but I must point out that even for the most experienced master of the Way, the errand you propose involves considerable risk. You would travel into the heart of an empire that would not only seek to silence you, but would think nothing of your execution. You would put yourself against governors, against priests, against teachers like your rabbi..."

"I know," Jesus said, "but it's worth it. It's what the prophets tried to do—to open people's eyes to the Kingdom of God around them. I want to stand in that tradition. I want to serve something greater than myself, calling the people back to justice and compassion. I've seen the truth, Master Gotami, and the truth has set me free. Now it's my job to share it."

Master Gotami studied him for a moment. "You have clearly given this a great deal of thought."

"I have."

For a long moment, Jesus thought Master Gotami was going to tell him it wasn't possible—that it was too dangerous. But she didn't. Instead, she gave another half-smile.

"Brother Abraham would be quite proud, I think," she said.

Jesus felt tears come to his eyes, and he made no motion to wipe them away. "I hope so," he said.

Master Gotami rose. "Very well," she said, offering him a hand and helping him to his feet. "We will discuss this again tomorrow. In the meantime, rest well and eat properly. Brother Judas will doubtless be eager to see you."

"Thank you, Master Gotami," Jesus said.

They made their way outside, where two residents waited to help Jesus up the stairs to see Judas.

# 41

"You're alive!" Judas exclaimed, pulling Jesus into a tight embrace.

"I am," Jesus gasped. "Alive and very weak, I might add."

"Oh, sorry," Judas said, letting go and stepping back to look Jesus over. "You made it, though! Did you have trouble? Are you all right? What happened out there?"

"Calm down," Jesus laughed, dropping his satchel by the door and making his way over to his mat. It was a welcome sight after forty days in a cave. "I've barely spoken since I left, and I just talked my throat raw with Master Gotami."

"I've been keeping an eye out for you," Judas went on. "I was ready to go out looking, but Moggallana said that might be premature. I was sure you'd been mauled by a tiger."

"No tigers," Jesus said. "A leopard and a demon, maybe, but no tigers."

"Pardon?" Judas asked, looking confused.

"What happened to *you*, though?" Jesus went on, remembering what Moggallana had told him. "You came back early?"

Judas's smile faltered. "I... I did," he said, lowering his gaze. "It was more challenging than I expected."

"More challenging?" Jesus echoed. "Which part? The fasting? The solitude?"

"No, they were manageable. I think I could've survived those. It was... something else."

The way Judas averted his eyes made it clear he was hiding something. Jesus waited for him to continue, but he didn't.

"Judas," he began, "did you see something out there? If you—"

"It's not something I wish to discuss," Judas said, keeping his eyes down.

"There's no shame in it," Jesus said. "If you knew what I saw out there, you'd—"

"I said I don't wish to discuss it," Judas snapped, then exhaled slowly. "I'm sorry," he tried again. "There are just some things I would rather leave in the wilderness, where they belong."

Jesus considered whether to push any harder, but ruled against it. Judas was clearly shaken, and Jesus didn't want to make it any worse. "All right," he said. "But if you ever change your mind, I'm here. It may help."

"Thanks," Judas muttered. "We're back now. That is what matters. It's over."

"It's over," Jesus agreed, "until the errand, of course. Have you spoken to Master Gotami about where you might go?"

Somehow, Judas managed to look even more miserable. He collapsed onto his mat, leaning against the wall. "I don't know that I will," he said. "Residents who fail to complete their rite of initiation aren't sent on errand, are they?"

"Could you just try again?"

"No," Judas answered, a frightened expression flickering across his face. "I'm not going back out there."

Jesus regarded his friend, wondering what could've disturbed him so badly.

"It's all right, though," Judas said. "I don't think I was meant to be ordained as a *bhikku*. Perhaps that path is not for me."

"Have you thought about where you might go?"

"Not yet," Judas said. "Back to the vineyard, maybe? I'm sure I'll come out all right, though. I always do."

Jesus didn't quite believe him. He knew there was one other option Judas hadn't considered.

"Come with me," Jesus said. "Come to Judea."

"Judea?" Judas repeated, confused. "What do you mean?"

As best he could, Jesus told Judas what had happened in the wilderness. He told him about the cave, the visions, and his conversation with Master Gotami. He told him about his change of heart and what he wanted to do. Judas's expression, which had been one of worry throughout the story, shifted to astonishment at the mention of his errand. "Judea..." he said in wonder. "That's so far. And you mean it? You would let me join you?"

"Of course," Jesus said. "We've come this far, haven't we?"

Judas sprang from his mat and began pacing their small cell. "I would see the Jordan... Jerusalem..."

Jesus watched him, surprised. "I didn't think it would mean so much to you."

"Are you serious?" Judas beamed. "To see my father's homeland? That would be wonderful! To see the Temple in person?"

Jesus let out a small laugh. "The Temple that made your father so angry he turned over the coffer? That Temple?"

"And your mission," Judas went on, paying no attention. "It would be..." he hesitated, searching for the right words. He stopped mid-step, his expression growing serious. "It would be the perfect way to honor his legacy. I always suspected he wanted to go back—to do the very thing you propose—now *I* would get to be a part of it."

He sat on his mat once more, invigorated. "Jesus," he said, "it would be my honor to go with you."

"They won't exactly be thrilled to see us," Jesus warned. "I don't want to give you the wrong idea. What we do... it would be controversial."

"They will see," Judas said, confident. "If we do this right, they will understand."

"I'm not so sure."

"Do you think Master Gotami will approve?" Judas wondered aloud. "I don't know if there's a precedent for something like this."

"Well, we'll just have to set one, won't we?" Jesus asked. "The journey will certainly be easier with the two of us."

Judas didn't answer. He was clearly lost in thoughts of Judea.

After a few moments, Jesus leaned over and extinguished their small lamp. "We should get some rest," he said. "We can keep discussing it tomorrow."

"I'm too excited to sleep," Judas said, and Jesus laughed.

They lay there for a few more moments, neither saying anything, but then Jesus broke the silence again. "Judas," he said. "You know that even if you didn't go to Judea, you would still have your father's blessing, right? Even if you didn't do all of this work to honor his legacy, he would love you just the same."

There was a long silence.

"If we're going to do this," Jesus said, "it's important you know that."

"Of course," Judas said after another moment. "I know that. I'm just eager, is all."

Jesus nodded, though Judas couldn't see him in the dark. "All right," he said, not entirely convinced. "Goodnight, Judas."

"Goodnight," Judas answered. "And Yeshua?"

"Yes?"

"Thank you."

Jesus couldn't help but smile. "You're like a brother to me," he said. "On a journey like this, I don't think there's anyone I would trust more than you."

That was the end of the conversation. Eager to hear what Master Gotami would say tomorrow, they slipped into sleep.

# 42

A WAVE OF SOUND reverberated through their room. The sound of home. "I never thought I'd say this," Jesus muttered, "but I'm going to miss that bell."

Across the room, Judas sat up and rubbed his eyes. "We could take a small bell," he suggested. "I could ring it next to your ear each morning."

Jesus shot him a look. "It's not too late to leave you behind, you know."

As they made their way to the meditation hall, nearly every resident paused to welcome Jesus back. Jesus was surprised to find that his frustration and suspicion had faded. He was glad of their support. He no longer saw himself surrounded by competitors, but companions.

The changes followed him into the meditation hall, where he sat with newfound spaciousness. The freedom he'd found in the cave was still there—solid and tranquil—and he could've remained in meditation forever.

Following breakfast—Jesus was now up to *three* mouthfuls of watery porridge—they approached Master Gotami about Judas's decision to come with Jesus, and after a brief discussion, she agreed. "As I stated before," Master Gotami told them, "each student chooses how they wish to use their errand. Brother Judas, you may not continue in formal training until you have completed your rite of initiation, but this does not mean you cannot assist Brother Issa in his."

"Thank you," Jesus said. "We'll begin preparations to leave. How long do residents typically wait before departing on their errand?"

"Forty days, Brother Issa," Master Gotami answered. "If you are ready and recovered, you will depart in forty days."

———

THEIR FINAL FORTY DAYS at Metta Valley passed quickly. Jesus steadily regained his strength until he could eat normally and felt ready to travel. This gave him time to process his experience in the wilderness more fully, as it gave Judas time to make the practical arrangements for their journey. While Jesus worked with Master Gotami to flesh out his intention for returning to Judea, Judas worked with Moggallana to negotiate the supplies they'd need and the route they'd take. Watching them work, Jesus was grateful Judas was coming. Without Judas's mind for numbers and practicality, he wasn't sure where he might've ended up.

Jesus saw the children again a few more times—meeting in the new location Master Gotami had chosen. He had new stories to tell them about spirits speaking from a pillar of fire and a carpenter's apprentice who traveled halfway across the world. As always, he delighted in their questions and their unabashed comments about how foolhardy the carpenter's apprentice seemed. He didn't disagree, but reminded them that some of the most worthy endeavors required more than a small amount of foolishness. "Sometimes," he suggested, tousling Kapu's hair, "you must be willing to lose your life in order to find it."

When the day of their departure finally came, Jesus rose early—earlier than the bell, even—and made his way to the Bodhi tree in the center of the courtyard. There, he decided to sit in meditation until it was time to go. He wanted to soak up as much of Metta Valley as he could to take with him—from the carvings on the rock walls to the smell of spikenard permeating the grounds. He was going to miss it all.

"Brother Issa," Moggallana greeted a few minutes later, moving mindfully across the courtyard. "You are up early."

"As are you," Jesus answered.

"Yes, well," the old monk said, "it is because I wished to prepare something for you—for your journey. If you have a moment, I wonder if you would mind following me?"

Jesus followed Moggallana to the supply room, where they'd first received their robes and bowls. "I wanted to give you these," Moggallana said, handing over the few clothes and possessions Jesus had given him on his first day. "I hope they help you to blend in a bit better than you might in your saffron robes."

"Good idea," Jesus said. "I wouldn't want to be stoned as an idolater on my first day back."

"I also wanted to give you this."

Moggallana reached up to a high shelf and brought down a bag Jesus didn't recognize. He handed it to Jesus.

"What's this?" Jesus asked, flipping it open and revealing a bundle of supplies. Nestled among the supplies was a wineskin. "Now, Venerable Moggallana," Jesus began, "you know perfectly well that the fifth precept forbids any form of—"

"Don't you quote the precepts to me, you overdecorated aspirant," Moggallana said. "You and I both know you have no intention of keeping that precept once you step outside these walls. Besides," he pulled the wineskin from the bag and turned it around, "this one is worth making an exception."

On the side of the wineskin, Jesus recognized a familiar insignia. *Shalom.*

"We never drank them," Moggallana said, "but the old fool would send us at least one a year. It was his way of teasing us, I think. He was more like you than you know, Brother Issa. Now, at last, I have a use for at least one of them."

Jesus stared at the insignia. "This really should go to Judas."

Moggallana grinned. "You think I mean for you to drink this on your own?"

Gingerly, Jesus accepted the wineskin. "Thank you," he said. "Really."

"Just promise me this. Whenever you drink it, remember him, all right? Remember his grace. Remember his spirit. Drink this in memory of him."

Jesus nodded. "You have my word."

"Good," Moggallana clapped him on the shoulder. "That might at least salve my conscience for this grievous violation of the precepts. Now, I've got to go retrieve your beloved donkeys from the stables. They are still in excellent condition, and we are glad to return them to you."

"You really don't have to—"

"Nonsense!" Brother Moggallana said. "I spoke to Brother Judas last night. He was all too glad to have them returned to his care."

Jesus forced a smile. "I'm sure he was overjoyed."

After morning meditation with the other residents, Jesus and Judas went to their room one last time to change into their old clothes. After a year, they felt strange—like wearing a costume. Jesus lingered for a moment, running a hand over the fabric of his saffron robe before leaving it on his mat beside his bowl. *While you are here, they shall be your only possessions,* Moggallana had told them. *Even then, we cannot say that we truly possess them. We are but stewards for a time.* He'd been right. Now their time was up.

Downstairs, Jesus and Judas found the other residents gathering, preparing to send them off. Moggallana and Master Gotami stood near the grand doors next to two donkeys Jesus would've been happy never to see again. Judas, meanwhile, hurried over and began patting them on the back. Both donkeys had been laden with supplies.

Two residents climbed up onto the platforms on either side of the massive doors, working with thick ropes. "Are you expecting an elephant?" Jesus asked.

"An elephant?" Moggallana answered. "Goodness no, Brother Issa. We merely needed a gate large enough for your pride to pass through."

"It is customary to open the gate prior to each errand," Master Gotami informed them. "Everyone deserves to see these gates open for them at least once, don't you think?"

Jesus stared up at the enormous doors, reminding him of the enormity of the journey they were about to embark on. This was likely the last time he or Judas would see this place.

"Remember," Master Gotami said, "you may often find yourself a sheep among wolves. Take refuge in your practice. Be wise as serpents and innocent as doves."

"Yes, Master Gotami," Jesus said. "We're ready."

Master Gotami nodded to Moggallana, who called everyone over. The residents crowded around them in a half-circle, prepared to send them off.

"Brother Issa," Master Gotami said when everyone had settled, "prior to embarking on your journey, are you prepared to take the great vow?"

"I am," Jesus said.

One resident handed Master Gotami a singing bowl. She struck it, sending a clear chime across the courtyard.

"Brother Issa," she began, "are you prepared to wake yourself and clarify your view—to teach the Way for the sake of awakening others?"

Jesus nodded solemnly. "I am."

She struck the bowl again, inviting another clear chime.

"On the journey to liberate yourself from every bond, are you prepared to work for the liberation of others?"

"I am."

"Through the peace and insight you discover through practice, are you prepared to show others the Way of peace and insight?"

"I am."

Once more, Master Gotami struck the bowl.

"Finally, having opened your eyes to see the realm of Nirvana—the Kingdom of God—are you prepared to help open the eyes of others that they might see? To help them cross the stream of suffering to arrive on the far shore?"

Once more, Jesus nodded.

"I am."

Master Gotami smiled. "In that case, it is my great honor to bless you on your journey, and to commission you to go out and make disciples of all nations, helping them take refuge in the wisdom and practice you have learned. Teach them as we have taught you, and remember that we are with you always, to the end of the age."

Moggallana signaled the two residents on either side of the doors. Their ancient hinges groaned, and inch by inch, the gates began to open. At the same moment, across the courtyard, the deep bass of the bell reverberated through the grounds.

Instinctively, Jesus hummed in harmony with the sound, and his hum turned into a familiar chant.

*"Open for me the gates of righteousness,"* he sang to himself. *"I will enter and give thanks to God. This is the gate of our God, and the righteous shall pass through..."*

The bell rang again, and Judas took one donkey's reins as Master Gotami and Moggallana stepped back to join the other residents.

Jesus took the reins of his own donkey, and together they moved forward.

*"I will give thanks, for God has answered my call,"* Jesus continued singing to himself, *"and God has become my salvation. The stone that the builders rejected has become the chief cornerstone—God has surely done this, and it is marvelous in our eyes. God has done all of this, and we will rejoice and give thanks..."*

A psalm for every occasion.

The bell rang one last time, and they passed through the doors, out of Metta Valley, and onto the same path they'd traveled the year before. It was different now, though. They'd seen it from the rooftop. It was no longer unknown—no longer overwhelming.

*There is a way that seems right to man,* the rabbi's voice warned, *but its end is the way of death.*

Jesus thought of at least a dozen retorts, but then he caught himself. Instead, he only smiled, reaching into his robes and clutching the Buddha stone in his palm.

"I see you," he muttered. "I hear you."

With that, Jesus set his face towards Jerusalem.

# Author's Note

I INHERITED A PARTICULAR way of telling the Jesus story. He was this John-Wayne-esque, ultra-conservative hero who seemed to exist for the sole purposes of balancing divine fire insurance equations and winning culture wars. If I'm honest, I found that story entirely satisfying growing up. Why wouldn't I? It gave me identity... clear enemies... kept me from murder and bank robbing and such... As I got older, though, something changed. I realized this story was causing more problems than it solved.

I started to suspect the identity it gave me had more to do with *control* than *faithfulness*... that my "enemies" were often the very people Jesus loved... that it wasn't the fear of disappointing Jesus that kept me from murder and robbing banks so much as a basic respect for my fellow humans... What's more, the more time I spent actually reading the Jesus story for myself, the more I realized two things: 1.) That Jesus didn't seem to care all that much about saving people from damnation (at least not in the way I was taught), and 2.) that the story I inherited seemed to have far more to do with consolidating and protecting power than honoring the teachings of the Jesus of the Bible. These realizations kicked off what would become a profound shift in the way I related to myself, the stories of scripture, and all things sacred.

The Jesus of the Bible was very different from the one I'd met in church. I mean, he was a radical... He was constantly at odds with religious institutions because he cared more about love than doctrine... He cared so deeply about justice and peace that he was deemed a criminal and executed by the government... By all accounts, this was *not* the kind of guy I was likely to find teaching my Sunday School classes. This left me with the eye-opening realization that if Jesus were to walk into a modern American church today, they would likely show him the door, preferring instead a more controllable idol of their own creation. In fact, the loudest faith leaders around me started to sound suspiciously like the religious elite that became so hell-bent on getting rid of Jesus in the first place.

I soon realized I wasn't the only one who felt this tension. I found resonance with a community who had sensed the same things—who became more interested in telling stories that fostered a healthy spirituality than upholding tradition and protecting the institution. These were people who realized the stories we'd inherited were tearing us apart individually and socially, and they were hungry for healing and truth.

When I was ordained in the mid-2010s, it was a wild time in the world of religion. People were leaving religious institutions in droves—disillusioned by years of scandal, politicalization, and exhausting battles over basic human rights. Meanwhile, interest in non-traditional expressions of spirituality was skyrocketing, with mindfulness apps becoming mainstream, conversations around psychedelics becoming bolder, and earth-based spirituality sections in Barnes & Noble booming. I became drawn to the writings of brilliant writers and thinkers who were working to honor that shift—to explore the new stories that were emerging and the ancient ones that were coming back to the surface like flowers through concrete. This included authors like Richard Rohr and Brian McLaren... Rob Bell and Sue Monk Kidd... people whose words kept me sane and helped foster a bold, new imagination for what a sacred story could be.

As a pastor, I saw it as my work to give voice to these new stories as skillfully as I could—especially the Jesus story, which I still stubbornly believed was worth telling. In sermons, short stories, articles, and book studies, I worked to help others reclaim their sacred stories—to re-imagine Jesus in a way that harmonized with the spirit he embodied in the gospels and let go of the blonde-haired blue-eyed paintings we'd seen hung in so many church classrooms. That work was surprisingly difficult, especially with so many cultural voices working tirelessly to protect the status quo. I quickly learned that there's a funny process you set into motion when you tamper with the Jesus story: Messing with the Jesus story means messing with the cultural-religious imagination... Messing with the cultural-religious imagination means messing with deeply ingrained hierarchies... Messing with deeply ingrained hierarchy means messing with people's grip on their power... And messing with people's grip on power means that they tend to get pissed. This whole thing can happen in the blink of an eye and often entirely unconsciously, but the reaction is strong, and it highlights just why re-imagining the Jesus story is such crucial work.

Somewhere during that struggle, though, the idea for *Metta Valley Gospel* was born. I realized I wanted to write the story of Jesus that I had always needed but could never find. Don't get me wrong, I could find it in the heart of books on theology and spirituality and philosophy... but never in the form of an embodied story that flowed with modern storytelling sensibilities and touched my imagination. I needed a truth that was "made flesh" in a good story, and I suspected I wasn't the only one.

The beginning of my work on *Metta Valley Gospel* coincided with my decision to step away from the church world, joining the masses of "spiritual but not religious" folks who found deep meaning in spirituality unbundled from its institutional religious trappings. I began working as a Humanist(ish), Buddhist(ish), Christian(ish) chaplain, exploring spiritual work in the greater context of a perennial wisdom tradition, and this shed a new light on the project of re-imagining the Jesus story. For example, I'd been exploring the practical truth of Buddhism for a few years, and I was continuously floored by the ways the teachings of the Buddha illuminated and informed the teachings of Jesus. It felt as though Jesus gave me the *what* while Buddha gave me the *how*. "Love your neighbor!" Jesus taught, then the Buddha would add, "And here's *how* you practice becoming the kind of person who naturally loves your neighbor..." (I learned the Buddha doesn't speak with exclamation marks. Jesus uses them a lot.) In realizations like this, I found that I wanted to write a story, not just about the Jesus I'd come to know in the gospels, but about Jesus in the context of that broader, practical, perennial wisdom tradition I was discovering. I wanted to talk about *how* Jesus had come to be the sort of person who lived as he did—what kind of spirituality informed the words and catchphrases that had become white noise to our ears (phrases like "The Kingdom of God" and "Christ")—and Buddhism offered just such a lens. That quest led me to the voices of teachers like Thich Nhat Hanh, Ram Dass, Eckhart Tolle, Aldous Huxley, Alan Watts, Anthony de Mello, Tara Brach, and Sharon Salzberg... all of whom show up in *Metta Valley Gospel* in one way or another. When I discovered *The Unknown Life of Jesus Christ* by Nicolas Notovitch—a 19th century work of "nonfiction" about how Jesus (a.k.a. "Issa") trained at a Buddhist monastery—I knew I had tapped an imagination deeper than just mine, and I set to work.

In short, I wrote *Metta Valley Gospel* for people like me—people who still care deeply about spirituality, but who have left the institution behind to find new ways of engaging the sacred. I wrote it to nudge our imaginations and to counter the destructive tradition of co-opting the Jesus story to protect power structures—a tradition that is smothering us as individuals and disconnecting us as a collective. I've taken some historical liberties (obviously) and I've been deliberately anachronistic in character and dialogue to serve the larger story. Mostly though, as a white male raised in the southern United States, I wanted to handle this story with as much cultural humility as possible. Insofar as I've painted Judaism, Buddhism, Hinduism, or Christianity in a negative light, it is only to show that *any* religion can be co-opted by narcissists, fearful people, and power-grabbers. They can be vehicles of abuse and harm, just as they can be vessels for justice and love. I hope this novel embodies both.

There are several people I'd like to thank for helping bring *Metta Valley Gospel* to life. First, thank you to my partner Claire, who is always my first reader and has been my primary conversation partner in all things spiritual since 2007. You were the first one to ask me, "Don't you think Christianity might have something to do with love, and not just... you know... being right all the time?" Turns out... yes. Thank you also to James and Pete, who remind me how to play—whether on a trampoline, at a computer, or rolling a d20.

Thank you to my wonderful beta readers—Laurie, Rebekah, Ellen, Beth, Lauren, Katie, and Brittany. Your feedback helped make this book what it is. Thank you also to Jamie and Andy, who listened to me fight with this story from its inception, and all those who offered me the encouragement, perspective, and guidance I needed as the book moved through its final stages of development.

Thank you to my Ko-Fi sponsors who went above and beyond in their financial support of this project—Alice Sawyer, Amy Bourne, Mike and Beverly Yeary, Brittany and Casey Ramirez, Dana R. Wise, Denise Gunn, Felipe Muñoz, Gregory Corrigan, Ian Briggs, Keith Sartin, Kim Turner, Kris Randall, Kristi Williams, Lauren Henry, Michael Nassar, Nancy S. Hagman and Rose Coon, Regina Sakalarios-Rogers, Susan and James Helton, and Suzanne Waller.

Thank you to my cover designer, Kari Brownlie, for the work you put into finding the right design for the story. There were many great drafts left on the cutting room floor.

Thank you to the faith communities who have inspired and challenged me as I've worked on this project—Lake Shore Baptist Church in Waco, Texas, Northminster Church in Monroe, Louisiana, Nashville Zen Center in Nashville, Tennessee, and The Unitarian Universalist Church of Pensacola in (you guessed it), Pensacola, Florida. Thank you to Jessica Evans and my Clinical Pastoral Education residency cohort, without whom this would be a much angrier and grief-filled book. Thank you also to the faith communities and institutions that supported and formed me before this. Even though we may not see eye to eye anymore, you helped me understand just how important these stories can be.

Thank you, finally to my grandparents, who formed my storytelling sensibilities by taking me to Blockbuster more times than I can count (but, sadly, not enough to keep them in business). To my dad, whose endless creativity in construction I've tried to translate into creativity with words. And to my mom, who asked for a short story about Jesus in Christmas of 2018, and got a two-part novel seven years later. Hope you enjoy.

I'll close by saying that writing *Metta Valley Gospel* led me to places I never imagined, and giving voice to this story has been a deeply formative experience. I hope that reading it has offered something of that experience to you. So, if bad religion has pushed you to the margins, I hope you can see yourself in this story.

If religion has brought you structure and life, I hope you can see yourself, too.

If you read this book and want to burn me for heresy... well, I hope that shows you something about yourself as well.

Thank you for your time and attention.

—Zach Helton

# About the Author

Zachary Helton is an ordained minister, Board Certified Spiritual Care Counselor, and author whose work explores the intersection of story and spirituality. He holds a Master of Divinity from Baylor University and a B.A. from the University of Alabama. Drawing on over a decade of service in progressive Christian and interfaith communities, his writing reclaims sacred narratives as spaces for healing, liberation, and awareness.

His work has appeared in *Braided Way* and *Flash Fiction Magazine*, and in 2024 he was nominated for the Orison Best Spiritual Literature Award. *Metta Valley Gospel* is his debut novel.

You can connect with him and discover more of his work at zhelton.com or on social media.

# Also by the Author

### Metta Valley Gospel: Book I

Jesus was brought up in a world of rules, control, and shame. Quick-witted and rebellious, he's always been the one asking dangerous questions. But when his pursuit of justice sparks a confrontation with a rabbi no one dares question, Jesus finds himself cast out of the only home he's ever known.

### Metta Valley Gospel: Book II

Jesus returns to Judea, burning with a vision of freedom and truth. But the world he reenters has little patience for his defiant spirit. Crowds grow as Rome and the Temple watch, and Jesus struggles to trust the Way as walls of opposition close in.

### Metta Valley Gospel: Book I Companion Guide

Reflections and Questions for Readers and Small Groups. Slow down and walk more deeply into the questions that linger after the story ends. Through guided prompts, open-ended questions, and moments of silence between the lines, you'll discover how the truths of Metta Valley live on inside your own story.

If this story resonated with you and you'd like to help other readers find it, consider leaving a brief review.

Reviews really do make a difference, helping the book show up for readers who might need it. Your review can be as simple as a few honest sentences about what stayed with you or how it made you feel.

Just scan the QR code or follow the link below to leave a review on Amazon.

Thank you for being part of this journey.

https://www.amazon.com/review/create-review?&asin=B0FMBXC5VK